The Benedictine Commando

The Benedictine Commando

JAMES McCONNELL

HAMISH HAMILTON
London

First published in Great Britain 1981
by Hamish Hamilton Ltd
Garden House, 57-59 Long Acre, London WC2E 9JZ

Copyright © 1981 by James McConnell

British Library Cataloguing in Publication Data

McConnell, James
  The Benedictine commando.
  I. Title
  823′.914[F]   PR6025.A1697

  ISBN 0-241-10613-3

Typeset by Elanders Ltd
Printed and bound in Great Britain
by Redwood Burn Ltd, Trowbridge and Esher

For precious friends hid in death's dateless night

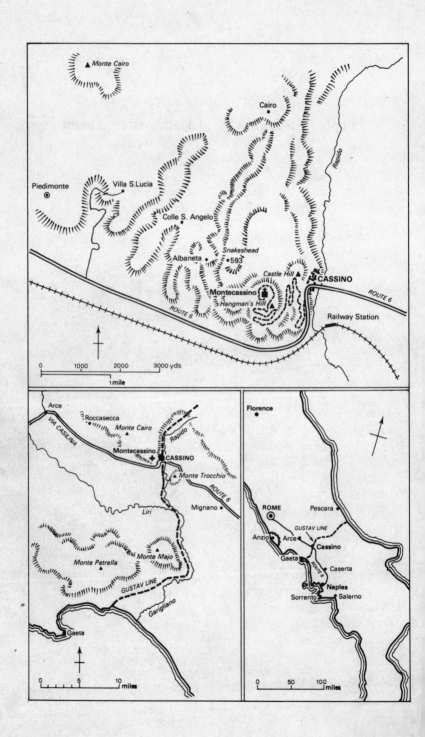

1

Binley's last day on earth had begun soon after midnight. At 0130 hours his platoon, No 3 in B Company, had moved up to their start line. Now they were crouching in a rocky hollow as the grey light grew, finding what shelter they could from rain, wind and shells.

'What's eating you, Binley?'

Fusilier Binley looked up into the leathery face of Sergeant Webb. He pushed out his lower lip and sucked in some of the mucus that was oozing from his nose.

'Nothing, Sarge.'

'You look like some old hen that's got an egg stuck up its arse.'

'I've got –' The shaming confession was tumbling out before he could stop himself. 'I don't know why, Sarge, but I just have this feeling my number's coming up today.'

'Fuck that!' Sergeant Webb knew he had to stamp on this right away before it spread to the others. 'We've all got our numbers coming up some day. You'd better get yourself sorted out before Mr Meredith gets back. Look at your greatcoat, man! It's like a fucking concertina.'

Binley nodded without conviction. He wiped the back of his hand across his nostrils. The dribble was starting to freeze on his skin. The peaks surrounding the battalion's position were covered with snow. An icy wind, laden with rain, whistled down the boulder-strewn slopes into the damp and cheerless hollow where he lay with the rest of the platoon. The Germans were subjecting the area to a desultory shelling. The Fusiliers winced every time a shell landed close by. Binley's uniform was sopping wet. He'd tied a couple of empty sandbags round his calves in an effort to fend off frost-bite. He hadn't taken his boots off for three days.

It seemed like a whole lifetime that the battalion had been fighting its way up the boot of Italy. They were very tired, with the kind of battle-weariness that goes beyond mere physical fatigue. The purpose of the war, even the objectives of the Italian campaign, had been long forgotten. Their world did not extend beyond their own unit.

Binley's loyalty, which was sterling in its quality, was to 'the lads', his immediate comrades, those other young men who had been pitchforked like him out of their humble but peaceable lives into this hell upon earth. With them he had shared the glory and the degradation, the terror and the boredom, the heat of summer and the chill of winter – all through the interminable months of August, September, October, November, December.

That was why he tried to fight his fear. It was the worst enemy of all because if it got the better of him he could never regain the respect of the lads. Yet this fear which gripped him was as bad as acute physical pain, an abominable and unbearable mental palsy which paralysed his mind. He had begun to shiver uncontrollably. He was afraid that he might soon start to blub.

'Cheer up, Binnie,' Corporal Lock called to him from the other side of the little hollow. Corporal Lock was Binley's section commander. He was a six-foot farmer from the Peaks and as strong as Achilles. Binley worshipped him. He possessed all the qualities which Binley himself knew he lacked, above all courage. He scorned enemy fire, through which he walked like a god. He seemed indestructible. 'Think of all that nice Italian crumpet waiting for you in Naples.'

Binley preferred to think about his home in Hurstbourne Tarrant and the plump but pneumatic girl he had left behind. What would he not give to be there now, doing his round with the baker's van, whistling a few bars as he walked up each path from the gate, knowing he'd receive a cheerful greeting at every house? He hated the very soil of Italy. Too often he had burrowed into it like a terrified animal.

He wished with all his heart that Mr Meredith never would come back, for his return would mean that the attack was about to start. He could not tell why, but there was something different about this particular feature. Bare Bum Ridge seemed to hold a special message for him personally. Jerry was up there somewhere, well dug in with machine-guns sited to cover every possible line of approach and his mortar crews hidden on the reverse slopes of the hill.

To stop himself thinking about it Binley unclipped his belt

and tried to pleat his oversized greatcoat in the approved fashion.

*

The Allied armies had invaded the mainland of Europe on 3 September 1943, the first troops splashing up the beaches of southern Italy exactly four years after Britain's declaration of war on Germany. Now, three months later, Christmas was approaching, and they had conquered less than one third of the long peninsula. They were bogged down on a ninety-mile front that extended from coast to coast some thirty-five miles short of Rome. Under directions from Hitler himself, the Germans were making skilful use of the mountainous terrain to delay the advance for long enough to complete their winter line, which would bar the approach to Rome.

It was named the Gustav Line, and Hitler had ordered that it was to be defended at whatever cost. The cornerstone of this formidable bulwark was a hill called Montecassino. On its summit stood the Abbey and Monastery of St Benedict, patron saint of Christendom.

One of the first Allied officers to set eyes on that gaunt and forbidding edifice was a Gunner major, who commanded a battery of the Greenshire Yeomanry. His name was Richard Stewart.

The Greenshire Yeomanry, as army troops, could be switched to give additional artillery support wherever it was needed. During the battle for the Mignano Gap Richard's own battery was supporting the first battalion of the Wessex Fusiliers. The Fusiliers had been given the task of clearing the enemy from an unprepossessing feature which the troops had christened Bare Bum Ridge. From an observation post the commanding officer's reconnaissance party looked out over the inhospitable landscape ahead. It was a sight with which they were all too familiar. An unending succession of mountainous slopes and summits stretched ahead as far as the eye could see, their peaks covered with snow and their flanks lashed by icy winds and continuous freezing rain.

The CO studied the ground for five minutes through his field-glasses, while his Intelligence Officer filled him in on what was known of enemy dispositions. When he lowered his binoculars he had already worked out his plan of attack.

He turned to Richard. 'We'll have to deal with that MG post

in White Farm before we can attack Bare Bum Ridge. It overlooks the battalion start line. Can you be ready to put down a stonk if I send in a platoon from B Company?'

'I'll use HE, Colonel. Do you want smoke as well?'

'Have it ready but don't use it unless I call for it. Trouble with smoke is it gets in the men's lungs.'

Richard nodded. The four men crawled back from the rocks behind which they had been sheltering and stood up.

'White Farm would make a good OP for the main attack,' Richard suggested. 'I can move up there as soon as your people have taken it, Colonel. Then we can register targets before you put in the battalion attack.'

*

Leaning against his command vehicle the CO gave his orders to the dozen officers forming a half circle round him.

'The battalion has been invited,' he told them with almost casual informality, 'to see Jerry off Bare Bum Ridge. I don't have to tell you that our old friends the Panzer-Grenadiers are likely to put up a stiff resistance. But we have been given additional artillery support for this action and I can promise you our attack will be preceded by a generous stonk.'

As the plan for the operation unfolded it became clear to Richard that Meredith's platoon had been designated for the stickiest task of all, the preliminary attack on White Farm. It was no different from the dozens of hamlets or farmsteads which the battalion had stormed during their advance from the toe of Italy. The disorderly but picturesque jumble of reddish roofs and off-white gables was perched on the flank of a hillock. There was no sign of life there now. At the approach of war the inhabitants had hoisted what they could carry onto carts, wheelbarrows or even the top of their heads, and fled to that traditional refuge of the Italian peasant – the mountains. The Gunners had given the buildings a preliminary softening up, blasting down a few more walls, sending a few more roofs up in smithereens. Now it was silent, apparently deserted. But Richard had enough experience to know that, placed as it was, it must inevitably form an important part of the enemy's defensive system. He was personally convinced that White Farm justified an attack on a bigger scale than just one platoon, but of course he could not say so.

'Don't worry,' Richard told the platoon commander, as they

made their way forward again. 'I'll see that you get plenty of artillery support.'

Meredith stole a glance at his companion. Stewart was wearing a sheepskin jacket and thick corduroy trousers tucked into a pair of brown American officer's boots. Scorning a helmet, he wore a battered peaked cap from which all the stiffening had been washed by continuous rain. Round his neck hung a pair of captured Zeiss binoculars. A map in its canvas and cellophane case dangled from his waist. Though only five years or so older than the platoon commander he seemed immensely more experienced.

'Are you coming right up to my platoon headquarters?'

Stewart nodded. 'Yes. I like to get as far forward as I can.' He looked into Meredith's eyes and smiled. 'If I'm up there with you, you'll know I'm going to take good care our shells don't fall short.'

A stray enemy shell crumped down a hundred yards away. Stewart paid no attention and Meredith found himself relaxing. It was a help to be in the presence of someone who seemed so unconscious of danger. He would need all the confidence he could muster when it came to giving his orders to Sergeant Webb and the rest of the platoon.

Platoon headquarters was in what was left of a stone shepherd's hut. While Meredith went into a huddle with his platoon sergeant and section leaders, Richard Stewart began to reconnoitre for a position which would give him a good view of White Farm and the ground below it. His own group consisted of a Tactical Assistant RA and a Lance-Bombardier wireless operator. For inaccessible positions such as this the regiment was using the reasonably portable Number 18 set. It was tuned in on the battery's firing net and kept him in contact with the battalion command post as well as the two Gun Position Officers back in the gun area. A field telephone and land line connected him with the headquarters of Meredith's company commander.

Before the three sections moved into position in readiness for the attack, Sergeant Webb spoke to Meredith about Binley.

'He's got a bad touch of the jitters, sir. I think he could go right round the bend like Hopkins did.'

'I'll have a word with him.'

Meredith found Binley crouching in the shelter of a rock.

11

The rain was pelting down more heavily than ever. Binley was very pale and shivering visibly.

'You all right, Binley?'

Binley scrambled to his feet, a damp, untidy and most unmilitary figure.

'Yes, sir.'

Meredith gave him a searching but compassionate look.

'You could report sick, you know,' he told him in a low voice. 'I'll send you back to battalion HQ if you like. You might feel better after a day or two's rest.'

'It's okay, sir,' Binley heard himself saying. 'I'd rather stay with the lads.'

Standing close behind the platoon commander, Richard had caught the gist of the conversation.

'Don't worry,' he told the Fusilier, nodding towards his observation post. 'I've got a whole battery of 25-pounders ranged on that farm, and if you run into trouble I can turn on every gun in the division.'

The confidence in the Gunner's voice seemed to communicate itself to Binley. Meredith saw his shoulders lift. He decided to leave it.

Richard's guns opened fire at 0955 hours, softening up the farm and seeking out the known positions of German machine-gun nests. At the same time Corporal Lock, Fusilier Binley and the rest of No 3 section heaved themselves to their feet and ventured out onto the bare, boulder-strewn hillside.

From his position near platoon headquarters, with the covering section, the three Bren gunners and the mortar crew for company, Richard watched them go. He never failed to admire the men whose job was to stand up and doggedly walk towards enemy positions, exposing their bodies to the storm of machine-gun fire which must inevitably come. At the moment all was deceptively quiet, except for the crump of his own guns' shells landing on their target. Thanks to the fire orders he was sending back the twenty-five pounders had got the range, forcing the German defenders to keep their heads down.

Ten minutes from the start Binley was panting for breath. The slope was steeper than it looked. It was hard to get a hand or foot-hold on the boulder-strewn hillside. The farm buildings loomed above them. They seemed alarmingly close, but the sight of shells bursting on them was comforting.

Then a machine gunner concealed in an unsuspected position

12

to their left opened up. He had been holding his fire for just this moment. As the bullets from the 'Spandau' smacked into the rocks around them and Fusilier Groagan went down gurgling, shot in the throat, the whole section dived for cover. But a mortar crew had also pin-pointed their position and bombs had started screaming down all round them. Splinters of metal and rock whizzed through the air.

Lock got to his feet.

'Come on, you fuckers!' he roared. 'Get on your bloody feet. I'm going to take you to that bleeding farm if it's the last thing I do. Fix your bayonets.'

Cowering among the boulders, hating themselves for their fear, they were grateful for the corporal's courage and the familiar comfort of his atrocious language. Each man withdrew his bayonet from the scabbard hanging at his waist and clamped the fifteen inches of steel onto the barrel of his rifle. Then they forced themselves to their feet to follow him.

Binley's trembling had ceased. He did not know whether he was frightened or not. He felt disassociated from his body, as if he were already dead. Some force beyond his own mind was driving him on through the shrieking metal and stone.

Back at his OP Richard had seen the section go to ground and through binoculars had spotted the unsuspected machine-gun nest. He quickly estimated its position on his map, worked out a six figure co-ordinate and picked up his mike.

'Hello 22. Section target, machine gun. 637514. I'll range with air bursts.'

'Right,' the GPO confirmed. 'Air burst coming up.' Then, a moment later, 'Shot 1. Time of flight fifteen seconds.'

'Number one ranging. Fire 3.'

Fifteen seconds later he saw the air burst. Long and to the right of the target.

'Left two hundred. Up four hundred. Number two ranging. Fire.'

Meanwhile number three section scrambled on towards their objective, the original eight now reduced to six. They had no way of knowing how the other section was progressing. They were isolated in a hell of their own.

They were only a hundred yards from their objective when the machine-gunner got Corporal Lock. Binley saw him go down and cried out in grief and despair. The section wavered, then, rifles in the 'on guard' position, they raced forward,

13

following their own steel towards the comparative shelter of the nearest building.

Binley grabbed the sleeve of Fusilier Deakin.

'We can't leave him.'

'He's dead,' Deakin yelled from a twisted mouth. 'Can't you see he's copped it?'

'Help me carry him, Jack. We've got to get him into the farm.'

But Jack Deakin had had enough of that exposed hillside. Alone Binley went back for Lock. He hardly cared if the machine-gunner got him too. More than a friend, Lock had been a protecting guardian, immune to bullet, bomb or shell. Now so suddenly he was no more than an untidy heap of khaki clothes, from which protruded a smashed head disfigured by the rictus of death.

Too late for Lock the twenty-five pounders had silenced the machine-gunner. A herdsman from the Black Forest was just as dead as the Derbyshire farmer, but his body was in smaller pieces. Binley slung his rifle and heaved his idol over his shoulder. Blood from the shattered skull was dripping down the back of his legs as he staggered up the hill to the shelter of the buildings.

Richard's guns had done their job thoroughly. The bodies of dead and wounded Panzer-Grenadiers cluttered the ground-floor rooms of the farmhouse where Binley deposited his burden. Their comrades had pulled out before the final assault.

In a daze Binley saw Mr Meredith and the other section dash in. Coming up the bed of the stream they'd had an easier time. Only one casualty; Fusilier Baker had copped a splinter up the arse.

'Consolidate!' Meredith shouted. 'Get to the windows! They may counter-attack and we've got to hold on till the Brens come up.'

Binley had laid Lock down on the flagstones of the farm kitchen. The stretcher-bearers would soon be up to take care of the wounded and in due course the Padre would come and bury Lock. Fuck Meredith and the counter-attack. Binley was going to spare a moment to say farewell to his hero. In the end it was old Binnie who'd been able to do him a good turn. Lock had sworn to take his section into the farm if it was the last thing he did and in a way Binley had helped that to come true.

By the time Richard moved up with Sergeant Webb and the covering section the Germans in their turn were mortaring the farm. Three more Fusiliers had been hit.

'For Christ's sake,' Meredith implored Richard. 'Can't you do something about those mortars?'

Richard looked round for a staircase that would take him to a higher point of vantage. He saw the narrow winding steps behind the fireplace. Drawing his revolver he quickly ran up them. In the single upper room a pallid, thin young German soldier huddled into the corner and raised his arms.

'*Kamerad! Kamerad!*'

Richard ignored him and moved cautiously towards the window that faced north-west. It was obvious that the youth's war was finished. They fought like demons, these young Krauts, and then when they came face to face they were suddenly frightened, fragile boys.

This hill on which the farm stood was a more significant feature than had appeared from the other side. The farm commanded an awesome view across enemy territory. To his right Richard could see an unending succession of peaks, rising higher and higher until their snow-covered summits were lost in the heavy grey clouds. Looking to his left he had a view clear up the valley that led towards Rome, as far as the point where it opened into a broad plain.

But what rivetted his attention was the sheer mount which rose steeply at the flank of that opening. On its summit, like a fort guarding the entrance to a harbour, stood an extraordinary building. Even at a distance of seven miles its size was redoubtable. Three times as big as Buckingham Palace and twice as high, it seemed to dominate the entire landscape. The sloping battlements at its base were those of a fortress, pierced by narrow slits that looked like firing embrasures. Above them, row upon row of windows glared across at the hillside where Lock had perished. The rain had momentarily ceased and over to the west the sun had found a gap and got through the clouds. Its yellow, watery rays struck the side of the building, imparting an almost luminous gleam to its golden stonework and striking flame-red reflections from the hundreds of windows.

He lowered his binoculars and moved back from the window. He had the uncanny sense of being watched by a hundred pairs of eyes.

Richard was not a particularly superstitious person, but the building exercised a strange effect on him. It did not seem to belong to this earth and its remoteness was emphasized by the band of mist which clung to the side of the hill, so that the walls seemed to have their foundations in the sky. He felt a strong sense of some presence up there and even during the few seconds before he drew back he experienced a strong and totally illogical premonition that his own life and fate were linked with that mysterious, golden *castello*.

Then he heard the whine of a salvo of shells and dived for the cover of the stout stone wall.

★

The blast from the first shell blinded Binley and a piece of shrapnel embedded itself in his thigh, shattering the bone. Sergeant Webb had come up with the Bren guns in time to position them before the counter-attack. He and Meredith propped the dead Fusiliers in the windows to make the place seem more strongly defended. The counter-attack was beaten off and remnants of one of the companies managed to get astride the rump of Bare Bum Ridge. But when they came under intense shell-fire and repeated counter-attacks the CO decided that the position was untenable. He asked his Brigadier for permission to withdraw this one company and Meredith's platoon under cover of darkness.

The stretcher-bearers had not been able to take Binley down the mule-track from the farm during daylight. It was too exposed to enemy fire. The whole of Bare Bum Ridge seemed to be under observation from the huge building across the valley. It was six p.m. before the two stretcher-bearers were able to set out on their three-hour journey to the Regimental Aid Post. The night was bitterly cold and by seven o'clock it was freezing hard.

Moving down the stony track with his small party Richard came up with the stretcher-bearers. He glanced down at the prone figure with the bandaged eyes. There was still enough of the face visible for him to recognize the Fusilier to whom he had spoken so reassuringly before the attack. The man on the front of the stretcher rightly interpreted his inquiring glance. He shook his head once.

'Do you need a hand?' Richard asked. He felt a need to do

something for Binley, even in the smallest way to make up for the false promise he had given.

'It's all right, sir,' the RAMC man answered, surprised at this offer from a Gunner major. 'We can manage him.'

Richard was reluctant to leave the wounded Fusilier. It was quite irrational but he felt a personal responsibility for what had happened. But his TARA and Lance-Bombardier had gone ahead and he was in danger of losing them in the darkness and confusion. He nodded to the stretcher-bearer and pushed on.

Before he lost consciousness Binley felt his dark world grow even darker. He fancied he heard the sound of a church bell ringing – very far away.

By half-past eight the stretcher party were nearing their destination. Exhausted, their hands numb with cold, they paused to rest. The NCO went to check Binley's pulse. The wrist was lifeless.

'It's all right, mate,' he said, his tone of assumed callousness masking his frustration and grief. 'No need to go so careful now. He's croaked.'

2

At the beginning of January 1944 the Greenshire Yeomanry were switched across to the left of British 10 Corps, which was pushing forward up the west coast of Italy towards the River Garigliano. During one of those lulls when the artillery of both sides seemed to decide mutually to give each other a rest, Richard Stewart attended Mass in the ruins of a village church. The RC padre from brigade headquarters had draped a white cloth over the bomb-damaged altar and some inventive soldier had rigged up a tarpaulin to keep the rain off his head during the service.

As Richard came out with the half-dozen others of all ranks who had taken Communion he was surprised to find his batman-driver waiting for him with the Jeep.

'CO wants you at regimental headquarters urgent,' Keast told him, and added reprovingly: 'We've been looking for you all over.'

Richard smiled at the implication that by going off to attend Mass he had been acting in a faintly disreputable manner. He climbed into the Jeep. Keast engaged four-wheeled drive. The track that led to regimental headquarters had been ploughed into a morass of mud.

Lieutenant-Colonel Dudley Fremantle had ensconced himself in a solid three-storey house a little forward of brigade headquarters. The fact that it was in full view of enemy territory and attracted regular attention from the German gunners did not worry him in the least. The important thing was that it had a roof capable of keeping out the atrocious Italian weather and walls thick enough to detonate shells before they penetrated. There was also the advantage that anyone who wanted to come and see him had to run the gauntlet. This discouraged visitations from base wallahs, who were the bane of Fremantle's life.

As the Jeep scurried up the exposed drive that led to the house Richard looked towards the north. Just for a moment he caught a glimpse, through a gap in the hills, of the great square building he had first seen from Bare Bum Ridge. He knew now that it was none other than the Monastery of Montecassino, of which he had heard so much during his schooldays. The awful thought suddenly occurred to him that this summons had something to do with Wilfrid. Christ, if anything happened to Wilfrid . . .

He felt in his pocket for the crumpled letter which had been delivered to him that morning. His father had got the BFPO number wrong again and it had taken two months to catch up with him. He read the last paragraph for the fourth time.

'Wilfrid has been promoted to lieutenant. Your mother and I are very proud of him, indeed of both our sons. He has applied to be posted to the Greenshire Yeomanry and hopes to go out to Italy as soon as his leave ends. I am not altogether happy about having both

18

my eggs in the same basket, but I have told Mum that you will look after your young brother.

Please write as often as possible. Your letters give us much comfort.'

Richard sighed as he tucked the letter back in the inside pocket of his battledress blouse. It was hard to visualize Wilfrid as a soldier at all, let alone an officer in a crack regiment like the GY. And how on earth was he supposed to 'look after' a nineteen-year-old dreamer like his younger brother in the freezing purgatory of the winter campaign? The regiment had lost too many officers lately, mostly in forward observation posts. Three had been seriously wounded and two killed in the last month.

In fact Wilfrid had arrived before the letter. Richard had seen him only briefly before he was posted to C Battery, under Major Stockwell. Fresh out from England he had looked desperately young and vulnerable, but the last thing Richard wanted to do was act the motherly elder brother. Far better to leave him alone for a while and let him get the hang of things for himself.

Richard found his Colonel in the downstairs room which had been converted into a surprisingly comfortable officers' mess. He was practising chip shots from a strip of carpet into a bucket with the hickory-shafted mashie-niblick which had accompanied him on all his campaigns. He was unfailingly cheerful and good-humoured and commanded his regiment as if they were a team engaged in a slightly dangerous form of sport.

'Ah, Richard, there you are. Where on earth have you been?'

'I was at church service, Colonel.'

'But I thought you were an RC.'

'I am, Colonel. But we have church services too.' With a smile he added: 'At Brigade level.'

'I see.'

There was a clang as the last golf ball went into the bucket.

'Well, one thing this war will have done for me. I'll be delivered from the worst evil that can befall a human being.'

'What's that, Colonel?'

'Shanking, dear boy. The secret is to keep the wrists cocked on the first part of the down swing.'

Fremantle leaned his club against a table and went towards

the little bar at the end of the room. Bottles with such familiar labels as Gordon's, Johnny Walker, Gilbey's and Plymouth Gin had been lined up neatly by the mess waiter.

'What'll you have? Whisky and soda or gin and something? I'm afraid we've only got some rather horrible Italian Vermouth.'

'Can I have a pink gin, please?'

Richard had expected to be the last to arrive for some sort of conference or order group, but none of the other battery commanders was there. Fremantle poured a generous measure from the Plymouth Gin bottle, splashed in a couple of drops of Angostura and held the water jug poised.

'Say when.'

'That's about right. Thanks. Here's cheers.'

'Cheers.' Fremantle lifted his own tumbler of whisky briefly. 'Your brother seems to be settling down well. Geoffrey tells me he's beginning to get his sea legs.'

'That's good.' Richard managed to conceal his relief. He had detected a note of caution in the CO's voice. He wondered how the very extrovert Stockwell was going to handle his new and disquietingly unpredictable subaltern. 'He may take a little time to adjust.'

'Mm. Take a pew, old boy.'

The two men sat down in a couple of the folding chairs which formed part of regimental headquarters' transportable stock of furniture. Fremantle studied Richard over the top of a thick, green tumbler which had been created from the bottom section of a wine bottle.

Though Richard was only twenty-eight there was the wisdom and maturity of a much older man in his face. He was always well turned out, close shaved and with a neatly trimmed moustache. Beside the North Africa Star on his chest was the white and mauve ribbon of the Military Cross which he had won during the attack on Longstop Hill before the capture of Tunis.

'You remember that time Alex came up to visit the regiment near Medjez?'

Richard nodded. He would not quickly forget the moment when, staring through binoculars at the shell-bursts from his own 25-pounders, he had heard a voice behind him and turning round had looked straight into the face of Lieutenant-General Sir Harold Alexander. The C-in-C had come up to the front, resplendent in scarlet-banded hat and field boots, to see for himself how things were progressing.

'You must have impressed him.'

'I can't see why,' said Richard, who had shared his observation post for half an hour with Alexander while an infantry attack went in.

'Well, he's asked for you personally.'

Richard's head jerked up.

'As one of his special liaison officers,' Fremantle went on. 'You're to report to AFHQ without delay. The message is marked Most Immediate.'

'Oh, Colonel; I can't go back to being a staff officer.'

'I shall be sorry to lose you, Richard, you know that. But it's a terrific feather in your cap to be picked out by Alex personally.'

'Do I have to go? There must be some way round this, surely? Couldn't you decline to release me, Colonel?'

Fremantle shook his head. 'It's a direct order. Alex may be able to charm the birds off the trees but I would not care to be the one to say him nay when he's made up his mind about something.'

A particularly well-aimed 88-millimetre shell struck the house on the far side exposed to the north. A shower of plaster fell from the ceiling. Richard dusted the fragments from his legs.

'Who will you give my battery to?'

'I thought Michael Higgins. He did very well during that show on Monte Lungo.'

'Yes. He's a good chap. I wouldn't mind handing over to him. When do I have to go?'

'Soonest, the message says. That means you report to AFHQ in Caserta tomorrow, I'm afraid.'

Richard had already accepted the inevitable. Life in the army consisted of a series of sudden, unexpected changes. He finished his drink and stood up.

'Colonel, you'll keep an eye on my young brother, won't you?'

*

Richard's orders required him to report to a Colonel Jenkins at Caserta. Even with his staff experience it took him half an hour to track down the GSO1 Special Intelligence Operations in the rambling Royal Palace which had been taken over as Allied Force Headquarters.

The Colonel was a bluff, balding officer with a rather fussy manner and a row of First World War ribbons. Richard recognized him at once as one of those staff officers who always has more to do than he can handle and is chronically behind on paper work. His desk was awash with documents and files.

'Ah, yes. Stewart. We're expecting you.' His eyes ran up and down Richard, shying away from the MC ribbon. 'Where's your kit?'

'I dumped it at the guard room, sir. The guard commander said he'd look after it till I know where I'll be billeted.'

'Yes. I see.' Jenkins caressed the lower left surface of his rib-cage as if he were concealing a patch of eczema beneath his service dress jacket. 'We can deal with that when you've seen General Alexander. I'll just try and find out from his ADC when you're to report to him.'

To Richard's surprise the C-in-C was ready to receive him almost immediately and appeared to be prepared to brief him personally. The ADC showed him into a large office on the third floor. The broad windows looked down the road that led from Caserta to Naples. The room was still equipped with the opulent furnishings appropriate to a princely residence which had aimed to match the splendours of Versailles.

Alexander immediately put down the paper he was studying and came out from behind his desk. He was wearing a plain battledress jacket above cavalry-twill breeches and brown leather field boots. Richard could not help thinking he looked a little improper, almost naked, without the peaked cap with its red band.

Alexander's slightly chubby face was already creased in a welcoming smile that immediately put Richard at his ease.

'Stewart? We have met before. On Longstop, I believe.'

Now in his fifty-second year, the Ulsterman looked fit and alert. Among the medals on his chest were the MC he had won at Loos and the DSO gained on the Somme. From the very first moment he struck a visitor as a highly professional soldier with the unassuming courtesy of an aristocrat.

'That's right, sir. I remember it very well.'

'So do I.' Alexander gave him a quick and searching inspection, then briskly turned to the matter in hand. 'You held a staff job for fifteen months but asked to be posted back to your regiment.'

'Yes, sir. They'd had a lot of casualties and needed officers –'

'Yes, I can understand your feelings. But your qualifications are rather unusual, you know. You speak three foreign languages with fluency – including Italian. I've been looking at your file.'

Richard made a wry face. All through his army career he had been dogged by his academic qualifications. Even after he had got his commission in the GY he had been singled out for a staff job and sent away for training at the Intelligence Corps Centre. When the war was carried to North Africa he had come out as a GSO2 on the staff of General Anderson's First Army. As it happened the GY were sent to the same theatre. When he heard about their heavy loss of officers in the fighting round Medjez-el-Bab he applied for transfer back to regimental duties. He had seen the end of the Tunisian campaign with the Yeomanry, had been with them all through the landings in Sicily and the advance up the boot of Italy.

Alexander saw his expression and smiled faintly. 'You must understand, Stewart, that I have a very difficult campaign on my hands. I have to make the best use of every resource I've got. You happen to be one of them.'

'Sir, I didn't mean to imply –'

'Now, sit down.' Alexander brushed the apology aside and sat down in one of the formal armchairs.

Richard took the other, removing his cap and placing it on the floor. He still felt awed at being in the presence of the legendary 'Alex' and did not really feel happy about sitting down.

'I'll explain what this is all about. Then perhaps you won't feel quite so bad.'

'Yes, sir. I mean, no.'

'I wonder if any general in modern history has had to command an army group containing so many different nationalities.' Alexander gazed thoughtfully out through the window for a moment, then turned his very direct gaze on Richard. 'How many nationalities do you think I have under my command? I mean complete formations and units.'

'Well, sir, there are the British and Americans, the French, the Canadians –'

23

Richard was fumbling to remember. A regimental officer is so absorbed in the small world of his own sector that he has little knowledge of the wider picture. Alexander helped him out, counting on his fingers.

'As you say, there are first the British formations which account for ten of the twenty divisions I have. Then there is the United States, which comprises the largest single nationality, but which is nonetheless a multi-racial force. From the Empire I have Indians and Nepalese, Canadian, South African and New Zealand divisions. The latter includes a Maori battalion. You mentioned the French, but remember that the other ranks are largely made up of Algerian, Moroccan and Tunisian colonial troops. Then there is the new Polish Corps, some thirty thousand strong. I even have a Brazilian unit. And of course we now have the Italians as our allies with a motorized brigade and the absolutely essential mule companies.'

To Richard's astonishment the General had ticked off fourteen fingers. He did not feel called upon to make any comment. When a Commander-in-Chief is in full spate a mere major does not interrupt. And he had enough staff experience to know that it was virtually unheard of for a Commander-in-chief to talk like this to a junior officer – especially in the absence of his Chief of Staff.

'Commanding such a force is a delicate task.' Alexander's eyes had moved to the large map opposite his desk. A connoisseur of art and a skilled painter himself, he'd had the map mounted on a stand so as not to cause any damage to the priceless wall coverings. It showed the Order of Battle of the Allied forces as well as all that was known of the Germans. He seemed to be talking as much to himself as to Richard. 'I have to be very careful not to step on corns. Of course, I have the closest possible links and understanding with my army commanders, General Clark and General Leese. But there are other very strong personalities on the scene. General Anders who commands the Polish Corps is a man of fiercely patriotic nature. General Juin who commands the French is a remarkably shrewd soldier who has accepted a lower ranking in order to fit into the command structure. General Freyberg, as you know, is a First War VC and has a very precise brief from the New Zealand Government.'

To emphasize his point Alexander tapped the arm of his chair. His fingers were delicate, almost artistic, the nails

24

carefully manicured. He wore a signet ring on his right little finger.

'Now, Stewart, this is where you come into the picture. Some very bitter fighting lies ahead of us. I need to know how the morale of this multi-national force of mine is standing up to the very demanding conditions. We have been having desertions from British units of the order of a hundred a month. It's not significant but it is a symptom of the physical and mental fatigue of the troops. We know that some hundreds of British reinforcements pitch-forked into the Salerno beach-head refused point-blank to fight for regiments they'd never heard of. Commanders of other nationalities are fiercely proud of their soldiers and might hesitate to report similar facts. But I need to know the spirit of my troops before I commit them to battle. In these conditions – appalling terrain and weather, almost impossible conditions for the bringing up of supplies and evacuation of wounded – morale is of prime importance.'

Alexander stood up and moved over to the window. There was a slight suggestion of swagger in his walk, perhaps a relic of his years in the Irish Guards. Richard wondered whether he also ought to stand up, but decided to stay put.

'Your job, Stewart, is to be my barometer, to keep me informed about the climate in my armies. It's a job that can only be done by an officer who has battle experience himself. I want you to visit front-line troops, talk to the men as well as the officers, find out what their mood is and gauge their battle-worthiness. You will report to me personally and I need hardly add that the greatest tact and delicacy will be needed –'

The General stopped as the door opened and a young Squadron Leader in RAF uniform came in. He was holding a sheet from a message pad folded in his hand.

Alexander took the message, unfolded it and read it.

. 'Thank you, Tommy. This came through very quickly. I wouldn't be surprised if I'm seeing this before its official recipient.' Alexander turned to Richard. It was obvious that his mind had switched to some new problem. 'Well, Stewart, you know what I want of you –'

As Thompson withdrew Alexander moved back behind his desk. Realizing that the interview was over, Richard retrieved his cap and stood up.

'Colonel Jenkins will look after the administrative side of your posting. He is the only other person who knows the real purpose behind your duties. As far as anyone else is concerned your job is to bring back first-hand reports of interrogations of prisoners of war and Italian refugees. You understand the position?'

'Yes, sir.' Richard put his hat on, moved to the door and pulled out his smartest salute. Alexander, already concentrating on the paper in his hand, merely nodded. But when Richard was already opening the door he called him back.

'Oh, Stewart – . You're a Roman Catholic, aren't you?'

'Yes, sir,' Richard said, for the second time in two days.

'You don't happen to know anything about the Abbey of Montecassino, do you?'

'It's the place where St Benedict is buried and therefore the focal point of the whole Benedictine Order. I suppose you could say it's one of the most revered shrines in Europe. It's been a place of pilgrimage since the sixth century, even for Popes and Emperors.'

'You've been there?'

'No, sir. But my school was run by Benedictines.'

'Oh? Not Downside, by any chance?'

'Yes, sir.' The General had taken Richard by surprise.

'That's a coincidence. My senior chaplain comes from there. But I can't help wishing St Benedict had not chosen the site of a fortress for his Monastery.'

3

Up in the Monastery of Montecassino on the day that Binley croaked Padre Nessuno also had heard a bell tolling, but his was a real one. It was four o'clock, the hour for Vespers.

He closed his books, carefully inserting markers in the passages he needed for reference. He was working on a thesis which would finally demolish the heresy that the bones of St Benedict reposed at Fleury in France and not beneath the high altar of the *basilica* here at Montecassino.

So immersed had he been in his work that he had hardly been aware of the distant thump of gunfire. That was a far-off world whose strife did not concern him. Here in the vast Monastery he could feel isolated from the conflicts of warring armies. As he stood up to replace his books on the shelf a shaft of late sunlight slanted through the window onto his face.

He closed the door of his cell and joined his fellow monks as they walked along the broad corridor towards the church. They were shadowy figures in their black cassocks, for there was little illumination in the building. After a low-voiced greeting they walked in silence, only the slap and shuffle of their sandals breaking the quietness of the long corridor.

Padre Nessuno decided that on this evening he would make his way to the church by the Loggia del Paradiso. He wanted to catch a glimpse of the sunset from the balustrade of the open cloister in the centre of the complex of buildings. It meant passing through the improvised quarters where some of the thousand or so refugees who had sought asylum from the approaching war were lodging. Simple folk, both old and young, they saw him as a symbol of divine protection and sought to kiss his hand as he passed.

Out in the open air the cold was already biting. There were other dangers too. Stray shells had already fallen within the Monastery and fragments from the anti-aircraft guns often spattered down on the roofs and open courtyards. As he crossed the Bramante Cloister he realized that he was not alone. Coming towards him was one of the young novices, who would soon have to decide whether to take his solemn vows, thus committing himself to the Monastery for life. Padre Nessuno suppressed his annoyance at this intrusion into the privacy he had sought. Felipe was only nineteen years old and he had adopted Nessuno as his mentor.

'Good evening, Dom. And how are your refugees?'

'We are running out of food, Father, and the shortage of water is becoming very serious. How long do you think we will have to keep these people here?'

'Not long. The fighting is coming nearer every day and soon

27

it will have passed beyond us. Then, may it please God, we can resume our normal life.'

'I am not so sure, Father. Have you heard the rumour?'

Padre Nessuno gave the young man a stern look. Rumours were not to be encouraged.

'Rumour?'

'That the Monastery is to be evacuated – by order of the occupying power.'

Even the suggestion shocked Padre Nessuno.

'Evacuate the Monastery? That is unthinkable. It would break the continuity of the community.'

'But *il segretario* told me that –'

'Felipe.' Padre Nessuno held up his hand to stop this idle speculation. 'Our Saint himself enjoined us to remember the words of the Psalmist: *"Custodiam vias meas, ut non delinquam in lingua mea; posui ori meo custodiam"*.' Nessuno was pleased to see that Felipe bit his lip and accepted the rebuke with due humility.

The last of the light was bringing out the golden tones of the arches and columns surrounding the Bramante Cloister. As Felipe hung back in deference to his mood, Nessuno walked to the balustrade and looked towards the west. The Loggia opened out onto the infinite. Most of the view consisted of sky and it was heavenward that Padre Nessuno usually gazed when he came here. But as he brought his eyes earthward the panorama that confronted him was awesome. To westward the sun had set behind the mountains and was dipping into the sea beyond. If he turned to the right he could see the snow-covered peak of Monte Cairo towering to five thousand feet against the darkening sky. Below him lay the flat plain of the Liri Valley stretching from the base of Montecassino to the Aurunci Mountains eight miles away. It was a fertile plain, speckled with small villages and farms. A few miles further north lay the towns of Pignataro, Pontecorvo and Aquino. The river Liri wound its way through small fields and low hillocks to join the Rapido, which flowed across the southern end of the valley.

In normal times that valley would have been studded with a thousand twinkling lights. Now it was dark, blacked out as some protection against the Allied Air Forces which dominated the skies. From time to time the detonation of a heavy gun broke the silence, the sound echoing forlornly round the hills. It was hard to believe that the gun area and supply dumps of the German army were down there and that in the mountains over his left shoulder another army was advancing to drive them back up the road to Rome.

Nessuno had not realized till now how deeply he loved this place. Felipe must surely be wrong. Yet he had to admit that there had been an intimation of some such development. Had not the Germans insisted on transporting all the moveable treasures of the Monastery to a safer refuge? And now he recalled the ominous words of the officer who had taken charge of the priceless manuscripts from the library.

'Hitler has ordered that the Allies are not to be allowed past this point,' he had told one of the monks. 'They will never take Rome.' Not long afterwards word had come up from Cassino town that the civilian population of the entire area was being evacuated.

Those had been evil omens but Padre Nessuno had tried to escape their implications. This Monastery was his whole existence. When he had taken his solemn vows nearly a quarter of a century ago, he had dedicated himself to a lifetime here in Montecassino. Benedictines do not move from one monastery to another. Once committed to a community they remain there until death. Padre Nessuno had been especially determined that he would live his whole life out in the place where St Benedict had founded his first community and where, as Nessuno was convinced, he lay buried.

The voice of Felipe brought him back to reality. 'Padre, we shall be late for Vespers.' Then, unable to resist the temptation to even the score a little, Felipe added: 'I believe the Founder said: "*Ergo nihil operi Dei praeponatur*".'

Padre Nessuno gave his companion a sharp look as he turned away from the balcony. He made a mental note to give Felipe a little lesson in humility. In silence the two black-cassocked figures passed between the statues of St Benedict, and his sister, St Scholastica. They ascended the broad monumental staircase that led to the forecourt of the church. There they kept close to the walls not only for protection from the biting wind but also from the danger which could fall from the sky.

The community was already seated in the church, the eighty or so monks occupying the intricately-carved stalls that lined three sides of the choir, behind the high altar. Nessuno and Felipe were the last to take their places, under the faintly reproving eye of the Abbot.

Nessuno searched the faces of his fellow monks, trying to read in them confirmation or denial of what young Felipe had told him, but with only the candles for illumination their faces were dim. He knew each one intimately, from old Padre Severino down to young Dom Michele, who had only taken his vows this year. Every age of man was represented here.

Many of the refugees had come to attend Vespers, but they were in the body of the church, on a lower level and out of sight beyond the high altar.

Padre Nessuno's mind and eyes kept wandering as the monks intoned the Magnificat, the almost hypnotic cadences of the Gregorian Chant rolling majestically round the vaults of the church. He was filled with a terrible premonition that this was the last time the community would ever be assembled together in the church he loved so well. In this light the colours of the inlaid marbled columns were even more beautiful, the orange, cream, yellow, golden and blue tints softened by the yellowish radiance of the candles. The vaulted roof with its gilded arches framing the frescoes of Luca Giordano seemed loftier and more mysterious.

Kneeling while the aged Abbot intoned the Pater Noster he raised his eyes to the cupola above the High Altar, then lowered them in reverence to the altar itself. This was the heart of the whole Monastery, its most sacred spot. It was here, in the presence of the saints' bones, that Emperors, Kings, Queens and Popes had come to kneel in homage. He could not believe that the Abbot would ever consent to abandon this.

It was with a sense of unreality that he heard the old man bid the community remain seated.

'Beloved in the Lord,' he told them, his failing voice shaking with emotion. 'I have sad news to break to you. Tomorrow the family of Saint Benedict is to be driven once again onto the path of exile, for this *excelsa domus* may become yet again a battlefield and a prey to death.'

Padre Nessuno, his mind in turmoil, hardly heard the rest. His lips automatically echoed his Abbot's closing words: 'Now and for ever may God's will be done.' His eyes were already dimming with tears when he heard his own name spoken. The Abbot was reading out the list of the half-dozen monks who would remain as custodians of the Monastery during the period of exile. Padre Nessuno's sorrow was replaced by a feeling of intense gratitude. So the continuity of the community would not be broken after all and he would be able to finish his thesis in peace.

Afterwards, Felipe asked him if he was not frightened.

'Frightened? Why should I be frightened?'

'If the Germans are evacuating the Monastery that means they are going to incorporate it in their defensive system.'

Padre Nessuno shook his head. 'You are wrong there. General von Senger has assured the Abbot that this is not the case. He is himself a devout Catholic and especially sympathetic to the Benedictine cause.'

The Commander of the Panzer Corps charged with defending the Cassino feature had made a most favourable impression when he had come to attend Divine Service in the Monastery on Christmas Day. It was he who had proclaimed the buildings out of bounds to German troops. He had even put a military police guard on the gate to ensure that the order was respected.

'He was so careful to respect our neutrality,' Nessuno reminded the young man, 'that he would not even look out of the windows of the Abbot's room, lest he should be able to see some movement on the Allies' side.'

'But if the Monastery is virtually empty,' Felipe insisted, 'will the Germans be able to resist the temptation to withdraw into it when they are subjected to severe attack?' Felipe, who had recent experience of the world of men, was perhaps inclined to be more realistic than Padre Nessuno.

'Even if they do, I don't think we have anything to fear. The Allies will simply pass on and lay the Monastery under siege. These are the days of Blitzkrieg, my friend.'

'I am not sure.' Felipe shook his head obstinately. At the University, before deciding to become a monk, he had dabbled in military history. 'The Italian Military Academy always chooses Cassino when they want to give an example of a perfect natural defensive position. You have heard those explosions outside the walls during the last few weeks? I am sure that the Germans are constructing a very strong defensive position here and this hill we are on is the key to it.'

When an older man has for long been in the position of guide and counsellor to a younger one, it is difficult for him to accept the fact that on certain subjects his pupil may be more expert than he. Besides, did not the Rule state that 'it becometh the

31

master to speak and to teach; but it befits the disciple to be silent and to listen.'

'These are the days of mobile warfare,' he said with authority. 'Tanks and aircraft have made a great difference to tactics. Besides, if the Germans have been so honourable about respecting the Monastery, how much more so will the Allies. After all, St Benedict is the patron saint of all Europe. His shrine is one of the most holy places on the earth.'

'All the same,' Brother Felipe said, 'I wish you were coming with us to Rome. I shall be worried about you.'

Padre Nessuno laughed. 'Hold to your faith, my son. Have you forgotten that St Benedict asked God to spare his monks? Even when the Saracens and Lombards sacked the Monastery and the earthquake destroyed it the monks were saved. God has protected us for a millenium and a half. He will not forsake us now.'

4

General Frido von Senger und Etterlin had taken command of XIV Panzer Corps on 8 October 1943 and had consequently become responsible for the defence of the western sector of the front, extending more than half way across the peninsula. He was an extremely cultivated man, who had won a Rhodes Scholarship to Oxford just before the First World War, in which he had served as an infantry officer. Being a member of an aristocratic family and imbued with the traditions of the old German army, he viewed the Nazi regime of Hitler with repugnance. Ironically, his job as a soldier required him to do all he could to keep the Fuhrer's enemies at bay and delay the fall of the tyrant. Von Senger was the kind of commander who believed in making himself familiar, by personal reconnaissance, with every feature of the line his troops were holding. He did not hesitate to expose himself to danger when visiting the front. Yet because his coldness towards Hitler was known, he was constantly under suspicion and surveillance from the officers of the SS.

A few days after the 90th Panzer-Grenadiers had bloodied the nose of the Wessex Fusiliers on the Reinhard Line, which screened the still uncompleted Gustav Line, a gleaming black 3.8 litre Horch swept up to the villa at Roccasecca where von Senger had his headquarters. It bore no less a person than Field Marshal Kesselring. He had come up to see for himself how the defensive works at Cassino were progressing. He was followed by a couple of Mercedes. The ADCs and staff officers were crowded into a Typ 320. A colonel from Himmler's Reich Security Head Office rode alone in the back of a 540K cabriolet.

Standartenführer Pohl was a right little dandy. His flashy uniform contrasted with von Senger's workaday grey-green outfit and the eccentric get-up of Baade. But what most interested von Senger were his plain black right-hand collar-patch, and the diamond-shaped black patch on his forearm, bearing the initials 'SD'. These two signs identified him as a member of the *Sicherheitsdienst*, sent from Himmler's RHSA to snoop on the generals in the field.

As he came out to receive his visitors, von Senger was accompanied by General Ernst-Günther Baade. This legendary figure was the inspiration as well as the commander of 90th Panzer Grenadier Division. The two men exchanged a glance as they saw the grey-uniformed SS officer step out of the second car.

'You and I are going to have to watch our Ps and Qs, Baade,' von Senger murmured. 'There's a gentleman who would be only too happy to see us hanging from a meat hook.'

Kesselring's eyebrows rose when he saw Baade's campaigning outfit, which included a Scottish-type kilt of khaki material worn over his breeches and, in place of the usual sporran, a revolver hanging from his neck by a cord. The rumour was still rife at OB Südwest's headquarters that Baade had accepted an invitation to dine on Christmas Day with his opposite number on the Allied side.

To avoid attracting the attention of any roving Air OP which might have penetrated the thick cloud base, the party covered the final ten kilometres to Cassino in a small convoy of Kübelwagen. The ADCs and staff officers were ordered to remain further back while the three generals moved to a good point of observation on the southern slopes of Monastery Hill, some way below the building itself. Out there somewhere, beyond Monte Trocchio, menacing but totally invisible on this dark day, was the Fifth Army of General Mark Clark. As usual, the rain was pelting down.

'I would have preferred to take my line of defence behind Monastery Hill to Piedimonte,' von Senger began, 'but the Führer was adamant that this feature should be defended. Of course, I bowed to his superior judgement.'

Kesselring looked sharply at the corps commander. For once the smile was absent from his blunt but chubby face. But there had been no hint of sarcasm in von Senger's quiet voice nor of disrespect in his scholarly features.

'The Führer is quite right,' OB Südwest stated emphatically. 'The characteristics of this feature are such that we cannot afford to dispense with them. Now, tell me what dispositions you have made.'

The burthen of von Senger's report was that the town of Cassino and the hill behind it had been turned into one vast fortress. The houses had been transformed into pill-boxes, their cellars and ground floors reinforced with concrete. Tanks had been concealed behind the walls of many of them and tunnels dug for underground communication by day. 16th Fortress Engineers had dammed the Rapido above the town. Its waters had been diverted so that the flat ground of the suburbs had become a quagmire. If the enemy tried to use tanks they would be bogged down. When the inevitable river crossing was attempted further downstream the sluice gates could be opened, releasing a flood of water. Even if some boats survived and elements did get across they would encounter a co-ordinated system of fortified farm buildings, concrete pill-boxes, tank turrets in ground emplacements, fields of mines, barbed wire entanglements and machine guns sited to cover every possible line of approach.

The hill they were standing on would be even more impregnable. Emplacements had been blasted in the solid rock. The natural caves had been enlarged, new caves had been created. At every bend of the zig-zag Via Serpentina machine-gun posts had been built. The thick and prickly gorse bushes had been reinforced with barbed wire and sown with mines. Von Senger and Baade were confident that the Panzer-Grenadiers could sit out the heaviest bombardment which Alexander's thousand guns could throw at them. They had just been supplied with new 'crabs', six-man steel shelters capable of withstanding anything except a direct hit.

'Yes, I can see that you have been more than thorough,' Kesselring cut in. 'I can report back to the Führer that you have created an impregnable position. Your defences are of fortress strength and you have excellent observation.'

'Yes, we can see everything that moves,' von Senger agreed. Kesselring's habitual optimism slightly irritated him. He was never sure whether it was a pose to impress Hitler – and the eyes and ears of Hitler. 'My observation posts will be on the forward slopes of the hill, more or less where we are standing.'

'Not in the Monastery?'

'From the Monastery one cannot see Cassino town,' von Senger pointed out quietly. 'Besides, we always place our OPs some way down the forward slopes.'

Kesselring had begun to move away. Von Senger followed him.

'If we can delay them on the Reinhard Line for another week,' the Corps Commander said, 'our defensive system will be complete. Then let them come. So long as I have troops to fire the guns they shall not pass.'

'I seem to detect a qualification in that statement, General.'

Von Senger looked at Kesselring seriously. 'The Führer has said that the Cassino position must be held at all costs. *All* costs. Every inch that is lost must be recaptured. Officers who fail in their duty will be disgraced. That is so?'

Kesselring nodded. For a moment they were out of earshot of the others. 'The Führer has good reason to insist on delaying the enemy's advance on every front. We are developing a secret weapon which will assure us of victory.'

'It will have to be a very special weapon,' von Senger commented drily.

'I can assure you that it is. The day after we use it the war will end. We will have the capacity to obliterate not only

35

London but every city in England. That is secret information, Frido. It is for your ears only.'

'The Führer's order will be obeyed to the letter,' von Senger promised him. 'These men will die here rather than retreat.'

To rejoin their vehicles the party had to pass close to the towering walls of the Monastery. From below its thick, slightly sloping base the building looked more than ever like a fortress. Kesselring waved his baton at it.

'I know that we have agreed to respect the Monastery, but in the last resort might you be forced back onto it?'

'No.' Von Senger shook his head emphatically. 'It is of no value to us as a defensive feature.'

'Herr General.' The smooth, almost purring voice came from behind von Senger's shoulder. Unnoticed the SS Colonel had caught up on the two Generals. 'Your attitude to this question is perhaps influenced by your religious convictions?'

Von Senger stopped and stared up at the Monastery, now deserted except for a handful of monks and civilian refugees. The rows of blank windows stretched away for a hundred yards in either direction. He dared not look at the SS Colonel in case he betrayed his feelings. What could a man like that know or care about the shrine of St Benedict? Already there were signs that after the Jews, the Catholics in Germany would become the prey of the SS.

'No, not at all,' he replied mildly. 'To use the Monastery for defensive purposes I would first have to demolish it – as we have done with the houses in Cassino. I can state categorically that I am able to defend this feature more efficiently without it.'

*

On 11 January 1944 the defences of the Gustav Line were complete. The German High Command gave their forces holding the screen of the Reinhard Line permission to withdraw under pressure into these well-prepared positions. As British 10 Corps on the western seaboard pushed forward to the River Garigliano the French Expeditionary Corps on the right began to filter across the Rapido and penetrate the mountains to the north-east of Montecassino. In the centre of the Fifth Army front 11 US Corps pushed forward to the banks of the Rapido and the outskirts of Cassino town.

The Germans were now ready, ensconced in the fortified block-houses of Cassino, sheltering deep in the caves and machine-gun pits on Monastery Hill, deeply dug in on the further bank of the Rapido and the village of Sant' Angelo, which commanded the crossing places. To the Allied soldiers who had been slogging up the Italian peninsula through a wretched winter, this was just another defensive line to delay them. The Intelligence services had let them down badly, seriously underestimating the strength of the Germans and their capacity to resist. There was nothing to forewarn them that they were now coming up against the most strongly defended feature of the whole campaign in Europe.

By the 15th Monte Trocchio, the isolated hill facing Montecassino from three miles away across the Rapido, was absorbed by the advance of 11 US Corps. Its summit offered a magnificent panorama of Cassino town, the mountains rising behind it and the inviting valley to the north-west. So much so that it became in time a sort of Dress Circle, from which a succession of distinguished visitors gazed out over the battle-field.

General Alexander was one of the first to avail himself of this extraordinary vantage point, which before the battles were finished was to provide cover for more than two hundred OPs. As was his wont he had come as far forward as he could to familiarize himself with the terrain.

The first thing to focus his attention as he peered out from the cover of the rocks was the great Monastery facing him from across three miles of flat ground. It appeared to be very much nearer than that. His experienced eye at once saw how the hill on which it stood dominated the whole picture.

Towards the north-west, parallel with the slant of the Italian peninsula, the flattish expanse of the Liri Valley offered what, to the commander of a mechanized army, must be regarded as the gateway to Rome. Along its north-eastern flank ran the ancient Via Casilina, now referred to as Route 6. This stretch of farmland and potential tank country was on an average five miles wide and thrust twenty miles deep into enemy territory. Three rivers, apparently insignificant from this height but destined to play a crucial part in the fighting, wound their way across the fertile plain. The Rapido, fed by many tributaries, normally looped round the town of Cassino. Now, diverted by the Germans, it had flooded several square miles of what had been the town's suburbs. It was met by the Gari a mile and a half south of the town. This tumid river joined the Liri, which

37

had meandered down from the north-east, just south of the village of Sant'Angelo. United together they formed the Garigliano, which found its way through the mountains to the Gulf of Gaeta.

On both its flanks the Liri Valley was dominated by mountains. To the south lay the Aurunci range, a jagged mass of great ridges rising to three thousand feet. From the north the Central Appenine range swept down to the five thousand-foot massif of Monte Cairo. From its snow-crowned summit the sky-line descended over crags and ravines to the seventeen-hundred foot outcrop of Montecassino. From there it plunged abruptly to the Via Casilina and the plain.

Upon this outcrop crouched the Monastery, as threatening to the eyes of a soldier as the Etruscan fortress it had replaced in the fifth century.

★

Richard's job as the C-in-C's Field Liaison Officer provided him with the sharpest of contrasts. One day he would be shivering with the troops in the most advanced and isolated mountain outposts, and the next savouring the flesh-pots of Allied Forces Headquarters. Colonel Jenkins had provided him with the indispensable Jeep and had allocated him as driver an Irishman named Mehan. Mehan had been a sergeant in the regular army of the Irish Free State and had deserted in order to join the Royal Inniskilling Fusiliers. Wounded in the house-to-house fighting at Centuripe in Sicily he had been medically downgraded and assigned to AFHQ as a staff driver. He was overjoyed when he realized that with Major Stewart he would again be getting a whiff of the sweet scent of battle.

Together, during the early days of January, they covered many hundreds of miles, often at little more than walking speed. The traffic of a mechanized army overcrowded the roads that followed the valleys, soon reducing them to deeply-rutted mud tracks. Richard discovered that for a staff officer to reach the forward areas demanded not so much courage as patience and persistence. It was not difficult to conceal the true purpose of his visits to units, for he always made his number with the intelligence officers who interrogated prisoners of war, or with the British Field Security and American CIC, whose job it was to deal with the Italian civilians who came across the lines. It was surprising how rapidly he built up a picture not only about the state of affairs on the Allied side but also what was going on behind the Gustav Line.

Every few days he would extricate himself from whatever unit he was visiting, struggle back through divisional and corps areas and return to AFHQ. Alexander liked to receive his reports in person so that he could ask questions.

Returning to AFHQ always meant smartening himself up, for one of the things that irritated him about the Headquarters was the dress-consciousness of the staff. Their insistence on correct military attire was in marked contrast to the eccentric and individualistic dress of the line regiments.

B3 Mess was peopled by a strange assortment of officers, both male and female. Many of them worked for the mysterious intelligence outfits which came under the aegis of Colonel Jenkins. They had a way of disappearing for days on end and then turning up again, very tight-lipped about where they had been and what they'd been doing. There were the 'Bourbon Colonels' of the OSS, who were operating spies in Rome and the northern cities of Italy. There were apparently junior officers like 'Tommy' Thompson, who somehow seemed to have the authority to say 'hands off' to officious senior officers. There were very silent, broodingly dangerous representatives of LRP, the long-range patrols which made Jeep sorties across the lines and deep into enemy territory. There were officers who talked about mule trains as if the wheel had not yet been invented, WAAF lieutenants who could take their pick of half a dozen proferred dates on any evening, psychoanalysts with Majors' crowns on their shoulders who spent their hours dreaming up the texts that would be fired at the Germans in propaganda shells.

Richard made particular friends with an American major who had a couple of rows of medals to prove that he had seen plenty of action in the 1914-1918 war. Now he was working for Allied Military Government of Occupied Territory.

'I know you youngsters think that AMGOT stands for Aged Military Gentlemen on Tour,' he said to Richard one evening at dinner.

Richard laughed, but he could not deny that it was true. 'I wouldn't call you aged, Major. If it weren't for the ribbons I wouldn't have thought you old enough to be in the first war.'

Major Steel always wore an impeccable green service dress jacket and knife-edged fawn trousers, but it was very easy to picture him in the jeans, chaps and broad-brimmed hat of a frontiersman. He had the kind of face that film directors seek out for the heroes of Wild West epics.

'I guess I'm old enough to be your father,' he replied with his slow drawl. 'What age are you, sir, if I'm not making too bold?'

'Twenty-eight.'

Steel nodded. 'My boy would have been twenty-eight this year.'

'Would have been?' Richard glanced at the American and saw a shadow pass across his face.

'He was killed at Pearl Harbor on the day we entered the war.' Steel bunched his fist and gently pounded the table. 'All I want is to follow him and I'm condemned to sit on my prat in a base area and account for sacks of corn.'

A pretty ATS officer came and took the empty seat on the other side of Richard. She gave him a smile as she sat down. He already knew her as a cypher officer. Her name was Diana Canning. Lieutenant Diana Canning.

'That's a tidy unit,' Steel murmured in his ear. 'Now, you just make the most of your chances.'

*

That night, when he had received his new Field Liaison Officer's report, Alexander spared five minutes to give him another brief insight into the kind of problems that beset a Commander-in-Chief.

'We cannot afford the time to let our formations re-organize,' he told Richard in response to the latter's suggestion that many units and formations were suffering acutely from battle casualties, illness and the hardships of a particularly cruel Italian winter. 'Perhaps you didn't know but I spent Christmas Day with Mr Churchill at Carthage. He protested about what he called the scandalous stagnation of the Italian campaign. I had to explain to him that his description of Italy as the soft under-belly of Europe did not accurately describe the kind of terrain we're fighting in.'

'It's a pity Mr Churchill couldn't have come to see what we're up against for himself.'

Alex gave Richard a quick look as if warning him not to say anything which might be critical of the man from whom he took his orders. 'I have invited him and he will be coming, but not till we have captured Rome. Meanwhile, we agreed on making a sea-borne landing further up the coast behind the German lines, forcing von Vietinghoff to withdraw his Tenth Army.'

Alexander picked up a pointer and moved to the large map opposite his desk.

'Now, this is top-secret information, but the landing will take place here at Corps strength.' He touched the coast of Italy at a point thirty miles south of Rome. 'The place is Anzio but the code name for the operation is Shingle.'

'Yes, I've heard Shingle mentioned.'

'You shouldn't have,' Alexander said mildly. 'But I suppose that's inevitable if you are in B3 Mess. Do you know the date?'

'No, sir,' Richard said truthfully.

'The first landing craft will touch down on the beaches at 2 a.m. on the morning of the 22nd. Before that happens we have to make sure that von Vietinghoff has as many divisions as possible committed to the defence of Cassino. Now you can see why the attack up the Liri Valley must go in without delay.'

'Do you mean the 22nd of this month, sir?'

Alexander nodded.

'But that's only a week away.'

'Yes, Richard, I know.' Alexander put down the pointer and gave something that in another man might have been mistaken for a sigh.

Perhaps emboldened by the fact that the C-in-C had addressed him by his Christian name for the first time, Richard ventured: 'Is all this to keep Mr Churchill happy?'

The C-in-C contemplated him, slightly lidding his eyes as if he were gazing across the tracts of the Libyan desert. Richard waited for a rebuke but the General relaxed. For some personal reason he had decided to take his young liaison officer into his confidence.

'The Prime Minister is himself under pressure. He wants to exploit our advantage in Italy as much as I do. But when he and Roosevelt met Stalin at Tehran in November, the Russian insisted on an invasion of France in May next. The Americans take the same view. They think we British are stalling on the invasion of France, using the Italian campaign as an excuse to delay it.'

Richard nodded. Though he had only been on his new job for two weeks he had seen indications of the rivalry and distrust which was building up between the American and British commanders.

'May is only four months away and they want every available landing-craft back in Britain at the earliest possible moment. We've only been able to keep the hundred and fifty landing-craft we need because Mr Churchill put in a personal transatlantic telephone call to Roosevelt. But we're not allowed to keep them a single day after the 22nd.'

Alexander picked up his swagger-stick and cap from a side-table and began to move towards the door.

'All that is confidential, of course, Richard. Top Secret in fact. But you can see now why I have to force the Gustav Line without delay and link up with our troops when they break out of the Anzio beachhead.'

The task of forcing this position would fall to Fifth Army. It was a multi-national army with a French, a British and a US Corps, and it was commanded by an American, Lieutenant General Mark W. Clark. Although the American attitude towards warfare in general and the Italian campaign in particular differed sharply from the British, Alexander was not the kind of Commander-in-Chief who breathed down the necks of his army commanders. He preferred to give them their objectives, then leave them to get on with the job.

At the headquarters of Fifth Army Richard was put in the picture about Mark Clark's plan for nipping the German Tenth Army out of the Cassino position. His strategy was geared to four principal thrusts. On 12 January the French Expeditionary Force would cross the valley of the Rapido and capture the high ground north of the Cassino Position. On the 17th British 10 Corps would establish a bridgehead across the Garigliano and secure the heights to the south of the Liri Valley. On the 20th 11 US Corps would force a crossing of the Rapido River south of Cassino and open the way for their armour to go rampaging up the road to Rome. Two days later, on the 22nd, the seaborne force would land on the beaches of Anzio.

If all went according to plan, Rome could fall within ten days.

*

As British 10 Corps were opening the offensive Richard went forward via corps and divisional headquarters. At Tac HQ of 78th Division he learned exactly where his old regiment was located. When he spotted the familiar frog emblem of the Greenshire Yeomanry he felt something akin to the pleasure of a home-coming. The gun area was on the southern side of the Garigliano and as he approached he heard the familiar crack of the 25-pounders firing a programme to soften up the enemy positions on the far bank.

Fremantle was directing operations from a wireless truck on the edge of the wood where brigade headquarters had been set up. This time there was no offer of a drink and the mashie niblick was nowhere in evidence.

The Colonel gave Richard a warm welcome and warned Mehan to park the Jeep under the lea of a bank.

'We were shelled half an hour ago. Lost one of my wireless operators. Sorry I can't offer you a drink, old boy, but I've got a regimental shoot on my hands. Tell me what you've been up to since I saw you last.'

During the periods when speech was audible and Fremantle was not talking on the Gunner wireless network, Richard told his old CO about his visit to the French Expeditionary Corps front. He had been with the 2nd Moroccan Division high up in the hills on the extreme right of Fifth Army's front when the first phase of the general attack went in. Thanks partly to his excellent French and to the proof of battle experience on his chest, he had struck up one of those quick and spontaneous friendships which develop between fighting men in the climate of war.

'I hear these Moroccans are very tough hombres,' Fremantle remarked. 'By all accounts the Krauts aren't too anxious to meet them on a dark night.'

'Neither would I, Colonel!' Richard laughed as he recalled the fearsome Goumiers with their dark skins, slightly Mongolian features and long, drooping moustaches. He had felt far from secure as he passed through their lines. Draped in their characteristic striped dressing-gown-like cachabias, they sat round their fires in groups, sharpening their knives and roasting small animals on spits. They had gazed at the British officer with malevolence.

'They prefer using their knives to guns. I was looked after by a captain in the French regular army who was commanding a tabor of Moroccan Goums. Chap called Marcel Duval. He asked me if I'd like one of his night patrols to bring me back a souvenir. Rather unwisely I suggested a German helmet. I knew someone at AFHQ who very badly wanted one.'

'Oh, what was wrong with that?'

'I got the helmet all right. The only thing was it still had the head in it.'

Fremantle's laugh was cut short by the whine of a shell passing through the air. Both men listened with interest, their experienced ears calculating whether it would pass over them or not. Then Fremantle nodded and grinned. Stones and earth were thrown up as the shell landed two hundred yards away. The detonation of the gun that had fired the round reached them at the more leisurely speed of sound.

'A 105,' Freemantle commented. 'This chap's beginning to be rather a nuisance. I think it's time we dealt with him. If you'll excuse me for a minute –'

'Colonel, before you start on that, can you tell me where to find Wilfrid? I'd like to have a word with him.'

'C Battery are supporting the Skins. Hang on and I'll give you the map reference.'

Battalion HQ of the Royal Inniskilling Fusiliers was in a farm just short of the river. Richard got there as darkness was falling and found the headquarters humming with the activity that precedes an attack. Stockwell was confirming the artillery programme with the Skins' CO, but he took time to greet the visitor.

'Your brother is with C Company, who are leading the assault. They're already moving up to their start lines.'

For Richard there was no alternative but to watch and wait, chafing at his own enforced inactivity.

The river crossing was due to take place at 9 p.m. The night was dark but reasonably fine. Over the front hung that strange stillness and expectancy that precedes an attack. Richard could not help thinking about Wilfrid, crouching out there in the pitch blackness somewhere, committed to the most hazardous of military operations.

It was a month since he'd had a letter from home and he knew the reason why. The letters were going to Wilfrid, who had always been the darling of his parents.

As the watch hands moved round towards nine o'clock Richard was sitting on his strapped-up bed-roll, trying to keep out of the way. The CO, Colonel O'Brien Twohig, had gone down to the river to supervise the crossing. The Adjutant made an entry in the battalion war diary, then came over to Richard. He too found this period of waiting hard to bear.

'An amazing fella, that brother of yours,' he said in a strong Kilkenny accent. 'When I first clapped eyes on him I thought we'd be having to kit him up with a rattle and a feeding bottle. You'd have thought it was the dog in charge of him instead of the other way round.'

'He's got a dog?'

'Well, you could call it a dog, I suppose, though to me it looks more like a cross between a sheep and a goat.'

Richard smiled. Wilfrid had been a passionate lover of animals since childhood.

'Where's the dog now?'

'Sure he's taken it with him. Everywhere he goes that dog goes too. He says it enjoys the sound of gunfire. As a matter of fact, the fusiliers like it. They say the dog brings them luck. It's a kind of mascot, you see. You can hear the beast barking on the wireless when he's giving his fire orders. You'd think it was putting him right on the co-ordinates.'

'How's he making out? Wilfrid, I mean, not the dog.'

'Bloody marvellous! He's as cool under fire as an Eskimo's tit.'

The thunder of a great cannonade made the rest of the sentence inaudible. The artillery barrage preceding the attack had opened up. The Adjutant went back to his wireless set. Richard resigned himself to a night of tension.

From the very first the attack went wrong. Owing to a guide's mistake most of the Inniskillings' boats had gone astray. One company managed to get across and seize a farm, but surprise had been lost. They were being heavily shelled by the German artillery.

The Adjutant switched to the Gunner wavelength. Richard heard Wilfrid's voice in Epitaffio Farm, directing a counter-bombardment shoot to try and minimize the effect of the German gunfire. Meanwhile Colonel Twohig dashed down to the place where the Wiltshires had made a successful crossing and arranged for the rest of his battalion to cross in the Wiltshires' boats.

By 3 a.m. the remaining companies were over the river. By 5.30 the isolated company was relieved and the position at Epitaffio Farm consolidated. Richard crossed the river with battalion headquarters to join up with the CO at Tac HQ. The

45

Adjutant sent a message to C Company to tell Wilfrid that his brother was there.

The cooks had rigged a tarpaulin between the walls of a ruined outhouse and as dawn broke the first cups of scalding-hot tea were being handed round.

Richard saw a young officer materialize from the gloom and stoop to come under the improvised shelter where the officers of battalion HQ were preparing to have breakfast. Not till the newcomer was within a couple of yards of him did he recognize his brother.

'Do you mind if Dante comes in?' Wilfrid asked the Adjutant.

'Not at all.'

Wilfrid gave a short whistle. A woolly mongrel about as high as his knee bounded up to him and nuzzled his hand. Then, as his master raised a warning finger, he sat on his haunches, laid his ears back and stared up, awaiting orders.

'Lie down there, boy. Over there.'

Wilfrid pointed to a bundle of hay by the wall. Dante padded over to it, circled twice and then flopped down. A single ear cocked up, while the other lay inert. His tongue came out dangling, and an eye surrounded by a patch of black hair eagerly scanned the surrounding faces.

'Hello, Richard.' Wilfrid greeted his brother as casually as if he'd just come down late for breakfast at their home on Gipsy Hill. 'Has Alex given you the sack?'

'Not yet, but I don't suppose it'll be long now.'

Wilfrid looked pale and there were deep shadows of fatigue under his eyes. Nothing else showed that he had spent a night under concentrated shell-fire. His battle-dress was rumpled and untidy, his tie askew, but that was in character. He was wearing the heavy sheepskin jacket favoured by many officers. His face was long and the boldest feature on it was the thin-bridged nose. The mound of soft flesh on his pointed chin was cleft by a vertical hollow. Dark, carelessly-cut hair framed a high forehead. The eyes were deeply recessed beneath black, mobile eyebrows. His mouth was not wide, but the lips were rounded and in repose slightly pushed forward as if preparing to give a low whistle of astonishment. His hands were thin and bony, the fingers unusually long with spatulate tips.

A Mess waiter handed him an enamel mug of tea. He started hunting for a spoon and eventually found one in the breast-

46

pocket of his battledress, along with a stained copy of Shakespeare's Sonnets.

'You had a rough night, by the sound of things.' Richard broke the embarrassed silence. 'I was listening in at battalion headquarters.'

'Yes,' Wilfrid agreed vaguely. 'It did get a bit sticky at one point. Even Dante was worried and that's unusual for him'.

'Why Dante? I can see the comedy bit but he's hardly divine.'

'He's been through hell,' Wilfrid explained seriously. 'I found him cowering in the cellar of a house the Skins captured. He seemed to want to come with me and he's been very easy to train.'

Wilfrid glanced affectionately at the animal who at once switched its gaze to him and swore allegiance with its eyes.

'Let's sit down here.' Richard squatted down on a bundle of brushwood with his back to the wall. Wilfrid folded his long limbs into a sitting posture beside him. The light was growing and a delicious smell of frying bacon filled the air. 'Have you had any news from home?'

'Your mail hasn't caught up with you?'

'No.'

'I had a letter from Angela. She said she'd written to you, too.'

'That'll be the day! Angela hasn't written to me for years.'

'Mum and Dad were bombed out.'

'Good God!' Richard blinked with shock. Wilfrid had picked up a dry stick and was poking the ground with it. 'Were they – ? Are they all right?'

'Just about. A thousand-pounder landed outside the sitting-room window. Everything round them was reduced to match-wood and the top storey's a gonner. Do you know they were sitting twenty yards from that bomb and never heard a sound. Just got up from their chairs and walked out of the ruins. But I understand Dad's badly shocked.'

'I should think he probably is! Where are they living now?'

'With Aunt Edie. Do you think one of us should apply for compassionate leave home?'

'We'd never get it. Not enough grounds. So many people have been bombed out.'

A cheerful shout came from the end of the shelter where the

47

cook had been preparing breakfast on a field stove. 'Grub up!'

The two brothers scrambled to their feet and joined the group at the trestle-table which the HQ Mess waiters had set up. The Skins had been on active service for long enough to have their creature comforts well organized. At a word from Wilfrid, Dante settled down into a crouch and laid his head on his front paws.

'I'm glad we had this chance to talk,' Richard said as a couple of enamel plates bearing bacon and liberated eggs were slapped down in front of them. 'I might not have found out about this for weeks.'

Wilfrid spread butter on one of the hard biscuits that came with the Compo rations. Keeping his voice casual he asked: 'Heard anything from Betty lately?'

'No. The last letter was dated three months ago. But I don't think she's going to change her mind.'

'Poor old Richard.' Wilfrid gave his brother a compassionate look. 'I think it's a rotten way to treat you.'

Richard's marriage had been a short one. He and Betty had gone to the altar a month after the outbreak of war. She was only eighteen then. A great many hasty marriages had taken place at that time as lovers prepared to part, not knowing if they would ever meet again. Richard's had been a real love match – or so he had believed. Saying farewell in a taxi outside Victoria Station before his posting to the BEF had been the most distressing experience of his life.

That had been four years ago. He had sensed how things were changed when the Regiment got back to Britain after Dunkirk, but had been totally unprepared for the letter which had arrived four months ago. She had written, with a kind of cheerful frankness, to tell him that there was someone else. He worked at the Board of Trade. They were in love. She said it was no fault of Richard's. It was just that she'd changed as she grew up. Vernon was fifteen years older and terribly sweet. He understood her so well. She knew Richard was big enough to forgive her.

By the time breakfast was finished the sun had risen. As Richard went outside with Wilfrid and Dante he looked towards the north and felt no surprise when he found that from this high position the Monastery was clearly visible. Wherever he went it seemed to follow him. Up with the Moroccan Goums he had seen it from the northern side. Now he was gazing at its southern aspect. The distance must have been a good eight miles, but it still appeared proud, aloof and formidable.

'Stockwell says we're due to pull back after this battle,' Wilfrid said. 'Might get a spot of leave.'

'Lucky you. My leave prospects look rather dim for some time to come. Where do you think you'll spend it?'

'I hear there's a rest camp at a hotel in Sorrento. That's not far from Pompeii. I've always wanted to see the wall paintings there. And I believe the Opera has started up again in Naples.'

Richard tried not to smile. It was typical of Wilfrid to plan his leave round art and music. Most officers had only one thought in mind and they weren't going to find what they wanted in a museum.

'Well, if I don't see you again before then, be good. And steer clear of the Neapolitan signorinas. By all I hear they're bad medicine.'

The warning was pure banter. Wilfrid was either too shy or too uninterested to waste any time on women. He had never developed a technique for getting past the purely formal stage with girls – nor any wish to, either.

'Where are you off to now?' he asked, as if he had not even heard the remark.

'To take a look at the Americans. Second US Corps are due to attack across the Rapido as soon as your people have established your bridgehead.'

Wilfrid put his already battered cap on his head and tightened the knitted scarf round his neck. 'Will we be seeing you again?'

'You may do. I have a kind of roving brief.'

'Hope so,' Wilfrid said, and with a short whistle to the dog was gone.

5

Getting back across the Garigliano was not so easy. The Germans, as always, were counter-attacking and their artillery had pounded the bridge which the engineers had constructed behind the Skins. It had to be rebuilt under continuous shell-fire. Richard was not able to rejoin Mehan till the afternoon.

At divisional Tac HQ he stopped as usual to get what information he could from the Intelligence Officer whose job was to interrogate prisoners of war. Although this was only intended to cover his real reason for visiting front-line formations, the reports he was bringing back on the interrogation of POWs and civilians were proving useful to the intelligence people at AFHQ.

'We did not take many prisoners,' the IO told him. 'Not more than twenty on the divisional front. We've identified them as from 29th and 94th Panzer Grenadier Divisions.'

'Any other gen?'

The steel-spectacled and studious-looking officer shook his head. 'They're very cocky, for some reason. We keep getting this story that Adolf Hitler has some fearful secret weapon up his sleeve that's going to completely turn the scales.'

Darkness had fallen by the time Richard left Tac HQ. He'd been offered accommodation for the night, but he wanted to get round to the area of 11 US Corps before the Americans put in their attack across the Rapido. It was timed for the night of the 20th.

Progress on the narrow track which served as the main

supply artery for the division was very slow. Most of the traffic was moving up towards the front. Mehan kept having to pull aside to let convoys of three-tonners jolt past. He took good care to stay within the white tapes which marked the area that had been cleared of mines.

They'd covered about five miles in an hour when they heard a heavy explosion ahead of them and a flash briefly illuminated the sky.

'Sounded like a couple of Teller mines going up,' Mehan commented. 'I heard Jerry's been laying double mines about three feet deep. They don't go up until about a hundred vehicles have passed over them.'

The reddish glow of a fire ahead confirmed his judgement. All movement on the track soon came to a halt. Presently word filtered back that a Scammel had run over a mine and brewed up. The increasing glare of the fire was conspicuous in the black night. It took the Germans about twenty minutes to get a battery of 105 mm howitzers ranged on it.

'I'm getting off this road.' Mehan engaged the low ratio gears. He was already in four-wheel drive. 'As soon as Jerry realizes the road's jammed he's going to plaster the whole length of it.'

He put the Jeep through a gap in the hedge. The game little vehicle bucked and porpoised its way across a couple of hundred yards of rough going towards a small copse. Richard and Mehan rigged a tarpaulin between the Jeep and two trees. The Irishman dug out his Benghazi Burner, primed it with petrol and made tea.

He was applying the rule of the Western Desert veterans: 'When in doubt brew up.'

It was not the first time Richard had been grateful for Mehan's resourcefulness. The back of the Jeep was loaded with gear so that they could make themselves comfortable if nightfall caught them away from a firm base. In addition to compo rations, water and bed-rolls, there were innumerable items which Mehan had 'won' from friendly quartermasters or abandoned Italian establishments.

At 7.30 precisely the night was made horrible by the tremendous din of an artillery barrage from the direction of Monte Trocchio, in the 11 US Corps sector five miles to the north. Sixteen field artillery battalions were pounding the

51

positions of the 104th and 129th Panzer Grenadiers in preparation for the attack by 36th US Division.

Richard swore. This meant that he was going to be late for the party.

'Looks like we're going to be here all night, sir. Shall I open a box of compo? I think there's one with some steak and kidney pie in it.'

'Good idea,' Richard agreed. 'And I'll open a bottle of that wine we got in Capua.'

There was no need to insist on distinctions of rank with so professional a soldier as Mehan. They had become a team, each with his own job to do, each respecting the other. Richard expected Mehan to keep the Jeep in perfect running order but he would never have asked him to perform such a menial task as clean his boots – even though he was officially his batman-driver. In fact, as often as not it was Richard who cleaned both pairs of boots while Mehan attended to the Jeep.

'Tell me, Mehan,' Richard said, as they stood eating in front of the Jeep, whose bonnet was serving as a buffet table for the scratch meal, 'is it true you're a deserter from the Irish Army?'

A grin creased the Irishman's freckled face.

'Aye, and I was a sergeant in it too. But I quit when it came home to me that they was going to stay neutral – even after the Jerries bombed Dublin. I knew I wouldn't see any of the fighting if I didn't do something about it. Then like an idiot I had to stop one in the leg at Tobruk. That's how I got my Grade C.'

'Did they give you any sick leave?'

Mehan shook his head. 'Daren't go home on leave, sir. The Irish Army has MPs at the docks in Dublin watching for the lads as they come off the boat. If they spot a deserter they'll have him in the glasshouse as quick as hell on stilts.'

'What'll happen when the war's over? You'll want to go back home, won't you?'

Mehan stared past Richard at the dim outlines of the hills. 'Sure, it'll be time to worry about that if the war ever does end.'

'They tell me you're quite an artist on the mouth-organ,' Richard said, after a pause.

'Would you like a tune?' Mehan's depression vanished

instantly. He put a hand inside his battledress blouse and drew out a harmonica. 'What do you fancy?'

'Macnamara's Band?'

'Macnamara's Band it is.' Mehan moistened his lips, cupped his hands round the instrument and began to play.

It was daylight before the jam on the road was cleared. Richard and Mehan, who had snatched what sleep they could under the tarpaulin, had to wait another two hours. The traffic control police were giving priority to the RAOC vehicles taking ammunition up to the Garigliano.

The delay meant that Richard did not get to 11 US Corps area until late in the evening. This time progress forward was slow. Priority was being given to the convoys of ambulances carrying wounded to the field hospitals. Many of them were moving at walking speed, easing gently over the deep ruts to save the occupants further suffering.

Things looked very bad.

The American troops he saw, usually so full of confidence and banter, had a whipped look. Richard, who was taking a spell of the wheel, ignored the signs pointing the route to Corps and Divisional HQ. He wanted to push as far forward as was possible. Without even talking to anyone he had picked up a sense of the mood that was in the air. It was not panic and it was not fear but rather something like a smouldering anger.

He had somehow got himself onto the railway track that curved round the southern base of Monte Trocchio before it ran on into Cassino town. The rails had been lifted and it was being used as an artery for vehicular traffic. The hump of Trocchio was looming high on his right when he pulled aside to allow yet another ambulance to sway past.

From the darkness at the side of the track a voice called out: 'Hey, Limey! Where do you think you're going? Don't you know this is the American sector?'

He looked round and saw a group of half a dozen soldiers squatting or lying on the bank beside the track.

'Are you 36th Div?' he called out.

'Were,' the Texan voice corrected. '2nd Battalion 141st Regiment. Or rather, what's left of it.'

In the eerie glow of the artificial moonlight he could see no more than a dozen men. He switched the engine of the Jeep off. The American who had hailed him struggled wearily to his feet and came towards him. The single bar of a lieutenant glinted on his shoulder.

Richard swung one leg out of the Jeep. 'My name's Stewart. Richard Stewart.'

The American nodded, still suspicious. 'Bob O'Hara,' he said automatically. 'You lost your way or something?'

Richard knew he was looking into the face of a man who has just come out of battle. The memory of horror was still in his eyes. He had not shaved for a couple of days. The steel helmet was askew on his head and his mouth was not too steady.

He said: 'I'm trying to find divisional headquarters.'

'You're way past it, buddy. You go much further on you'll be in the Panzer-Grenadiers' headquarters. You got any identification?'

Richard had to admit that a British Major pushing his way forward into an American sector in the dead of night was likely to arouse some suspicion. He produced the special pass with which the C-in-C had provided him. O'Hara held it in front of the masked lights of the Jeep.

'Allied Force Headquarters,' he read out, then straightened up. 'Hey, Sarge. Know what we got here? A staff officer from AFHQ.'

A burly figure squatting on the bank rolled to his feet and sauntered towards the Jeep. Richard could see the stripes on his arm. He had the features of a professional boxer but the same look of total exhaustion. His uniform was soaking wet and covered with mud. Half a dozen of the GIs stood up and came over to form a half-circle round the British officer. The rest were either too disinterested or too tired. They had the haunted expression of men who have seen their comrades slaughtered at their side and still cannot believe they have come out of it alive.

Mehan had quietly climbed out of the Jeep on the other side, pushing into the pocket of his battledress trousers the Biretta he had taken from an Italian prisoner in Cyrenaica. He had been carying it illegally ever since. He did not like the way this conversation was building up, knowing from personal experience that troops fresh out of a battle that had gone wrong can be very unpredictable.

'A Limey staff officer?' the sergeant growled. 'You're the guys who dropped us in the shit. You were supposed to clear that high ground on our left before our attack.'

'Yes, we let you down,' Richard admitted. 'The Germans opened the sluices further upstream and the current washed a lot of our boats away.'

The frank admission seemed to mollify the sergeant a little. He peered more closely at Richard's chest.

'Say, that ribbon you're wearing, I seen one of them before. That's a Military Medal, aint it?'

'Military Cross. You know, they dole them out with the rations. But I did used to be a real soldier at one time. You people look as if you'd had a rough time.'

'Rough time?' The sergeant gave a short laugh. 'You can say that again.'

'What went wrong?'

'Everything. It was a foul-up.' O'Hara's eyes went out of focus as he stared over Richard's shoulder in the direction of the Rapido. 'We took casualties even before we reached the river –'

'When our own artillery started their barrage the Krauts guessed what was happening,' the sergeant cut in. 'They caught us as we were moving up to the river. We lost our guides, got ourselves bogged down in the mud, saw half our boats blown to hell –'

'Goddam boats!' A high-voiced GI with a prominent Adam's apple pushed forward excitedly. 'When we did get them in the water we couldn't hold them. The stream was running at eight knots. And all the time the Krauts were pouring shell-fire and mortar bombs and machine-gun fire onto us.'

'It took seven hours to get two battalions across.' Lieutenant O'Hara took up the story again. 'By dawn we had dug in on the far bank. Then when daylight came they gave us everything they'd got. Jesus God, it was murder! We could not even get our wounded back. We had to pile the stiffs outside our fox-holes to make room for ourselves.'

A brief silence fell. They were remembering. At the back of the group one of the GIs choked back a sob, tried to turn it into a cough.

'Tell him about the Monastery,' said a small, dark GI who had been staring at Richard with unnaturally bright eyes.

'Oh, yeah. The Monastery.' O'Hara wiped an eye with the knuckle of his hand. 'That was the freakiest thing of all. When daylight came we looked up and there was this kind of Grand Hotel staring down on us. I counted one hundred and twenty windows in the part I could see and I'll bet there was a Kraut at every one of them. It was too easy for them. Like spitting cherry stones out of a top-floor window onto someone in the garden below.'

'Cherry stones shit!' commented the sergeant.

'If the bridges were knocked out, how did you get back?'

'We swam it. Me and two others from my platoon, the sergeant with four from his. There was a few others from other companies. Oh, yes. And our prisoner!'

'You brought back a prisoner?' Mehan asked incredulously.

'He brought himself. It was spooky. We were preparing to withdraw just after dark when this Kraut came crawling into our fox-hole. He was calling to us in English: "Don't shoot, I'm surrendering".'

'I wanted to stick a bayonet up the bastard.'

'It's a funny thing,' O'Hara said. 'But when you're in a situation like that you feel less hatred for the enemy than for your own generals who've sent you into it. This Kraut told me the Gestapo were after him and he'd rather be a prisoner of ours than theirs.'

'So what did you do with him?' Richard asked with interest. 'Where's he now?'

'Handed him over to the MPs. I guess he's in the POW cage. Must be lonely for him. He's the only prisoner we took.'

A couple of Studebaker six-wheel drive 2½-ton trucks came feeling their way nervously down the track. The black driver of the leading vehicle stopped level with the Jeep and put his head out of the window.

'You guys any idea where the 141st are?'

'We're the 141st,' the lieutenant told him. 'Are you our transport?'

'That's right. There's another four trucks on the way.'

'You can send them back,' the lieutenant said. 'Come on, fellas. Climb aboard.'

'Where's the rest of the regiment?' the driver enquired plaintively.

'There aint no rest.'

The soldiers were all piling into the front truck.

'Say, I got plenty of room too,' the driver of the second truck called out.

They took no notice but crowded in together, anxious to

remain a close-knit band of comrades, because no one else in the world had shared their experience nor could guess at what they had gone through.

From the Liri Valley came the occasional desultory boom of a cannon and the crump of the odd shell landing, but the front had lapsed once again into comparative quietness. The first battle for the Cassino Position was over.

6

The almost deserted Monastery was now completely cut off from the outside world. The vast building, designed to house a community of several hundreds, was occupied by only a dozen members of the religious order and four families which had been allowed to remain, for the simple reason that most of them were too sick to move.

The German authorities, when they had evacuated the entire civilian population from the Cassino area early in January, had tried to evict the remaining monks. They refused to go.

'You promised us that our decision to remain would be respected,' the German officer was told. 'If you want to move us you will have to do it by force.'

'Then on your own heads be it,' the officer stated baldly. 'We decline to accept responsibility for what may happen to you.'

From that day on the military guard was removed from the entrance and the great doors, the only means of access from the outside world, were closed and barred. The Monastery and those inside it were isolated.

Padre Nessuno was not unhappy. With the departure of the flood of refugees it was possible to return to something approaching a normal monastic existence. The monks, under their aged Abbot, did their best to continue living, working and praying according to the Rule which governed their lives. It was not easy. Shells were now falling within the precincts of the Monastery so frequently that it was dangerous to venture into the garden and open cloisters. The Luca Giordano fresco at the entrance to the church had been seriously damaged. A refugee drawing water from the well in the Bramante Cloister had been killed, the blast pulping his bones beneath the unbroken skin.

The twelve monks had for safety taken refuge in the lowest and oldest part of the building. It so happened that the most secure place was also the most sacred. When St Benedict had come to Cassino one thousand four hundred and fifteen years before, the whole of this part of Italy had been ravaged by war. Because he intended to establish the first real monastic order in Christendom, he required a site aloof and high above the plains where men fought their battles. St Benedict's purposes were totally different but he chose his location with the eye of a war lord siting a fortress. Although in the year 529 a temple of Apollo stood upon the summit of seventeen hundred foot high Montecassino it had indeed prior to that been an Etruscan fortress.

The cyclopean foundations of those pre-Christian fortifications had consisted of stone blocks four feet long. They were still in place when Benedict built his first Monastery and they were still in place in 1944. The Saint chose as his own cell a small chamber about twelve feet by ten in the old fort. That part of the original structure survived the ravagement of the Monastery by the Lombards in 581, by the Saracens in 883 and by the great earthquake of 1349. To this tiny, austere chamber where the Patron Saint of Europe laboured to perfect his Rule for Monks, the religious and secular potentates of Christendom had come in pilgrimage. Now, as danger threatened again, the Abbot directed that the Most Holy Sacrament be brought from the basilica and placed with reverence on the altar of what had become the Chapel of St Benedict.

'We must try to see the will of God in all that befalls us,' the Abbot had said. 'Were we not reduced to such a small number we could not gather together to celebrate the Divine Office in this most holy place.'

So, as the Allied armies drew ever nearer, the monks

continued the regular services that brought them together seven times a day; and the measured rhythm of the Gregorian chant, echoing in those underground passages, seemed to prevail above the rumble of war.

Padre Nessuno had obtained permission from Abbot Diamare to leave his books in his own cell and to continue work on his thesis there. No real danger was involved as he could reach it without having to venture out under the open sky. He derived a strange feeling of pleasure and fulfilment from pacing along the empty corridors, feeling the immense building enclosing him like a womb.

More than ever Montecassino seemed to stand aloof from the horror and fury of man's warfare as a symbol of spiritual values and the peace of God. It was a privilege to have been one of the few chosen to maintain the continuity of the community through another of the great crises of the Order's history. And though he tried not to harbour uncharitable thoughts he could not help feeling a certain relief that he was now spared the argumentative questions of Felipe.

He had got into the habit, on his way to and from his cell, of paying a visit to one of the families which had been allowed to remain. Laura Montini's husband had been one of the seventy civilians killed in the first bombing of Cassino town on 10 September 1943. Soon afterwards the Abbot had brought her up to the Monastery with her two sons, Franco and Sandro. When the majority of the refugees were evacuated from Montecassino, Laura had been allowed to stay. The six-year-old Sandro had been struck down by a mysterious illness and was too sick to be moved. Nessuno had helped the little group to settle into a small storeroom near the bakery, where the cold was not so intense.

One evening before Compline he paid a visit to the little room, dimly lit by a low-burning oil lamp. Laura was squatting beside the improvised cot where Sandro lay. He stopped at the door, gazing at her. With the soft light moulding her features she looked exactly like Leonardo's Mary, in the Madonna of the Rocks.

'Close the door,' she whispered. 'I don't want him to catch a draught.'

Nessuno shook off the spell that had suddenly held him. He was convinced that his concern for Laura and her sons was totally disinterested. But the young mother was in the full flower of womanhood – and God had given him eyes to see with.

'I've brought some water for you.'

He put the carafe down on an upturned box. It was cool from the well and the warmer air was condensing on the glass.

'Thank you. He is drinking such a lot. I am worried about him, Padre. He complains that he has pains all over his body. I think his fever has risen, but an hour ago he was as cold as ice.'

'He is asleep now?'

'Yes, but he is very restless and his skin is so hot and dry.'

'Where is Franco?'

'He has gone to get some bread. Dom Eusebio said there might be some to spare.'

Laura straightened up. She was, inevitably, dressed in black, a colour she was now condemned to wear for the rest of her life.

'The fighting is very close now, Padre, isn't it? Do you think that the Monastery will be attacked?'

'No, my child. You are safe here. Since the Germans have respected us there is no reason for the Allies to attack the Monastery.'

'I pray that you are right.' They were talking in whispers and she was gazing up at him with those very dark eyes. 'But why should they have bombed Cassino and only killed civilians?'

He would like to have put an arm round her shoulders to comfort her. It would have been an impersonal, fatherly gesture. Yet he held himself back.

'They were probably trying to hit the railway. Is there anything you need for Sandro?'

'I do not know.' She turned to look down at the restless, shivering child. 'He ought to be in hospital, with proper nursing.'

'I will bring you some more blankets. And a little dried fruit from the store, if the kitchener will let me have it.'

'You are very good to us. God bless you!'

Laura impulsively moved towards him, took his hand and kissed it. He felt the soft warmth of her lips on the back of his fingers.

He returned the blessing, turned away quickly and opened the door.

From then on his visits became more and more frequent.

Franco, to whom he had begun giving lessons, had channelled towards him the affection he would have given a real father. Sandro, during his periods of lucidity, called him *mio padre*. The first time he used the phrase Laura glanced at him shyly, with an almost conspiratorial expression. They were indeed becoming a little bit like a family, with Nessuno filling the role of the male parent. And in these circumstances, he told himself, it cannot be wrong to play the part of foster-father. Had not St Francis, that most ascetic of Saints, once made effigies of a wife and children to comfort himself in his vowed celibacy?

But Sandro's condition was giving more and more cause for concern. He had become terribly apathetic, drowsy by day yet unable to sleep at night. His abdomen was swollen and his urine was bright yellow. Nessuno knew that Laura was right. The boy needed proper medical care. He began to hunt through the books in the dispensary for clues as to the nature of the illness.

One evening – it was 19 January and the same day as Richard had said farewell to Wilfrid – Padre Nessuno called in at the little room beside the bakery on his way to Compline. He brought a little goat's milk that had been scalded and another carafe of thoroughly boiled water. Franco came running to clasp him round the legs and Sandro turned his head to give him a weak smile.

'Let me go, Franco,' Nessuno protested, trying to maintain his balance. 'Have you learned your five times table for me?'

Sobered by the question Franco released his prisoner. Laura and Nessuno exchanged a glance and smiled.

'Five ones are five,' Franco began. 'Five twos are ten.'

He was half-way through the table when a tremendous concussion shook the walls. The window burst open, glass tinkled on the sill outside and the door crashed back on its hinges. A shell had hit the wall outside.

'Santa Madonna!' Laura cried out and in an instinctive movement flew towards Nessuno. He opened his arms to receive her, his hands meeting in the small of her pliant back. As he held her there in the darkness left by the snuffed-out candle, he could feel her soft femininity pressed against him. And in his own body there kindled the flame of an emotion which he believed he had mortified two decades ago.

★

For three days after that he did not go back to the little room. He even adopted a new route to his cell so that he did not pass the door. Work on the thesis came to a halt. He lay awake for long hours at night and when he did sleep his dreams took forms which he could not control. What was occurring within his spirit was some kind of rebellion. All his early teaching and the principles that had governed his life as a monk argued that his feelings towards Laura were lustful and wicked. But an obstinate voice declared that this love which possessed him was not evil, that it was another facet of the divine love on which his religion was based. He found it desperately hard to conceal the depth of feeling which certain phrases in the daily psalms awoke in him. Fortunately the light in the Chapel of St Benedict was dim, and he was able to conceal the quivering of his lower lip.

'When evil thoughts come into one's heart,' the Rule commanded 'to dash them at once on the rock of Christ and to manifest them to one's spiritual father.'

Nessuno did not want to take this problem to the Abbot, although he knew that such was his duty. Instinct told him that the true solution could only be found by himself and within himself. This was too powerful, too big a thing to be resolved by the familiar platitudes.

He searched the Rule for guidance, though he was already well versed in its seventy-three chapters. Curiously enough, though it gave specific instructions regarding the administration of a religious community, it did not offer much in the way of moral guidance, after enumerating *quae sunt instrumenta bonorum operem* – the Tools of Good Works.

Thomas à Kempis's *Imitation of Christ* was more specific, though it was hardly comforting. On Resisting Temptations, Thomas had this to say: 'This the poet Ovid writes, "Resist at the beginning, the remedy may come too late." For first there comes into the mind an evil thought; next a vivid picture: then delight, and urge to evil, and finally consent.'

Nessuno meditated on that sentence for a long time. If the emotions he felt were indeed evil he had already passed the second phase in the progress of a temptation. He must apply the remedy before it was too late; he must separate himself from the cause of temptation.

At 7.30 on the evening of 20 January the monks had already said Compline and retired to bed. They were awakened by the thunder of the cannonade which preceded the bloody battle on the river Rapido. For three days the windows of the Monastery rattled to the concussion of the guns. Entirely cut off from the outside world the monks could only try to guess what was happening from the din of battle. Even when an ominous silence descended on the Rapido and the Liri Valley the fighting still raged in the hills to the north. Once a staccato crescendo of machine-gun fire told them that an assault had almost reach the walls of the Monastery, only to wash back again like a spent wave.

It was on the afternoon of the 22nd, a freezingly cold Saturday, that Nessuno found Franco hanging about near the monks' temporary sleeping quarters.

'Franco. What are you doing? You know you are not allowed down here.'

'Mamma sent me. Padre, why have you not been to see us? It is three whole days.'

'I have been very busy,' Nessuno replied untruthfully.

'Sandro is calling for you. He says he wants to see his *padre*. He is very ill. Mamma thinks he is going to die.'

'To die?' Nessuno was shocked. 'Oh, no! He must not die.'

'Then will you come, padre?' Franco was pulling at his arm. 'You must tell God to stop him from dying.'

'No one tells God,' Nessuno answered reprovingly. 'We can only pray to him and then accept whatever is his will.'

Nevertheless he went with Franco.

There was reproach in Laura's eyes when she saw him come in.

'We thought you had forgotten us.'

'I could never forget you,' Nessuno said with a fervour that he had not intended.

'Then why have you kept away from us? Have we done any wrong?'

Although she said 'we' he knew that she meant 'I'. He could tell by the way she was looking at him that she was remembering those moments when he had held her in his arms.

'Franco told me Sandro is worse.'

She nodded and looked down at the little cot where the child lay. Sandro was muttering incomprehensibly to himself, plucking feebly at the blanket with his fingers. His eyes were almost closed and he kept rolling his head from side to side.

'He has been having violent nightmares, even dreaming with his eyes wide open. And his fever is so high his forehead is burning. When I look at his tongue it frightens me, it is so red and cracked. All yesterday he was asking for you. "Why does *mio padre* not come any more?" he kept saying.'

She was standing with her hands joined in front of her, her back to the oil lamp. Her face was in shadow but the light filtered through the edges of her hair. He thought it looked like a kind of halo.

He said: 'Franco, will you go and find Dom Eusetio and ask him to give you some aspirin tablets for Sandro?'

'Where will I find him?'

'Try the little room beside the hall we are using as our refectory.'

When Franco had gone he bent and touched Sandro's burning forehead.

'Your *padre* is here, Sandro.'

Sandro did not seem to hear him. He called out quite loudly: '*Libera per me.*' But it was part of some dream. Nessuno felt helpless to do anything for him. He straightened up, facing Laura. For the first time he was alone with her. He might never again have the chance to speak his heart to her.

'Laura.' He paused. It was the first time he had used the Christian name. 'If I have stayed away from you it was not because .... You must try to understand.'

'Understand what, Padre?' Her voice was so low that he was sure she understood a great deal already.

He moved around a little so that she would turn her face into the light. She met his eyes with a grave expression, looking up at him through her lashes.

As she took a step towards him he put up his hand quickly.

'No. You must not touch me.'

She stopped dead, as if he had slapped her on the face. 'But that other time, when you held me in your arms—'

'I know. But I have thought much about that. We must not let it happen again.'

'But why? I know you are a priest but you are also a man. And we will all soon be killed. Is it wicked to feel as we do?'

He shook his head, fighting the longing to reach out and

64

touch her. 'No. I cannot believe that it is wicked. But many years ago I made a promise, Laura. You must help me to keep it. I beg you to help me.'

7

After his very revealing conversation with Lieutenant O'Hara and the remnants of the 141st, Richard would like to have made a personal report to the C-in-C but when he called AFHQ the Chief of Staff told him that Alexander was too preoccupied with Operation Shingle to see him just at present. Would he please submit his report in writing? Richard felt that the matters he wanted to report could not be expressed in writing. Alex had explicitly stated that Richard's reports were for his eyes and ears only. He decided that he would fill in time by taking a look at the sectors of 34th U S Division.

This formation had achieved greater success than the luckless 36th and had managed to fight their way onto the slopes north of Montecassino. Visiting the forward units meant following mule tracks on foot and penetrating into a landscape that belonged more to some deserted planet than to this earth. The Americans had performed unimaginable feats of bravery and endured acute hardships to secure a foothold on the diabolical natural rock fortress which looked down on Monte-cassino from the north. They had christened it Snakeshead Ridge, because it curved round to a flat head raised like a cobra's to strike at the Monastery.

The French were on even higher ground to the right of the Americans, the formidable Goums in their woollen cachabias

65

huddled against a cold as intense as anything they had met in their own Atlas Mountains.

Cassino town was still untaken and no attack had yet succeeded in dislodging Baade's Panzer-Grenadiers from their well-fortified strongholds.

Wherever he went Richard found that Montecassino and the Monastery which crowned it dominated not only the battlefield but the minds of the soldiers fighting and dying beneath its windows. From colonels down to privates all ranks hated the Monastery. Day and night they lived, or tried to remain alive under its baleful stare. It was a constant presence, seeming to pry into their every activity, bringing down a terrible retribution on any move they made. To the units in the Liri Valley, along the Rapido and, most of all, in Cassino itself, the Monastery had become an obsession, a phobia. More even than the German army it was the great square edifice which seemed to be denying them the way to Rome.

It was on a typically rainy Wednesday evening that Richard finally drove back to Caserta. After changing into some cleaner, dryer clothes he went to the Royal Palace to see whether General Alexander was available to receive a verbal report. As he passed through the long corridors he called on a GSO3 of his acquaintance to find out what progress was being made at Anzio.

'Bogged down, old boy. They've missed their chance. Instead of advancing and capturing the hills dominating the beach-head they dug in on the sea-shore and sat tight. So Jerry took over the hills and now they're sealed in.'

'Weren't they supposed to threaten the rear of Tenth Army and force them to retreat from Cassino?'

'That was the rough idea, old man, but it hasn't worked out that way. As you rightly say, Shingle was launched in order to take pressure off the Cassino front. Now it looks as if we're going to have to attack on the Cassino front to take pressure off the beach-head. Never a dull moment, is there?'

Alexander's ADC told Richard that the C-in-C was in conference with Generals Clark, Freyberg, Juin and Leese. They should be finished soon but Alex had just come back from a visit to the beach-head where he had been trying to put some pep into the local commander. He was very hard pushed for time.

'If you don't mind waiting in the ante-room, I can ask the General whether he wants to see you or not,' said the ADC.

However, it turned out that Alexander did want to see Richard in person. When he came out of the room where he had been waiting he found Colonel Jenkins with the ADC.

'Apparently he wants to see us together,' Jenkins said, nervously fingering a sheaf of papers he had brought. It surprised Richard that a staff officer who worked at AFHQ should be in such a twitter about seeing the C-in-C. He did not know that Jenkins had served under Alexander on the Somme as a very junior subaltern and ever since that day had worshipped the ground he walked on. 'I haven't the faintest idea what this is all about. Have you had a – er –?'

The ADC put his head out of the holy of holies. 'Colonel, will you and Stewart come in now?'

Jenkins nodded. 'Come on, Stewart,' he muttered.

Richard thought that the C-in-C looked tireder and more worried than he had seen him on any previous occasion.

'Yes, I do want to see you, Richard, especially about this business of 36th Division on the Rapido. But you'll have to make it brief, I'm afraid.'

Richard gave him a quick rundown of the conditions under which troops in the front line were operating and their reaction to them. He dwelt for rather longer on his encounter with the survivors of the 141st and wound up by trying to give Alexander some idea of the irrational awe in which the troops held the Monastery of Montecassino.

'Yes, I've heard quite a lot about that,' Alexander cut in briskly. 'I'm afraid it means we're going to have to knock it out.'

Richard could not believe that he was hearing right. 'I'm not sure what you mean, sir.'

'We may have to ask the Air Force to destroy it.'

'But you can't, sir! It stands for everything we're fighting to preserve!'

The words had come bursting out before he was able to stop them. In the shocked silence which followed he could hear clearly the ticking of the chronometer on Alexander's desk.

Richard, appalled at what he had said, bit his lip. He had heard Jenkins draw in his breath. Out of the corner of his eye he could see the Colonel's face glowing redder than ever.

67

The C-in-C had done no more than turn his head through forty-five degrees to fix Richard with his eyes.

'Major Stewart, are you telling me what I may or may not do with the forces under my command?'

This was a different Alexander. The eyes, usually gentle and friendly, had hardened. He had not raised his voice but behind that acid question had been all the power of a man who commanded two million soldiers, sailors and airmen.

'Sir.' Richard found himself standing to attention as if he had been called out as right marker on parade. He knew that he must speak his mind, even if it meant a court-martial for insubordination. 'With respect, I thought we were fighting to save civilization, not destroy it. I thought that was what this war was all about.'

He'd made his declaration. Now he waited for the inevitable storm.

The General's eyes had narrowed so that they were almost closed. He seemed to be staring not so much at Richard as through him. Richard, though his knees were trembling, held that steady gaze with his own eyes.

It was Jenkins who could not forbear to break the tension. 'I think Stewart's over-wrought, sir. If you'll permit me to have a word with him –'

'It's all right, Percy. I'll deal with this myself.' Alexander nodded at the papers Jenkins was holding. 'We'll discuss your plans some other time. You'll be in your office if I need you?'

The blood that had rushed to Jenkins's cheeks was concentrated in two scarlet spots and the bald dome of his head shone with an unnatural gleam.

'Yes, sir. Very good, sir.'

With an admonitory glance at Richard, he got himself to the door and, as he was hatless, merely stiffened into an attitude of attention before letting himself out.

Richard was still standing with his arms rigid at his sides. He had not felt like this since a day twelve years before when he had stood in the head master's study waiting to receive six of the best.

To his astonishment Alexander relaxed and gave a deep sigh.

'Sit down, Richard.'

'Sir?'

'I said sit down.'

Completely mystified by the General's apparent change of mood, Richard took the chair he had occupied when the C-in-C had first interviewed him. He knew that he had stepped far beyond the limits permissible to an officer who was barely of field rank. He was not familiar enough with King's Regulations to tell whether his offence was serious enough to justify a court martial. More likely he would be ignominiously 'returned to unit'.

The General took a turn towards the window, came back to the middle of the room and gazed at the campaign map on its stand.

'You used the phrase "what the war is all about". You said it with all the arrogance of a junior officer who never has to face the decisions of higher command. Do you realize what that can sometimes involve?'

Alexander's tone was not so much angry as sad. The question was a rhetorical one, but Richard felt that he had to make some response. He chose the safest one.

'Sir.'

'I think you understand, because I have put you in the picture, some of the pressures we are under here in the Mediterranean. It was very important for us to achieve a quick success with Shingle and the attack on Cassino. Unfortunately, 6 Corps have not been able to break out as I had hoped, and you are only too well aware of what happened on the Rapido.'

'Yes, sir.'

Having said what he felt he had to say, Richard was content to play the role of listener. He still could not quite fathom Alexander's mood. The General was talking to him as if he were – well, almost a colleague of similar rank.

'Hitler has instructed Field Marshal Kesselring that "the British and Americans are to be flung back into the sea in a welter of Anglo-Saxon blood".' Alexander smiled. 'Those are his exact words. Charming, isn't it? As for the Cassino Position, his instructions are no less bloodthirsty. Though I was rather amused to hear that on January 24th the name of the Führerriegel was changed to Sengerriegel. Our attack achieved something if it persuaded Hitler that he had better not stake his reputation on the Winter Line.'

It was on the tip of Richard's tongue to ask how on earth Alexander knew the exact wording of Hitler's messages to

69

Kesselring. He guessed that he had inadvertently been given a glimpse of that mysterious and inviolate world of secret intelligence.

'Now, something you don't know, Richard, is that I am going to have to lose seven divisions to Overlord and Anvil—'

'Sir?'

'The two invasions of France. Overlord on the north coast and Anvil on the south. Three American divisions and the whole of the French Expeditionary Corps will be diverted to France.'

'So the Italian campaign is to become a side-show?' Richard could not keep the bitterness out of his voice. He was thinking of the bloody battles Alexander's armies had fought to reach their present line, the men who had sacrificed lives, limbs or liberty to conquer the hundreds of hills which now lay behind them.

'It won't become a side-show as long as I am in command,' Alexander snapped back tersely. 'I have the best fighting organization that exists anywhere in this war – Germans and Russians included. Fifth and Eighth Armies are now finely honed machines and I intend to take them onto the soil of Germany itself.'

The General moved closer to the map and altered the position of one of the flagged pins that had been stuck into it by his Chief of Staff. As he stepped back there was a knock at the door and the ADC put his head in.

'Brigadier Henderson is here, sir. He's been waiting for ten minutes.'

'Take him down to the Mess and give him a drink, John. I won't be long now.'

The ADC gave Richard a mystified glance. It was obvious that he wondered why a brigadier was kept waiting while Alex talked to a mere major. Richard wondered too. Once again the C-in-C was setting protocol aside. Perhaps he was trying to sort things out in his own mind by talking aloud, or possibly testing his arguments against an ordinary soldier. Whatever the reason it was intensely interesting to be given this glimpse into the workings of a great commander's mind.

'Now, you know that 11 U S Corps has taken a very severe mauling.' Alexander resumed his exposition as soon as the ADC had withdrawn. 'The French are holding the mountains to the north of Cassino and British 8 Corps are fully committed on the Garigliano. So I am going to have to use my reserve corps against the Cassino Position.'

'The Polish Corps?'

'No. They are not ready yet. I mean 2nd New Zealand Division and 4th Indian. You have visited both these formations so you know what I am talking about.'

Richard nodded.

'The Indian Army are all volunteers. They are soldiers by vocation, members of the martial races of India – Sikhs, Punjabis, Mahrattas, Rajputs and, of course, the Gurkhas from Nepal. They are the most professional under my command and their officers are among the best.' Alexander turned and looked straight at Richard. 'How important to them is a Christian shrine? How could I justify sending them to be cut to pieces by these fanatics of Hitler unless I had taken every possible step to reduce the enemy's defences?'

Richard remained silent.

'The New Zealanders also are volunteers. They are more than just another division. They are a complete expeditionary force with their own supply, ordnance, medical and welfare services. Did you meet General Freyberg?'

Richard admitted that, no, he had not met General Freyberg. He had, however, caught a glimpse of him and knew the awe and affection in which he was held by his troops. Though far from pretty to look at he had the ability to melt everybody by his charm.

'A wonderful soldier.' Alexander raised his chin, staring out of the window, his mind for a moment casting back in time. 'I wish I could read you the citation for the VC he won in the '14-'18 war. Did you know that as GOC of the New Zealand Expeditionary Force he is responsible not to Mr Churchill but to the Prime Minister of New Zealand?'

'No, sir, I didn't.'

'The home government can recall the expeditionary force at any time. And they have said they will do so if casualties in any battle exceed one thousand.'

'36th Division had over fifteen hundred casualties in that attack over the Rapido.'

Alexander glanced at Richard with slight surprise, as if the comment had reminded him that he was talking to another soldier and not the walls of his office.

'Casualties.' He spoke the word with distaste. 'The news-

71

paper reports talk glibly of advance, retreat, attack, casualties. For some reason once men have been put into uniform they are no longer regarded as individual humans. They become statistics. My task is to kill Germans, but to do so without sacrificing one more of my own soldiers' lives than I can help. I saw too much needless slaughter on the Somme.'

Alexander, as he passed the little table on which his scarlet-banded hat lay, moved it to a more symmetrical position. In a very offhand voice he asked: 'Do you know Wilfred Owen's poems? There is one entitled "Greater Love" –'

Surprised, Richard looked up, but the General had turned his head away. Richard had always been moved by this particular war poem and the first two stanzas had remained startlingly fresh in his memory. They had flashed through his mind a few weeks before as he had watched Fusilier Binley borne away on his stretcher.

> Red lips are not so red
> As the stained stones kissed by the English dead.
> Kindness of wooed and wooer
> Seems shame to their love pure.
> O love, your eyes lose lure,
> When I behold eyes blinded in my stead!
>
> Your slender attitude
> Trembles not exquisite like limbs knife-skewered,
> Rolling and rolling there
> Where God seems not to care;
> Till the fierce love they bear
> Cramps them in death's extreme decrepitude.

He had never imagined that he would find himself recalling them with the Commander-in-Chief of an army group on active service. But then, nothing about this strange interview was according to the book.

'So you see,' Alexander, returning to his brisk manner, had decided it was time to bring the subject to a close. 'I cannot allow sentimental consideration for a mere building to accept my decision. The lives of soldiers are more important.'

Richard still remained silent. The General, despite the emphasis with which he had made his statement, was looking at him as if he expected some comment.

He said: 'May I speak my mind, sir?'

'Yes. Say what you think.'

'Well, sir.' Richard tried to find words in which he could put forward his opinion without sounding insubordinate. 'We came into this war because we knew that the Nazis were evil. If the expression anti-Christ can apply to anyone it applies to them. That's why many of us joined up at the very beginning. We felt that we were going to fight in a just cause –'

'Yes, yes. I understand that. Hitler and all he stands for must be crushed. The way to do that is to destroy his armies, and the sooner the better. Everything else is subordinate to that principle objective.'

'That's the old justification, if I may say so with respect, sir,' Richard persisted doggedly. 'I can't believe that in a fight against evil one should sink to the level of one's opponent –'

He stopped, knowing he had gone too far. Alexander's brow had darkened.

'You know, Richard, if I had not read your record I'd be wondering whether you were a conscientious objector of some sort.'

'I often wonder about it myself, sir. When we've fired an artillery programme I can't help thinking about the men we've blown to pieces. Usually one doesn't see them, but once when we followed up an attack –'

Alexander cut in sharply. 'It happens to us all, I assure you. But I concern myself more with our casualties than the enemy's. That is why, if the necessity arises – and it may – I must put sentimental considerations aside. That Monastery of yours forms part of the most formidable defensive system I have ever encountered.'

'But, sir, if you destroyed the Monastery and it turned out that there was nobody in it you would arouse the indignation of the whole civilized world! How could we maintain afterwards that we were the saviours of civilization? We *can't* show ourselves as barbaric as them!'

Richard had stood up and his eyes were on a level with the General's. He had been invited to say what he thought and he had certainly done so. Alexander contemplated him reflectively. His expression was very stern, very serious. Richard knew that the blood had drained from his own cheeks. His legs were shaking but that could be due as much to anger as to nervousness.

73

'Tell me something, Richard.' Alexander's voice was very quiet. 'How would you feel if it was your own life that had to be sacrificed to save the Monastery?'

'You could have it with pleasure, sir,' Richard answered without hesitation. 'That place represents everything we've been fighting for. If we destroy it when the Germans have respected it, I'd rather not be alive to see our victory.'

Alexander turned his back on Richard and walked towards his desk. He moved behind it and faced the younger man across its shiny surface. The gap between them was still only fifteen feet but Richard felt that he had been exiled to a great distance.

'I don't think we can usefully continue this conversation any longer. You may dismiss. Ask Colonel Jenkins to come up and see me. And regard yourself as confined to this headquarters.'

8

Richard had three pink gins in the Mess before dinner, but they did not help much to banish his depression. When he recalled the outspoken way in which he had addressed the Commander-in-Chief he felt a flush come to his cheeks. How *could* he have had the nerve to talk to Alex like that?

He was just putting his glass down and preparing to follow the other officers into the dining-room when he felt a hand on his shoulder.

'Good to see you, Richard! When did you get back?'

Major Steel was as immaculate as ever in his dark green jacket and fawn trousers. His shrewd eyes appraised Richard, guessing from his manner that all was not well.

'Hello, Nick. Let me buy you a drink. It'll give me an excuse to have another one myself.'

'Okay. Make it a Scotch.'

When the Mess waiter had set up the drinks Steel raised his glass. 'Good health. You don't look your usual cheerful self, Richard. Did you have a rough trip?'

'It was a fascinating trip, Nick. But I've just cooked my goose with Alex.'

Steel spun the whisky in his glass and contemplated Richard for a moment. 'Do you want to tell me?'

The American was just about the only person at AFHQ in whom Richard felt like confiding at that moment. He gave him a blow by blow account of the interview with Alexander. Steel listened to him with a serious expression. When Richard had finished he polished off the rest of his whisky and ordered two more drinks.

'I think you did just the right thing, sir,' he said with his slow drawl. 'It's no good fighting a war on the basis of moral principles if you don't remain true to those principles. I admire you for speaking up as you did.'

'Thanks, Nick. That's all very well, but you didn't see Alex's face when he dismissed me. I'm confined to this headquarters. I'll be lucky if I'm not court-martialled for insubordination.'

Steel shook his head. 'From what I've heard of Alex you won't be court-martialled for saying what you think. He asked for it, didn't he?'

'The least that can happen is that I'll get RTU.'

'RTU? What in hell does that mean?'

'Returned to unit. It's about the most ignominious thing that can happen to an officer. God knows what my commanding officer will think. It reflects very badly on the regiment.'

'You're taking too pessimistic a view of this, Richard.' Steel put a fatherly hand on his shoulder. 'Let's take our drinks in to dinner.'

As they moved from the ante-room into the dining-room, Lieutenant Diana Canning was coming out. She'd eaten in a hurry because it was her week as night duty officer in the cypher room.

When she saw Richard she paused. 'Nice to see you back again, Richard. How were things at Cassino?'

'Rough. But I've got your German helmet for you.'

'Oh, wizard!' The ATS beamed, showing all of her somewhat large front teeth. 'When can I have it?'

'As soon as I've had a chance to clean it up.'

'Oh. I don't mind if it's dirty,' the young lady assured him. 'A bit of mud and grime will make it even more realistic.'

'It's not ordinary grime,' Richard said. 'You see, when I acquired it the original owner's head was still in it.'

*

Richard and Steel were the last pair to leave the dining-room. They finished their apricots in silence. Richard was still feeling ashamed of himself. Major Steel had pointed out how ungallant it was to cause an ATS full lieutenant to lose face by almost fainting in the Mess.

The Mess waiters were already moving round the tables to clear them as they passed through into the ante-room to partake of what passed for coffee.

Richard was just filling a pipe with Dunhill 965 when the Mess Corporal came over to him.

'Major Stewart, sir?'

'Yes.'

'Message from Colonel Jenkins, sir. He wants you to report to his office forthwith.'

Richard swallowed his coffee and put his pipe away.

'This is it,' he told Steel. 'Wish me luck.'

'Now, don't you go creeping into the tall grass, son. You know Daddy Jenkins thinks the sun rises and sets from Alex's ass, but we don't all share that view.'

*

Where office furnishings were concerned Jenkins had done himself proud. He had a shrewd eye for antiques and had surrounded himself with elegant pieces which he had either purchased on the all-pervasive Italian black market or won by much the same methods as Mehan had acquired his more practical collection.

'Well, Stewart!' Jenkins leaned back in a button-upholstered desk chair and surveyed Richard with grudging admiration. 'So – you've been telling the C-in-C exactly what he can and can not do.'

'He did invite me to speak my mind, sir.'

76

Richard had stood up to a lieutenant-general. He was not going to back down for a mere colonel.

'You certainly seem to have done that.'

'I suppose this means I'll be RTU.'

'Well – .' Jenkins put his bald head on one side and adopted a judicious expression. Like many staff officers doing a comfortable desk job at rear headquarters he was slightly defensive in the presence of officers whose duties took them into danger – even if they were of lower rank. 'I managed to get in a good word for you. There may be a way to avoid returning you to unit.'

'I can't believe he'll keep me on as LO.'

'No, you've had it where that's concerned.' Jenkins picked up a beautifully-carved ivory paper-knife and ran his finger down the blunt edge. He seemed to be choosing his next words carefully. 'I understand you told Alex that you would be willing to sacrifice your own life to save the Monastery of Montecassino from destruction.'

Richard did not answer at once. He could not remember exactly what he had said in reply to the C-in-C's quiet question. Phrased in Jenkins' words the statement held significant implications. He felt a shiver at the back of his neck, like the caress of a premonition.

Jenkins took his silence for agreement. He raised his eyes and pointed the tip of the ivory knife at Richard.

'Well,' he said, 'we're going to give you the opportunity to do just that.'

*

It took Jenkins half-an-hour to explain precisely what he meant. When he had finished he pushed his chair back and went to the inlaid mahogany corner-cabinet where he kept his private supply of drink.

'How about a spot of brandy? I managed to get hold of some Italian stuff that's not at all bad. Doesn't compare with cognac, of course, but I suppose we shouldn't complain.'

Richard accepted. He felt he needed a bracer. What he had heard did not quite amount to a sentence of death, but it was hardly a recipe for a long life. He nodded his thanks as Jenkins put an elegant little liqueur glass on the table beside his chair.

'Mind you, Stewart, this is not an order. You are free to

accept this assignment or turn it down. In a sense you would be going as a volunteer.'

For the first time Richard felt resentment. Jenkins must know that he could not turn this down. After the declaration he had made with such confidence to Alexander he was going to have to go through with it.

'Of course, I'll take it on,' he said, with perhaps too much emphasis. 'But may I ask some questions?'

The assignment Jenkins had offered him amounted, in its starkest terms, to leading a patrol into the Monastery itself. If Alexander was in possession of a first-hand report from one of his own officers that the enemy were not occupying the place, it could be taken for granted that he would not consent to the bombing.

The problem was, how to get into the Monastery? It formed the key point of a defensive system which the entire weight of Mark Clark's Fifth Army had been unable to penetrate.

Jenkin's idea – and he was at pains to point out that he had sold it to Alex in order to give Richard a chance to restore his reputation – was to approach Montecassino from the other, the enemy side.

'For some time,' he explained, 'I've been trying to persuade Alex to approve a plan to send a Jeep column through the lines to make contact with the Italian partisans.' It was the first time Richard had heard of these bands of young men who had taken to the mountains after the Armistice of September 1943 to continue resistance to the Fascists and Germans in the unconquered parts of the peninsula. 'They need arms, explosives, radios and above all moral support. We saw what a Fifth Column could do to help the Boches when they over-ran Western Europe. If we can co-ordinate these partisan groups we'll have something like an army behind the enemy's lines.'

The unit to which Jenkins intended to entrust this mission was the Long Range Patrol. Practically every nationality fighting on the Allied side was represented among them, and there were even a few from nations that were officially enemies. Richard's own little unit would be a separate entity of perhaps half a dozen men. The LRP, who had plenty of experience in that direction, would help them to get through the lines. Once they were well inside enemy territory the LRP would link up with the partisans while Richard's group tackled the apparently impossible problem of getting into the Monastery of Monte-cassino.

'You said I'd have a unit of half a dozen or so,' Richard said thoughtfully. He could not share Jenkins' enthusiasm for the idea and wondered whether the Colonel realized just how many practical difficulties stood in its way. 'Where are these people going to be drawn from?'

'I don't see why you shouldn't ask for the people you want – provided they are willing to come and their units release them. Can you let me have a list – pretty pronto, it'll have to be.'

Richard nodded and finished off the rather sweet liqueur. 'How long have we got for this job? There must be a deadline.'

'Two weeks.' Jenkins answered so promptly that Richard was sure he knew the date planned for the next attack on the Cassino Position. 'One to mobilise and one to get into Montecassino. That will give you four days to extract yourself. No attack is planned before the 20th.'

'It's not long.'

'No. Alex wants you to be on your way within a week. Within that time I've got to mobilise your personnel, arrange stores and supplies, appropriate the explosives and arms for the partisans, fix you up with wireless communication and transport –'

'I presume we continue to wear our own uniforms even behind the lines. That may create problems.'

'If you're caught in anything else you'll be shot as spies,' Jenkins said cheerfully. 'But the LRP always wear their own uniforms. There are as many different odds and sods on the German side as there are on ours. Strange uniforms don't cause much comment in the rear area. But I can issue you with cyanide tablets if you like.'

'Cyanide tablets? What on earth for?'

'Just as insurance. In case you find yourselves in a situation there's no way out of. You simply crack one between your teeth and – ' he raised both hands with fingers spread, like a priest at the communion table blessing the bread and wine ' – it's curtains within seconds.'

'No, thanks.' Richard declined the offer hastily. 'What about vehicles? British vehicles are more likely to be conspicuous.'

'Ah.' Jenkins nodded sagely. He had begun to look very pleased with himself. 'Now, there I've got something special up my sleeve for you. We have a little pool of captured German vehicles. You can't risk being caught wearing a German uniform but so far as I know nobody has been shot yet for driving a German vehicle.'

Richard nodded a little gloomily. Perhaps later he would be able to share Colonel Jenkins' enthusiasm for this mission. Alex might have approved it, but he had obviously left the details to Jenkins. None of the planning he had heard so far bore the stamp of the C-in-C. He wondered to what extent he was now *persona non grata* with the General; he would have liked to see him just once before setting off on a mission from which he saw little prospect of returning.

This was obviously not the moment to raise that question. Jenkins had stood up and was replacing the liqueur bottle in his corner cupboard.

'One thing we've got to do is decide on a code name for this party of yours. Any ideas?'

Richard stood up and pondered for a moment.

'What about Operation Abbey – or Plainsong?'

But Jenkins had already made his mind up. He straightened, more flushed than ever after stooping.

'I thought we might call you the Benedictine Commando.'

*

It was typhoid fever. There could be no doubt about it any longer. Nessuno had searched through the book he found in the dispensary, comparing Sandro's symptoms with those de- scribed there. When he saw a dozen or so pink pin-head spots on the boy's skin he knew he had final confirmation.

He did not mention the dreaded name of typhoid to Laura, but he warned the Abbot that all water drunk in the Monastery must from now on be boiled, and that more attention than ever must be paid to hygiene.

It was impossible under the circumstances to put into effect all the measures recommended in 'The Family Physician', but he did what he could to create hygienic conditions in the little room by the bakery.

'You can give him milk and water,' he told Laura. 'But the water must always be boiled and the milk scalded. And he must have no food.'

'He has been begging for an orange or some other sort of fruit. It is hard to refuse him.'

Nessuno shook his head. 'No food. That is very important.'

He did not add that it would almost certainly be fatal. No purpose would be served by making her even more frightened.

'And he must not move more than is necessary. On no account let him get out of bed or walk.'

'He'll have to get up to do wee-wee. He's not able to do it lying down.'

'Not even to do wee-wee. He must learn to do it into that spare carafe I brought you. And it must always be carefully scalded afterwards. You have two sheets now. They must be changed every day and the soiled one thoroughly washed.'

Laura reversed the moist cloth she had laid on Sandro's brow. 'But I cannot get it dry in one day.'

'No matter. A damp sheet won't harm him. It will help to keep him cool.'

She was looking up at him with that expression of trustfulness which he found so hard to resist. 'Nessuno, is he going to die?'

Something rose from his chest to the back of his throat, blocking his power to speak. He felt a great rush of tenderness and protectiveness for her. He could not bear the thought of her having to suffer this new loss.

He managed to master it and after a moment was able to speak naturally. 'I've found some laudanum. If we give him half a grain every hour he should recover.'

He did not feel as confident as he tried to appear. The next day his fears were justified. Sandro was frighteningly listless. He was scarcely able to move. He had become incontinent. Working together now as a team Laura and Nessuno began the fight for his life. It went on day and night and there was little room in the monk's life for anything else except the daily services which he knew he must continue to attend.

That was a strange climate for a great love to burgeon in – the little room with its guttering candle, the supine boy, the unpleasant smells, the constant cleansing and emptying. They had little time to think about anything but the constant chores and yet this ordeal was forging between them a bond stronger than any lover's knot tied in leafy lanes on summer evenings.

Franco had been adopted temporarily by one of the other families. Nessuno had read that children are more prone to the infection than adults. So, as Sandro had now gone beyond awareness, they were virtually alone. Only occasionally, as they worked together, they paused briefly and their eyes met.

On the third day after Nessuno had first seen the pink spots he came back from Vespers to find Laura standing in the middle of the room looking down despairingly at her child. She was holding the empty carafe in her hand.

'He's not able to wee,' she whispered. 'What shall I do?'

This was what he had feared. 'An instrument may have to be used,' the medical book had said. But there were no such instruments in the beleaguered Monastery.

He knelt and put his hand on the boy's head. His fever had risen alarmingly.

'We must somehow get his temperature down. We must put cold packs round his body.'

They improvised cold packs by wetting cloths and wrapping them in waterproof material. Sandro was so hot that they had to be changed every half hour. His abdomen was swollen, tight and tender.

'Keep him from turning,' Nessuno warned Laura as he left her to attend Vespers. What he most feared now was that some violent movement would lead to perforation of the bowel.

As he went down to the Chapel of St Benedict he was already praying: 'Merciful God, spare her this new affliction.' Had he not known that to move Sandro would have been fatal he would have carried him out of the Monastery in his own arms, risking the gunfire, and walked on and on till he found some medical post where he could receive help.

Everything in the service of Vespers that evening seemed to have a special significance for him personally. As the monks sang the Magnificat he found his mind going back to the mother in the little room by the bakery. By a strange coincidence the Psalm was the twenty-fifth. Nessuno's neighbour glanced round at him fleetingly, for when they came to the fifteenth verse he suddenly choked and lost his voice. He could only listen to the words, their prayerfulness intensified by the rhythms of the Gregorian chant.

> Mine eyes are ever toward the Lord
> for he shall pluck my feet out of the net.
> Turn thou unto me and have mercy on me
> for I am desolate and afflicted.

The troubles of my heart are enlarged,
O, bring thou me out of my distresses.
Look upon my affliction and my pain,
and forgive all my sins.

The Abbot alone intoned the Pater Noster and Nessuno wondered whether he was only imagining that the old man's eyes were turned more frequently than usual in his direction.

After the Blessing and the final Amen he slipped away unobtrusively. Hurrying back towards the bakery he was trying to work out a thought that had come to him during Vespers. Why had he felt it all so much more deeply this evening? Why did every message now have a profounder, even if more painful meaning? Would he have had this insight, this intimation of mystery, if his monastic life had not been touched by the realities and passions of the outside world?

He was still deep in thought as he opened the door and entered the dimly lit room. He knew at once what had happened.

She was standing in the middle of the room. Her fingers were locked tightly together in front of her breast. She was staring upwards as if seeing something beyond the dark corner of the ceiling. The candlelight caught one side of her face. Something like a pearl on her cheek glistened and then slid downwards over the skin. A fresh pearl burgeoned in its place. Slowly she moved her lower lip to gather in her own tears.

Nessuno's heart swelled.

The figure on the bed was absolutely still. Sandro had shrunk. Around him was that strange cocoon of emptiness where once had been the aura of a living spirit.

Not for some moments did Laura turn her head towards the doorway. Her face was unnatural in its composure.

'E morto. Mio bambino é morto.'

She drew in a long breath, then appeared unable to let it out. Padre Nessuno opened his arms to her. She went to him, was enfolded as she pressed her face against the black serge of his habit.

*

They buried Sandro the next morning in a small makeshift coffin, laying him in the central grave of the presbytery. It had to be done swiftly, because on that 5th of February the top of

Monastery Hill was being subjected to an unusually heavy concentration of artillery fire. Not only were the German positions round the walls and on the slopes below being pounded but many shells were falling within the buildings themselves.

Against this thunderous background the monks only gradually became conscious of a strange drumming noise. For a long time they could not identify it.

Then *il segretario* exclaimed: 'It is the great door. There are people at the great door.'

From a window on that side Nessuno looked out onto the shell-blasted space outside the main entrance. Down below he saw about forty women, shrieking and crazed with fear. They were clamouring for admittance to the safety of the great building.

'They must have been hiding in Sant' Agata and San Rafaello,' the secretary said when he heard Nessuno's report. 'Merciful heavens, what they must have endured!'

'We cannot admit them.' Abbot Diamare shook his head, bowed by this new and unexpected problem. 'Tell them we have not enough food and water for ourselves. We cannot let them in here.'

But the women would not be turned away. With shells bursting on the slopes behind them they screamed defiance at the faces in the window.

'Let us in or we will put fire to the door and burn it down.'

The threat was not a very real one but the Abbot decided, if only out of common humanity, to admit them.

When the great door was unbolted Padre Nessuno was at the window above, watching. As the huge oak panels swung back he witnessed an extraordinary spectacle.

A host of terrified people, men, women and children, sprang into view from the hollows, caves and ruined buildings where they had been hiding. They raced towards the doorway, as strong in numbers as two battalions of infantry. It was impossible to close the doors against this human flood.

By the time the last child had squeezed through the archway behind the doors, at least a thousand demented human beings had thronged into the Monastery, seeking what to them seemed a sure sanctuary from the fury of war.

9

As January gave way to February the Italian winter tightened its grip. In the mountain sectors conditions were appalling. Freezing rain turned to snow. Soaked garments froze on men's bodies. Frostbite became commonplace. At times the winds rose to such velocity that mules on the supply routes were swept off their feet and hurled into the deep canyons beside the tracks. It was a problem merely to stay alive in such conditions. To fight in them was hell.

But for Germans and Allies the fighting went on. Kesselring was still being exhorted by bloodthirsty messages from Hitler to defend the Cassino Position against any onslaught and to hurl the invaders at Anzio back into the sea. Alexander was constantly nagged by the Chiefs of Staff and by Churchill, whose icily polite enquiries about the lack of 'an aggressive attack' on the Italian front could not conceal his impatience.

The German High Command felt that they had the situation pretty well in hand. Von Mackensen's Fourteenth Army, AOK14 in German terms, had the task of containing the Anzio beach-head. Von Mackensen did not consider that General Clark had landed sufficient forces either to occupy the Alban Hills south of Rome or to make a thrust at the Eternal City itself. He was now preparing his counter-attack, for which four large battle groups – Pfeifer, Graser, Conrath and Raapke – were standing ready.

Von Vietinghoff's AOK10 was responsible for the ninety-mile front stretching from coast to coast across the dinosaurian back of the Appenines, and the Cassino Position still lay within the sector of Von Senger's XIV Panzer Corps. It was here that the main thrust was being received. Early in February von Senger gave Baade, as Commander of 90th Panzer Grenadier Division, control of the whole Cassino Position. Baade, with his kilt and his dog, took up residence in a cylindrical concrete dugout on Route 6, containing two bunks. It was part of the defensive system a mile or so back from Cassino. The Americans of 34th Division were still stubbornly fighting their way onto Snakeshead Ridge and the high ground north of the Monastery, supported by their fearsome artillery. So effective was their gunnery that 132nd Grenadier Regiment were pulverized and the second battalion of 361st Grenadier Regiment, moving up as relief, were reduced to a mere handful. Nonetheless, the stout-hearted Baade believed that, given fresh troops, he could hold the Cassino Position.

As fresh troops he was allotted 1st Parachute Division. During the early days of February the Parachute Machine Gun Battalion and 1st and 3rd Parachute Regiments were moving across to the Cassino Position. Thus the stage was being set for the bitterest battles of the whole war, for these Fallschirmjäger were the toughest soldiers in the German, and perhaps in any army.

Alexander also was in desperate need of fresh troops. He decided to milk 8th Army, which had adopted a defensive role on the Adriatic. On the 3rd February he had created the New Zealand Corps. It was this development which made the whole question of the Monastery of Montecassino more immediate.

Initially the new corps consisted of only one division, 2nd New Zealand. As Lieutenant-General Sir Bernard Freyberg had been promoted to corps commander, Kippenberger took over this division. It consisted of 4th N Z Armoured Brigade and 5th and 6th N Z Infantry Brigades, including 28th Maori Battalion. There was also a cavalry regiment mounted on Staghound armoured cars, as well as a Machine Gun Battalion, N Z Engineers and N Z Artillery. To increase the punch of the gunners four British Royal Artillery regiments had been allocated to the division.

A few days later Alexander added 4th Indian Division to Freyberg's corps. That brought into the picture its very forthright commander, General Tuker. Tuker had seen this formation through many battles all the way from Egypt to the Rapido. The fact that the recurrence of a tropical illness was forcing him to relinquish active command to Brigadier Dimoline did not stop him taking a dogged interest in the fate of his formation.

The Indian division consisted of 5th, 7th and 11th Infantry Brigades. Each of these brigades contained two Indian and one British battalion. For instance, 7th Indian Infantry Brigade consisted of 4th Bn 16th Punjabi Regiment, 1st Bn 7th Gurkha Rifles and 1st Bn Royal Sussex Regiment. To this last battalion was to fall the task of taking over Snakeshead Ridge from the Americans.

The divisional armour was provided by the Central India Horse and the Machine Gun Battalion by 6th Rajputana Rifles. The field companies of the Royal Indian Engineers came from the Bengal, Madras and Bombay Sappers and Miners. Two Indian animal transport companies were reinforced by one American, one French and one Italian company. For the attack on Cassino, Dimoline, now promoted to Major-General, was allocated additional units. Among them were the Greenshire Yeomanry, recently withdrawn from 10 Corps.

*

On February the New Zealand Division moved up to Cassino to take over from the 34th United States Division. The sector they went into was a strip of about eight thousand yards just south of the town. The Kiwis therefore found themselves literally beneath the windows of the Monastery, which towered seventeen hundred feet at a neck-craning angle above their heads.

At the same time Alexander and Clark agreed that 4th Indian Division should take over the position held by US 36th Division in the hills to the north of Monastery Hill. Brigadier Lovett went forward to reconnoitre the terrain and saw with his own eyes the exhaustion of the American troops on those frozen slopes and the appalling conditions in which they were subsisting. He came back to recommend that the Royal Sussex should relieve them as soon as was humanly possible.

It was to Brigadier Lovett's 7th Indian Infantry Brigade that the Greenshire Yeomanry was assigned. Major Stockwell's battery was detailed to support 1st Royal Sussex, and Captain Wilfrid Stewart was warned that he would be required to establish a forward observation post on Snakeshead Ridge.

Richard was too immersed in his own preparations to be aware of these regroupings taking place away over his head. Within half an hour of his leaving Jenkins after that first briefing, the Benedictine Commando had acquired its second member. When Richard had told Major Steel confidentially what he had volunteered to do, the American instantly declared that he was coming with him.

'No, sir, you're not going to bone me out of this,' he stated with serious emphasis. 'It's the chance I've been waiting for – to do something tidy in this war instead of doling out blankets and corn, like some hick clerk in a grab-and-run. 'Sides, this is an AMGOT job.'

'How's that?' Richard asked, surprised.

'Preservation of monuments and artistic treasures. That's part of our job, just as much as handing out dry-dees for babies and sanitary pads for their mothers. If what we're doing is going to save that Monastery from destruction I'll be able to – . Well, I won't have any children to tell it to but I can go back home and say I've done something tidy. Unless you don't want to have me along?' The major stared at Richard, horrified by his own thought. 'Maybe you're thinking I'm too old for this –'

'I'd be glad to have you, Major,' Richard said truthfully. He could see that Steel was fit and tough despite his years. It would be a comfort to have someone whose wisdom and friendship he could trust if he was going to cross the lines with a group of unknowns. 'If you can square it with Daddy Jenkins.'

The next morning Richard asked Mehan if he would be willing to come with him on a dangerous mission into enemy territory. He had discovered that Mehan was a trained wireless operator. The Irishman's answer was a broad grin which displayed a very uneven set of teeth.

'Just try and stop me, sir. If we get back from it perhaps the MO will give me my A1 grading again.'

It made Richard feel better to know that he would have these two familiar faces with him. Daddy Jenkins had been no match for Major Steel's persuasive powers and the American had been given the job of quartermaster to the little unit. Leaving him to liaise with Jenkins over supplies, weapons, transport and communications, Richard set off on his own private recruiting tour.

When he came back four days later he had enlisted a representative from the New Zealand Division, the French Corps, the Italian co-belligerent force and the newly-formed Polcorps. Jenkins had said the force was to be as international in composition as possible.

He could only hope that it would live up to its usurped title of Commando.

Steel had not been idle in his absence. Claims and Hirings had alloted him a small and virtually undamaged villa on the outskirts of Caserta. This would give them a base to assemble personnel, vehicles and equipment. It had the additional advantage of being within half a mile of the LRP headquarters.

'Hi, Major!' Steel greeted him, as he climbed out of the Jeep at the door of this temporary headquarters to which the duty officer at Special Intelligence Ops had directed him. 'I have news for you. Seems things are beginning to move faster. Daddy Jenkins says we have to move out by Wednesday 9th at the latest.'

'That's a day earlier than my original instructions. It won't give us any time for proper briefing and familiarization.'

'That's what the man said. As I understand it, there's a lot of pressure from the Chiefs of Staff for more action on this front.'

They were going into the villa, which had been stripped of furniture, when a stranger came out of one of the rooms opening off the hall. Richard checked instinctively. The man was in German uniform. When he saw Richard he stiffened to attention and clicked his heels.

'What the hell's this?' Richard muttered to Steel. 'We don't want a bloody Kraut hanging about the place. I know Italian POW's are being used as Mess waiters but–'

'Take it easy, Richard. He speaks English.'

Richard looked more closely at the German. He was a better type than most POW's, tall and fit-looking with strong, handsome features and close-cut fair hair. His uniform had been through the mill but he had obviously made great efforts to clean it up and get creases back into the trousers.

'Oberleutnant Rudolf von Reifenbach,' the German stated stiffly. 'At your orders, sir.'

Richard nodded, still wary. 'An officer. What's he doing here?'

'He was captured by the 141st on the Rapido,' Steel explained. 'Or rather I understand he gave himself up.'

Richard's memory went back to that conversation on the road near Trocchio.

'Are you the person who said he would rather be a prisoner of ours than of the Gestapo?'

'That is correct,' the German said, still stiff. 'But I am not prepared to give information about the German army.'

'Nobody asked you to,' Richard said sharply. The man's English was good but there was still a guttural quality in his speech which made his hackles rise.

'Come on in and I'll put you in the picture,' Steel said quietly. 'We've fixed up a kind of office in here.'

One of the front rooms had been equipped with a folding table and chairs. Steel had scrounged a few odd sticks of furniture from shelled or bombed houses which had been abandoned by their owners. They included a very beat-up arm-chair and a dilapidated sofa.

The American shut the door behind him.

'I wanted to tell you about this before you met him, but you caught me by surprise. I didn't expect you back quite so soon.'

'Things went more smoothly than I expected. The chaps I wanted were very keen to come. With Alex's signature on the message there was no problem about getting them released. Now, what about this German?'

It had been Jenkins's suggestion, Steel explained. The intelligence officer at the Army POW cage had sent through a report that a most unusual prisoner had come in. Technically he was a deserter from the German army, but he was not the low-grade type which had lost the stomach for fighting. The reason he had given for surrendering to the Americans was that he'd been tipped off by his superior officer that the Gestapo were after him. His uncle, an aristocrat and an officer in the old German army, had been accused of plotting to assassinate Hitler. He and several others had suffered the standard fate of all who threatened the person of the Führer, which was to be hanged against a wall with a meat hook through the lower jaw. Every member of the traitor's family was being hunted down by the Geheimstaatspolizei. It did not help Rudi von Reifenbach that his mother was an Austrian Jewess.

Just after Christmas he had heard from a cousin that she had been dragged from her house at dead of night and taken away in one of those grim trains of sealed carriages which departed for unknown destinations from which no one ever returned. Three weeks later had come the warning that members of the Gestapo were at the headquarters of his Panzer-Grenadier regiment demanding that he be hauled out of the line and handed over to them.

'He's convinced now that the sooner Germany loses the war and Hitler gets kicked out the better for his country. The interrogating officer thought that one of Jenkins's cloak and dagger organizations might be able to make use of him. Daddy decided that he was just the job for your Benedictine Commando.'

'Good Lord! We're going to have problems enough without that. How do we know he's not a plant?'

'Why don't you talk to him yourself? There's a scroogy coincidence in all this.'

'What sort of coincidence?'

'You see if you can figure that out for yourself.'

'All right.' Richard moved round to the chair behind the bare desk. 'You can wheel him in.'

Richard did not approve of the casual, almost friendly way Steel handled this former enemy. He made him stand to attention in front of the table while he questioned him. Steel flopped into the arm-chair behind the German.

Richard first took von Reifenbach through the part of his story which Steel had told him. The answers came as crisply and concisely as machine-gun fire.

'All right.' Richard leaned back after ten minutes of close questioning. He was beginning to be impressed by the tall, flaxen-haired young man. 'You can stand at ease.'

For the first time the German relaxed, but he seemed to know the difference between 'at ease' and 'easy'.

'Where did you learn to speak English so fluently?'

'My father was a diplomat at the Embassy in London. When he was sent to South America he left me at boarding school in England.'

'Where?'

'Ampleforth.'

Richard caught Steel's eye. The American winked.

'That's a Benedictine school. Are you a Catholic?'

91

'Yes. As a matter of fact I am a confrater of the Starnberg Benedictine Monastery near Munich.'

There was fatalistic streak in Richard's nature. When a coincidence such as this occurred he tended to believe that fate was deliberately dealing the cards in a certain way. From that moment he knew that the Benedictine Commando was going to have one German member.

*

That evening Richard went down to the headquarters of the LRP to meet the people who would be accompanying his own party. There would be four of them, using two Jeeps. The commander was a tall Scot named Bill MacDonald. He introduced his second-in-command, a South African called Erle Johnson, then took Richard out to the back of the building where the other two were loading guns, ammunition, explosives, radios and rations onto the Jeeps. One was an Indian with white teeth flashing in a dark face, the other a squat Canadian with a downward-drooping moustache. Richard tried to memorize the names – Ram Savarkar and Tucker Barr. No rank had been mentioned.

'We're moving off at sparrow-fart tomorrow,' MacDonald explained. 'We'll be going through in the Canadian sector. That's well away from Cassino and up there in the high mountains the troops are much thinner on the ground. You'll rendezvous with us at 3rd Canadian Div headquarters Monday evening. That'll give us time to work out a route through the mountains. Why don't you stay and have dinner with us? We've got a sucking pig and some very good wine.'

*

For the monks in the Abbey the morning of Wednesday the 9th began as usual with Matins and Prime, followed quickly by Terce and Mass. There was a terrible amount of work to be done and it was becoming more and more difficult to fit in the religious services which were as essential to them as the maintenance of life itself.

When St Benedict had said: 'No one in the house of God should be troubled or sad,' he could hardly have foreseen the conditions which now prevailed in his Monastery. The thousand refugees who had flooded in four days earlier had settled down as best they could on the great entrance staircase,

92

in the carpenter's shop under the ancient library, in the porter's lodge, in the post office, in the corridors – anywhere they could find space. Some of them were in the rabbitry, many beneath the basilica itself.

There was little order and therefore no discipline. The monks had been invaded by a migration of demoralized and extremely vocal cuckoos. It was hard to maintain an attitude of Christian charity towards people who had so little regard for each other and so little idea of the principles of hygiene. In places the smell of humanity, excrement and urine was overpowering. There was a shortage of water and to obtain supplies from the well in the Bramante Cloister meant running the gauntlet of shell-fire. Food was carefully rationed and the few animals remaining after the German requisition had to be guarded vigilantly. To add to the difficulties a mysterious sickness was spreading among the refugees. Many of them had become so ill that they could not move, even to perform the most basic human functions. Nessuno was sure it was typhoid.

The needs of the refugees, as well as their own problems of survival, kept the monks busy from dawn till dark. Through it all they managed to preserve one little island of sanity and contemplation, the tiny cell of St Benedict, into which they withdrew for their worship.

Padre Nessuno had been put in charge of the welfare of children. He enlisted the help of Laura and together they made the rounds of the numerous families, many of whom were ignorant peasants needing help or advice in the treatment of childish ailments. Franco often came along too. The death of his brother had affected him deeply and it was essential to prevent him from sitting and brooding.

Nessuno found it hard to fight back despair. He was forced to witness so many heart-breaking sights. What he found most distressing was the patient resignation of the very old – men and women with toothless gums, deeply wrinkled faces and beady little eyes that stared at him with an almost bovine appeal.

'What shall we do, Padre? What is to become of us?'

All he could offer them were the standard reassurances. 'We must trust in the mercy of God. Have faith and all will be well. Remember the Children of Israel and how God delivered them.'

One day, weakened by these ceaseless unavailing efforts and

the lack of food and sleep, he allowed his sense of despair to get the better of him. In an outburst of emotion that was almost anger he allowed Laura to see his true feelings.

'I cannot believe what I am saying to them any more! How can I go on telling them to have faith in God when we can all see that God has abandoned us?'

No sooner were the words out than he clapped his hand to his mouth.

'Oh, Laura! What am I saying?' He sank down on a bench and began to rock to and fro in an agony of self-recrimination. .

Laura stood watching him for a moment. Then she stooped and took his head between her hands and laid it against her breast, comforting him. Gradually he calmed and when he had himself under control he lifted his head and looked at her very steadily for a long time. His eyes were shining with unshed tears. All of a sudden the restraints broke and out came the confession he had been unable to make to anyone else.

'Laura, I love you. God help me, I love you more than anything on earth or in heaven.'

10

The two-vehicle convoy of the Benedictine Commando moved out of Caserta before first light on that same Wednesday 9 February. In one day less than the stipulated time Richard had assembled the international force which Jenkins had insisted on. In addition to Nick Steel, Pat Mehan and Rudi von Reifenbach he had a New Zealander, a Frenchman, a Pole and an Italian.

Marcel Duval was very much the colonial type of French officer, with sun-bronzed cheeks, vivid blue eyes and a lady-killer's smile. Fen Greeley, a sergeant-major from the NZ corps, had been a prop forward in the All Blacks team. His gentle voice was surprising in a man with massively broad shoulders and the battered features of a prize fighter. Viktor Zygalski, an aristocrat and former cavalry officer, was one of the thousands who had been released from Russian-occupied Poland. He had a long, aquiline face and sensitive hands. But Richard knew that he was an expert in silent killing, either with those same hands or certain other weapons he had in his armoury. Baldovino Cantelli looked like a character from *opera buffa* with his supple leather boots, jet-black moustache and feather sticking up from his Bersaglieri head-dress. He had greeted Richard by embracing him on both cheeks. As he was barely five foot in height he had to stand on tiptoe to do so.

There had been some awkward moments while this widely assorted bunch were turning up at Caserta. Baldovino had been arrested as a suspicious character by the MP while wandering around AFHQ. Viktor had encountered Rudi before Richard had time to warn him and only the intervention of Fen had prevented him from attacking the German physically. But all differences had been smoothed over during the evening meal, largely thanks to the strong red wine which Mehan had conjured up.

For transport Daddy Jenkins had supplied two captured German vehicles. The first was a Steyr 1500 A/01. It was an 8-seater personnel carrier powered by a V-8 air-cooled engine. With its high and low-ratio gear-box and optional four-wheel drive it was an excellent cross-country vehicle. Its junior companion was one of the ubiquitous Kübelwagen, the little personnel carrier derived from the Volkswagen, or People's Car, which Dr Porsche had devised on orders from Hitler. With its 25 hp engine it could be persuaded to do about 50 mph, and though it lacked four-wheel drive it had a reduction gear on the back axle which improved its cross-country performance.

For communications the 'Commando' had one of the latest Type A, Mark III suitcase-type wireless sets which had been developed for the use of spies, and a brand new Number 18 set. This had been included on Richard's insistence. The spy set had a range of 500 miles, but it could only be used for Morse code. Their armoury consisted of Tommy guns and *38 Smith and Wesson revolvers on the basis of one for each man. There was a box of 36 grenades and a couple of dozen of the very light bakelite grenades which could be thrown like a cricket ball. Ten boxes of Compo rations assured food for eight men for three weeks. There was also a wad of forged currency for use north of the Gustav Line.

Ahead of them lay a journey of no more than forty miles as the crow flies, but experience warned that it could take most of a day to move across the lines of communication and then work forward into the high mountain areas where they were to meet up with Bill MacDonald's Long Range Patrol. That sector was being held by the newly-arrived Canadian Division, and Bill had gone ahead to work out a route through the lines.

As they left the last houses of Caserta behind, Richard had an uncomfortable sense of unfinished business. His final meeting with Jenkins had been unduly hasty. The Colonel gave him the impression that his mind had moved on to other enterprises and that Richard's insistence on trying to tie up so many details was a little tiresome. He would have liked to see Alexander just once before departing, but Daddy Jenkins replied that the C-in-C was far too busy and, when pressed, said he believed he had gone to the Anzio beach-head.

Jenkins' last gesture had been to hand him two letters which had been addressed to him through SIO. One was from Wilfrid. It had been written before the Greenshire Yeomanry had been posted to 4th Indian Division. Much of it concerned Dante, who had been recommended for a Canine Military Medal, in spite of cocking his leg against the Brigadier's field boots. The other was from his mother and was very brief. She was worried about Dad, who had not been the same since that thousand pounder had landed so close.

The two letters were buttoned away in the inner pocket of his battle-dress jacket. They would accompany him wherever he went. Nothing from Betty. He was not sure whether he was glad or sorry. In a way it was a good thing that he did not have to worry about his wife. Sometimes men hesitated to accept missions of this kind not because they lacked courage but because they felt that they had an obligation to avoid the most extreme dangers for the sake of the one who would be left alone. Richard did not have that problem.

The roads leading northwards towards the Canadian sector were in atrocious condition. They had been required to bear the full brunt of a mechanized army on the move; the damage caused by heavy lorries, transporters and tracked vehicles had been compounded by the unrelenting rain. On both sides of the road were houses ruined by shells and bombs. The villages they passed through were terribly damaged. Baldovino could well exclaim *Povera Italia!* Not till they were out of the valley did they pass through hamlets and towns that were intact.

Mehan, at the wheel of the Steyr, was leading the way. Following behind in the Kübelwagen, Richard could see the members of his 'Commando' through the open back of the German vehicle. The camouflage battle jackets they were all now wearing gave a certain uniformity to their appearance, but as they retained their own head-dress they looked as distinctive and eccentric as the cast of some all-male pantomime. More than once they were stopped by MPs or security-minded officers who were suspicious of the two German vehicles with their improbable passengers.

They took a day to travel first across the supply routes of 2nd US Corps and the French Expeditionary Force, then through the rear area of the Canadian Corps and lastly, ever more laboriously, up to the headquarters of 3rd Canadian Division.

This was a region of high mountains, most of them snow-covered, where only a few farmers could eke out an arduous existence. Troops were thinner on the ground here than nearer the coast. As darkness was already falling, Richard left his party to make themselves comfortable in a farm below Div HQ, while he went to find out the whereabouts of Bill MacDonald and the LRP.

He found Bill in the back of a three-tonner which had been fixed up as a mobile office by the G3 Intelligence. The tall Scotsman was checking over the latest information about German movements and positions and arranging for the LRP to pass through the Canadian lines.

'I think I've found a way through for us,' he told Richard, with his strong Galashiels accent. 'Some of the local farmers are still around and I was able to talk to them. This is largely a region of forest but in summer the shepherds from the coastal plains bring their flocks up to pasture on the higher slopes. They follow trails called *trattürs*, wide strips of open ground cut through the forests. They are not marked on any map. There's one that leads through the hills to San Gregorio. That's

97

a village about ten miles beyond the line held by Jerry. I've got a farmer standing by to guide us through tonight.'

By the time Richard returned to the farm a two-course dinner was ready. Paddy Mehan and, surprisingly, Nick Steel had become the self-appointed cooks of the party. The farmer had dug up a demi-john of wine from under his barn and there was a certain festivity in the air. The Bennies had not only made friends with the LRP men but had done some bartering with the Italians, exchanging tins for cheese and salami sausages.

After the meal Richard assembled his seven men under a Tilley lamp slung from a beam in the kitchen. It provided enough light for everyone to see the map which he unrolled. The tang of Marcel's Tunisian cigarette was as strong as joss-sticks.

'Bill got the Canadian intelligence officer to mark the German positions up on this map. They're thin on the ground so if we stick to our routes there should be no problem. Just in case we run into Jerry patrols we are going to split into two groups. Then if one group goes for a Burton the other can complete the mission. So it's essential for everyone to know our rendezvous point with the Italian partisans. It is here.' Richard pointed with his chinagraph pencil to a point on the map. 'The village of Peroli. Memorize its position and name but don't write it down.'

He looked round the ring of faces. The festive atmosphere of the supper table had vanished and they had all sobered to a professional attentiveness. Rudi, holding back a little from the ring, looked tense and apprehensive. The sound of his own guns firing from beyond the dark hills and the crump of the shells on the slopes below the farmhouse had made him very nervy. Baldovino, who like Steel was a good ten years older than the others, hardly seemed to be listening. Richard wondered why his thoughts were so far away.

He had taken the precaution of assigning one watch-dog each to the German and the Italian, simply as an insurance policy during the crucial period when they were crossing the lines. Fen would be watching Rudi; Marcel would be watching Baldovino. At any hint of betrayal to the enemy they would be shot.

'I have agreed with Bill MacDonald that we shall carry the bulk of the supplies for the partisans in the Steyr. That will allow us to divide our numbers up more equally between the vehicles. As there are twelve of us, it works out at three to each vehicle.'

'Four in one of them, the Steyr, I suppose,' Marcel corrected him. 'You have forgot to count Maria.'

'Maria? Who's Maria supposed to be?'

Marcel stared at Baldovino accusingly. 'You have not told it to him?'

Baldovino shrugged his shoulders under the sheepskin jacket which he had slung over them. He had taken off his Bersaglieri hat and the bald dome of his head was shining in the light of the Tilley lamp. He spread his hands and wrinkled his brow in that attitude of helpless innocence which Italians adopt instinctively when their conscience feels guilty. 'I not have the chance. *Mi deve scusare, maggiore.*'

'Come on!' Richard said angrily. 'What is all this? Who is Maria?'

'Eh!' Baldovino's shoulders rose further and his fingers spread wider.

He turned for support to Tucker Barr, the French and Italian-speaking LRP man, who was standing at the back listening to the briefing.

'She is an Italian who got separated from her family by the fighting. Her parents are in San Gregorio, just the other side of the German positions. She was trying to go back through the lines but was stopped by the Canadians, and she's been living with the farmer here since then. When she realized Baldovino was an Italian officer she latched onto him, got him to agree to take her through the lines. I told him he'd need to square it with you.'

Richard glared at Baldovino, who dropped his eyes and would not look at him.

'She may be a spy for all we know.'

'No, *maggiore.*' Baldovino shook his head energetically. To make himself taller he had stood on an up-turned box. 'She is not a spy. She is an educated girl, a trained nurse. If we run into trouble a trained nurse can be very useful to us.'

'I am of the same advice. We will be a long way from medical help.' Marcel came into the argument so promptly that Richard began to suspect that there had already been some collusion about including the Italian girl in the party. It was the sort of thing that happened very often in a world of men who had been deprived of female companionship for years. Sometimes the temptation to take a willing woman along outweighed all considerations of discipline or security. The German intelligence staff were well aware of this and frequently sent good-looking Italian girls across the lines to carry out tactical spying missions under the guise of refugees.

'We can't take the risk. This task is dicey enough as it is. Besides, a woman would create all sorts of problems.'

The second argument was a mistake. Viktor took it up at once. 'What sort of problems? I do not understand that. She is a nurse and we are grown men.'

'Why don't you see her and talk to her?' Fen suggested in his quiet voice that was always audible.

Richard reckoned that there were at least four of them in it – the Italian, the Frenchman, the Pole and the New Zealander. He turned to Steel.

'Did you know anything about this, Nick?'

The American shook his head, but his eyes were twinkling. 'It's a new one on me. Nothing to stop us taking a gander at her, though.'

Baldovino took that as his cue. Without waiting for Richard's response he got down off the upturned box.

'I fetch her. Then you will see, *maggiore*.'

'Where is she?' Richard asked, as the Italian hurried out through the door. He had an uncomfortable feeling that things were moving out of his control.

Marcel and Viktor answered at the same time. 'Waiting in the kitchen.'

When Baldovino came back a subtle change passed over the eight men in that small room. It was something deeper and more pervasive than merely sexual lust. The presence of any woman has a strangely humanizing and comforting influence on men who have for too long been dedicated to the task of killing other men. When the woman looks as if she had escaped from one of the paintings of Botticelli the effect is powerful enough to banish reason.

Maria Valdisponda's auburn hair was heaped severely on her head in a tightly-plaited bun. She was wearing black voluminous garments which could not altogether conceal the lithe movement of a slim body. She seemed unconscious of the way the eyes of every man there were clamped on her.

'This is Maria,' Baldovino introduced her in a hushed voice

in which there was more than a hint of pride. 'Maria, *questo è il maggiore Staywart, il nostro capo.*'

Richard decided not to let her know that he spoke Italian. He did not want to open the floodgates of eloquence and entreaty.

'How do you do?' he said, with a politeness and formality which, even to his own ears, sounded ridiculous.

Maria smiled. Baldovino beamed. The faces of the other six cracked into self-congratulatory grins. Richard hastened to disillusion them all.

'It's no good,' he said, shaking his head firmly. 'Under no circumstances can we take a woman along with us.'

He could understand Baldovino snapping up such an extraordinary piece of good luck. But the presence of a blazingly attractive woman in the midst of eight sex-starved men could only cause dangerous tensions. Even as he shook his head he knew that the damage had already been done. Maria saw the gesture and rightly interpreted his tone of voice. In an impulsive and sincere display of emotion she went down on her knees in front of him on the bare flagstones. She placed the palms of her hands together in a gesture of prayer.

'*Vi supplico,*' she said in a low voice which trembled with emotion. '*Per l'amor di Dio, vi supplico.*'

'Tell her to stand up.' Richard had to make an effort to keep his voice hard. 'I'm not some bloody deity.'

'To her you are,' Baldovino said. 'You hold the keys of life and death.'

'I certainly don't. She should be taken to the Field Security people at Div HQ. They'll know what to do with her.'

'If you do that she is probable to kill herself.'

'What is harm in helping her?' said Viktor, and added rather illogically: 'Why are we fighting this war?'

'All what she is asking is a lift across the lines,' Marcel said with gallic persuasiveness. 'We have room and to spare.'

There was a general murmur of agreement. Richard remembered the doubts he had felt when he had seen this group assembled round the table at Caserta the night before. Though he was accepted as the leader of the mission he knew that he could not impose his authority on them unless he had their confidence and agreement.

He looked round at Nick Steel. The American had remained

101

silent but he had a knack of influencing things without having to make a positive statement.

'What's your opinion, Nick?'

'Looks like you're in the minority, Major.' Nick was getting a lot of amusement out of the situation. 'And as Baldo pointed out, a trained nurse could sure come in handy.'

Richard was still hesitating. He found himself looking into the face of Pat Mehan. The Irishman had taken no part in the argument and had stayed in the background. There was a serious expression on his pale cheeks and Richard knew that his trusted driver had been trying to catch his eye and convey some message.

When he saw that the major was looking at him he gave two emphatic nods. Richard understood that Mehan felt certain he had to bow to the majority opinion.

'All right. On your head be it, Baldo. She can travel in the Steyr with you. But once through the lines she goes her own way.'

'*Cos'ha detto?*' Maria had been following the argument, switching her gaze from face to face. Now she looked up, questioning Baldovino.

'*Dice che tu puoi venire con noi.*'

Maria rose from her knees. She half ran towards Richard, seized his two hands and began to kiss them. He could feel her warm tears wet on his knuckles.

★

Wednesday 9 February was also a day of decision for Lieutenant-General Sir Bernard Freyberg.

Since the beginning of the month he had been devoting his very experienced mind to the Cassino Position. As soon as he was given his objective he had gone forward on one of those front-line reconnaissances so dreaded by the officers whose duty was to accompany him. He knew that, although the American artillery were pouring shells into Cassino town, including the heavy metal of their 8-inch howitzers, the defenders were not to be dislodged from their deep shelters. He knew that in the area north of the Monastery the American and German infantry were clinched, exchanging blow for blow with blind yet heroic pugnacity; that whenever the US troops attempted to storm Monastery Hill they became exposed to murderous cross-fire.

He and his two divisional commanders, Kippenberger and Tuker, had surveyed the position from the top of Monte Trocchio. They did not like what they saw – the flooded valley, the universal grey-brown desolation, the hostile mountains tightly packed behind Montecassino.

His final plan, reduced to its simplest terms, was to use the Indian Division in the mountains and the New Zealand Division in the valleys. The Indians would capture Monastery Hill, sweep southwards down it and then turn eastwards towards Cassino. The New Zealanders would advance along the shallow causeway which had carried the old railway from behind Monte Trocchio and seize the southern end of the town. When the two divisions met, Cassino and Monastery Hill would be isolated and the hundred and eighty tanks of US First Armoured Division would burst into the Liri Valley.

The plan sounded good and looked good on paper. The Indians were experienced mountain fighters, none more so than the Gurkhas. They had proved their worth in Eritrea and North Africa. But Monastery Hill was the most fearsome defensive position they had ever tackled.

General Tuker was brooding and angry.

'Those Nazis will use the Monastery,' he said. 'They may swear blue they won't but they'll use it in the last resort.'

Freyberg turned to Kippenberger. 'Your men have had a taste of what it's like being under the Monastery. What do they think about it?'

'There's no doubt in their minds,' Kippenberger stated emphatically. 'They don't think the place can be captured till the Monastery is destroyed.'

'Tell me, Bernard,' Tuker said. 'How do you rate our chances of success? We're being asked to attack with two divisions where two divisions have already failed.'

'Not more than fifty-fifty.' Freyberg spoke very seriously. 'But Alex is under pressure from the Chiefs of Staff as well as Winston. And we know that the counter-attack on the Anzio beach-head is imminent. We've got to pull this off, but I'm going to see that we get every possible support.'

That afternoon Freyberg went to the headquarters of General Mark Clark at Presenzano. There was little love lost between the American Generals and the British, and the old rivalry was becoming very apparent. The Americans, having entered the war much later, felt that the British were trying to show them how to conduct a campaign. The British were critical of the American Generals for not being personally familiar with conditions at the front. Brigadier Lovett had been especially angry to find that no high-ranking US General had been up onto Snakeshead Ridge.

Mark Clark's dog, which was very obviously expecting a litter of puppies, gave Freyberg a warmer welcome than her master. Freyberg came to the point without delay. He wanted the Monastery bombed. Clark did not consider that this was a military necessity. Freyberg reminded him of the directive issued by General Eisenhower on 29 December 1943.

'If we have to choose between destroying a famous building and sacrificing our own men, then our men's lives count infinitely more and the building must go. Nothing can stand against the argument of military necessity. That is an accepted principle.'

'Yes,' Clark agreed. 'Don't forget that Eisenhower added: "But the phrase is sometimes used when it would be more truthful to speak of military convenience or even of personal convenience."'

'You do not consider this is a case of military necessity?'

'No. I do not.'

Clark was supported by his staff and Freyberg departed fuming.

Tuker was so angry when he heard of the Army Commander's decision that he had to sit down.

'Not a military necessity!' he growled. 'Don't they know what their own men are having to put up with?'

'Kippenberger had suggested that the Monastery might be more use to the Krauts bombed than unbombed.'

'He's not been invited to attack it! I have.' Freyberg was concerned at how ill Tuker looked. The old tropical illness had chosen a bad moment to hit him again. Dimoline was a good commander but he did not have Tuker's capacity to galvanize the division. 'Why is there so little intelligence available on this Monastery, Bernard? We've had practically nothing about it.'

'Our intelligence has let us down badly on this whole Gustav Line position. They gave us no warning about what we were up against. Even predicted we'd be in Rome by now! But I'm going to take this up with Alex. That Monastery must be destroyed.'

104

11

'This is where I leave you. The Germans are on that ridge to our right front, but our patrols report no enemy in the forest ahead.'

The Canadian company commander spoke in a low voice. The landscape in front of them was silent and desolate. The mountains rising to northward could be felt rather than seen. It was difficult to believe that there were any enemy out there.

Richard checked his watch. It was just coming up to midnight. In a few minutes the noise cover which had been promised by the GOC of the Canadian division was due to begin. Already the beams of a couple of searchlights aimed at the clouds overhead gave enough reflected light for the track leading towards the forest to be visible.

He had temporarily swapped the Kübelwagen for one of the LRP Jeeps. Bill MacDonald had agreed that one of the sturdy American cross-country vehicles should be with each group. The German vehicles were still something of an unknown quantity, whereas the Jeep had proved itself capable of traversing terrain previously considered impossible for wheeled vehicles.

Richard had Rudi in the seat beside him. He'd decided to keep the German close to him during the line-crossing operation. In the back were the Italian guide and Fen Greeley, sitting directly behind Rudi. This time the Steyr was following, loaded with gear and carrying Pat Mehan, Maria, Baldovino and his watchdog, Marcel. Reluctantly Richard had decided to leave Nick with the second group. He and Viktor would follow with the LRP an hour later.

Exactly on the dot of midnight he heard half a dozen tanks start up a mile behind him. The roar of their exhausts, mingled with the shriek and clanking of their tracks, sounded very loud in the still night air. At the same moment the drone of aircraft came from the south, growing louder at every moment. Beaufighters, by the sound of them.

'In an hour's time we'll be creating a diversion on that hill over there.' The Canadian captain grinned as he pointed to a snow-capped peak. 'We'll make as much noise as we can.'

'Thanks.' Richard started his engine and waved a signal to Mehan. Behind him he heard the Steyr cough into life. 'How far ahead are your furthest outposts?'

'About half a mile. Once in the woods you're in Jerry country.'

Richard nodded and let in his clutch. The Canadian saluted and stood back as the little convoy started up and moved away into the gloom.

The nervousness of the Italian farmer was almost palpable. He was heartily regretting the moment of bravado in which he had volunteered to act as guide to these mad *Alleati*. Richard wondered how Rudi must be feeling as he approached his own army from the direction of the enemy lines. He appeared unmoved and fearless but Richard knew that the hand he kept tucked into his tunic was gripping the revolver loaded with the single bullet he had requested.

The Canadians in the forward positions were lying low. There was no way of telling where the two vehicles passed the last sentry, but after half a mile Richard began to have that unmistakeable sense of cold and prickly loneliness which pervades the no-man's-land between the lines. His mouth became dry and the familiar desire to urinate became almost uncontrollable.

Somewhere to the left a Canadian Bren gun opened up. It was answered by the harsh roar of a Spandau. A flare went up into the air a mile away and lazily floated to the ground. The tanks were still kicking up their rumpus, moving away to eastward. The Beaufighters were prowling over the peaks of the hills as though seeking targets.

Their occupants tense and silent, the Steyr and the Jeep ploughed on and entered the dark forest. Leaning forward

106

between him and Rudi, the Italian urged Richard up the steep gradient of a barely discernible track covered with grass and stones. The Jeep, already in low ratio and four-wheel drive, bucked and fought for grip, its passengers holding on so as not to be thrown out.

They'd gone less than a mile when Fen tapped Richard on the shoulder. Behind them the Steyr had stuck.

Everybody except Pat at the wheel had to dismount. Richard, Marcel and Baldovino put their shoulders to the Steyr and shoved. The farmer kept exclaiming 'Forza, forza!' and prodding ineffectually at the front wing. Marcel stood guard with his Tommy gun at the ready. Maria peered unnervingly down the alleyways between the trees as if she could see phantoms behind every bole.

The Steyr could not be persuaded up the bare patch of rock which had stopped it and there was no way round the obstacle.

'Nothing for it but to turn her round and winch her up in reverse gear on the starting handle,' Pat stated, leaning out over the driver's door.

Richard switched the engine of the Jeep off. Pat got the Steyr turned and they started to put his theory to the test. To Richard's surprise the Steyr, with its engine turned off and reverse gear engaged, began to move backward inch by inch as Pat laboured on the starting handle. They'd got it half way up the ten-foot strip of bare rock and the only sound in the forest was their gasping and panting when Marcel made a high-pitched hiss through his tongue.

Everybody froze.

'Keep still,' the Frenchman said in a loud whisper. 'I heard voices.'

Above the noise of the questing aircraft and the tanks performing their aimless manoeuvres came the sound of boots trampling the undergrowth. Then Richard heard the low guttural tones of German voices. A patrol was coming down the hill towards them.

Marcel, Pat and Fen, cradling their Tommy guns, crouched into firing positions facing the enemy. Richard pulled the paralysed farmer down beside him, pressing a finger on his lips. Rudi melted away into the dark shadows.

'Get her down!' Richard hissed at Baldovino. Maria was

107

standing as if turned to salt, her eyes searching the trees. Baldovino dragged her to the ground.

All six of them lay there on the wet earth, listening. The patrol was coming straight down the path, moving fast. Left to itself on the sloping rock the Steyr was slowly hiccuping back to the place where it had stuck. The vehicles, already mud-spattered, were further camouflaged by the dappled shadows cast through the trees by the artificial moonlight. The patrol would not see them till they were almost on them.

Richard could not yet discern any figures, though the crunch of their boots and the clanking of the grenades at their belts sounded very close.

'Don't fire till I do,' he whispered to Marcel and Fen. 'We'll let them get really close.'

He knew that they could not afford to miss. The Tommy guns were useful for close-quarter combat but no match for the fire-power of a German fighting patrol. To engage them too soon would mean being out-gunned.

The patrol was within a hundred yards when from a hill away to the right came a series of detonations. They were followed by the moan of mortar bombs in flight and the thud of their bursts. Immediately a Spandau opened up, this time firing long, angry bursts. It was answered by the stutter of a Bren gun and the crackle of rifle fire. The Canadian company commander was creating the promised diversion.

Richard heard the leader of the patrol give the order to halt. He could picture them standing there, interpreting the sounds of the battle just as he himself was. Then came a brief command. They began to move again. This time they were going laterally across the slope of the hill, heading towards the battle.

The prone men waited till the sound of footsteps had died away before scrambling to their feet. Richard looked round for the farmer. The Italian had vanished. He knew that was the last they would see of him.

'Jesus!' Fen exclaimed. 'I forgot to watch Rudi.'

There was no sign of the German.

'He has probably taken his chance to join his comrades.' Marcel applied the safety-catch of his Tommy gun.

'He's under the Jeep.' Pat jerked his head in that direction. 'I saw him go to ground in there like a scalded rabbit.'

As Richard walked towards the Jeep he saw Rudi crawling

out from under it. He stood up and pushed the revolver back into its belt holster.

He smiled at Richard but his rawboned face was chalky white. 'A close call. That was a fighting patrol.'

It took twenty minutes to cajole the Steyr over the sloping rock. After that the going levelled out, though there was no longer any discernible track. The noise of battle continued to the north, growing in volume as the artillery of both sides joined in. Richard pushed on, with Fen using a compass to keep them moving on up hill in the direction the farmer had indicated.

Just before three they hit the *trattür*. The Jeep abruptly emerged into a broad corridor running through the forest. Richard stopped. Pat ran the Steyr up alongside and cut his engine. Everybody got out and stood staring.

The undulating grass highway, at least a hundred yards broad, stretched away to right and left. Beyond it the forest gave way to snow-covered peaks which almost touched the luminous clouds. Here and there snow lay in patches, but it was easy to imagine the summer sun smiling down on the lush grass and the flocks of sheep tumbling across the hillocks and hollows of this ancient trail. The din of battle on the hill further back had died away and now the night was eerily still and silent. They were through the German lines.

The going was easier from now on. The *trattür* followed the most favourable contours of the ground, but it was not intended for wheeled traffic. The vehicles rocked, plunged, climbed and slid over the uneven terrain. Now and again the passengers in the Steyr had to get out and put their shoulders behind the rear wheels or bounce on the bumpers to help the tyres to bite.

They had been going for an hour and a half and had covered about six miles when Fen said: 'Pat has stopped. I think they've seen something.'

Richard pulled into the cover of the trees and halted. On the other side of the *trattür* the Steyr had melted into the shadows of the forest.

'Can you see anything?'

'Yes.' Fen was peering ahead with puckered eyelids. 'It looks like a patrol coming in open order along the *trattür*. There's about a dozen of them.'

'They are not German.' Rudi had climbed onto the bonnet of the Jeep to get a better view. He seemed to have excellent sight in the dark.

'Better play safe,' Richard said. He took his Tommy gun and placed himself behind a tree. Fen did the same. Rudi went to ground. There was no sight or sound of the other group on the far side of the *trattür*.

The dozen or so figures came gradually closer, only dimly discernible as there was no longer any artificial moonlight to improve visibility. When they were only a hundred yards away one of them must have seen the glint of a vehicle or a weapon. They halted and then began to race for the shelter of the woods.

Baldovino shouted to them in Italian. They halted, replying in a dialect Richard could not understand. Then, as Baldovino continued to call reassuringly to them, they came tentatively on.

'Is all right,' Baldovino shouted across the open space. 'Are Italians. Refugees trying to go through to the Allies.'

They were a pathetic and frightened bunch, mostly old men and women. Baldovino questioned them before sending them on their way with a dire warning not to say they had seen Allied soldiers.

He came across the *trattür* to speak to Richard. 'They have not seen no Germans since San Gregorio and then it was only a patrol which moved on.'

'Has the village been evacuated?'

'Not yet. But the news are not good. The rumour say that the SS are coming to stop this movement of refugees. And the parents of Maria are there.'

They had hardly got moving again when Richard stopped and switched off his engine. From a few miles back had come the sudden harsh roar of a Spandau. It was followed by the stutter of a less raucous weapon and then the thud of grenades. The exchange lasted for about half a minute. Then there was silence again.

First light found them on the slopes above San Gregorio. Here they would leave the *trattür* which curved away into the hills. Richard decided to lie up here for the day. The vehicles were run into the forest, this time on the same side, and camouflaged with branches.

As usual, Pat Mehan quickly got himself organized and by the time it was fully daylight had cooked up a passable breakfast. As they had now been on the move for twenty-four hours and everyone was ready for some sleep. Bed-rolls were unloaded and the more experienced campaigners looked around for ways to make themselves as comfortable as possible.

Richard arranged a roster of sentries and took the first watch himself. He was worried about the second party and kept hoping they would turn up. His own group had been so much delayed that the others should have caught up by now. That brief half-minute of firing had been ominous.

The diminutive Baldovino and Maria made themselves comfortable in the back of the Steyr. Pat stretched himself across the front seats. Fen, Marcel and Rudi spread ground-sheets under the trees or in the lea of the vehicles.

Richard placed himself with his back to a tree at the edge of the forest and lit his pipe. From the direction of the Steyr came the sound of Baldovino snoring. Pat had brought out his mouth-organ and was playing it very quietly. The plaintive notes of *The Rose of Tralee* crept out over the Italian valley. It was for once a fine day, though still bitterly cold. He sat there looking down the valley, watching the sun come up from behind the hills. The scene could have been taken from the background of one of Giorgione's paintings. There was a glistening of frost on the ferns and plants. Here and there the beaded dew on a spider's web had stiffened into a crystal tracery. Smoke rose lazily from the little village away below. Faint sounds of human activity floated up in the still air – the clangour of goat and cattle bells, an axe cleaving logs, a woman calling to a child.

It was beautiful enough to be painful. The sight awoke in Richard emotions of tenderness and aesthetic yearnings which had been repressed by months of active service. He had forgotten he could feel like that. An immense longing for peace and a return to the civilized way of life swept over him.

He shook the mood off and forced himself to think about his Bennies. There had been a moment back there when the German patrol was bearing down on them when he had become very aware of how exposed he was. Apart from Pat Mehan, all his companions had been unknown quantities – three Italians and one German. Marcel, for all his Parisian swagger and panache, had the instincts of a soldier. Fen, as was to be expected, had kept his head; the dour New Zealander's physical strength was maximised by great moral toughness. Baldovino had been a little too slow to inspire confidence but

111

he had not panicked. Rudi had passed this first crucial test. Richard was sure that if the patrol had bumped them he would have put a bullet in his own brain.

His head jerked round at the swish of feet through the long grass. Maria was coming towards him, pulling a shawl tight round her. She smiled at him shyly, gazing down at him with an enquiring expression. She had unplaited her hair and combed it out so that it fell in an undulating cascade over her shoulders and down her back to waist level.

He took the pipe out of his mouth.

'Baldovino tells me you speak Italian,' she said in her own language.

Richard admitted that he did.

'But you speak very well! Why did you pretend that you did not?'

He shrugged.

'You do not mind if I talk to you?'

'Not at all. I like talking Italian.'

She sat down on a flat stone beside him. 'I wanted to thank you for allowing me to come with you. You cannot understand what that meant to me.'

'Baldo told me your family live in that village.'

'Yes. San Gregorio. I pray that they are safe.'

'Did you come across by this *trattür*?'

'No. I was working in a hospital at Cassino till the Germans evacuated the town. Then I went north hoping to make my way home. But the Allies advanced and I was cut off.'

Richard shifted round so that he could see her face. She was staring down at the village, her eyes troubled.

'You were at Cassino? Do you know the Monastery?'

'Yes. I went there often to help with the sick refugees.'

'Did they evacuate the refugees from the Monastery?'

'Yes. Everybody was forced to leave. Only a few of the monks were allowed to stay.'

'There are still monks in the Monastery?'

Her eyebrows rose at the sharpness of his question. 'Yes. Unless the Germans have made them leave. Does that surprise you?'

'No. I suppose not. Now that the Monastery is in the front line it's hard to imagine.'

'They are in no danger. The building is as strong as a fortress and the Allies will not harm it.'

112

She stayed talking to him till it was time to wake Marcel for the next watch. The hour and a half passed very swiftly. He was glad of the chance to reacquaint himself with Italian. Many words and phrases he had forgotten came to life again. She was intelligent and well-educated. He found that she shared his enthusiasm for the operas of Verdi, the paintings of Giotto and the sonnets of Petrarch. It was a long time since he had talked like that to a woman.

*

Richard was woken at about three by the sound of excited voices. Propping himself up on one elbow he saw a couple of dozen Italians moving up onto the *trattür* from the direction of the village. They were chattering excitedly and throwing fearful backward glances down the valley. They never saw the vehicles hidden in the trees and soon passed out of sight along the *trattür*.

There was still no sign of the following group. Pat had had all the sleep he needed and was, predictably, brewing tea. Baldovino was sitting up, yawning and scratching himself. Maria, Marcel and Rudi were still asleep.

After those who were awake had shaved and had some food, Richard asked Baldovino to scout down to the village and find out whether it would be safe for the little convoy to pass through. As far as could be seen from up here on the hill there was no way of circumventing it, for it lay in a cleft between precipitous slopes forming a bottle-neck through which they would have to pass.

Baldovino buttoned his sheepskin jacket tightly round him and donned his feathered hat at its jauntiest angle. He had scarcely disappeared down the track which led to the valley floor when Fen came to report that a lone Jeep was coming along the *trattür*.

As it drew nearer Richard saw that there were four men in it. Bill MacDonald was at the wheel with Nick Steel beside him. Viktor Zygalski and the Indian, Ram Savarkar, were in the back.

Bill swung in under the trees, switched the engine off. He stared expressionlessly into the thickening shadows of the forest.

'Is the Kübelwagen following?'

Bill's eyes swung to Richard, but they remained blank.

113

'We ran into a Jerry patrol. They hit the Kübelwagen with the first burst and it brewed up.'

'Erle and Tucker?'

'They bought it. Tucker was hit by Spandau fire as he baled out. We only got out of it because Erle waded into them chucking grenades like confetti. Gave us time to get the Jeep turned round.'

'Any chance they took him prisoner?'

'No. We saw him go down. He got a burst in the chest from their Spandau.'

Richard nodded. He had a sudden vivid picture of the fair-haired South African with his lop-sided smile and eyes crinkling at the corners.

'We heard firing and grenade bursts behind us. You must have bumped that patrol which just missed us.'

'We recovered Tuck's body and took it back to the Canadians.' Bill hoisted a long leg out of the Jeep. 'That delayed us. Then we decided to use a different route to the *trattür*. Nobody fancied that track again.'

Nick, Viktor and Ram were dismounting from the Jeep, silent as men are when they have seen comrades killed.

Nick put a hand on Richard's shoulder. 'Good to see you, Richard. When we met that farmer running shit-scared we got worried about you. But he calmed down enough to show us another way up to the *trattür*. Bill decided to risk moving by day so's to catch you up.'

Richard was very relieved to see the American again. With his experience and humour, he was a comforting and steadying presence.

The loss of the Kübelwagen was serious. A third of the supplies for the partisans had gone with it. Bill squatted down beside Richard as Pat doled hot stew out into their Mess tins.

'I'm afraid I'm going to have to ask for my Jeep back. Any chance of your lending me one of your chaps? I've suffered fifty per cent casualties and we've hardly started yet.'

It was understandable that the Scot considered his own mission far more important than the Benedictine Commando's. He could not understand all this fuss about a pile of bricks and mortar. Richard was spared answering the question by the return of Baldovino, who arrived panting and exhausted by his climb up the hill.

The news from San Gregorio was unpleasant. Maria put her

hand to her mouth and listened appalled as Baldovino gave his report.

The *Feldsichersheitspolizei* had got wind of the flow of refugees through the village. They had evacuated the entire population in trucks and had set up a road block.

Maria was weeping as he finished. He moved over to put an arm round her shoulders.

'It could be much worse, Maria. In other places they have shot civilians out of hand.'

'Is there any way round the village?' Bill asked.

'No. Not with vehicles.'

'Only one thing for it, then.' Richard looked at Bill. 'We'll have to thump them. We'll leave Rudi out of it. Okay, Rudi?'

Rudi shrugged his shoulders and muttered: *'Feldsichersheitspolizei!'*

Richard knew that the only way to run this Commando was on a democratic basis. That was why he had decided not to play too much on rank and to encourage Christian names. What followed was not so much an order group as a conference, with each man being given a chance to state his opinion. Richard summed up the consensus of opinions and when Bill had suggested some changes in detail it was agreed.

Nick and Pat stayed with Baldo, Maria and Rudi at the camp-site with the vehicles while the other six made their way down to the outskirts of the village.

Fen had been a poacher in his spare time. His massive physique had not prevented him from mastering the art of silent movement. He went ahead and found the village was deserted except for the small school where the detachment had set up their headquarters. The half-dozen who were off duty had looted a keg of wine from the *trattoria* and were settling down to a well-oiled sing-song. They obviously did not expect to be troubled by anything worse than the odd Italian refugee. The two sentries were stamping to keep their feet warm on the roadway opposite the one and only shop.

It was all very simple. Ram and Viktor took the two sentries. Ram disposed of his man by the approved Indian thug method. He used a silk scarf with a knot in it, taking the sentry from behind and strangling him. At the same moment Viktor slid a long stiletto under the ribs of his victim, clapping a hand across his mouth to stifle his death-cry and cradling him in his arms as he fell.

While Marcel and Fen covered the street in case any of the other buildings were occupied, Richard and Bill dealt with the school house. It consisted of a single room with buildings along one side. Bill moved to the door, holding his Tommy gun at his waist. Richard went round to the side of the building, crouching below the windows. Inside he could hear lusty voices raised in song.

Enemy voices.

He lifted a large stone, stood up and for a second stared at the men inside the room. He was not thinking of them as people. Then he smashed the stone through the window. The singing stopped abruptly and every head turned towards the crash. At that moment Bill flung the door open and, firing from the hip, sprayed the room with bullets. As those still alive jerked their heads towards the door, Richard pulled the pins from two 36 grenades and lobbed them through the gash in the glass. He was flat on his face as they exploded. The remaining glass flew out and a few metal splinters pierced the wooden walls of the school.

There was no sound from inside the room. As Richard moved round to the front of the building he heard a few more single shots fired inside the schoolroom. Bill was making sure there were no survivors.

Richard ran quickly to the doorway, just in case he needed covering. The Scotsman was inside, moving quickly from one dead body to the other, stooping and lifting the limp arms. He seemed unaware of Richard watching him.

Outside in the road Fen put two fingers in his mouth and blew a piercing shepherd's whistle. The agile Ram was already climbing the telegraph pole at the end of the village to make sure that there would be no telephonic communication with San Gregorio.

Richard had only gradually become aware of pain at the side of his left buttock. Now he remembered a fiery twinge as he'd gone to ground after flinging his second grenade. He could feel a trickle of wetness on his thigh. He put a hand down to feel the spot. His fingers came away sticky, marked with a dark stain. But he told himself it was only a nick and immediately forgot all about it.

Ten minutes later the three vehicles came rolling down the

road into the village, with Rudi at the wheel of a Jeep. By then the dead sentries had been hauled into the blasted schoolhouse. As soon as the Steyr halted Maria climbed out and ran to the open front door of a house near the *trattoria*. It took her only a moment to find out that it had been looted of all its contents. She came back sobbing. Baldovino put his arms round her.

'What are you going to do with her?' Bill asked Richard in a low voice.

'We'll have to take her along with us.'

'Christ!' Bill exploded, his pent-up tension bursting out. 'Is this a military operation or a Sunday school outing?'

'We can't leave her here alone with eight dead Germans,' Marcel pointed out with dangerous calm. 'If the PAI find her here they'll skin her alive.'

'You should have thought of that before. She should never have come in the first place.'

'Well, it was my decision and I take full responsibility for it.' Richard kept his voice calm. After the blood-letting everyone was tense and tempers were ready to flare up.

'That's all very fine, but I'm not going to let your decision foul up my operation. These explosives and weapons have to reach the partisans. When I agreed to see you through the lines there was nothing about you bringing a Kraut and a Wop along, let alone an Eyetie female.'

'Steady on, Scottie,' Fen warned in his deep voice.

Ram had gone to stand behind Bill's shoulder, his white teeth gleaming in the dark skin of his face. Pat ranged himself behind Richard. Nick, sensing trouble, climbed out of the Steyr and came slowly towards the group. The water of the fountain in the dark village square continued to splash noisily.

'We need Rudi and Baldovino to help us achieve our mission, and Maria –'

Bill did not let Richard finish. 'You're on a fool's errand. It's only a bloody monastery. A Roman Catholic one at that. Probably stuffed with the bones of saints and chunks of the true cross –'

He stopped abruptly. Pat had moved past Richard as lightly as a dancer, his fist bunched to knock the Scotsman down. Bill made a quick movement and in an instant the .38 was in his right hand. From near the fountain another revolver blasted. The .38 in Bill's hand went spinning through the air. He

117

grabbed his right hand with his left, his jaw dropping in abject amazement as he stared at Nick.

The American walked calmly forward, holding his revolver in the position from which he had fired it, exactly in front of his navel. At that moment the military uniform was incongruous. He might have been some hard-bitten sheriff stepping out of a Wild West movie.

'Douse it, everyone! We won't get nowhere if we start locking horns among ourselves.'

There was a long silence before the two separate groups relaxed.

'I forgot he was a Mick.' Bill was still gazing in disbelief at the revolver in Nick's hand. 'Christ, do you realize you might have killed me?'

'Not a chance. Now, you were both at fault, so I suggest you just forget about the whole thing.'

'Fair enough.' Mehan drew the back of his hand across his nose. 'I'm terrible sorry.'

'*Sorry!* When another rank offers to strike an officer!' Bill stooped to recover his revolver.

Richard could see he was still in a belligerent mood. He said loudly: 'When are we going to have the share-out, Bill?'

'What share-out?'

'The Jerry watches. I hope you've got one for each of us.'

'Oh, yes, the watches.' As he straightened up Bill's eyes swung towards Richard and he knew he had made an enemy.

12

Richard calculated that although Peroli was only thirty miles away as the crow flies they faced a journey of about a hundred miles by road. Because of the mountains their route would follow an S shape. The village where they were supposed to meet the partisans lay twenty miles back from Cassino on the German side.

He had assigned Fen to ride with Bill and Ram in the second Jeep. Nick and Rudi would accompany him in the leading vehicle. Rudi had proved he could handle a Jeep so Richard let him take the wheel. It could be advantageous to have a German driver if they were stopped. He wanted Nick with him to discuss the ugly situation which had arisen with the LRP leader. The rest of the party – Pat, Marcel, Baldovino, Viktor and Maria – were assigned to the Steyr. Pat drove with Viktor beside him. The Pole's German was probably good enough to deal with traffic control police.

Bill accepted Richard's decisions with an ill-graced nod. His silence made it clear that the sooner he got shot of the Benedictine Commando and their half-arsed mission the better he'd be pleased.

The three-vehicle convoy set off at fifty yard intervals. They were going to travel at the highest speed possible with hooded lights. Rudi took the Jeep up to 45 m.p.h.

'When did you learn to handle a revolver like that?' Richard asked Nick over his shoulder.

'I was in the Detroit police mid-thirties. If you couldn't shoot

119

straight you didn't stay alive. I've kept in practice since then by joining a gun club.'

'Do you think Bill was going to shoot?'

'There's a special look comes in a man's eyes when he's ready to kill. Bill had it.'

'We've got problems enough without that.'

'I guess it'll blow over. Bill's a wild one. A mite wooky, I'd say. I wonder how many missions he's done for the LRP.'

'Half a dozen, I believe. He led the group which blew up those aircraft on the Catania airfield.'

'How come you knew he had those watches?'

'I saw him helping himself after we sorted out the Krauts in the school.'

'That was a lousy way to behave. I just hate looting.'

'I've known people get like that. Especially these special service chaps. It becomes a compulsion, like nicotine or whisky. I suppose it's got some psychological explanation, like kleptomania. I expect his mother put alum in his feeding bottle.'

Nick laughed. 'It's probably time he had some furlough. Anyhow, we'll be going our own ways after tonight.'

'He wants me to detail two of my chaps to him. All he can think about is his own side of this mission.'

'You going to?'

'Pat's out, obviously and I'd be loath to part with Fen. He doesn't say much but he's solid and reliable. That leaves Viktor and Marcel.'

'I'd say Viktor is a good man in a tight spot.'

'Marcel's no slouch either. You have to be good to command those Moroccan Goums.'

'Could be,' Nick said dubiously. 'I guess you've seen the way he looks at Maria?'

Richard did not answer. Rudi was slowing down. The little road that led up to San Gregorio had ended and they were coming to a main road running from east to west. There was heavy traffic on it. Rudi had to wait for nearly five minutes at the T junction before there was a gap which allowed the three vehicles to slip out and insert themselves in the flow. It was obvious that a large German formation was being transferred from the Eastern end of the line to reinforce those containing the Anzio beach-head or defending the Winter Line at Cassino. The domination of the skies by the Allied air forces made it impossible for the Germans to carry out any large-scale movement during daylight.

Richard felt his skin prickle with tension as the Jeep jostled along in close company with enemy vehicles. He felt that the squat little American machine must be blatantly obvious to the helmeted troops he could see in the lorries. But there was a tremendously varied assortment of transport, from big Opel and Daimler-Benz lorries to the lighter Wanderers and jaunty little Kübelwagen. All of them were painted buff yellow, some with brown or green camouflage streaks.

'This is a parachute regiment,' Rudi told Richard, as they came up behind a half-track motor-cycle towing a 105 mm gun. 'You can see the Luftwaffe eagle on their smocks.' Two of the seats faced backwards. The pair of soldiers sitting on them held their rifles pointing at the sky. They wore the special, pot-shaped helmets of the Fallschirmjäger units. These made them look surprisingly different from the normal German soldier in his neck-protecting Stahlhelm.

Apart from the incident at San Gregorio, this was the closest Richard had been to German soldiers. He found it unnerving to sit under the unblinking stare of these lethal-looking thugs.

A BMW motor-cycle and side-car carrying three soldiers swept past them and overtook the slow-moving Kettenrad.

'Darf ich – ' Rudi began, then corrected himself. 'Should I overtake?'

Richard twisted round. The Steyr and the second Jeep had closed up to thirty-yard intervals. The choice was whether to stay behind the Kettenrad for God knows how many miles or risk losing the following vehicles. The two Germans were beginning to talk about the Jeep. One of them pointed to the front bumpers.

'Pass him.'

After that they overtook whenever they could, Richard looking back to make sure the others followed. It was surprising how anonymous they soon began to feel in the general bustle and movement. The Germans in any case were using a lot of foreign vehicles, many of them captured or commandeered from occupied countries. Here, as on the Allied side, everybody was intent on his own job. Drivers had only one thought in mind and that was to reach their destination before dawn caught them on the open and exposed road. The last thing any

121

of the Germans was looking for was a British vehicle miles behind their own lines.

Richard soon began to experience a sense of elation, knowing that he was deep inside enemy territory, wearing a British uniform and driving a British vehicle. It was particularly satisfying to be waved through the traffic jam in Alfedena by a German military policeman.

He wondered what Wilfrid was doing and what he'd say if he knew that his brother was twenty miles behind Jerry lines.

Just after the small town of Opi they ran into the first real snag. The route Richard had selected turned left and crossed over the Meta Mountains to Sora. The alternative road, going straight on, involved a detour of about a hundred miles.

At the junction a military policeman stood under the drenching rain directing all traffic to take the longer route. He was muffled up to the ears in a voluminous motor-cycle coat of grey-green waterproof canvas. A pair of goggles had been snapped up onto his helmet. As Rudi made to turn left he held out his red and white disc on the end of its handle.

'Can't you see the sign?' he shouted. 'This road is restricted.'

Rudi pulled up just past him. As the Jeep had right-hand drive he was on the ditch side of the road.

A quick-fire exchange in German followed. The MP was telling Rudi that all vehicles without special authorization must take the longer route. The mountain road had been bombed and was further deteriorating under the atrocious weather conditions.

'We have verbal authorization from General von Vietinghoff,' Rudi barked at him with all the authority of an officer addressing another rank. 'I am giving you a direct order to let this convoy through.'

It is difficult for a German soldier to resist a direct order from an officer, but a military policeman is different and this one had definite instructions. As the conversation escalated into an altercation Richard put his head out to peer back past the hood. The Steyr, only dimly visible in the darkness and pelting rain, had halted about twenty yards back. He thought he saw the second Jeep disappearing up the other road. Either Bill had missed the turning or had decided not to get mixed up in the argument.

What happened next made Richard think that the LRP man

had made a wise decision. A staff car had turned off the main road and was halting alongside the Jeep. It was a powerful cabriolet with a long, black bonnet. On the radiator was the three-pointed star emblem of Mercedes-Benz. Sitting in the back was an officer. He leant forward and wound down the window. To judge by his leather coat and the arrogantly up-swept cap with its shiny peak he was of high rank. Richard, on the advice of the LRP men, had been brazenly wearing his own fore and aft cap with the Greenshire Yeomanry badge. He whipped it off and thrust it between his knees.

'What is the hold-up here?' the German officer shouted.

The MP saluted deferentially and explained his dilemma. The officer's head jerked round and he stared at the Britisher.

'You!' he bawled. 'What is your regiment? And where did you get this vehicle?'

Richard's mouth had gone dry. He groped in his mind for German numerals and the names of the formations he had seen on the Order of Battle map at AFHQ.

'*Fünfzehnte Panzer-Grenadier Division, Herr General,*' he yelled in the stentorian tones of a German soldier replying to such an enquiry.

'Then what are you doing here? You should be at Nettuno on 14th Army front. And you are improperly dressed. Why are you not wearing a hat?'

Richard was dimly aware that a shadowy figure had moved up the ditch behind the military policeman. Another had darted behind the rear of the Mercedes-Benz.

'Answer my question!' the officer commanded. 'What are you doing in this sector? And what vehicle is that?'

'*Herr General, ich habe eine –*' Richard's voice trailed away as he floundered for words. He turned to Rudi for help and saw a heart-stopping sight. The lethal form and face of Viktor Zygalski surged up from the ditch behind the military policeman. His hands were gripping two wooden handles, but the wire that joined them was invisible. His clenched fists described a circle on either side of the MP's head, then jerked back and crossed. The German's eyes bulged. His mouth opened but no sound came. He fell backwards, twisting face downwards in Viktor's grip.

Richard dragged his eyes away from the gruesome sight and turned back towards the road. The officer was just getting out of the car. Everything about him spelt trouble for somebody. He had just put a foot to the ground when the figure behind the car moved like a flash of black lightning. Marcel had learned some of the techniques of his Goums. A long blade flashed dully and Richard heard the thump as it struck the German's midriff, just above the belt. Marcel, white teeth bared, took his weight as he keeled forward and thrust the body ahead of him onto the floor of the rear seat. He jerked his knife free and put the bloody blade behind the ear of the paralyzed driver.

'*Gerade aus!*' he told the terrified man as he slammed the door. '*Schnell! Schnell!*'

Somehow the driver found a gear. The Mercedes-Benz roared off up the road leading into the mountains.

'Help me with this!' Viktor Zygalski was dragging the body of the MP from the ditch by his shoulders.

'What's the idea?' Nick demanded. 'Leave him there. We want to move on.'

'He'll be found if we leave him here.' Viktor was panting with physical effort. 'And we want his uniform.'

Nick vaulted out and took the legs of the dead man. Together they swung the body once, twice, then slung it into the back of the Jeep. As they clambered in on top of it Rudi let in his clutch and accelerated up the hill after the staff car. The German's face had gone absolutely white, as on the previous night in the wood. Richard looked back. The Steyr was following.

'That was necessary, Rudi. We'd have been in the bag if Viktor and Marcel hadn't turned up.'

'A *Kettenhund* and an SS Colonel,' Rudi said dispassionately. 'Did you see the death's head on the *Standartenführer's* cap? Those are the swine who are bringing dishonour on Germany.'

Three miles later they came upon the Mercedes-Benz parked by the roadside. The driver was standing with his back to a telegraph pole and his hands were clasped behind it. Marcel was just tying his wrists with the tow-rope. The man was so frightened that he had lost retention and wet his trousers.

'We won't harm him,' Richard promised Rudi, wincing as he climbed out. The blood on his backside had congealed, glueing his underpants to the open cut.

Marcel and Viktor dragged the body of the SS officer out of the Mercedes-Benz. They began to strip him of his uniform.

Under the long leather coat he was wearing a tunic and breeches of soft, light ash-grey. His legs were encased in burnished jack-boots. On his head he wore a high-fronted peaked cap with a silver eagle and the silver death's head badge which had aroused Rudi's anger. The tunic was heavily garnished with regulation branch identification – silver-cord straps above the patent-leather peak of the cap and green piping round the crown, silver braid on the shoulders and lapel, a metallic-embroidery badge on the sleeve. With his sheer white shirt he wore a black tie, as if in mourning for a slaughtered multitude.

'Mind how you handle this one,' Viktor warned as they turned to tackle the MP. 'Their sphincters usually open when you strangle them.'

By the time the Steyr came fussing in low gear up the steep gradient the job was done. The bodies and the unusable trousers of the MP had been concealed in the undergrowth.

'What happened to Bill's lot?' Richard asked Pat, as he climbed down from the driver's seat.

'They went past when they saw the staff car stopping by you.'

'We can't wait. It's two o'clock already and we've still a long way to go.' Richard nodded towards the Mercedes-Benz. 'Rudi, do you know this type of car?'

'Of course. It's the eight-cylinder 54OK, the supercharged model with the M24 Daimler-Benz engine. Probably requisitioned from some rich Jewish businessman. Do you want me to drive it?'

'Yes, please. Marcel, will you go with Rudi and follow the Steyr? I'll have Viktor with Nick and me in the Jeep.'

'Good,' said Viktor, unholstering his revolver and advancing on the shivering German driver. 'We can't leave this one here, though.'

'No, Viktor!' Richard called out sharply.

Viktor stopped and looked at him in surprise. Richard jerked his head towards Rudi.

The Pole nodded. 'All right to tie him up and dump him a bit further from the road?'

'Put him against that tree.' Rudi indicated an oak a hundred yards away. 'He will be visible there when daylight comes.'

While Viktor went to deal with the driver Rudi slid behind the wheel of the Mercedes and began to check over the controls.

Richard started the Jeep and moved to the head of the column. He kept looking back down the road half hoping to see the second Jeep appear and half fearing to be overtaken by a German convoy. Without that MP to head them off the Paratroopers might decide to take the short cut over the mountains.

A couple of minutes later Viktor climbed into the back behind him and Nick.

'Did you gag him?' Richard asked.

'I gagged him the best way I know.' Viktor's voice sounded hoarse. Richard glanced round, saw his face, and knew for certain that Viktor had given the driver his quietus. He let in the clutch and the Jeep jerked forward.

He soon realized why access to the pass was being restricted. The damage caused by bombing and continous rain had made it almost impassable. There was a line of burned-out vehicles near the summit. They had been caught on the exposed mountainside by RAF fighter-bombers.

At Sora they rejoined the heavy traffic moving towards the Anzio and Cassino fronts. Richard reckoned that if Bill had taken the longer route round he might be as much as a day behind them. This time he did not pass any German vehicles. Traffic was moving along at a steady pace. He did not want to attract unnecessary attention or run the risk of separating the convoy.

There was still an hour of darkness left when they reached the turning for Peroli. It was a narrow, minor road that climbed into a mountainous region. Arce, the town which lay sixteen miles to the rear of Cassino, was another ten miles further along the road they were on.

Nick, with the map on his knees and a torch in his hand, had been studying the faintly discernible contours of the hills. The turning was three-quarters of a mile after a bridge and just opposite a faded sign which said: *Roman Theatre*.

'I guess this is it.'

'Hope you're right. Check that the others follow us.'

'It's okay,' Nick told Richard a moment later. 'They've all turned off.'

Peroli was five miles from the main road and about two thousand feet above it. The sky was lightening as the three vehicles negotiated the endless series of zigzags. They met several German military vehicles coming down, but they too

126

were in a hurry to reach their destination before the Allied aircraft began to prowl the sky.

The grey light of a dry but overcast morning revealed the jumble of houses perched on the hillside a mile before they reached it. Anyone who might have been in the single street had vanished by the time the leading Jeep drew up in the tiny *piazza*. The inhabitants had naturally assumed that the visitors were Germans and had made themselves scarce.

Richard called Baldovino and told him to knock up the owner of the *trattoria*. The little Italian came back five minutes later, gesturing eloquently. He was accompanied by a pale youth with a strip of black beard round his chin. He was wearing a beret with a badge stuck in it. There was a bandolier across his chest and from his waistbelt dangled a couple of grenades. A sheathed stiletto was stuck into his belt and he carried a double-barrelled shot-gun. It was Richard's first sight of a *partigiano*.

The young man was very thrilled to see his first Allied soldiers but at the same time extremely scared. Richard wanted to ask him not to point the shot-gun straight at his head but he kept his mouth shut.

'General Toro and the whole of the Gruppo Manzoni have moved into the mouutains further north,' Baldovino explained excitedly. 'It seems that the Germans were informed about them and have been making *retate*.'

'What are *retate?*'

'They are round-ups of Italian males by the German and Fascist Italian police. This boy has taken much risk to stay here for making contact with us. He can guide us to the new headquarters of General Toro. It is near Fiuggi.'

'We don't want to go any further away from Cassino.' Richard was thinking quickly. Waiting for Baldovino he had experienced an uncomfortable conviction that something very nasty had already happened or was soon to happen in this place. 'It's the LRP's job to contact the partisans. Does he know anywhere we could lie up for a day?'

As the young man answered Baldovino's question, pointing back down the road and then gesturing towards the hills, Richard got the gist of his reply. On the way up he had seen a track leading into forest about half a mile before the village. He'd restarted the Jeep before Baldovino had finished translating, and was turning it round as the Italian climbed aboard the Steyr.

Back down the hill at the opening to the track he stopped for long enough to find a chalky pebble and print the word BENNIES on a board that had fallen from somebody's private signpost. He propped it up so that it was visible to a vehicle coming up the hill.

'Don't you think that might interest the Krauts too?'

'We'll have to take that chance, Nick. Our *partigiano* friend isn't going to hang around much longer.'

After a mile or so the rough and stony track emerged from forest onto a bare hillside. There, nestling in a hollow, was a typical Italian farmhouse, with pinkish walls and a rusty-red roof of interlocking tiles. Woodsmoke rose from the chimney. A cock, some hens and a few geese strutted in the yard. There was a donkey tethered on the hillside and a woolly dog whose bark was more of a greeting than a warning. A man and woman came running out of the door at the sound of the vehicles then stopped in fear when they saw the buff-coloured Steyr. They were typical peasant stock and it was hard to tell their age.

Baldovino put on his Bersaglieri hat with its cheeky feather and strutted off to speak to them. Richard glanced over his left shoulder. The view was stupendous, looking across the valley to the mountains on the other side. Far below he could see the road they had left. It was empty of vehicles now. From somewhere along the valley out of sight came the drone of an aircraft. He felt in his ear-drums a faint concussion, not unlike excessively loud heart-beats. It was the sound of gun-fire, borne on the wind from Cassino.

'He is friendly,' Baldovino came back to report. 'We can stay here and draw water from his well if we hide ourselves in that wood. He says he has been hiding an escaped British prisoner-of-war since last September.'

The pine forest offered good cover. The three vehicles were parked to form three sides of a square across which the tarpaulins could be rigged. Rudi and Marcel cut branches to camouflage them thoroughly while Nick and Pat set about preparing breakfast. Viktor, putting first things first, was checking his weapons and making sure they would be within reach if he needed them in a hurry.

Richard was trying to pin-point their position on the map when Maria came back from the farm with a bucket of water. She was not alone.

It was hard to believe that the figure accompanying her had

128

once been a British soldier. He was wearing cast-off civilian clothes and a three-days' growth of beard. He introduced himself as Number 4023521 Private Spragg of the London Fusiliers. His first enquiry was, had they any fags?

Puffing at one of Richard's State Express 555s, he told his story. He had escaped, or more likely been released, from the POW camp in Fiuggi at the time of the Armistice. His efforts to reach the Allied lines could not have been very energetic as he had only covered twelve miles before finding a friendly farmer on whom he could batten.

'What are you lot on, then?' he asked, squatting down and eyeing Maria in a way Richard did not like. 'You Commandos or summink?'

'We're trying to contact the Italian partisans.' For some reason Richard did not want to tell Spragg very much.

The ex-POW sneered. 'You won't see much of them. They come down to the village and take away most of the food then scarper back to their mountains. The last thing they want to see is a Jerry.'

More to test him than for any other reason, Richard said: 'You can join this Commando, if you like. We can fix you up with kit and weapons.'

'Me a Commando?' Spragg shook his head in disgust. 'Not fuckin' likely, mate. I'm stayin' here till the Allies liberate me. I've had all I want of the fuckin' war.'

Richard knew that of all the circle who were listening to this exchange with a kind of appalled fascination none was more interested than Rudi. But he controlled his anger. He was in no position to make more enemies.

The smell of the breakfast which Nick and Pat had now finished preparing was wafting over from the cookhouse they had improvised on the other side of the Steyr.

'Smells like bangers,' Spragg hinted.

'Would you be prepared to stand guard while we get some sleep?'

'Okay.'

'Then you can join us for breakfast, if you like.'

Spragg drew the back of his hand across his lips.

'Cor! Never thought I'd have a mouth waterin' for Compo.'

After breakfast Richard sent him down to the place where the track emerged from the wood. Everybody else prepared to make themselves comfortable, spreading their bed-rolls where the ground looked most promising. Richard made Maria take his groundsheet and greatcoat. He showed her the trick of scooping out a hollow to accommodate her hips and lining it with moss. She lay down between him and Baldovino.

He was almost asleep when he opened his eyes. She had turned towards him, and her eyes were also open. Her face was very thoughtful and she did not smile. Though she was staring straight at him her expression did not change when she saw him watching her.

He closed his eyes but the picture of that face framed by the auburn hair remained imprinted on his mind. He resisted the temptation to open them again but, dog-tired though he was, it took him a long time to go to sleep.

13

Alexander was under renewed pressure. A week earlier the American Chiefs of Staff had commented that in spite of a weakening of German forces on Fifth Army's front 'there has been no heavily-mounted aggressive offensive.' The C-in-C had replied that he had high hopes of a break-through in the near future. As seen on small-scale maps and from OPs on the top of Monte Trocchio the situation did indeed look promising. The Americans on Snakeshead Ridge were within a few hundred yards of the crest of Monastery Hill. They were only a mile and a half from Route 6. It seemed that one more squeeze would crack the nut.

Meanwhile, the Ultra messages which Alexander was receiving through Squadron-Leader Tommy Thompson – 'from a

Most Secret Source' – indicated that von Mackensen was preparing his *coup de grâce* against the Anzio beach-head. The Germans at Cassino had to be kept fully engaged so that troops could not be switched from there to the beach-head. So the pressure was passed down the chain of Command – Alexander to Clark, Clark to Freyberg, Freyberg to Tuker and Tuker to his Brigadiers. The Brigadiers told their battalion commanders that they must be ready to attack as soon as possible.

What could not be seen from Monte Trocchio was the appalling nature of the terrain facing Tuker's division – the natural rock fortresses, the precipices and chasms, the cruel brambles, the boulders, the stench of unrecovered bodies, the freezing wind, the cold, the cold. Nor did they know that into those deeply blasted machine-gun positions were now creeping the most deadly fighters in the German forces. As so often it was *esprit de corps* and not patriotism that would inspire men to heroic deeds. These men would give their lives to prove that the air force's Paratroopers could surpass anything that the army's Panzer-Grenadiers had done to fulfil the Führer's order to stand at Cassino.

On Saturday the 12th Tuker fired his broadside. In the absence of adequate intelligence information he had set about repairing the omission himself. The subaltern he had despatched to scour the bookshops of Naples had found a book which was a mine of information on the Monastery of St Benedict. Armed with this the commander of 4th Indian Division drafted his memorandum to the corps commander. The points he made were as resounding as the blows of a battering-ram.

'The Monastery was converted into a fortress in the 19th century . . .

'The walls are of solid masonry at least 10 feet thick at the base . . .

'MONTE CASSINO is therefore a modern fortress and must be dealt with by modern means – by applying blockbuster bombs from the air . . .

'I would ask that you give me definite information *at once* as to how this fortress will be dealt with as the means are not within the capacity of this division.'

Freyberg, though courageous as a lion, was an extraordinarily gentle man who cared as a father for the troops under his command. Those who did not know him well were surprised to find that he could quote Jane Austen as readily as the speeches of Winston Churchill. Tuker was different, a professional soldier to the tips of his finger nails but much more aloof, less approachable. He shared one characteristic with Freyberg and that was a passionate affection for the troops under his command – Punjabis, Sikhs, Mahrattas, Nepalese, British.

On the evening that he received this memorandum Freyberg picked up his telephone and asked for Fifth Army headquarters. He used the green 'scrambler' telephone with which headquarters from Corps upwards were now equipped. When both parties pressed the button on the instrument they still heard clear speech but their words were reduced to gobbledegook to anyone listening on a line tap. He knew that Mark Clark was away at the Anzio beach-head checking the measures being taken to repulse von Mackensen's imminent counter-offensive. So he was not surprised when Clark's Chief of Staff, General Gruenther, came on the line.

'We want to have the Abbey attacked,' Freyberg told the American bluntly. 'I'd suggest a force of thirty-six aircraft using heavy bombs.'

'You know the Army Commander's view on this,' Gruenther replied with equal stiffness.

'The divisional commander who is making the attack feels that the Abbey is an essential target.' Freyberg spoke slowly and distinctly, but without heat. 'And I agree with him.'

After a pause Gruenther said: 'Very well. I will speak to the C-in-C.'

But the C-in-C was not available. Gruenther spoke instead to Alexander's Chief of Staff, General Harding.

'Freyberg,' he told him, 'wants to have the Monastery softened up.'

Harding replied that he would speak to Alexander about it.

Later that evening, when Clark came back from the beach-head, he learned of Freyberg's request. Angry that the approach had been made during his absence he told Gruenther to speak to Harding again and re-state his personal opinion that the bombing of the Monastery was not a military necessity.

It was late that evening when Harding 'phoned back with Alexander's decision. In the outcome the German propaganda machine made a meal of this decision and more than one historian has judged Alexander harshly for it. But afterwards, sitting on the slopes of Monte Trocchio and gazing across at the Monastery, he confided to the Roman Catholic chaplain who was his close friend that it was the most difficult choice he had been called to make in the whole of his military career.

He made it alone, pacing the carpet of his office.

There was no reliable information available to confirm or deny the belief that the Germans were using the place. He privately agreed with Tuker that the intelligence services had let them down over this. The demand for quick results from Churchill and the Chiefs of Staff as well as the necessity to take pressure off the Anzio beach-head made a final decision necessary now. One thing was certain: his soldiers believed that the Monastery was a hostile presence opposing them. If he declined to have it reduced and they suffered horrible casualties how could he ever face them again?

Which was more important? The preservation of a monument of great architectural, artistic and religious value or the lives of those thousands of men shivering on the hills around it?

The memory came back of his interview with the young liaison officer who had so passionately argued against the destruction of St Benedict's Abbey. In a way that argument had helped to clear the matter in his mind. He regretted now having dismissed him so summarily. Like everyone else he had assumed that the C-in-C of an army group was devoid of religious sentiment, even if he was regularly seen at church parades.

The conqueror of the Afrika Korps smiled a little wryly. There was one secret which he carried with him and which he would carry to the grave. Not even the Roman Catholic chaplain who was his close confidant and friend knew that he had been accompanied throughout all his campaigns by a talisman which some of his fellow countrymen would have been inclined to regard as a piece of popish idolatry. Protestant Ulsterman though he was, he never put on his uniform without tucking into an inner pocket a small crucifix. It had lain against his chest through all the battles of North Africa and Italy and he never moved without it.

He touched it now through the cloth of his battle-dress, felt the sculptured figure press into his flesh. But no guidance came from that direction either. This was a decision which a man must make on his own.

Yet he seemed to hear a word whispered somewhere out in the dark night. And the word was 'Paaschendaele.'

Not long afterwards the telephone on Gruenther's desk rang. It was Harding.

'General Alexander agrees to the bombing of the Monastery if General Freyberg thinks it is a military necessity.'

Gruenther asked Harding to wait while he relayed the message to Clark.

'General Clark wants you to remind the C-in-C,' he said into the 'phone a few moments later, 'that in his view the bombing is not a military necessity.'

'General Alexander has made his decision,' Harding stated flatly.

A few minutes later, as Clark walked away, Gruenther telephoned Freyberg.

Choosing his words carefully, he said: 'General Alexander has decided that the Monastery will be bombed if you think it is necessary. General Clark does not think that this is a case of military necessity.'

'I do consider it is necessary,' Freyberg stated.

'Right,' said Gruenther, feeling that he had now done all he could to make everyone's position clear. 'Then it is authorized.'

*

Richard's sleep was disturbed by the sound of aircraft engines. Fighters had swooped low over the forest. A few seconds later came the roar of their cannon shooting up some vehicles which had ventured out onto the road below. Maria had started up in terror.

'It's all right,' he reassured her. 'They're attacking the traffic on the road.'

She calmed at the sound of his voice, but it was not only the aircraft which had frightened her.

'I had a terrible dream. It was about my parents. They were in a place surrounded by barbed wire. There were men with dogs and whips.'

He tried to reassure her. 'Dreams reflect fears, not reality. I expect they're being looked after all right.'

The others had turned restlessly at the sound of the aircraft, then gone to sleep again. Baldovino was snoring loudly. Maria glanced towards him, then smiled at Richard. As he moved into

134

a more comfortable position he winced involuntarily. She saw his face twist.

'What is the matter? You are in pain. What is it?'

'A grenade splinter. Grazed my hip.'

'You were wounded and you said nothing about it?' Maria chided him. 'I must look at it at once.'

'It's in a rather embarrassing spot.'

'Don't be silly. Have you forgotten that I am a trained nurse?' She had already turned the blanket back. 'Where is the first-aid kit?'

'Under the rear seat of the Jeep.'

She brushed aside his objections. His underpants were stuck to the wound with congealed blood. Very gently she damped the material and eased it away. She was totally concentrated and dispassionate as she washed the wound, applied disinfectant and a dressing.

'There. Have you clean clothes?'

'I've got clean underpants.'

'Then put them on.'

She busied herself packing away the first-aid kit while he got out his holdall and put on a clean pair of pants.

'Give me the dirty ones and I'll wash them.'

Reluctantly he handed her his blood-stained underpants. 'You shouldn't be doing this for me.'

'You men are so funny! When you did so much for me what is it to wash your *mutande*?'

After four hours sleep Richard already felt completely refreshed. It was three o'clock in the afternoon. Maria went down to the farmhouse to see what washing facilities there were. Richard took advantage of the opportunity to shave and wash with the water that was left in the bottom of the bucket. Rudi immersed himself totally in the icy water of a nearby stream he had found.

'First thing we have to decide,' Richard told the seven members of the Commando when they had all woken up, 'is whether we wait for Bill, Ram and Fenton to show up.'

He quizzed the semicircle of faces. They had gathered round Nick's campfire with the mugs of tea which Pat had dished out. It was already dark enough for the firelight to throw shadows on their faces. He had made up his own mind what he wanted to do, but he sensed that everything would go more smoothly if he gave every man a chance to speak his mind.

135

'*If* they do turn up.' Nick picked up a stick and inserted it into the heart of the fire. 'Three guys in Allied uniforms riding an American vehicle. There were a lot of MPs on that road.'

'How long have we got?' Marcel asked.

'I'm not sure. Just before I left I heard that things were beginning to hot up. We were originally given a fortnight. That would have taken us to the 16th.'

'Just permit me to make this clear in my mind,' Marcel said in his slow, distinct way. 'We have to penetrate the Monastery, ascertain whether it is occupied and then come out again. You will signal the information from the Monastery itself?'

'Yes. We'll have to take the suitcase set with us. The Number 18 is in Bill's Jeep.'

'How far are we from Cassino now?' Viktor asked.

'About twenty miles as the crow flies. Say, thirty by road.'

Nick emptied the dregs of his tea on the ground beside him with a grimace.

'I get the impression that you have some sort of a plan in your mind, Richard. If that's the case let's have it.'

'Well, try this for size. Anything detailed would be stupid. We don't know what we are going into. My idea was that Viktor, Marcel, Pat, Rudi and myself should try to reach the Monastery tonight, using the Steyr. There will be a lot of traffic on Route 6 and we ought to be able to get near Cassino by road. We'll probably have to do the last bit on foot, but we have fourteen hours of darkness to work with.'

'You are not taking me?' Baldovino protested vehemently, but Richard wondered if this was only to cover his relief.

'Now, hold it.' Nick came in with his slow drawl. 'Did you say Viktor, Marcel, Pat and Rudi?'

'Yes, Major. I want you and Baldo to look after our base here. That's very important. The others may turn up any time. And we don't need Baldo because there won't be any Italians in the forward zone. They've all been evacuated.'

The truth of the matter was that Richard had decided to leave out the two older members. He did not believe they had the stamina to climb a 1700 foot hill under conditions which might be less than ideal.

After only a short argument Nick and Baldo agreed to accept Richard's decision. Maria had not been mentioned, but he guessed from the way the Italian kept glancing towards the farm that Baldo was not averse to the idea of acting as her guardian for a few days.

'Just one point,' Nick said, when such details as weapons, rations and dress had been decided. 'Suppose your theory that the Germans are not in the Monastery is wrong and you find it's full of Panzer-Grenadiers. You may not get a very friendly welcome.'

'If the Germans are in the Monastery then this whole operation loses its point. We'd make our way back to our own lines. But I'm gambling that I'm right.'

Richard saw Nick exchange a glance with Pat Mehan. As usual the Irishman had listened intently but had not contributed to the discussion.

Richard caught his driver's eye. 'How does all that suit you, Pat?'

'Sure, it suits me fine.'

Maria came up from the house to say that the farmer had invited them all to supper.

'That's very kind of him, Maria, but—'

'You cannot refuse. He has killed a kid and dug up his best wine.'

'We have time,' Marcel assured Richard. 'We will be better prepared to face Route 6 and Monastery Hill if we have a good meal inside us.'

By six o'clock the whole party was crowded round the table in the farmhouse kitchen. Spragg was not one to miss a square meal and Baldo had volunteered to stand guard on the track through the forest. The Bennies had contributed half a dozen tins of Compo rations. Short of food as they were, the Italians had taken it upon themselves to feed six hungry men.

When Richard said as much the *contadino* laughed, showing an uneven set of teeth.

'Better for you to have the kid than for the *tedeschi* to confiscate it.'

'Or the partisans,' Spragg muttered.

The tablecloth, plates and glasses were of surprisingly good quality. Richard was sure that their hosts had brought out carefully preserved wedding presents, which were only used on very special occasions. He found the peasant's face fascinating. It had the strength and shining honesty of the simple folk Velásquez used as models in his more earthy paintings. His wife's eyes sparkled with good humour. All these unknown

137

soldiers might have been her sons. Her black hair was drawn away from her face to a small tight bun at the back of her head. Both their faces were hardened and tanned by exposure to the weather; they were lean from unremitting hard work or deprivation, but this only emphasized their qualities of dogged courage and a touching resignation to whatever fate had stored up for them.

Maria, sitting opposite Richard, offered a striking contrast. The light from a blazing log fire fell on her alive and intelligent face. She felt his gaze on her and as she drank wine from her glass she seemed to be toasting him privately. It was the first time he had seen her laughing.

As once or twice before in his life, he felt intensely aware of this moment and this place and knew that he would remember every detail of it for the rest of his life.

*

By seven o'clock the sun had set and the fourteen-hour night had begun. Nick walked up from the farmhouse to see the party off. He stood watching as Rudi climbed in behind the wheel of the Steyr and Richard took the seat beside him. Viktor, Marcel and Pat sat in the back, the Irishman carefully nursing the wireless set. The windscreen and side-screens had been spattered with mud so that the occupants were virtually invisible from outside. Only a small half-circle of clear glass permitted the driver to see forward.

'Don't fall out of any windows!' Nick shouted, as the engine of the Steyr started up.

He stood watching it as it bounced down the track towards the forest. Not till it disappeared did he turn to walk back to the farm where Baldo, Maria and Spragg were still gathered round the fireside with the farmer and his wife.

As he walked up the rough track, the sound of the Steyr faded in the forest. The waiting was going to be very long.

*

On Friday the 11th, 1st Royal Sussex, the British battalion in 5th Indian Brigade, moved to their harbour area at San Michele, four thousand yards from Cassino across the floor of the Rapido Valley. The role of the Greenshire Yeomanry in this operation was unusual. 1st Royal Sussex had their own regular artillery support in the form of a battery from 31st Field

Regiment. However, as there was space for only a limited number of infantry on Snakeshead Ridge and no possibility whatsoever of deploying tanks, the guns would have to take a greater share of the work than normal. It was for this reason that Dudley Fremantle's regiment had been put under command of 4th Indian Division. Stockwell's battery had been allocated to 7th Brigade. If he was called upon to support the attack on the Monastery he would want to have his own forward observation officer up with the leading company, though the guns themselves would remain in the valley below. As it could take nine hours to get up onto Snakeshead and then only by night, the FOO would have to be positioned in advance. It was a measure of Wilfrid's growing reputation in the regiment that he was chosen to man the battery OP in this difficult operation.

Rather than rely on another regiment's communications Wilfrid had his own Number 18 set and a signaller to operate it, as well as a Technical Assistant RA. As usual Dante came too, occupying his customary place on the floor of the Jeep under the legs of his master.

The weather at San Michele was extremely unpleasant – torrential rain and icy conditions. Three of the six-wheel drive American trucks which had been allocated to the battalion got ditched. They were carrying the blankets and greatcoats. The infantrymen, who were wearing full battle equipment, were soaked. The day was spent drying off clothing. 'At 18.30,' the regimental diarist recorded with masterly understatement, 'to Cairo and subsequent areas.'

The little party of Greenshire Yeomanry set off on foot with C Company headquarters across the quagmire of the Rapido Valley on the seven-mile hike to Snakeshead Ridge.

The only crossing point on the river was a Bailey bridge. It had been registered by the German gunners and frequently became a shambles of dead, dying and panic-stricken mules. During the intervals of shelling the Jeeps, with chains on their wheels, made a fiendish noise, the wooden slats beating a tattoo under their weight and the chains slapping the boards. Wilfrid and his two assistants raced across during one such lull.

Cairo was a village at the base of the hills running north from Cassino. It was now deserted and in ruins. The Germans had registered it and were throwing shell and mortar-fire down on it. The Royal Sussex sat for five hours under this intense bombardment, waiting for the mule-trains which would carry their heavy equipment up the tortuous track that led into the hills.

It was during this pause that Wilfrid noted a peculiar quirk in the behaviour of the infantrymen. They preferred immunity from the wet to immunity from shell and mortar-fire. Given the choice between sitting in a water-filled fox-hole or lying on open, drier ground they almost always chose the latter. The risk of being hit was preferable to the certainty of getting soaked.

Dante was shivering. Wilfrid rubbed him down and tried to shelter him under his greatcoat. The dog jerked his head up to lick his master's face in gratitude. His tongue was warm. Wilfrid smiled at Lance-Bombardier Bliss, the signaller who was carrying one of the Number 18 sets.

Bliss winked and said: 'Good old Dan. I've got a dog a bit like him at home. Cor, if the wife could see me now!'

The hitch which had delayed them lengthened from five to twenty hours. Daylight on the 12th found them still waiting at the foot of the hills. One of the company commanders came over to explain to Wilfrid what was happening.

'Jerry attacked last night on Monte Castellone and began infiltrating south towards Terelle. It looked so serious that the Brig sent two battalions to help the Americans.'

'When do we move on?'

'Tonight. If we can get enough mules. I hear they lose thirty per cent of the mules on each trip up to the forward positions.'

It was going to be another day of waiting. Wilfrid would use it to learn a few more of the Sonnets off by heart and to teach Dante some of the drills he needed to know.

When they at last got moving again the following night he soon saw why the toll of mules was so heavy. The supply route was one single track which climbed and wound up the steep slope. It passed over precipitous rock barriers with sheer drops at the side. As they climbed higher these surfaces became coated with ice, which made them even more treacherous. Even Dante found it hard to get a grip and once he nearly fell over the edge. After that Wilfrid improvised a harness on him.

'It's going to be worse coming down this than going up,' Bliss commented, as he struggled up a particularly steep patch on hands and knees.

'We'll be going down the other side – to Route 6,' Wilfrid

140

said with an optimism he did not feel. He was wondering how the stretcher-bearers were going to transport the wounded down these two thousand feet of goat tracks.

By 4 a.m. the battalion had managed to struggle up onto the high ground to the north of the American positions. There was no prospect of carrying out the relief in daylight. Up here anything that moved was plastered. They made use of the remaining hours of darkness to dig in and build sangars as protection against the hail of fire which would inevitably descend on them when the sun came up. Wilfrid chose a position fifty yards from Company Headquarters and supervised the construction of a sangar from the boulders which littered the hillside. Dante, who had been trained to react to the commands, 'Dig in' and, 'Take cover', got busy digging a hole for himself, scooping the earth out between his back legs. As he worked deeper his nose grew blacker and his behind stuck up more and more immodestly.

Wilfrid was drinking a cup of tea which the TARA had brought over from the cookhouse as daylight came and the low clouds lifted from the hills.

'Jesus!' he heard Lance-Bombardier Bliss exclaim. 'Look at that bleedin' Monastery! All them windows!'

Wilfrid moved to a position from which he could see along the flank of the hill. The Monastery was below him now and for the first time he was looking down on it. The distance, he knew, was about one mile but it appeared startlingly close. And from its own separate hillock it gazed as dispassionately over these bare uplands as it had stared down on the valley below.

As daylight grew and the CO of the Royal Sussex made contact with the Americans he had to readjust all his plans in the light of two unpleasant surprises.

Snakeshead Ridge, to use the American name, was a rocky, uneven hump shaped like a boomerang. It was about a thousand yards long. One end plunged into Death Valley. The other, curving to the left, overlooked the Monastery. At the bend in the boomerang was a high, rocky dome known as Point 593. The Germans had turned it into a fortress. It commanded fields of fire which swept the surrounding rocky landscape.

Lieutenant-Colonel Glennie's information had been that Point 593 had been captured by the Americans. It was so marked on the maps at Corps HQ. He found now that the 90th Panzer-Grenadier Division still held their powerful strongpoints on the cliff-like slopes of the rocky dome. The capture of Point 593 was an essential prelude to the attack on the Monastery itself.

The second shock which awaited Glennie aroused both compassion and pity. The men of the 34th US division had been facing the Panzer-Grenadiers since the beginning of February, with often no more than a few yards separating them. These men, crouching in shallow pits, could not move. They were still alive but frozen into immobility. They could hold a gun and aim it at the enemy but they could not walk. At least two hundred of them would have to be lifted out of their positions by the Royal Sussex, placed on stretchers and carried down the long trail to the valley.

This could only be done under cover of darkness and the relief could not proceed till it had been accomplished.

Glennie reported the situation to his Brigadier, C. de T. Lovett. Lovett's orders had been to attack the Monastery on the night of the 15th/16th. He now asked for a postponement of that attack till the 16th/17th. He needed to clear Point 593 of the enemy first. Freyberg was not prepared to over-ride the decision of so experienced a commander.

The Royal Sussex and those accompanying them prepared to endure a day of intense shelling and mortaring, their positions overlooked by the enemy on the slopes of Monte Cairo towering behind them.

14

It was just before dark on Saturday evening when Spragg, who had been made to take a two-hour watch, came rushing into the farmhouse to tell Nick that he had heard booted feet coming up the track.

'They sound like Jerries!' he said, his eyes wide with apprehension. 'The partisans don't move like that. They keep off roads and tracks. Shall I wake the others?'

'Take it easy.' Nick picked his Tommy gun off the kitchen table and started for the door. Maria, drying her hair in front of the fire, had straightened up and was trying to guess what was being said. 'Let's find out first what is going on.'

Bill, Ram and Fen had driven up to the farm that morning just after daybreak and almost exactly twenty-four hours after the first party. They had not slept since leaving the *trattür* and were absolutely exhausted. After a quick breakfast they had thrown themselves down on their bed-rolls and immediately fallen asleep.

Now, as Nick, Baldovino and Spragg ran to cover the exit from the forest with two Tommy guns and a .38 revolver, four weary figures came into view.

Nick came out from behind his rock when he saw who they were. Rudi and Richard were supporting Pat, who had an arm round each of their shoulders.

Viktor trailed behind. All four of them were completely played out. Baldo and Nick ran forward to relieve the others of Pat's weight.

'Has he been hit?'

'No. It's an old wound that started playing him up.'

'Where's Marcel?'

'He's not with us. I'll tell you all about it when I get these boots off. It's been a bloody fiasco.'

★

'Everything went all right till we got to Via Casalina – you know that's the Italian name for Route 6. There was plenty of stuff on the road but it was about the same as that first night. But when we joined the road coming down from Rome – ye gods!'

Richard was sitting in front of the farmhouse fire. His boots were off, his blistered feet washed and dried. Maria had examined Pat's leg and said it needed several days' rest. He was very disgusted with himself and deeply distressed that his old wound had let him down. It was goodbye to that A1 medical grading. Maria had insisted on putting him on the bed in the loft which Spragg had been using. From up there came the strains of an ancient Kerry lament. The Irishman was seeking solace from his mouth-organ. Now Maria was sitting on the floor with her legs tucked under her, combing out her hair with long strokes.

Viktor and Rudi were making inroads into a jug of Emmanuele's wine while his wife, Costanza, improvised a hot meal from tins of Compo rations and some of her own potatoes. Ram and Fen were still sleeping but Nick had wakened Bill. He sat across the table from Richard, listening intently to his story.

'It was like Piccadilly on a Saturday night, only without the lights, of course. There's something brewing at Cassino. Vehicles were nose to tail – ammunition lorries, personnel lorries, SP guns, tanks. Oh, yes, and a lot of horse-drawn stuff. Marching men too, files of them for miles on either side of the road. Rudi talked to the driver of a lorry we got stuck behind in one of the traffic jams and found out that 1st and 3rd Parachute Regiments were moving up to Cassino. That accounted for the volume of traffic.'

While he talked Richard found his eyes going back again and again to Maria. She was watching him with an intent expression even though she did not understand a word he was saying. But what was fascinating him was the graceful and repeated sweep

144

of her arm as she combed her hair and the way it rippled with a life of its own as the comb passed through it.

'1st and 3rd Parachute Regiments,' Bill repeated. 'That's vital information. They'll be glad to know about that at AFHQ.'

'You think you'll be able to make contact with the Number 22 set?'

'Should do from this height. Maybe not after dark but we should be within range in daylight. What happened to Marcel?'

'I'm coming to that.' Richard took a long swallow of tea, and put another match to his pipe. 'We were only making progress at about four miles an hour. Then one of our aircraft dropped a flare about a mile ahead and shot up the column. Luckily he didn't get as far as us but we could see vehicles blazing. Of course, our own guns opened up to add to the fun. It took them about two hours to clear the road so that we could move on.'

Richard saw that Bill was getting impatient. He realized that what was so vivid in his own mind might not hold much interest for the LRP man. The full story of that night's drive would have to wait till some other time.

'Well, to cut a long story short, we were still only level with Aquino when it began to get light.'

Nick asked: 'How far is that from Cassino?'

'About five miles. That's when we ran into real trouble. The MPs had put a check-point on the road there. There were too many for even Viktor to handle.'

'You turned for home?' Bill asked rather scornfully.

'We were looking for a side-turning to get off Route 6. We'd decided to do the last five miles on foot. But as daylight grew there was a terrific panic on everybody's part to get off Route 6 and under cover. Suddenly the road was empty and we were the only vehicle in sight. Then some FOO on Monte Trocchio must have seen us because a heavy stonk came down. We went into the ditch fairly fast and I can assure you we did not hang around. Lucky we didn't, because he got an air burst very near the Steyr with his next shell. Poor old Marcel wasn't quick enough. A piece of shrapnel got him in the leg.'

'You left him?'

'It wasn't as simple as that, old boy. We were all for going on to Cassino on foot, but the wireless set was knocked out by the shelling. Not much good getting to the Monastery if we

145

couldn't send any messages. We decided to come back here, pick up another set and try again. I think we've got a better plan for next time.'

'And Marcel?'

'Marcel knew he couldn't walk the twenty miles back here. He was right too. It's taken us twelve hours travelling across country and keeping away from roads.'

'You didn't let him surrender?' Bill's tone was still scornful.

'He calculated we were only three miles from Terelle where the French Corps are. It's over the hills but he reckoned he could just about make that distance. That's what he wanted to do so we made sure he had water and grub before we started back. Then after about ten miles Pat's leg gave out. The last half of the journey was a little tedious.'

Costanza called from her stove that the meal was ready. Maria scrambled to her feet and helped her to bring it to the table. Richard, Viktor, Rudi and Bill grabbed knives and forks and attacked the stew ravenously. Maria took a plate up the narrow wooden steps to the immobolized Pat.

'You still feel this task of yours is worth while?' Bill asked, after they had been munching in silence for a few minutes. 'Don't you think you'd do more good if you came with my boys and joined up with the partisans?'

'It's more important than ever.' Richard helped himself to a third potato and began to peel it. 'We met up with some refugees moving north like us and keeping away from the main roads. Some of them had been up near the Monastery. They told us there were no Germans in the place but that several hundred civilians had taken refuge there about a week ago. One man said he thought it was nearer a thousand.'

'That's not possible,' Bill stated bluntly. 'You can't believe what these Eyeties tell you. Montecassino has been in the front line since the middle of January. We know that the Germans evacuated the whole area.'

'There's a chance that it's true,' Richard said quietly. 'The only way we can check it is by going up there to see.'

'You know, I can't understand you, Richard.' Bill shook his head. 'Why does this place matter so much to you? It's just a building. Do you *want* it left intact for the Krauts to use against our own chaps?'

'It's not so simple as that, Bill. What I do know is that Alex

146

wants positive information about this and I've been given the job of getting it for him.'

Bill cast his eyes upward and began to pick at his teeth with a pointed matchstick.

'What's this alternative plan, Richard?' Nick wanted to know.

Baldovino, who had been relieved by Spragg at the sentry post, bounced into the kitchen and stood there trying to pick up the drift of the conversation.

Richard pushed away his now empty plate and helped himself to some more of Emmanuele's surprisingly good wine.

'We'll have to pay this chap something, Nick.'

'I've given him a certificate to show to AMGOT when we liberate this part, and I intend to make sure personally that these people are looked after.'

'Good.' Richard took another appreciative sip and put his glass down. 'Rudi thinks we'll never get as far as the Monastery unless we do something so crazy that everyone will fall for it.'

'Crazy – like how?'

Baldovino laughed with delight when he heard Richard's plan and slapped his thigh. He began to translate for Maria's benefit what had been said.

'That certainly is one crazy plan.' Nick had joined in the laughter. 'So crazy that it might work. Will you try it tomorrow night?'

'Tomorrow morning. The roads are jammed at night but there's practically nothing on them by day. Given a good run we could do the fifteen miles from the road junction at Arce to Cassino in half an hour.'

Nick looked sceptical. 'Our air force is strafing that road regularly and our artillery OPs will have you under observation for the last five miles.'

'We'll just have to run the gauntlet. But if we can make radio contact tomorrow morning we'll ask them to leave Route 6 alone for half an hour.'

Bill had pushed his chair back and stood up.

'It ceases to be a military operation at all. I wouldn't let any of my chaps dress up in pantomime costumes like that.'

'I'm not asking you to, Bill. All I want from you is the Number 18 set which you've got in your Jeep. The SIO signals unit at Mignano is only seven miles from the Monastery. The

18 set should manage that distance in daytime, especially as we'll be transmitting from high ground.'

'Then you'll be disappointed. We're short of wireless sets since we lost the Kübelwagen.'

The hostility in Bill's voice rocked Richard for a moment.

Baldovino and Maria had fallen silent, sensing the tension between the two men.

'You actually *want* the Monastery to be destroyed, don't you?' Richard said with angry bitterness.

'Of course I do! And so do about a million other Allied soldiers.'

Richard met Nick's eyes. For the first time he was wondering whether this whole mission was a terrible mistake. But there was something in the American's face which gave him heart.

'It's not just a Monastery,' Nick said. 'Not if there's a thousand civilians in it.'

'I'll tell you what I'll do.' Bill put one foot up on the chair and pointed a finger at Richard. 'If you let me have Fen to fill the gap left by Erle and Tuck I'll give you an 18 set.'

It was an outrageous suggestion but Richard did not dismiss it. The partisans were an unknown quantity and he could understand Bill's reluctance to go into their territory with only Ram to support him. The New Zealand sergeant-major was of sterling quality but he was a very obvious Anglo-Saxon type and he had the disadvantage of not speaking German or Italian.

'It's a deal,' he said.

The party which would make the second attempt to reach Montecassino automatically selected itself. Viktor Zygalski was enthusiastic about the idea of masquerading as an SS Colonel. He was about the right size to fit into the uniform, though his aristocratic looks and hooked nose contrasted with the coarse features of the dead *Standartenführer*. Baldovino had already resigned himself to the loss of his moustache and was practising giving blessings in a semi-falsetto tone. Richard was sure he himself could fill the military policeman's jacket and trench coat. Rudi's uniform was beginning to show signs of wear but it was still authentically German. Nick was so pleased at the prospect of being included that he made no objection to trying on Emmanuele's best suit and the stiff collar he wore on Sundays.

While Richard put his head down to snatch some sleep Baldovino set off to try and scrounge a priest's outfit.

Emmanuele and Costanza had told him that the Vatican maintained a house near Peroli which was used by both priests and nuns. Richard did not realize till Baldovino had departed that Maria had gone with him.

*

He awoke suddenly but did not know where he was. The dream vanished swiftly from his mind and he was aware only of an obstinate reluctance to face the world of wakefulness. He knew that on the coming day he was going to have to do something very unpleasant. He was looking at a rough wall which he did not recognize. It was the smell of woodsmoke which reminded him that he had put his bed-roll down in a far corner of the farmhouse kitchen.

A strange snip-snipping noise puzzled him. He turned on his back and putting his weight on his hands levered himself out of his sleeping-bag into a sitting position.

The kitchen was in shadow, the only light coming from a lamp on the table near the fire and from the logs burning in the fire itself. Maria was sitting on the floor in front of it, her head bowed as she worked at something.

He slid out of the sleeping-bag, put on his trousers, socks and the pair of slippers he always carried in his kit. This end of the kitchen was cold. He shuffled on his battle-dress blouse and walked towards the fire.

Maria's head was bowed. Before her in a heap of glowing russet lay a coiled mass of severed tresses. She snipped again and another skein of hair fell to the floor.

'Jesus, Maria! What are you doing?'

She started and turned at the sound of his voice. The shears seemed huge in her hands.

'Baldovino and I managed to get a nun's habit from the Vatican house.'

'What do you want a nun's habit for?'

'I am coming with you. They will be less likely to stop you if there is a nun with you. And besides, I have a feeling that you are going to need me.'

'No, Maria, you can't. You can't.'

'You cannot refuse me now. You cannot tell me I have cut off my hair for nothing.'

Unable to help himself he too went down on his knees beside her and picked up a double handful of the hair. It was springy

149

and resilient to the touch. The firelight sparkled on it. In death it had taken on an even more magical brilliance.

'You shouldn't have done this.'

'But whoever saw a nun with long hair? And what does it matter anyway? You risked your life today. What are a few locks of hair?'

He shook his head in despair. She had cut it close to her scalp, savagely and without skill. Tufts of the stuff seemed to be sprouting at uneven lengths. The job was three-quarters done.

'Can I finish it off?' she asked him, hanging her head on one side.

'You might as well – now that you've ruined it.'

He remained kneeling while she snipped at the remaining locks. He picked up the last one and drew it slowly across the palm of his hand.

'I'm going to keep this.'

She put the shears down and gave her head a vigorous shake. The shortened hair jerked into new patterns, determined still to have a life. She reached out a hand and grasped his, enfolding the hair and his fingers at the same time.

15

It was still dark when the Mercedes 540K moved away down the track. The time was six o'clock, two hours before Bill was due to call up AFHQ on his 22 set. He had failed to make contact the night before. It was always more difficult during darkness as the sets were down and also there was a great deal of traffic on the German side. It was obvious that something big was brewing.

'That's a real snip about the parachutists moving up,' Bill had said. 'We've got to let AFHQ know about that.'

'You won't forget to tell them about the civilian refugees in the Monastery?'

'No. Rudi said it was 1st and 3rd Parachute Regiments, didn't he?'

'That's right. And you won't forget, will you?'

'It's from nine to nine-thirty you want this cease-fire, isn't it?'

'Yes. Nine to nine-thirty.' Richard had briefed Bill to request AFHQ to order a lull in artillery and air bombardment on Route 6 so as to give them a chance to get close to the Monastery. 'I can't really ask for more than half an hour, but that should give us long enough.'

'The 540K is capable of over the ton so you could almost be in Naples in half an hour.'

Bill gave them a salute as they left and even went so far as to wish them luck.

The robing ceremony in the kitchen had provided a moment of comedy. Viktor had not only slipped into the SS Colonel's uniform but into his personality as well. He put Rudi on the mat, bawling him out in Prussianized German and promising the direst penalties because the knot on his bootlace was a grannie. They wound up in each other's arms, helplessly laughing.

'Only one thing wrong.' Rudi had stepped back to run a critical eye over the ash-grey uniform. The flared breeches were a little loose on Viktor's slim hips but his broad shoulders amply filled the jacket. He had put on the heavily adorned cap at a rakish angle.

'You mean the bloodstain?' Viktor squinted down at the hole where Marcel's knife had gone in. It was surrounded by a dark mark, which even vigorous scrubbing had not erased. 'It won't show when I am sitting down.'

'No. I mean you do not look enough of a shit to be wearing this uniform.' Rudi reached forward to straighten the cap and adjust the knot of the black tie. 'This bastard was *Sicherheitsdienst*. You can tell by the green piping round the crown of his cap, this plain black collar-patch and the SD badge on his sleeve. He must have been a Nazi way back before 1933.'

151

'Is that what the eagle on his left arm means?'

'No. You can tell from the *Ehrenwinkel*.' Rudi pointed to the silver chevron on the upper right sleeve. 'He may also have been in one of the *Einsatzgruppen*. They don't usually advertise the fact.'

'The SS murder battalions,' Viktor explained when he saw that the word was new to Richard. 'They followed the German advance and quickly filled mass graves with Jews, local administrators, commissars and anything else that moved and thought.' His face seemed to contract. 'This bugger may have helped liquidate the Warsaw ghetto.'

Rudi was now at the wheel, really enjoying the feel of a superb motor-car under his hands. Viktor occupied the passenger's seat and Richard was on a cushion between them, his legs swung sideways so as not to foul the gear lever. The upper and outer garments of the military policeman fitted him reasonably well and he hoped not to have to show his British battledress trousers. Except for Maria and Rudi they were all extremely uncomfortable, as they were wearing their own uniforms under their disguise.

The 'Vatican' party was in the rear, with Maria in the middle. In her nun's habit she had looked so like one of those ravishing actresses who play the part of nuns in films that Costanza had instinctively crossed herself. Shorn of moustache, Baldovino looked very tame and harmless but in the priest's high-buttoned cassock and flat hat he had quite a venerable appearance. Nick was the most incongruous of them all. Even the deep stiff collar, which was so tight that he could hardly breathe, and the black serge of Emmanuele's suit could not mask his honest Westerner features.

'The Red Cross sure hire some real dudes,' was his comment as he'd inspected himself in the mirror. 'Say, if I talk Injun dialect will they take me for a Swiss?'

Daylight was growing as they travelled along the main road towards the junction just below the fortress town of Arce, and at the same time the traffic was thinning out. A high wind was keeping the clouds moving fast and for once it was not raining.

Richard had wanted to get to the junction with Route 6 before it was fully daylight, but he did not want to make the run down it until Bill had had a chance to transmit his message requesting a cease-fire. That necessitated a very nervy wait of over half an hour hidden behind a wall one mile from Arce. In the distance could be heard the thump of gun-fire round Cassino and the occasional rasp of a strafing aircraft.

It was the finest day for some time. The clouds were high and there were even patches of blue sky. Richard decided to lower the top of the cabriolet so that the occupants would be visible enough to make the required impact. When the mohair cover had been fitted over the folded hood he stood back to admire the car with a pride that was almost one of ownership. The Mercedes was a mouth-watering motorcar, developed from the all-conquering sports and grand prix racing cars. The hemispherical mudguards thrust out a couple of feet forward of the bonnet and then swept back gracefully to the running-boards. The upright, V-shaped radiator was flanked by a pair of large Bosch headlamps. The spare wheel was recessed into the left front wing. The chrome on the wheel spokes, lamps and radiator had been kept bright and the black cellulose was highly polished. The whole outfit seemed set for a fast holiday trip down the *autobahn*, heading for the alpine ski-slopes.

During one of the tense silences Nick asked: 'How much ice do you think this will cut if they take us prisoner, Rudi? I mean wearing our own uniforms underneath.'

'It depends.' The German stared at a buzzard which was wheeling over the hillside ahead of him. 'If you can get rid of the disguise before they catch you, you will be prisoners of the Wehrmacht. You will be questioned, of course, but you will be treated correctly. But if you are caught like that – ' He shook his head sombrely. 'You will be handed over to the Gestapo. I would not then like to be in Viktor's shoes.'

'They will never capture me alive,' Viktor assured him. He examined his hands, as if remembering all the men he had killed with them. 'I have taken precautions against that.'

It was with relief that soon afterwards they heard Richard say: 'Time to move.'

It was ten minutes to nine on Sunday, 13 February.

Rudi pressed the self-starter and the eight-cylinder engine came to life. He eased out onto the empty road and turned the long, slim bonnet towards the Via Casilina. Cassino was thirty kilometres, less than twenty miles away.

The first crisis came almost immediately. A military policeman was on duty at the point where Highway 82 joined the Via Casilina. Behind him was a sand-bagged shelter. He

153

stepped out into the roadway when Rudi signalled his intention to go straight on. Rudi stopped beside him. Richard felt the familiar dry sensation in his mouth.

'Only authorized traffic is allowed up this road in daylight.' The MP's eyes were taking in the three incongruous figures on the back seat as he spoke. 'What is your destination?'

Rudi said: 'Montecassino. The Abbey of Montecassino.'

'You cannot get to Montecassino. The road goes through Cassino town and it is closed. What is the purpose of your journey?'

Only then did Viktor deign to turn his head. 'We are a special delegation from the Vatican,' he snapped. 'Authorized by the Pope and Hitler personally. We are proceeding to Montecassino to verify that it is not being used by the German army for defence, nor by civilians for espionage. You will let us pass immediately.'

The MP saluted but his attitude remained firm. 'You are coming from the wrong direction, Herr Standartenführer. That is the road from Rome.'

He pointed up the road which had come in at right-angles.

'We had to make a detour via Isola del Liri. A stupid military policeman directed us that way. That is why we were delayed. We had intended to make the journey in the dark.'

Viktor's accent was holding up well, but Richard wondered whether a real SS Colonel would have been prepared to offer so many explanations. The MP kept glancing at Richard. Naturally he expected a colleague to make some contribution to the conversation, but Richard dared not trust his German in this situation so he remained silent. In the back Baldovino was gazing benignly at the MP as if he was about to bestow a blessing on him, whilst Nick stared with unconcern at the houses of Arce above the road. Maria wore an expression of angelic and unruffled purity.

It was with his eyes on her face under the nun's black band and cowl that the MP said: 'You are too late now. I cannot allow you to go down this road in daylight. The Americans have it under observation. Anything that moves in daylight is bombed or shelled.'

'It is essential that the Colonel reaches Cassino Monastery without delay.' Rudi came into the conversation tersely. 'There are reports of Allied spies among the refugees.'

154

Richard nodded his agreement and risked a phrase that he knew carried weight.

'*Es ist ein Führerbefehl.*'

That made an impression on the MP. He again ran his eye over the six in the Mercedes-Benz, then went to the front to check the registration number. For a horrible moment Richard was sure that the dead SS Colonel had been posted as missing and the number of his car circulated to all military police.

'You must wait here. I will check with my headquarters.'

He was just turning towards the shelter when the air was rent by a tearing sound. The MP looked over his shoulder then dived for cover. A Lightning went over at a height of no more than a hundred feet, moving southwards at a good three hundred miles an hour. Either the pilot had failed to spot the Mercedes or he was seeking a fatter target, for he fired neither cannons nor rockets. He had disappeared down the road to Cassino in a few seconds.

'Let's go, Rudi!' Richard said.

Rudi let in his clutch with a jerk and the Mercedes shot forward. Richard looked at his watch. The hands were on exactly nine o'clock. He hoped Bill had made contact on the eight o'clock call.

Richard had no illusions about the foolhardiness of what he was trying to do. Waiting there by the roadside he had weighed up the chances and reckoned that the odds were about ten to one against ever reaching the Monastery. Now that they had survived their first brush with the Military Police the odds had shortened. Perhaps five to one against. There was still a strong probability that they would be stopped at a check-point further up the road and subjected to a more searching examination. And who could tell what the reaction of front-line units would be to the appearance of a cabriolet full of 'tourists'? Moreover, the Mercedes could only get them within striking distance of Montecassino. To reach the Monastery they would have to continue on foot over some of the most bitterly contested terrain of the whole campaign. Most unnerving of all, however, was the domination of the skies by the Allied air forces and his personal knowledge of what the Allied artillery could do to any vehicle moving up Route 6.

Things went smoothly for the first five miles. They passed an armoured column moving up towards the front, the large angular tanks mounting the long 75 mm gun. Their crews wore the black Panzer uniform with silver-grey curly-winged Luft-waffe eagles on their jackets. Richard tried to memorize their markings as the Mercedes screamed past.

A mile further on came the side turning that led to the village of Coldragone. Here again stood the now familiar figure of an MP in his long, rainproof coat and with goggles snapped up on his helmet. This time there could be no argument. The road was completely blocked by a blazing ammunition lorry. It had been hit by the Lightning. They could see the black smoke curling up and hear the detonations of the shells exploding.

'How long·is the deviation?' Rudi asked the MP.

He saluted Viktor and stared in amazement at the occupants of the back seat, but was too preoccupied in watching the sky to ask any questions.

'About two miles. You rejoin Route 6 on the other side of Coldragone.'

Richard checked his watch. Seven minutes of the precious half hour had gone by. As soon as they came to Coldragone he swore. The streets were crowded with vehicles and troops. It looked as if a train-load had recently arrived and the men were being hastily dispersed to billets or camps.

As Rudi tried to blast a way through with his horn Richard tried to derive some advantage from this serious setback. This was a treasure-house of intelligence about the enemy forces. If he ever got back to his own lines he would have a mine of information.

He took a mental photograph of an officer in a blue-grey cap with a silver wings-and-cockade badge on the band and an eagle on the crown, a group of other ranks wearing shoulder-straps with a blue-grey cross, eight Panzer-Grenadiers in a parked Horsch open truck, a column of troops in thigh-length field-grey tunics wearing peaked field caps with a metal edelweiss badge on the side. The mental effort did something to alleviate the tension of moving in an open car at walking speed through a crowd of enemy soldiers.

They all stared open-mouthed at the Mercedes. Richard's theory was being proved correct. The spectacle was so utterly improbable that the Germans shook their heads in sheer disbelief or burst out laughing. In the centre of the village an officious captain walked out in front of the Mercedes and held up his hand.

Rudi and Viktor gave him the familiar treatment. He was

156

hostile and resentful towards the man in the SS uniform but in the end reluctantly waved them on.

It was 9.18 by the time they cleared the village.

'For God's sake step on it, Rudi.'

The track was pitted by deep potholes. Rudi was showing too much respect for the precious German staff car, flinching whenever it bottomed on its springs.

'Here,' Richard said at last, his impatience getting the better of him. 'Stop and change places with me.'

Rudi did not query the order. He stopped and got into the back while Richard took the wheel. He gave the Mercedes full throttle in bottom gear, not caring if the rear suspension crashed down on its mountings and the three in the back seat had to hang on tight so as not to be thrown out.

It was 9.21 when he swung the Mercedes out onto the comparatively smooth surface of Route 6. The distance to the turning for Santa Lucia was ten miles away and there were only nine minutes left of the cease-fire time – assuming Bill's message had got through. He changed up through the gears, brought in the supercharger and pushed his speed up to 90 m.p.h. It was hard to believe this was the same road as he had crawled along in the dark thirty hours before.

A cluster of signs at the turning for Roccasecca indicated that there was an important headquarters up there, but they went past too quickly to read any of them. The road surface had been repaired with gravel in places; several times he had to control wild skids. Every now and then they passed burned-out vehicles in the ditches. At one bridge an MP leaped for safety as the Mercedes-Benz bore down on him. A few vehicles coming the opposite way, also running the gauntlet at full speed, flashed past at a meeting velocity of 120 m.p.h. He overtook a company of Panzer-Grenadiers in open Opel troop-carriers as if they were standing still.

In the back Baldovino was holding his flat cap on with both hands and Maria had bent forward into the gale of wind. Nick, with screwed-up eyes and wind-swept hair, was watching the sky. It was innocent of aircraft. No shells were bursting on the road ahead, but Richard felt an empty sensation in the pit of his stomach at the thought that he was racing towards a battle-front at more than a mile a minute.

As the hands of his watch moved to 9.30 they were still three miles from Cassino. The broad plain of the Liri Valley stretched away to the right and on the left the mountains were swinging down to the outcrop of Montecassino. The supply dumps, hospitals and assembly areas to the rear of the front had given way to more purposeful emplacements. They were coming into the gun area and there were fewer soldiers to be seen.

'Only another mile to the turning,' Richard shouted over his shoulder. The high-pitched whine of the engine echoed back from a church at the roadside.

Then came what he had been dreading, but in a more terrifying form than the day before. A shell flying on a low trajectory landed on the road ahead and bounced clean over them. He heard it explode as it landed behind. He realized instantly what was happening. Some crafty gunner had discovered that his gun was on a prolongation of Route 6 and was amusing himself bouncing shells down the highway. It was a good trick. The shells might explode at the first, second or third bounce, a bit like skimming flat stones over a lake. It would also be possible to achieve air bursts.

'Can't you buggers give us a few minutes grace?' he yelled aloud at the top of his voice.

To know that you are the target for even one gun is a very uncomfortable sensation. He could see the top of Monte Trocchio ahead of him now and knew that someone in an OP was watching Route 6 through a pair of binoculars. He put his foot hard down. The whine of the supercharger rose to a high scream. The Mercedes bucked and weaved, but the speedometer needle crept to 105 m.p.h. The next shell went over the top of them before exploding in the air after its first bounce on the road behind.

As a gunner Richard was sure that a troop and perhaps a battery would soon be in on the act. He was right. Shells were landing very close during that last mad mile and a half. As he slowed for the turning to Santa Lucia, a mile from Cassino Town, a stonk came down on the road junction. Earth and gravel sprouted round the car as Richard changed down and took the corner in a broadside turn. The rear wheels spun as they tried to get a grip on the loose surface. Dirt and stones from shell bursts landed on the occupants of the open car but it had still not been hit. He changed up and gave the engine maximum revs as he fled from that road junction. The horrible crump-crump fell behind and a minute later they were under the lee of the hill and out of sight of Monte Trocchio.

The area to the west of Monastery Hill, like that behind Monte Trocchio, was densely populated by guns and their crews. Richard spotted a number of 88 mms, a few 75 mms and a couple of 105 mm howitzers. They were well camouflaged, only their wicked protruding barrels giving them away.

The staff car was the only vehicle moving on the road and it was obviously not popular with the guns' crews. Soldiers were shouting angrily and pointing at the sky. Richard looked up and saw a Piper Cub circling over the hills. The Germans liked to keep quiet and out of sight whenever the Allied gunners had an Air OP up.

'You'd better stop or we will be lynched,' Rudi advised.

Richard pulled in under the cover of a large tree by the roadside. At that moment a shell landed beside a copse a hundred yards away. He saw the body of a German soldier projected up into the air by the blast. It rose to the height of a telegraph pole, turned lazily and then plummetted to earth.

'*Oh, Dio!*' Maria exclaimed behind him. '*Poverino!*'

'Look.' Nick reached forward and touched Richard's shoulder. 'Am I seeing things?'

Richard followed the line of his finger. On a flat field below the road half a dozen Italian peasants – women and old men – were quietly and methodically tilling the land. Their horse or ox had been requisitioned and they were doing the job with spades and forks, apparently oblivious of the shells landing all around.

'Do they not realize the danger?'

'For them death by starvation is as great a danger as shellfire,' Baldovino said. 'They must plant and raise a crop this spring if they are to survive.'

Richard was more concerned with the artillery *Oberleutnant* who was striding angrily towards them. He was white with anger.

'What the hell do you think you are doing?' he shouted as soon as he was within earshot. He was too furious to be worried about rank. 'Do you realize you were the cause of that bombardment?'

'What rank is he?' Viktor hissed at Rudi.

'*Oberleutnant.*'

'It's all right, *Oberleutnant*,' Viktor assured the German with ill-founded confidence. 'We have a special mission.'

The officer gaped as he registered the passengers in the

159

offending staff car. When he realized that he was talking to an
SS Colonel he stiffened and saluted.

'Where are you trying to go, *Herr Standartenführer*?' he
asked, unable to take his eyes off Maria. 'This road leads to our
forward positions.'

He was battle-stained and weary, his face showing the strain
of being constantly under shell-fire. Richard felt a sudden surge
of fellow-feeling towards this German gunner.

'We must get to the Benedictine Monastery,' Viktor
continued in his officious tone. 'How close can we go by
road?'

The officer shook his head. 'You cannot go up there. It is
impossible. The Monastery is out of bounds to troops. Besides,
it is in full view of the enemy.'

'Nevertheless, it is necessary that we go. We are under orders
from the Führer.'

'The Führer! You have some authorization?'

'We have come from the Vatican, *Oberleutnant*,' Rudi
chimed in. 'This is Dom Baldovino, a papal nuncio. Sor Maria
Valdisponda represents the Italian Government and Monsieur
Nicolas the Swiss Red Cross. The *Herr Standartenführer* is
concerned with the security aspect of the situation.'

The gunner blinked as he tried to assimilate this rigmarole.

'What is your name, *Oberleutnant*?' Viktor asked him
sternly, taking the notebook out of the breast pocket of the
SS uniform.

'*Oberleutnant Wilhelm Peifer, zum Befehl, Herr
Standartenführer*,' he rapped out, stiffening to attention.

Viktor wrote it down. His hands were rock steady.

'Regiment?'

'1/16 Artillery Regiment. Battle Group Stumpel.'

'I will commend you for your alertness, *Oberleutnant*.'
Viktor completed the entry and closed the notebook. The
German relaxed, relieved that he had not got into the bad books
of the SS. 'Now, how close can we come to the Monastery by
road?'

'A quarter of a mile on you will come to a lane which winds
round the flank of the hill to Albaneta. But I would advise you
not to take your vehicle beyond the first farm. The track
becomes very rough and it is constantly shelled.'

'Then we will have to proceed on foot.'

'I doubt if the sister could manage it.' The German's eyes

160

rested with concern on Maria. 'It is very steep and rocky and you would be under observation by the English. Their artillery fire is very accurate.'

'But there are German troops up there?'

'Yes.'

'Then if they can endure it,' Viktor stated pompously, 'so can we.'

The German shrugged. He obviously thought that the Colonel and his companions were mad, but he had done what he could to warn them. If they were determined to walk straight into a hail of fire that was their affair.

The Air OP had moved east, back towards Cassino town. There was a momentary lull.

'Tommy must be having his morning cup of tea,' the *Oberleutnant* remarked with a laugh. 'Go now while it is quiet.'

Richard had just turned off the road onto the track which the *Oberleutnant* had suggested when the wind swept a storm of icy rain down from the hills.

'Let's have this convertible top up,' Nick called out. 'I'm catching a rusty neck.'

Richard stopped the car while Nick and Rudi jumped out to remove the cover from the hood and erect it. The rain was heavy enough to reduce visibility to a hundred yards and he could not see clearly where this track was leading. A sign bearing a skull and crossbones had made it clear that it was not a recommended route.

The mission which had appeared to be a practical possibility at AFHQ in Caserta was now assuming a totally different complexion. The optimism he had felt after they had survived the first military policeman had dissolved. Admittedly they had achieved their first objective of getting within striking distance but that stonk at the road junction had given them all a taste of what lay ahead. He knew that he could rely on Viktor to see it through with him but he felt he ought to give the others a chance to express an opinion before they reached a point from which there was no return.

He waited till Nick and Rudi resumed their seats.

'You all heard what the *Oberleutnant* said. We're going to have to do the last part on foot and probably under fire. Do you think it's still on, Nick?'

'Sure,' Nick said at once. 'So far's I'm concerned. You don't want to quit now, do you?'

'How about you, Baldo?'

'We are nearly there now, Richard. I think I would rather go on than drive back down that road again.'

'What about Maria?' He switched to Italian. 'Do you understand what we are up against?'

She answered angrily: 'If those peasants have the courage to work their fields under shell-fire, then I have enough courage to go on.'

Richard did not want to risk insulting Viktor by asking him the same question but he had to give Rudi the option.

'Rudi, you've done wonders in helping to bring us so far but I'm not sure that there's much more you can do for us.'

'I am under your orders,' the German said firmly. 'I go with you.'

'That's it, then.' Richard reflected that even if he had felt like chickening out he could hardly have done so when an AMGOT Major, an Italian, a German and a nurse were willing to go ahead. 'We push on.'

The track soon began to climb the flank of the hill. The surface was very rough and he had to use all his skill to keep the Mercedes going. The rear wheels were spinning and the sump frequently scraping the centre of the rutted track. He had to turn the steering wheel energetically to avoid the worst hollows and humps. In the back his passengers were grunting as the car bucked and heaved. It was unlikely that the Mercedes had ever before been subjected to such brutal treatment, but it kept going.

And the rain kept sloshing down, more heavily than ever. Now and again they met a string of mules with Italian drivers returning from a trip with supplies to the front line. Once Richard had to pull over for a Kübelwagen specially rigged to carry a couple of stretchers. It was evacuating two badly wounded soldiers, easing its way down the hill metre by metre.

As they climbed higher they overtook groups of Paratroopers trudging up the hill. They were recognizable by their pot-shaped helmets and the long thigh-length camouflaged smocks which fastened between the legs. Their blue-grey trousers were tucked into fancy jump-boots and their shoulder straps and ammo pouches were of black leather. They were much more heavily armed than the British infantryman, with special collars of rifle-clip pouches hanging round their necks. Some of them carried the redoubtable MG 42 machine gun, nicknamed 'Spandau' by the British, and many were armed with MP 40 sub-machine guns. They looked very tough but the majority were surprisingly young and at close quarters much more skinny and pale than the average British soldier's idea of 'Jerry'.

All of them stared at the Mercedes in total disbelief. They would have been less surprised if Elijah in his chariot of fire had come down from heaven. But they made no attempt to interfere with it. Richard had gambled on this psychological aspect of his plan. The front-line zone was very different from the base area. The minds of these men were absorbed by fighting and survival. They knew little about espionage, security, documentation. And like all front-line troops they could not have cared less if some brass-hat was stupid enough to drive into enemy shell-fire in his staff car.

Richard could hear them making ribald comments as the Mercedes jolted past. He prayed that he would not meet a high-ranking officer, but the only man who stopped them was a Feldwebel with three seagull-shaped symbols on his sleeve. Spurning a helmet, he wore a ski-type cap with a long peak. He was a handsome fellow with a cheerful, swashbuckling manner.

'You have lost your way?' he enquired with ironic politeness. 'There is a war on around here, you know.'

'We have to get to the Monastery,' Rudi told him. Richard felt very conscious of the hostile gaze of half a dozen Paratroopers who had crowded round.

'The Monastery? You want to go to the Monastery? You're crazy.'

'We have a very important mission. It is a *Führerbefehl*.'

Once again the magic phrase worked wonders. The Feldwebel shook his head in pity.

'Then I advise you to go on foot. You cannot take your car beyond that big rock with the olive tree on it. From there you are under observation.'

There was so much moisture on the windows that he had not been able to see into the interior. Viktor put away the revolver he had been grasping. Richard drove on.

He did not stop at the big rock. The rain was heavy enough

163

to prevent any observation from Monte Trocchio. Thereafter the track became less steep as it cut across slopes terraced to provide level strips for the olive groves. Several hundred yards on, just as Richard was negotiating a hairpin bend, the rain-storm ceased as abruptly as it had begun.

'Chrisamighty!' Nick exclaimed. 'Just take a look at that!'

Richard had only time for a quick glance over his shoulder but that was enough. They had climbed higher than he had realized. Now that the cloud had cleared the plain of the Liri Valley was exposed, a thousand feet below. The narrow ribbon of the Rapido wound across it. But what had shaken him was the sight of Monte Trocchio staring directly at them. He knew it was three miles away but in the clear, rain-washed air it looked near enough to touch. Blinded by the rainstorm they had come round the flank of the hill onto the side facing Fifth Army. The whole battlefield lay below.

He felt his flesh tingle. He could imagine a dozen pairs of binoculars trained on the vehicle labouring up the exposed hillside, could hear in his mind the directions the officers in the OPs would send to their GPOs to bring the fire of their batteries to bear on it.

'Spank 'er tail,' Nick urged.

'She won't go any faster than this.'

The first of the ranging shots came twenty seconds later. It burst about a hundred yards ahead. The second fell the same distance short. Those gunners knew their job. They would soon have the Mercedes registered, even though it was moving.

'Drive onto that terrace! The next one'll hit us.'

Richard spotted the terrace at which Nick was pointing just before the windscreen was starred. The third shell had been very close and just to the left. He knew what he would have done if he'd been commanding that battery. He would have fired an air-burst.

Praying that the thought would not communicate itself to the gunners on the other side, he aimed for the curving terrace which would take them under the cover of a rocky outcrop. His mouth had gone absolutely dry and the desire to pee had become almost irresistible. The Mercedes seemed to be hardly moving over those last yards, but after an age it bounced onto the terrace. The space was so narrow that whilst on one side the bodywork was scraping the wall, on the other the wheels were overhanging the drop. The surface was stony enough

164

to give purchase to the wheels but after twenty yards the way was completely blocked by a large olive tree with spreading roots.

When Richard stopped just short of it nobody needed telling to bale out and go to ground in the shelter of the retaining wall on the downhill side. Richard bundled Maria into the space between an olive tree and the stones and covered her with his body. He hoped that they had just about got out of sight before the tree stopped them and that the gunners were firing by guesswork.

As shells landed behind them and the air was filled with the whine of shrapnel and rock fragments, he could feel her trembling under him.

'Oh, Madonna! Che paura! Che paura!'

He could actually hear the detonations of the four guns firing at them from behind Monte Trocchio, but the shell had got there long before the sound and just before the whine of its passing through the air.

The Allied guns peppered the area for a minute then moved their fire along the terrace to the left. After five minutes they abandoned it altogether in favour of some more juicy target. Slowly and a little shamefacedly the five men got up from the places where they had taken cover. It seemed incredible that none of them had been hit. Baldovino and Rudi undid their fly buttons and, turning away from Maria, urinated against the wall.

Maria scrambled up, wiped her eyes and touched Richard's hand.

'Grazie, Richa. Senza di te non avrei potuto resistere.'

He could see now that just before the tree stopped them they had come under the shelter of a boulder-strewn slope and passed out of sight of Monte Trocchio. The gunners must have assumed that they had continued moving across the hill.

'Looks like this is journey's end for the car.' Nick brushed dirt off Emmanuele's Sunday suit. 'Even if we could reverse out we'd only come under fire again.'

'You've got a wireless set in the luggage compartment,' Viktor suggested. 'Can't you ring them up and tell them to leave us alone?'

'Even if I knew their frequency the Germans might intercept the message on monitoring sets. Then we'd be in the bag.'

'Do we start walking, then?'

'You know what Pat would say if he was here? When in doubt brew up. He made me bring his Benghazi Burner. It's in the boot.'

16

That dreary Sunday morning amid the bleak and brooding sadness of the landscape below the Monastery a BBC war correspondent prepared his equipment to record another of those commentaries which would give to listeners of the Home Service some inkling of war conditions overseas. He had noticed a padre preparing to conduct Matins in a field behind the sheltering skirts of Monte Trocchio. From the back of the C of E Jeep were unloaded a portable organ, a folding table and the paraphernalia of Divine Service. The padre donned his white robes, a few servicemen rolled up. Worship began with a hymn.

To the accompaniment of an occasional shell-burst, the distant drumming of the *Nebelwerfers* pounding Cassino and the slightly flat-sounding chords of the organ, a dozen male voices reached for the higher notes of *Abide With Me*. Against this eerie background Frank Gillard made his 'voice over' commentary.

' ... and there, solid-looking and severe as ever, stands the Monastery itself, still undisturbed, crowning that mountain top and dominating everything. But for that Monastery and our wish to preserve it undamaged, the efforts of this past week's fighting might have produced more concrete results.

'One wonders what fate holds in store for that huge golden building on the hill.'

To Lieutenant-General Ira C. Eaker, the American Commander of the Mediterranean Allied Air Forces, had gone the order to level the Monastery. Eaker was about to make military history. For the first time the heavy bombers of strategic air forces were to be used in massive strength to support ground forces. The destructive power which had flattened German cities was to be concentrated on the single building atop Montecassino.

The air forces had been asked to do a job and they were going to do it properly.

Later that day, despite the storm rampaging round the Appenines, Eaker decided to make a personal reconnaissance of the target. He was not unaware of the importance of the event, though he was sceptical of its usefulness to the ground forces. But it would provide valuable experience for the forthcoming big show, the invasion of Europe. Piloting a Piper Cub himself he was accompanied by the deputy to the Supreme Allied Commander Mediterranean. The two Generals, Eaker and Devers, flew over Montecassino at a height of no more than two hundred feet. The German anti-aircraft guns kept quiet as a spotter plane was up. To fire would bring down instant tribulation from the much more numerous Allied batteries. Peering down through binoculars, Eaker saw the machine-gun posts right up against the Monastery walls, saw figures, which he believed to be German soldiers, moving in the cloisters.

He made two important assumptions from that reconnaissance. Only the heaviest bombs would breach those walls. And, if Flying Fortresses were to be used, they would need clear weather to pin-point the target from their operational height of fifteen thousand feet. Less than half a mile separated the Monastery from the Allied troops besieging it.

Back at base he gave the orders which would alert the crews of 135 Flying Fortresses, 47 Mitchells and 40 Marauders – a force more than six times greater than Freyberg had requested.

★

Even though the terraces behind gave some protection against the north-east wind it was bitterly cold on that bleak hillside. As the one enamel mug was handed round each member of the group warmed his hands on it for a moment before passing it on. They had chanced on a deserted area due to the fact that no attack was expected from this direction. A section of Route 6 was visible far below. Beyond it the Liri Valley appeared to be completely deserted, though a whole army was hidden there in bunkers and pill-boxes.

Now and again from the direction of the road up to Santa Lucia came a series of staccato cracks as a German battery fired a salvo. It was usually repaid with interest from the other side. Half a dozen mortar crews could be seen lobbing mortar bombs from their multi-barrelled *Nebelwerfers* over the top of Monastery Hill onto the town of Cassino beyond.

Further to the right, under the hill, columns of porters or mules were following the stony tracks which the olive growers used to reach their terraces. Those moving up were transporting boxes of ammunition and rations but the downward traffic consisted largely of stretcher-bearers carrying men wounded by the merciless American artillery. Amongst the porters Richard saw figures in voluminous djellabas and white turban-like headgear.

'The Jerries must be using prisoners from the French Corps as porters. I wonder if Marcel managed to get through. Do you think he had a chance, Rudi?'

Rudi shrugged but did not answer. He was staring down at the files of stretcher-bearers with sombre eyes. Richard had felt a change in him while they'd been squatting there. He did not think it had been caused by the shelling, nor by his own decision to take over the wheel of the Mercedes. He believed he understood the real reason. The sight of those Paratroopers going up to the front line had given Rudi a nostalgia for his own comrades in the 'Hoch und Deutschmeister' Division.

Then the clouds came down again and suddenly visibility was reduced to fifty yards. Instead of rain the olive groves were submerged in a drenching mist. Richard scrambled to his feet.

'Come on! This is our chance.'

The Benghazi Burner and the mug were quickly packed away and the Mercedes was reversed and manhandled out onto the track again. The only damage it had sustained was half a dozen shrapnel holes in the body work. The smell of cordite still hung in the air, an unpleasant reminder of what would happen if the mist cleared.

It covered them for another quarter of a mile, till they came to the stone building which was the justification for the track. This was a temporary home used by the olive growers during the harvesting season to save themselves the long daily journey up and down the mountain. Here the track ended.

There was nothing for it but to abandon the Mercedes-Benz and tackle the remainder of the journey on foot. With the others pushing it from behind, Richard coaxed it into a low lean-to at the side of the house. They camouflaged it with its own net and a heap of brushwood they found there, then for good measure built a solid dry-stone wall across the entrance. The job took a good hour and still there was no sign of troops on the surrounding hillside.

They split the gear up among them. Rudi humped a box of Compo, Viktor the Benghazi Burner and a can of petrol to fuel it and Nick a can filled with water. Maria was given a haversack with a few essentials such as tea, sugar, field dressings and cigarettes. Richard put his arms through the shoulder-straps of the 18 set. Luckily its instrument panel was protected from the weather by a box-like canvas screen.

'How far are we from the Monastery?'

'As far as I can tell from the map, Viktor, about 1,500 yards. I'd say we've climbed about 1,200 feet from Route 6. That means we've only got 500 to go. We could probably see it if there wasn't this mist.'

Richard was leading the file when half an hour later he reached the top of the hill. He saw at once why there were so few troops on it. This was not Monastery Hill at all, but a hill to the west of it. A deep valley, more like a chasm, separated them from their objective.

Viktor and Rudi came up the last few yards and stood beside him, staring at the huge building two thousand yards away. The mist had risen and it was clearly visible.

'Keep under cover of this rock,' Richard warned Nick and Baldovino, as they helped Maria up the last steep slope. She had hitched the long nun's habit up to knee length and was using the cowl to shield her face from the wind. 'You can see now why they're not using this hill for their supply columns. There's a deep gulley between us and Monastery Hill.'

There was no sign of life around the walls. The greenish dome over the church stood out above the surrounding red-tiled roofs. Several columns of smoke drifted up from inside the complex of buildings.

'It is as a small town,' Viktor commented. 'Or a medieval walled city.'

'Problem is, how the heck do we get in – *if* we ever make it that far?'

'Where's the entrance, Maria?'

'The main entrance is on the right.' Maria's cheeks were chapped and raw from the biting wind. 'You see the road going up to it? Look! There is a tank moving up it now.'

'It is an armoured car,' Viktor corrected her.

Richard pointed to the north-west corner. 'Isn't that a small doorway about twenty feet below the lowest windows?'

A bark of machine-gun fire drew their attention to the dome-like Point 593, dominating the Monastery from the north. It underlined the fact that up there the infantry of both sides were dug in, vigilant if not visible.

'We can't approach that place in daylight. We'll keep under cover till the mist comes down again. Then we can use the rest of daylight to work our way round the north end of this chasm. There's a mule track up to the Monastery from there. We might even borrow a couple of mules to hump this stuff up the last steep bit.'

'You have ever tried to drive a mule, Richard?' Baldovino enquired. 'Would be easier to push the car up the hill.'

Darkness was falling and the temperature had dropped to well below zero as Rudi, who was at the head of the file, whispered back that he had reached the mule track.

'It must be in use,' he reported. 'There is blood and fresh mule-droppings on it.'

There was not long to wait before the sound of hooves became audible. The first of the supply columns were moving up. At the same time the Allied artillery began shelling the track further down on the off-chance of hitting anything that was using it.

The column began to go past, dim shapes in the gloom. Richard could just see the mules, eager beasts with heads down firmly planting their feet on the rough surface. Their haunches strained to thrust the weight of the slung boxes up the steep gradient. He could hear the creaking of the leathers and the throaty 'Ah! Ah!' of their drivers urging them on. The air became bitterly aromatic with a strong animal smell.

He had to wait twenty minutes for the chance he wanted. It came in the shape of a couple of mules which had been left straggling some distance behind the others. The diminutive driver was walking at the head of the leading animal, talking softly to it in his own dialect.

Richard stepped out onto the track in front of him.

'Halt!'

The muleteer stopped dead. His mouth opened, his eyes rolled in terror. Viktor had moved out behind him. He had discarded the SS uniform and was once again in British battle-dress.

'Your name?' Richard rapped out.

'Gia – Gia – Giacomo Antonelli.' The words came out in a hoarse whisper, as if the man was already being throttled.

'You are now a prisoner of the Allies, Giacomo. But you need not be afraid. Turn round.'

Giacomo turned all in one piece. His neck had gone rigid with fear. When he saw the figure of a priest and a nun standing at his elbow he drew in his breath in a long hiss.

'*Santa Vevgine!*' He crossed himself and began to recite the Lord's Prayer.

'Have no fear, my son.' Baldovino addressed him in Italian and held up a hand. 'You are a Catholic and I am a priest. The Allies are fighting for Christianity. We are on a mission for the Holy Father. You have been chosen to help us and if you do so your reward will be great.'

'*Si, reverendo. Cosa debo fare?*'

He was a simple man trained to respect the clergy and to obey any order from an officer. It took only a few moments to off-load the ammunition boxes which were slung on either side of the mules' backs and to replace them with the Commando's gear. They were on their way before the head of the next column caught up.

The trail dipped before climbing up again. Seen from the hollow the great square hulk of the Monastery towered up against the sky. From the Allied side searchlights were still being directed on the clouds and the jumble of roofs was clearly outlined. The occasional flash of a gun lit the sky like summer lightning but they were well ahead of the gun area now, entering the eerie world of the front line. The mules were a help in more than one respect, for the sound of their hooves was familiar to the German soldiers up here and it gave cover to their own slithering footsteps.

Where the track forked, the left-hand route going on up to the German lines, Richard signalled Giacomo to take the right-hand one. This struck up more steeply towards the Monastery itself. On Maria's directions he was making for the flat plateau on its south-west side, where there were two chapels and various ancillary buildings.

He was expecting at any moment to be challenged by German sentries or to hear the angry roar of a Spandau. But they reached the flat ground without incident.

The mules halted and the others closed up, waiting for directions. The Monastery was only a couple of hundred yards away.

'We'll take shelter in the porch of that church while we get our bearings,' Richard whispered.

Round the side porch of the church there was a small walled enclosure. Giacomo led the mules into it. The rest of the party had just followed when the engine of an armoured car started up close to the Monastery. It came slowly down the hill, as if searching. Richard could imagine its gun turret swivelling towards the church. Every member of the group held their breath as it cruised slowly past and went on down the hill.

Groping his way into the porch in the darkness Richard had felt his toe touch something soft on the ground. The sickly-sweet stench told him what it was. As soon as the armoured car had passed he switched his torch on. The bodies of half a dozen civilians lay in grotesque attitudes, just as they had been flung down by the blast of a shell-burst.

He had a strong conviction that there were machine-gun posts nearby. He'd fancied already that he had heard the voices of their crews talking. The mules were standing patient and immobile, their heads hanging as they nuzzled the ground in search of grass. Giacomo was patting them, congratulating them softly for performing their task so well.

He signalled to the others to squat down round him in the angle formed by the porch and the outside wall. Something was stopping him from going into the church itself.

'We know there are people in the Monastery because we saw the smoke,' he whispered. 'The question is, how do we get in there?'

As he had hoped, Baldovino offered himself. Like all good

Italians, he rejoiced in the opportunity to achieve individual glory. 'I will go. They will admit a priest. And when I am in there I am sure I can persuade them to admit the rest of you.'

'I will go with Baldovino,' Maria said at once. 'No, please let me. I could not stay here with the smell of death all round me. And Baldovino will get in more easily if I am with him.'

It was no time or place for an argument and besides, there was force in what Maria had said. Viktor and Richard escorted them to within a hundred yards of the walls and then watched them walk up the last open stretch to the great gate. Before the two dark figures in their long swirling robes reached it, they passed out of sight behind a wall. Inside the Monastery a clock chimed four quarters and then struck the hour. It was seven o'clock.

The four who were left waited three long hours. They dared not make a fire of any kind, nor even smoke. As they grew more accustomed to the sounds of the place they were able to locate machine-gun posts on the eastward side of the Monastery.

Twice a patrol tramped past on the road fifteen yards away and at nine-thirty punctually the armoured car made another trip as far as the Monastery. It waited up there for five minutes before coming back down the hill again. All the time could be heard the confused sound of the supply columns moving up the tracks. On Snakeshead Ridge it was strangely quiet.

Rudi had become increasingly nervous. Richard even wondered if he was thinking of making a bolt for it. If he tried to do that Richard knew he would have to shoot him and risk the noise. Rudi had fulfilled his purpose with the Commando. He was not really needed any more. But if he was persuaded to talk to German interrogators they could all land up in Gestapo hands.

The clock in the Monastery had just struck ten when a dark shape slipped into the enclosure. Richard rose to meet him.

'Where is Maria?'

'In the Monastery,' Baldovino answered in a whisper.

'Who else is in there?'

'Perhaps a dozen of monks and God knows how many hundreds of refugees. The Abbot is still in charge, but is very old and – *sta per crollare.*'

'Are they willing to let us in or are we going to have to use persuasion?' Nick asked.

'The Abbot will admit no one more but I found a friendly

173

monk. I told him the real reason of our mission. He and Maria will admit us at midnight by that small door we have seen. But there is a condition. No one in military uniform.'

Richard glanced round at Viktor, who was at his shoulder listening.

'The answer to that is easy,' the Pole said. 'Our Italian friends will not feel the cold if we borrow their garments.'

Richard tried not to breathe as he wrestled the jacket off one of the dead men in the porch of the church. He could hear Rudi retching as he did the same. In five minutes the three in uniform had exchanged their military jackets for threadbare civilian garments. The smell they exuded was nauseating.

'Shall I deal with him?' Viktor asked, nodding towards the muleteer. He was already groping in his pocket for his strangling wire.

The idea of murdering the trusting Italian sickened Richard. He shook his head.

'We're going to have to take him with us.'

'We cannot risk it. To reach that doorway will be the most dangerous part of this whole exercise.'

'All the same,' Richard insisted, 'I am not going to have him killed. We can loose the mules. They'll find their own way back.'

Viktor glared at him. Even in the darkness he could see the resentment on his hawkish face.

'When we have come this far you are squeamish about an Italian soldier? He is on the enemy side, remember. I will gag and tie him and sling him across one of his mules. They will probably stay here till morning.'

Richard agreed to that. With Rudi in an unpredictable mood he could not afford to antagonize Viktor.

As the Pole moved away to where Giacomo was standing between his mules, he beckoned Nick.

'Let's stick close together, Nick. I'll cover you and you cover me.'

'You're worried about Rudi?'

'Yes. And I'm not too happy about Viktor.'

Nick nodded and tapped the bulge in his jacket pocket.

Richard was thankful now that he had looked carefully at the west side of the Monastery from the other hill. As he remembered it they would have to traverse the whole length of the building, following the base of the lower sloping wall where

174

it met the steep hillside. As the ground fell away they would be moving along a kind of ledge, their dark figures outlined against the light-coloured stone. Mercifully the machine-gun posts they had located were on the north, south and east, but there was no telling what lay in the deep valley below the western facade.

He waited till eleven before giving the signal to move off. Viktor had dealt with Giacomo. His inert form was slung across the back of a mule, wrists tied to ankles under its belly. No sound was coming from him and he did not move.

'You lead, Viktor,' Richard whispered. 'I'll bring up the rear.'

'No. You lead. I will watch your rear. If anything happens do not wait for me. Get into the Monastery.'

'That's a better idea, Richard,' Nick said. 'I'll come behind you, then Rudi. Baldo and Viktor can bring up the rear.'

Richard nodded his agreement. He was carrying the 18 set and it was therefore more important for him to achieve an entry than anyone else. The four others lined up beside him in the agreed order. They had left their Tommy guns at Peroli but each man had his revolver and a couple of the little bakelite grenades. Most of a case of Compo rations had been split up and the tins distributed about their persons. The petrol, water and Benghazi Burner had been reluctantly abandoned.

He listened carefully for three minutes then ventured out and crossed the roadway. The five men adopted a zigzag pattern as they moved across the rough ground towards the Monastery. It consisted of bare rocks on which stood huge boulders. There was an occasional wall and a few hardy trees. Nearer the walls there were cultivated patches where vegetables were being grown.

So far from being a refuge the base of the sloping wall felt very exposed. As he began to move along the ledge that led to the doorway Richard knew they were getting higher and higher in relation to the ground falling away below. Though this side of the building was the darkest, the whitish radiance of the 'artificial moonlight' cast its faint glow into every corner.

'Pass the word back to space out a bit,' he whispered to Nick.

Before he had gone half way Richard became convinced that he would have a better chance of survival if he were walking the plank. His eyes were continually drawn to the dark valley

175

below. It must be crawling with Germans. Even now half a dozen Spandaus could be aimed at them, awaiting an order to fire. On Snakeshead Ridge a flare went up, and it seemed that the blaze of light was being beamed directly on them. As it slowly sank to the earth three long bursts of machine-gun fire jarred the night. Richard thought he heard the scream of a man hit in the guts.

After that the darkness seemed deeper. He had inched forward another twenty yards when Nick hissed.

'Psss.'

Richard stopped. The sound of an engine had suddenly grown in volume as a vehicle came round a bend on the road a hundred feet below. It was the same ugly eight-wheeled armoured car. His eyes were now well enough tuned to the darkness for him to see its 20 mm gun and the machine gunner with his head and shoulders sticking out of the turret.

All he had to do was look upwards towards the Monastery and he must see the five figures standing on the parapet.

The armoured car ground slowly past and disappeared from view round the south side of the building.

The doorway was only fifty yards away now. Richard had to fight the urge to scramble towards it at panic speed. He was finding it necessary to moisten his lips, make saliva and swallow. This cat-walk in semi-darkness and total silence was the most unnerving experience he had ever endured – worse even than being shelled on that hillside below.

He thought of Daddy Jenkins in his cushy billet at Caserta and cursed him. He recalled the mocking words of Bill MacDonald and once again felt that depressing surge of doubt about the validity of this mission. The picture of Wilfrid materialized before his eyes. Where were the Greenshires now? Had his brother got the leave he'd been looking forward to?

Concentrate! he told himself. He was so near to accomplishing what had seemed an impossible task and here he was letting his mind wander. He forced himself to think of Maria. He pictured her waiting for him behind that door. Only forty more yards to go.

When at last he reached the comparative shelter of the niche into which the door was set he looked at the luminous face of his watch. 11.53. They were seven minutes early. As Nick, Rudi, Baldovino and finally Viktor joined him he signalled them to squat down beside him. No one spoke, but he could tell from their breathing that they had been just as petrified as he.

They sat there, listening to the furtive but purposeful sound of the mule trains. They had delivered their supplies and were now on their way down again. When the clock in the Monastery struck midnight its chimes seemed to be coming from Snakeshead Ridge. It was the trick of an echo.

There was an unreal quality in the sound of that bell tolling its twelve strokes, as it had done every midnight for countless years. The sound was so peaceful and measured. It awakened memories of village churches, Mexican *estancias*, small Tuscan towns visited on holidays long ago.

As the last note died they were all looking at the locked and bolted door.

'Come on, Maria!' Baldovino murmured. 'Come on!'

There was no sound from inside the Monastery, neither of footsteps, drawn bolt nor key. The temperature was dropping fast. They were becoming frozen stiff. The searchlights had been switched off at midnight and the darkness was more intense. Every now and then, from beyond Snakeshead Ridge, came the crump of shells landing. The Germans were hitting the Royal Sussex supply route.

At half-past twelve Viktor stood up, went out as far as he could onto the narrow parapet and stared at the sloping surface of the wall above him.

'That window is only twenty feet up,' he told Richard. 'There are plenty of hand and footholds.'

'Give it a bit longer. There may be some hitch inside.'

'If I wait any longer my hands will be too frozen to do it.'

Nick said, still in a whisper: 'It's worth a try. We can't sit on our tails the whole goddam night.'

'Okay, Viktor. Have a go. And good luck.'

Richard moved out onto the parapet as Viktor rubbed warmth into his hands before reaching for his first hold. He was helped by the fact that the stones were large and rough and the wall sloped inwards. It was obvious at once that he was also an experienced climber. He progressed quickly and was within six feet of the window-ledge when there came a sharp crack from the door.

The bolt had yielded suddenly to the pressure of whoever was drawing it, and shot back against its stop. The noise had sounded very loud in the surrounding stillness. The unseen

177

person, realizing that speed was now more important than silence, turned the key in the lock with a deafening rattle.

The door swung open onto a black, vaulted chamber.

'*Avanti! Avanti! Subito! Subito!*' an urgent voice urged them.

Richard had seen Viktor flatten himself against the wall at the crack of the bolt. At the same time he had heard excited voices in the valley below, then a barked order.

Immediately after the door had swung open came the first burst of machine-gun fire. He heard the crack of it through the air above his head, the slap of the bullets on the stones an instant before the roar of the gun.

Viktor's body jerked out from the wall, plummetted past him. It hit the sloping shale fifteen feet below and went sliding down out of sight into the undergrowth at the side of the road.

He felt his arm grabbed as Nick hauled him into the niche and then dragged him through the door. It was closed with a bang, just before a hail of bullets slammed into the thick oak. The firing lasted for a minute. Then outside there was silence.

Richard stood in the pitch blackness, too shocked and grieved to feel any elation that he was at last inside the Monastery.

17

Half a mile away from the Monastery on that same night the Royal Sussex moved forward to relieve the Americans. Over two hundred of them had suffered so extremely from exhaustion and exposure that they were unable to walk. The British soldiers had to lift them out of their foxholes and place them on stretchers for the long journey down to the Rapido Valley. So difficult was it to pass casualties down the ice-covered, twisting route that relay parties had to be installed at frequent intervals.

Many of those who had survived the mortaring and machine-gunning of Snakeshead Ridge were killed by shell-fire on that nightmare journey down the mountain.

Otherwise the relief went 'according to plan' and was completed by 5 a.m. There was one unusual circumstance. The casualties suffered by 34th US Division had been so severe that companies were relieving battalions and battalions were relieving brigades.

By daylight the Royal Sussex were ensconced in the comfortless foxholes, sangars and weapon-pits which had been vacated by 'the cousins'.

The Gunners also had taken over the same forward observation posts as the Americans. Wilfrid found himself sharing a miniature fortress made of boulders with a Captain from 31st Field Regiment. Both forward observation officers had their own communications, so that each system duplicated the other. Like the 31st Wilfrid was on net to his own battery commander at battery headquarters and to his GPOs.

He spent the morning ranging on targets so that his guns would have them registered during daylight in preparation for a shoot at night.

One of the targets, Point 573, entailed very accurate gunnery. The guns in the Rapido Valley nearly two thousand feet below had to fire over the top of Snakeshead Ridge with a very low crest clearance. In such circumstances it was more important than ever to test sights regularly and carefully and to 'lot' the ammunition. The charges varied fractionally from one batch of shells to another and it was essential to register targets with the same charge lots as you were going to fire on your programme.

Unfortunately, owing to supply problems, the necessary requirements in ammunition had not yet been met.

'There's nothing we can do about it,' the GPO told Wilfrid. 'If we have to shoot before we can lot the ammo we'll just have to pray that the charges aren't different.'

179

It may have been the shock of Viktor Zygalski's death – the roar of the machine-gun, the smack of bullets on stone, the body crashing past him in the darkness – or it may have been the eerie transition from the exposure and fear of the parapet outside to the fastness of the great building with its massive walls. Whatever the reason Richard felt a sense of total unreality as he followed the small flame of the hurricane lamp along the dark corridor.

Behind him the thud of bullets on the door had ceased. An unearthly silence enveloped everything.

Round a corner, in a small low chamber, the monk who was leading the way put his lamp down on a table. Its light, cast upwards, shed an orange glow on the faces gathered round it.

'What about Viktor?' Nick was still keeping his voice to a whisper.

'Gone for a Burton. They got him with the first burst. He fell about forty feet onto the hillside below. Where's Maria?'

'She's up in the Monastery. Richard, this is Padre Nessuno. It's thanks to him we've got you in.'

Richard bowed gravely to the short figure in its long, black cassock.

'La ringrazio sinceramente, Padre.'

'Lei parla italiano?'

'Un po.'

'Ah, meno male!' the monk exclaimed and then poured out a stream of Italian so rapidly that Richard had difficulty in following what he said. The gist of it was that he had disobeyed his Abbot's instructions in letting them in and had done this only because Baldovino had told him that the purpose of their mission was to save the Monastery. He was relying on them not to give him away.

'He has shown to me a small room where we can hide ourselves and rest,' Baldovino explained. 'We can do nothing till daylight. In the dark it is impossible to move without stepping upon bodies.'

'It's true there are civilian refugees here?'

'Yes. Hundreds of them!'

Nessuno led them by a tortuous route through basement cellars and corridors and up stone staircases till they reached the habitable levels of the building. Richard could never have found his own way back to that small doorway.

It was the odour of humanity rather than the murmur of voices which warned him that he was now being led into the passages where the refugees were encamped. Here and there groups were huddled round small fires, prepared to endure the sting of the enclosed smoke rather than the bitter cold. In other places anonymous forms lay on the ground, clasping each other close for warmth. Following Padre Nessuno's lamp the four men had to pick their way carefully, putting their feet down in the spaces between the recumbent bodies.

Richard felt that he had stepped over a hundred men, women and children before Nessuno at last opened a small door and beckoned them to come quickly inside. When they had passed him he closed the door of the refuge and bolted it.

There was already a lighted candle burning in the room. After the gloom of the corridors the place seemed quite light. Two women and an eight-year-old boy were sitting on a couple of truckle beds. When she saw him Maria came forward impulsively and took one of his hands in both of hers.

'Oh, thank God! I was so afraid for you.'

She had thrown back the cowl and with the light behind her cropped head might almost have been mistaken for a young monk. She gazed at him very intently for a moment, then pulled him forward by the hand.

'This is Laura – and her son, Franco. She has lost both her husband and her youngest son.'

Laura turned towards him, but not before he had seen the look which passed between her and Padre Nessuno – a look which in a mysterious way was very akin to the glance which he had exchanged with Maria.

'You have come to save us?' Laura asked, holding Franco close to her skirts.

'That's what we hope,' Richard answered. He looked round at Nick, Baldovino and Rudi.

'Where is Viktor?'

'You tell her, Baldo. I seem to have run out of Italian.'

Now that they were inside a building the smell of the dead men's clothes they were wearing had become nauseating. They took off their borrowed jackets, rolled them up in a tight bundle and put them in a corner. The wireless sets and compo rations were carefully placed against the wall.

'We've got to get a message through about these civilians,' Nick said as soon as that had been done. 'That's a first priority. If they bomb this place now it will be a massacre.'

'No good trying to signal till tomorrow morning. And we still have the best part of a week in hand. Today's only the 13th, or rather early morning of the 14th.'

'I wouldn't be too sure you've got all that much time in hand. I've a feeling they're going to advance the date for the attack. Why do you have to wait till to-morrow morning?'

'These sets die at night. They're not much good for more than a mile or two when it's dark. There's a lot of interference. Sounds like Chinese music. Anyway, Nick, I want to be able to report on whether Jerry is using the Monastery or not. That was the object of this exercise.'

*

The first thing Richard saw when he woke was Laura sitting in a chair, cradling her son who had his head on her shoulder. The sky was still dark behind the high window.

He scrambled up, wiping the sleep from his eyes, and woke the others. They performed their ablutions as best they could and then cooked a breakfast of powdered eggs, porridge improvised from the compo biscuits and mugs of tea. Richard felt slightly guilty, knowing there was a starving multitude outside, but it was vital to keep his own group in a condition to function efficiently.

Leaving Maria and Laura to clear up the remains of the meal he gathered the other three surviving members of the Benedictine commando round him.

'I'm going to try and make contact at the eight o'clock reporting time to make a preliminary report and tell them I want to report again at 1400 hours. By that time we must have as much information as we can get.

'Baldo, I want you to make contact with the Abbot. Find out from him exactly who is in this place and how long they've been here. I specifically want to know if the Germans have been or are using it. Rudi – .' Richard hesitated. The German had been avoiding his eye for some time now. His mind seemed to be on something else. For the first time since they had crossed the lines Richard was wondering if he could rely on him. He decided to give him a task that was not of vital importance but would keep him occupied.

182

'Yes, Major.' Rudi had snapped out of his reverie and with an obvious effort was concentrating on Richard's orders.

'I want you to circulate as much as you can among the refugees, see if by any chance there are any German soldiers among them. Nick, I want you to come with me. I'll show you how to operate the 18 set. You ought to know, just in case anything happens to me.'

'Right. We'd better move fast. It's already a quarter of eight.'

'I know. I wish the Padre was here. I'd like to get to an upper floor.'

'Franco can guide you.' Baldovino jerked his head towards the bright-eyed boy who was so eagerly watching the group of soldiers, trying to understand their strange language. 'He has been in the Monastery for months. He knows every inch of it.'

'That's fine. If his mother will allow him.'

Even if his mother had disapproved there would have been no stopping Franco. He was thrilled at the prospect of participating in the operations of these strange and glamorous beings who had come so unexpectedly into his life. As Baldovino and Rudi set off on their appointed tasks, he led them towards the stairways to the upper floors.

Darting ahead and then waiting for them to catch up, Franco led Richard and Nick to a staircase which mounted to the upper floors. To disguise the wireless set from the apathetic stares of the refugees, Richard had covered it with some pieces of material he had pulled off the chair in the small room.

The place was a labyrinth of cloisters, corridors and courtyards. There were refugees everywhere, most of them formed into little self-contained groups. They were folding up the improvised bedding they had lain on during the night, preparing their scraps of food on the crude cooking arrangements they had set up. There were women of all ages and many children, but the men were old and wizened. Few males of military age had slipped through the nets of the German and Fascist police forces. They all had the haunted, apprehensive expression of people who had suffered extreme terror and had little confidence in what the future might hold for them. As shells were landing intermittently in the open cloisters or on the roofs, they had sought refuge as deep down in the Monastery as possible, within the protection of the massive lower walls.

It was past five to eight when Franco brought them out into a long, broad corridor with a row of dark wooden doors on either side. He had obviously been here many times before because he went unhesitatingly to the third door on the right-hand side and turned the handle. It opened into an empty monk's cell, with a bed, chair, table, chest of drawers and wash-stand.

Franco pointed to the window: *'Di qui si può vedere Cassino.'*

Richard crossed to the window and caught his breath. Instinctively he moved back a step. The town of Cassino lay immediately below. He felt that he could have opened the window and thrown a stone down into its shattered streets. A haze of smoke lay over the ruins, and even as he watched another salvo of Nebelwerfer bombs crashed down near the church. The flooded Rapido had oozed out over the marshland to the south-east of the town forming a dirty, grey lake. The ribbon of main road led straight out of Cassino till it curved round the base of Monte Trocchio and vanished. Nothing moved on the visible stretch of road nor in the countryside to either side of it. Had it not been for the occasional spout of earth thrown up by a bursting shell you would have thought it an empty and deserted landscape. There was no sign of the defending army nor of the vast host waiting to attack.

He wondered if ever before in the history of warfare it had been possible to stand at a window on the fourth floor of a building in the front line and look down on enemy positions from almost directly above. It was the kind of OP that gunners dream of. He wondered what sort of man would not only resist the temptation to use it but go so far as to put a guard on the gate to keep his own soldiers out.

'How's the time, Nick?'

'Two minutes of eight.'

'Will you open the window while I get the thing set up?'

The moment Nick opened the window an icy blast swept into the room. Outside the weather was as atrocious as ever. Richard placed the 18 set on the table. He unclipped the extension rods and fitted them together to form an aerial about ten feet long. He had to cant the set sideways so that it could be poked out through the window. He plugged in the battery lead, put the ear-phones over his head and picked up the hand mike. As eight o'clock came up on their watches he switched the set on. The dial showed that the power was coming through. He began to transmit on the SIO frequency.

'Ben calling Jenny. Are you receiving me? Over.'

He listened for a few seconds, then switched again to transmit.

'Ben calling Jenny. Repeat Ben calling Jenny. Are you receiving me? Over.'

The air was as full of voices as Prospero's island, but from Jenny there came no reply.

'Blast them!' Richard exploded, after trying in vain for five minutes. 'What the hell are they up to?'

'Perhaps your set's not powerful enough.'

Richard shook his head. 'It can't be that. Mignano's seven miles at the most. Nick, you see how simple this is to work. If I leave you here, could you try every half hour or so to raise them? I want to make a thorough inspection of the Monastery.'

'Okay. Sure.' Nick squatted down in front of the chair while Richard quickly showed him how to operate the British set.

'Don't transmit for long, and if you make contact simply tell them to stand by for my report at fourteen hundred hours. We'll meet down in the room at ten.'

With Franco as his guide, Richard set out on his tour of the building. He walked along empty corridors, peered into the deserted refectory, tiptoed reverently through the library, from which the most precious parchments and ancient books had been removed. He tramped through the section of the buildings which had been used as a school, prowled up and down staircases, opened the doors of empty classrooms.

It was all made more eerie and unreal by the muffled sounds of warfare from outside and the occasional louder detonation of a projectile striking some part of the Monastery. It was easy to understand why the refugees had crowded into the lower levels, leaving the upper floors deserted.

Franco knew the private route by which the monks could gain access directly to the choir without passing through the public part of the church. Richard followed him as he pushed the door open and dipped his fingers in the font of holy water before crossing himself. The two of them tiptoed across the marbled floor and Richard craned his neck to peer at the frescoes on the ceiling. Even in the gloom of an overcast winter's day the coloured marble on floor and walls glowed with its own inner light.

Franco pointed to the high altar, a miracle of sculptured marble.

'The bones of St Benedict and St Scholastica are under there,' he whispered, as if the two saints might overhear if he spoke too loudly.

The explosion of a shell out in the Bramante Cloister reminded him that their only protection was the thin skin of the dome over their heads. As he shepherded Franco towards the door he glanced at his watch. The time had passed more quickly than he had realized. It was not surprising. He felt that he had walked miles.

Inspecting the lower levels was a very different matter. It was not easy to make a way through the encamped refugees. They crowded every available inch of space. The only clear area was in the vicinity of the little Chapel which the monks had reserved for their own use. Even in an extremity such as this the continuation of the Opus Dei was of primary importance.

As he and Franco made their way back towards the small room for the ten o'clock rendezvous they met a strange procession. Even the refugees had fallen silent and edged back to leave a free passage. Four monks were carrying a plain wooden coffin on their shoulders. One monk walked in front and another followed behind.

'What's happened?'

'It is Dom Eusebio.' Franco's mouth quivered and he blinked back tears. 'He was nursing the sick and caught their illness from them. Mama said he worked himself to death.'

Richard stood back, pressing against the bodies of the people behind him to let the coffin and its bearers go by. The sepulchral spectacle seemed to be no more than a natural part of the atmosphere of doom which hung over the whole place. As the funeral cortège passed on towards the Chapel of St Anne he grabbed Franco's hand and hustled him back to the little room beside the bakery. Baldovino and Rudi were already there. The German had lost his expression of absent-minded aloofness. It had been replaced by one of anger.

'There is not a single German soldier in the place,' he stated. 'I have searched everywhere. Nothing except Italians. The neutrality of the Monastery is being respected by the Germans but your artillery either do not care or their gunnery is very inaccurate. I saw a man drawing water from the well blown to pieces!'

'Thank you, Rudi,' Richard said crisply and forebore to comment. 'What did you learn, Baldo?'

Baldo had seen the Abbot, who had confirmed that there were only eight members of the religious community left but as many as a thousand refugees.

'What about Germans?'

'No German has set foot in the Monastery since the beginning of January.'

Rudi nodded energetically in confirmation of this statement.

'Did you tell the Abbot who we are?'

Baldovino shook his head. 'It would not be wise. He has great faith in the Germans and their promise to respect the Monastery. All this shelling has not made him very pro-Allied. And besides, for an old man of eighty he has enough problems already.'

'I see. Thank you both.'

Richard would like to have gone off somewhere quiet to think. With Rudi and Baldovino staring at him, waiting for some decision, he got out his pipe and tobacco and began to fill the bowl. For the past week the difficult task of getting into the Monastery had been an objective in itself. At times it had appeared so impossible that he still found it hard to believe that they had done it. Since the wooden door had closed behind him, sealing him off from the bullets and the war outside he had become to some extent a victim of the euphoric confidence in the building as a place of sanctuary which affected the monks and refugees. Even now, when the belief he had expressed so confidently to General Alexander had been confirmed, he had to keep reminding himself that all the Benedictine Commando had achieved so far would be pointless unless he could get the message across.

It was imperative for Alex to know that the Germans were not making use of the Monastery; that, on the contrary, it was serving as a sanctuary for a thousand refugees. If the C-in-C approved the bombing of it under those circumstances, the damage not only to Alexander's own reputation but to the whole credibility of the Allied cause would be incalculable.

He had just got his pipe going nicely when Nick came in. He was looking harassed and irritated.

'Not a cheep until just now. I tried every half hour, like you said. Then all I heard was "Jenny calling Ben. Pass your message. Over."'

'So what did you say?'

'I said "Stewart will make his report to you at fourteen hundred hours. Please listen then."'

'Did you receive an acknowledgement?'

'The guy just said: "Roger Wilco Out".'

Richard nodded.

'Who is Roger Wilco?' Baldovino wanted to know.

'It meant they'd received and understood the message. This means I can make my report at two o'clock and then we can start planning to get out of here again. I want to get back to Caserta as fast as I can so that I can confirm the situation to Alex in person.'

As there was still no sign of Maria Richard went off in search of her with Franco again as his guide. He found her in the deepest and most ancient part of the Monastery near the former cell of St Benedict, in another chapel which had been converted into a makeshift hospital ward. She had created some semblance of order in a chaotic situation. The mere presence of a competent nurse had brought tremendous comfort to the twenty or so sick and wounded refugees. Many of them, stretched on improvised pallets, followed her every movement with an expression of dog-like trust in their eyes.

She was just knotting a bandage on the knee of a girl of about sixteen. When she saw him she smiled, straightened up and came to the doorway.

'There's some food waiting for you in the room. You ought to eat something.'

'I will later.' She looked despairingly at the rows of helpless forms. An old man was groaning with pain and an infant boy screaming for his mother. 'These people are in desperate need of help. Some of them ought to have morphia. I only have torn-up sheets for bandages and very little disinfectant.'

'Is it true that there are some cases of typhoid?' he asked her in a low voice.

'I am afraid so. In these conditions it is not surprising and there is danger of it spreading. Richard, do you think the Germans would let us evacuate the worst cases?'

'It's hard to say. I know the situation seems bad enough

already but my concern at the moment is to prevent it becoming a lot worse.'

'How could it be worse?'

He did not answer that question. 'I must go now. I'm trying to get a message through to our own people about the situation here. Please take a break for some food soon. Can't Padre Nessuno relieve you?'

'He and Laura have been helping me but he had to go off to attend a service.'

Feeling a little irritated that the monks should be persisting in their regular devotions while there was so much human suffering on their doorstep, Richard left Maria and began to make his way back towards the staircase which led to the upper floors. He had not gone far when he heard the incongruous sound of voices raised in song.

'Come and see,' Franco urged him. 'They are in the Chapel.'

A group of refugees had crowded round the doorway of the small chapel where the half-dozen monks were assembled. Richard had to stand on tiptoe to see over their heads. The black-cassocked figures were standing in a half-circle facing the altar, intoning the Psalms ordered for the day. As he listened to the familiar and comforting cadences of their voices, faithful to the rhythms and eloquent pauses of the Gregorian Chant, he realized that they were right to continue their worship in this way. Their singing brought an element of sanity and order into circumstances which were verging on hysteria.

It was close to two o'clock when he reached the cell on the upper floor. Nick was already there. He had opened the window and extended the aerial through it. Richard smoothed out the paper on which he had written a terse message in telegraphese.

At two o'clock exactly he switched the set to transmit.

'Ben calling Jenny. Are you receiving me? Over.'

'Jenny calling Ben. Am receiving you. Pass your message. Over.'

'To Colonel Jenkins. SIO. AFHQ. Am inside Monastery. NO, repeat NO occupation by enemy. One thousand refugees in building. Stewart. Message ends. Over.'

'Roger. Out.'

As Richard switched the set off Nick said: 'Is that all?'

'It's enough, isn't it? These radio operators have been trained

189

to be very security minded. Though even if the Germans had time to intercept the message it would not help them much.'

Nick watched Richard retract the aerial and pack the set up for transportation.

'So what now?'

'We've done what we set out to do. That message should be on Daddy Jenkins' desk within a few minutes. But I still want to get back to Caserta as quick as I can so that I can give Alex an eye-witness account of what we've seen here.'

'You say I. You don't think you're going it alone, do you?'

'I was banking on you coming with me, Nick.' Richard hoisted the set onto his shoulders. 'I don't know how keen Baldo and Rudi will be on the idea. And I just pray no one has discovered the Mercedes.'

*

The signals officer at Mignano decided to give Richard's message a Top Secret rating and Most Immediate priority. It was brought to Jenkins' office as soon as he returned from a somewhat delayed lunch.

He slit the outer envelope with the ivory paper-knife, saw the envelope marked Top Secret inside.

'That's all right, Henderson,' he told the messenger.

When the door had closed he used the paper-knife again and drew out the message sheet. He read the brief report three times, then laid it on his blotter. He pushed his chair back and walked as far as the window and back, trying to make up his mind. Then he stared at the green telephone for the best part of a minute before he picked the receiver up.

'Chief of Staff, please.'

He had to talk his way past a GSO I before he was put through.

A crisp voice said: 'Harding.'

'Jenkins here, sir.'

'Jenkins?'

'Yes, sir. SIO.'

'Ah, yes. What can I do for you, Jenkins?'

'Can we scramble, sir?'

'Yes. Hold on.' There was a pause while each man pressed the button. Then Harding's voice came through again, sounding only a little more fuzzy. 'Right. Carry on.'

'I just wanted to ask you, sir. Has the bombing of Montecassino been fixed definitely?'

'Yes. It'll be tomorrow. General Eaker has had a favourable weather forecast so the green light's on. As a matter of fact, I've just been asked the same question by Gruenther. It seems General Juin went to Fifth Army Headquarters in person to try and stop the bombing. But it's too late to change anything now.'

'I see. Thank you.'

'Why do you ask? Your people aren't involved in this, are they?'

'No, sir. I just want to brief one of my agents to send back a report on how effective the bombing is.'

'I shouldn't bother, Jenkins. The C-in-C is going to Cervaro to see the results for himself.'

Jenkins hung up and stood with bowed shoulders. The Top Secret message on his pad stared at him accusingly, surrounded by the piles of 'bumph' which he never seemed able to clear. His brief as director of SIO gave him a great deal of independence. The excuse of secrecy protected his operations from too close scrutiny by senior officers. He realized now that the whole idea of the Benedictine Commando had been a mistake.

It had been his own brainchild and he had not told the truth either to Alexander or Stewart.

Alex had said that if Jenkins could provide him with irrefutable proof that the Germans were not in the Monastery he would be able to resist Freyberg's pressure to have it destroyed. Jenkins wanted to prevent Alex from making a mistake which could become a blot on an otherwise impeccable career. But he had not confided to the C-in-C that he was sending his former liaison officer on a most hazardous line-crossing mission. And he had misled Stewart when he had told him that the Benedictine Commando was Alexander's conception.

Without being aware of what he was doing he had moved to the drinks cupboard and brought out the bottle of Scotch. As the pressures had built up round him he had been using whisky as a fuel more and more. Lately things had been so hot that he'd got into the way of starting the day with a slug.

'Too late, Stewart,' he muttered and knocked back the two

fingers he had poured. 'Too bloody late. You and your precious Monastery have had it.'

The room appeared to rock slightly. He screwed up his eyes and with his free hand smoothed the permanent wrinkles between his brows. He'd had quite a few of these turns lately. Overwork. Pressure. Perhaps he ought to get the MO to check up on his heart. Trouble was, he worried too much about things.

He moved round to read the message once again, focussing with an effort. Then he picked it up, took it to the fireplace and stooped before the grate. He put his lighter to the flimsy sheet and when the flame had consumed all but the last corner he let it go. There was enough draught to draw the ashes up the chimney.

18

On their way back from sending the message Richard and Nick had to cross an open courtyard. It was always wise not to dawdle, but on this occasion Richard heard an unusual sound. He stopped to look at the sky. An aircraft was passing over the Monastery, flying just below the cloud base. It was bigger than the Piper Cub used for Air OPs. Probably a Kittihawk, he thought.

The machine was directly overhead when he saw something tumble from its underbelly.

'God! A land mine!' was his instant thought, remembering London.

But the object only tumbled a couple of hundred feet before bursting open and disgorging hundreds of leaflets. As they drifted down, twisting like a covey of slaughtered white birds, the wind caught them, carrying them away over the roofs of the buildings.

'What in hades can that be?'

'God knows. Propaganda leaflets of some kind. But why here?'

They soon found out. Before they had time to reach the little room panic was already spreading among the refugees. They had to fight their way through a surging mass trying to get to the Abbot's quarters. In the thick of it was Baldovino, moving with the tide of people.

'What's happening, Baldo?'

'They have dropped leaflets. I go to try to find out.'

'We'll wait for you in the room,' Richard shouted as the Italian was borne away.

It was ten minutes before Baldo returned. He was very pale. In his hand he held a muddy sheet of paper.

'I managed to take hold of one of the leaflets. The bomber was not very accurate. None of them fell on the Monastery. The wind carried them all beyond the walls. Two boys ran out to collect some. It was a very brave act. Anything that moves out there is fired at.'

'What does it say, for Pete's sake?'

Baldovino took a grip on himself. He handed the leaflet to Richard. He gave it a quick glance.

'Jesus Christ!'

'Come on, come on,' Nick urged impatiently.

Richard read the text of the leaflet aloud, translating as he went:

'Italian friends,

WARNING!

Up till now we have tried by every means to avoid bombarding the Monastery of Montecassino. The Germans have taken advantage of that. But now the fighting is closer round the sacred precincts. The time has come when against our will we are obliged to direct our arms against the Monastery itself.

We are warning you so that you can have a chance to save yourselves. This warning is urgent. Leave the Monastery. Go away at once. Take notice of this warning. It has been given to help you.

The Fifth Army.'

In the silence that followed Nick muttered: 'Jesus H. Particular Christ.' Richard handed the leaflet to Laura. She read it and gasped. At that moment the door opened and Rudi came in. He was very angry.

'You have seen the leaflet?'

Richard nodded. He could not bring himself to say anything.

'Then what was the point of mounting this operation at all? I believed our purpose was to save the Monastery. You deceived me, Major.'

'Believe me, Rudi, this has surprised me as much as you. I just can't believe it.'

'Then your own command has deceived you! It is clear they intend to bomb the Monastery.'

Baldovino took the leaflet from Laura and studied it again. 'It depends what is meant by the word *bombardamento*.

'The wording is *puntare le nostre armi contro il Monastero stesso*. To my mind "point our weapons" indicates an artillery barrage rather than bombing.'

'That is still bad enough,' Rudi protested. 'The Americans have 8-inch howitzers now. That is a very big shell.'

Rudi had expressed thoughts which Richard would not have put into words.

'They'll call it off when they learn that there are a thousand refugees here – and no Germans.'

'You are confident of that?' Rudi challenged. 'The leaflet emphasizes that the bombardment is imminent.'

Nick said. 'I think we've got to contact your friends at Mignano again.'

'We can try,' Richard said wearily. 'But I'm not too confident that we can raise them before tomorrow morning.'

*

The Abbot was being besieged by a panic-stricken crowd. As head of the community it fell to him to make some decision as to what they should all do. Though, God knows, he had never aspired to be head of a community such as this. His hopes of ending his days peacefully in the Monastery which had sheltered him for more than half a century were becoming very faint.

He decided that his only course was to try and make contact with the German authorities. That would not be easy. The last link with the outside world had been severed when a German pilot, anxious to show his acrobatic skill by flying under the funicular linking town and Monastery, had crashed into the cables.

Two boys, members of the families who had been there longest, volunteered to venture forth to try and find a German officer. But they were not hardened to shell-fire. They had gone no more than a hundred yards when they were driven back. A little later, when there seemed to be a lull in the gun-fire, they tried again. This time they carried a white flag. But the shelling was coming from the Allied side and the white flag was not visible to the observers on Monte Trocchio. Once more the boys were forced to flee to the shelter of the Monastery.

And now dissension broke out among the half-crazed peasants clamouring round Abbot Diamare. One man more coherent than the rest stood up on a chair to command attention as he shouted:

'Our only salvation will be to open the main door and go out all together under the protection of a white flag. The Americans will hold their fire when they see we are harmless civilians.'

'Even if they do see the white flag,' a woman retorted stridently, 'it is more likely that they will wait until we are in the open and then massacre us all.'

'To stay here is certain death,' maintained one of the younger women, the mother of two children. 'We have had the warning.'

Pandemonium broke out as they began to quarrel among themselves. One vociferous faction went so far as to spread the outrageous suggestion that the monks were in collusion with the Germans and that the whole thing was a trick to eject them from the Monastery.

It took many minutes for the Abbot's secretary to quieten them enough for the old man to make himself heard.

'You must all do what you think is best,' he told them. 'If you wish to risk your lives in the open, then do so. But I advise you to remain within the shelter of the Monastery. Tonight we will try again to make contact with the Germans.'

★

During the last hours before darkness made movement difficult, Richard transferred his 'headquarters' from the small room near the bakery to a vaulted space he had noticed near St

Benedict's cell. The chapel which Maria had converted into a hospital ward was just above it. This crypt-like chamber was beneath the most ancient and massive section of the whole complex of buildings and formed part of the ancient fortress, or Toretta. The walls consisted of massive chunks of rock. Substantial stones provided a very firm arch overhead. The advantage of this refuge was not only that it gave better protection against bombs or shells, but also brought him closer to the Abbot and the remaining monks. Though Padre Nessuno was still the only one who knew the true identity of the Benedictine Commando, Richard felt that at any moment he might need to declare himself to the Abbot, who was the only source of authority in the whole of that crazy bedlam.

It also gave him the opportunity of keeping some kind of watch on Maria. Since she refused to leave her patients to eat or to rest he had to take food to her.

A final and by no means minor consideration was that if the refugees discovered that there were representatives of the Allied Forces among them they would probably appoint a lynching party.

Nick was up on the third floor again, trying vainly to raise some response from the signals station at Mignano. As darkness descended on the bleak landscape the 'Chinese music' filled the ether once more. He realized that there was no hope of making contact with the 18 set until the following morning. While he could still see his way, he descended the stairs, leaving the 18 set in the empty cell, ready for the morning's transmission.

As soon as darkness had fallen two more young men, who had offered themselves to the Abbot for this venture, crept out through the Monastery door. They knew that every night a German armoured car patrolled up as far as the entrance. This time they were lucky and managed to attract the attention of the crew without being shot at.

The sergeant commanding the patrol listened in astonishment while one of the boys, speaking in halting German, explained the predicament of the refugees and monks.

He thought quickly and made his decision.

'Tell the Abbot he can come out and meet my officer at 5 a.m. tomorrow morning. He must be accompanied by only one other person. If there are more, we will open fire.'

With that the armoured car turned round and drove back down the road. Badly shaken by their encounter with the

196

uncompromising face of war, the two youths crept back to give the Abbot the news.

Padre Nessuno and Laura had not abandoned their work among the refugees. While Maria did what she could for the really serious cases they continued their rounds succouring the many families whose children were sick, frightened or in any other kind of acute distress.

But Laura had refused to move with Franco from the little room to the more secure refuge Richard had chosen under the Toretta.

'Will you come and persuade her, *maggiore*?' Nessuno pleaded, when the monks had said a very delayed Vespers.

Richard and Nessuno found Laura preparing Franco a good supper based on one of the food tins which he had pressed on her. She listened carefully to all his arguments and then gently shook her head.

'I cannot leave this room.' She was looking at Nessuno as she spoke. 'I feel I am still near Sandro here. And other things have happened in this room from which I do not want to be separated.'

Franco was switching his gaze from his mother's face to the monk's. They formed a trio from which Richard felt excluded. There was some secret here which he could not fathom, but he knew instinctively that Nessuno was controlling his face with a great effort.

'It's your decision. But if there's heavy shelling or bombing I think you should move down.'

He turned and went out, leaving the three of them alone.

*

After Compline, the last service of the day, the rule for the Benedictine monks was silence. That night they sang the hundred-and-fortieth Psalm and as Padre Nessuno left the little chapel the words were still re-echoing in his mind. Over the refugees too had fallen an apprehensive hush in which the wailing of a baby could be clearly heard. The very stones of the Monastery seemed to be watching and waiting. Throughout that long night the building was as sleepless as a condemned man before his execution. Even the din of war was muted. Cassino Town was still and a brooding silence lay over Snakeshead Ridge. The artillery of both sides seemed to have taken the night off.

When he visited Fifth Army Headquarters on the afternoon of the 14th February, Freyberg had learned that the bombing of the Monastery was scheduled for the next day. It so chanced that after weeks of foul weather the clear skies which would be needed were forecast for Tuesday 15 February. The bombing would have to take place then or never. On the 16th the air forces had an appointment to hit von Mackesen's Fourteenth Army besieging the Anzio beach-head and blunt the anticipated counter-attack. Yet Eaker and his British deputy, Jack Slessor, delayed giving the final order for a mission they found distasteful. They were prepared to unleash the full destructive power of a modern air force but in their heart of hearts they hoped the request would be withdrawn.

Back at his own headquarters Freyberg urged the commander of 4th Indian Division to advance his main attack to the night of 15th/16th. Dimoline maintained that he could not order his brigadiers to change their plans. Lovett had been up onto Snakeshead Ridge himself to survey the position with the CO of the Royal Sussex. He and Glennie had looked at the terrain from forward positions and agreed that Point 593 had to be captured first in order to give 7th Brigade a fair chance. Moreover, it was pointless to mount an attack until the second brigade was in a position to reinforce it; and 5th Brigade were still back at San Michele.

That Monday night Colonel Glennie sent out patrols into the no-man's-land of the ridge. If the word patrol conjures up the picture of an orderly echelon of soldiers, with rifles at the 'port arms' position, advancing through a copse or across a meadow, then it was hardly appropriate in this case. And if no-man's-land suggests a sea of mud with shell holes and barbed-wire entanglements precisely defined by the trench-lines of the 1914-18 war, then that phrase too must be discarded. The lads from Bolney, Ditchling, Lewes, Haywards Heath and all stations to Brighton who ventured forward from their foxholes into the blackness did so on hands and knees with sacking tied round their boots and balaclava helmets on their charcoal-faced heads. Black was already beautiful that night on Snakeshead Ridge. And the terrain they entered was a hell of a different quality from the slough of Flanders' Field. Instead of mud there was rock. Instead of shell-holes there were sudden chasms or little precipices. Barbed-wire there was, to be sure, but it was thickened by the thorny brambles that flourished on these uplands. Nor had Jerry neglected to lay mine-fields.

In the watchful and menacing silence of that freezing night the slightest sound – a dislodged stone, the scrape of a boot against rock, the clink of a bayonet – would bring down a stream of scything machine-gun fire.

The reports the patrols brought back were confused but to the CO they spelled out one clear message. On the narrow spine of the ridge there was not room to mount a battalion, let alone a brigade attack. Point 593 would have to be taken by one company.

General Eaker had no inkling that the air strike he had planned was to be the prelude to an attack by only one company. Nor did Colonel Glennie know that the bombing had been scheduled for the next day. This was war. And war, as anyone who has been involved in it knows, consists largely of grand military cock-ups.

That night at 9.50 p.m. the final order went out to 12th and 15th US Army Air Forces. On airfields on the islands of Sardinia and Corsica and at Amendola, Tortorella, Lucera and Celone ground staff began to trundle the trailer-trains of bombs out to the waiting Flying Fortresses.

*

Rudi had slipped out through the main door while it had been opened for the boys who were trying to contact the German patrol. No one had seen him go.

He knew from observation that there were machine-gun posts dug in close to the Monastery on the southern and eastern sides. The defenders were concentrating their depleted forces on the flank from which the attack was expected, leaving the north-western corner to the armoured car patrol. He was not ready yet to make contact with his own people. His plan depended on finding the dead paratrooper he had seen on the way up the mountain.

There had been plenty of time for him to think since he had made his decision to evade the Gestapo by deserting to the enemy. The secret police had already established a horrific enough reputation for the news that they were after him to throw him into a panic. It would in fact have been more honourable to do as his commanding officer had suggested and

199

shoot himself. His motive in accepting the invitation to join the Benedictine Commando had indeed been prompted by a desire to prove that he was not a coward. But a number of things had disillusioned him.

In the first place he despised what he regarded as the slip-shod discipline of the Allies. And how could anyone respect a commander like Stewart, who encouraged his subordinates to call each other by their Christian names, irrespective of rank? Rudi did not like being asked to do things. He preferred a direct order. And that incident when Mac-Donald had challenged Stewart's authority. A German major would never have lain down under that kind of insubordination.

It was when he had come in such close contact with the German Paratroopers that he had begun to feel a kind of homesickness. At that point the purposes of the Benedictine Commando had still seemed worthwhile. Rudi shared one characteristic with Richard; he would have made considerable personal sacrifice to prevent the Monastery being needlessly destroyed. But the infamous leaflet had put an end to that.

Now he had a plan which would enable him to recover his honour, at any rate in his own eyes. If it led to his death it would be more acceptable than an ignominious death in a concentration camp or suicide by his own hand.

It took him several hours to find the corpse he had seen lying half hidden near the mule track. He had to lie low whenever the mule trains were coming up, and once had to move fast to avoid being challenged by a reconnaissance patrol. It was midnight before he found the young German. He had been killed by a shell when he'd turned off the track to relieve himself.

He was about the same build as Rudi and the photograph in his identity document showed a not dissimilar face. Rudi had to harden himself to strip the uniform off the stiff body, complete with the vital identity disc. The cold was intense enough to set his teeth chattering as he took off his own uniform and put on the dead soldier's. When that was done he had shed the identity of Rudolf von Reifenbach and donned that of Gefreiter Hermann Brendel. He concealed the cast-off uniform under a rock and made his way back to the track.

It was at about 3 a.m. that the sentry guarding one of the paths leading up Monastery Hill from Cassino saw an unarmed

200

figure come swaying towards him. When challenged he replied in German. The sentry escorted him with raised hands to the sergeant in his section command post.

Rudi liked the look of the sergeant, an honest soldier of the old school. He decided to tell him a story that was very close to the truth, concealing his real rank and name.

'Gestapo bastards!' the sergeant growled, his suspicions allayed. 'Yes, you can stay with us. God knows we need every man we can get. I'll fix you up with some job where you won't be noticed. How do you fancy being a stretcher-bearer?'

'I'd rather carry a gun.'

'You needn't think it's a soft job. Not in the parachutists.'

The sergeant looked up at the gradually lightening sky. 'Better come inside the cave. Tommy usually shells this hill before he has his breakfast.'

Platoon headquarters was in a small cave about six feet wide. The Panzer-Grenadiers who had occupied it had further excavated it and piled rocks at the entrance. By the light of the German version of a Tilley lamp Rudi could see that the sergeant was a surprisingly studious-looking type, not at all the kind of tough you associate with the Paratroopers. He wore spectacles, had a sensitive mouth and thoughtful brows. But the other soldiers in the small headquarters were little more than boys.

'You'll find the paras are different.' The sergeant had produced a Bavarian pipe with an ornamented bowl and was filling it with tobacco. 'You see, in our parachuting days we all used to jump together – the officer first. Colonel Heilman jumped with us at Catania and he was first out. We all muck in. At Crete the cooks and bottlewashers who had never jumped in their lives piled into the air transports so as not to be left out. You've joined a family, my friend, but a family who live dangerously.'

'That suits me.'

The sergeant's spectacles glinted in the light as he studied Rudi's face thoughtfully. 'You speak with an Austrian accent. What formation were you with, Hoch und Deutschmeister? No, don't tell me. I'd rather not know. It's no good putting you in a combat unit. Us Paratroopers have different ways of doing things and you'd never get away with it. But you'd fit nicely into the Medical Section.'

'Can't you fix it for me to be in the front line?'

'You'll be in the front line, *mein lieber Freund*, make no mistake about that. I'm going to send you to Colonel Dr Elders as a volunteer stretcher-bearer. Listen. There goes Iron Gustav.'

'What?'

The sergeant laughed at Rudi's perplexed expression. 'He's the spotter plane for the Allied artillery. He's up early this morning. That's a sure sign it's going to be an eventful day.'

*

At five o'clock in the morning the Abbot was wrapped up warmly, ready to venture out into the pre-dawn light with his German-speaking secretary. He was spared the ordeal. The German officer came into the building for the meeting.

His name was Leutnant Deiber. While the secretary interpreted he stated stiffly that he had brought his superiors' instructions for the total evacuation of the Monastery.

The Abbot made the pathetic and rather naive suggestion that the refugees and the monks should be allowed to go in opposite directions – the refugees towards the town of Cassino, the monks towards Rome.

'That is absolutely out of the question,' Deiber told him. 'Major Schmidt has arranged for the mule-track leading down to the Via Casilina through San Richizio-Colloqiuo to be opened for you between midnight and 5 a.m. tomorrow. You and your people must make absolutely no noise. Anyone attempting to go towards the Allied lines will be shot.'

'Not until midnight?' The Abbot shook his head and glanced at the lightening windows. 'That may be too late.'

'It is the best we can do. It will soon be daylight. Already there is too much visibility for so many people to come down now. That would be certain to attract enemy fire.'

The Abbot shrugged and spread his hands in a gesture of resignation. Then he saw the German officer's stern face soften. His voice was different as he put a question to the secretary. Diamare did not try to hide his surprise as he listened to the translation.

'He is asking if he would be allowed to visit the church.'

'The church?' The old man looked into the eyes of the officer and realized that beneath the uniform and the assumed insensitiveness was a young man far from home.

'Of course,' he said. It was a Benedictine tradition never to refuse hospitality, and certainly not a request which indicated sincere religious convictions.

Leutnant Deiber was accompanied to the door of the empty church. The interior was dark. Using his regulation pocket-torch to light his way he stepped inside and stood in silent contemplation for a few minutes.

He was the last person to say a prayer beneath that superbly vaulted and frescoed ceiling.

19

'Full many a glorious morning have I seen.' Wilfrid was endeavouring to recall a sonnet which he had learned by heart on the Garigliano. He'd been waiting a long time for a suitable day to declaim it. 'Flatter the mountain tops with sovereign eye.'

Lance-Bombardier Bliss turned round. He was shaving as best he could with half a pint of water heated in a food tin. The left side of his face was white with lather.

'Did you say something, sir?'

'Just talking to myself.' Wilfrid lowered his voice before groping in his mind for the next line. 'Kissing with golden face the valleys green, Gilding pale streams with heavenly alchemy.'

Dante's tail swished to and fro. He was squatted on his hind quarters, front legs braced and trembling slightly. He stared up into his master's face, one ear cocked, desperately trying to interpret. He had caught the change in rhythm, the slightly different tone in Wilfrid's voice.

'All right, Dan. We'll be getting some breakfast in a minute.'

They were under the shelter of a large rock, screened from the German positions. Wilfrid was sitting on a ledge gazing down the slopes towards the Rapido Valley. The sun was fifteen degrees up from the horizon and its warmth was already enough to raise steam from the leaves of evergreen plants. Globules of ice gleamed like crystal buds on the bare branches of the Judas trees which grew in profusion. The sheen of light sparkled from rock and stone.

Overhead the sky was an elusive blue of wonderful purity. It faded to a frosty grey closer to the earth. From somewhere on the ridge came the faint sound of music. Some signaller had tuned his set to a civilian station. The Air from Bach's Suite in D. Wilfrid tried to locate the source, but could not pinpoint it. The Germans were close enough for it to be one of their sets. He thought that the Air had never sounded so beautiful.

It was strange that he should experience such a welling up of happiness at this moment and in this place. There *was* here something far more deeply interfused, some motion or spirit that impelled all objects of all thought –

'Grub up, sir!' the TARA called out cheerfully.

'Good show,' Wilfrid responded. He did not get up to go over to the cookhouse at once. He clung to the fleeting thought as one clings to a dream that fades too rapidly. Perhaps it had something to do with contrast. The ugliness, the fear and danger of war made beauty all the more intense when it appeared. The closer to death the closer to truth.

The Lance-Bombardier and the Technical Assistant exchanged a meaning glance and cast their eyes eloquently towards heaven.

'Come on, Dan.' Wilfrid got to his feet. Dante careered round in small circles and then fell into place at his master's heels.

To the rear the Royal Sussex were settling down to another day of waiting, made endurable by such activities as were possible in the circumstances. They cleaned their weapons, washed and shaved with the severely rationed water, read *Eighth Army News* and laughed at the latest cartoon of the Two Types, smoked the cigarettes which the Americans had given them, wrote letters home.

Back at battalion headquarters the CO was relaying to

brigade the information gained from his patrols. A deserter who had come in during the night, thought to be from 4th Parachute Regiment, was being sent back for further interrogation. Those wounded on patrol had been successfully evacuated. The battalion was desperately in need of grenades. Mortar bombs were also in short supply but it had been found that American bombs could be fired from German and Italian mortars captured by the Royal Sussex in North Africa.

When Glennie offered to go back to Brigade HQ to discuss that night's attack, Lovett told him to stay put. The Brigadier would come up himself to Tac HQ at 1400 hours for a conference.

By half-past nine Wilfrid was back in the OP, staring across Snakeshead Ridge at the Monastery. The faint morning breeze was in his face. It brought with it the sickly sweet odour of the unrecovered corpses in the disputed territory ahead. Jerry and Tommy both smelled much the same when they were dead. The sunlight was illuminating the Monastery with a golden luminosity which made it stand out against Monte Trocchio behind it. The light appeared to come from within the stones themselves.

Only gradually did Wilfrid become aware of the low rumble. It began as a distant drumming that might have issued from the bowels of the earth. Then, as it grew in volume, he realized that it was coming from the sky and recognized the sound of aircraft engines.

'It's Flying Fortresses!' Lance-Bombardier Bliss pointed towards the sky to southwards. 'Look, you can see the vapour trails.'

Wilfrid followed the direction of the pointing finger. Very high up, at eighteen thousand feet, he could see the faint trails, like lines ruled with white chalk on the blue background. And at the forefront of each trail the silvery outline of an aircraft. They were flying in echelons of three abreast. Each trio was followed along the same ruled white lines by more and more and more.

'B25s,' announced Lance-Bombardier Bliss, who had excellent sight. 'They're coming this way.'

The rumble grew to a roar and the watchers craned their necks further and further back. Dante had started shivering. He slunk under Wilfrid's legs, pressing himself against the back of his calves.

When the leading echelon seemed to be directly overhead the first bombs were released. They tumbled lazily from the bomb-bays, flying at first like torpedoes parallel with the aircraft. Then, as their fins found a purchase on the air, their noses dipped and they plummeted towards the building on the hill-top far below.

The first strike hit the church fair and square. Wilfrid observed the pulverizing explosion just on the far side of the green dome. Fragmented masonry spurted into the air. A grotesque sculpturing of black smoke reared itself into the air. The green dome had miraculously survived the first bomb, but it had only seconds to live. When the smoke from the second flight of bombs rose, the church, the dome were gone.

Then came explosion after explosion. Vast as it was, the building shuddered at every merciless punch. The noise was deafening. Dante was whimpering and even hardened soldiers squirmed deeper into their foxholes.

At Tac HQ Glennie picked up the field telephone which connected him to Brigade. He was prepared to deliver a very forthright comment but the Brigadier forestalled him: 'All right, old boy. We didn't know, either.'

A huge pall of smoke now rose hundreds of feet over the Monastery. The hill seemed to have become a volcano. Some of the bombs were falling outside the walls. The orange flash of their bursting was bright in the smoky gloom. The quirky effect of the blast drew masonry towards the centre of the explosion for an instant of time before hurling it outwards.

Staring in horrified fascination Wilfrid felt the hair on the back of his head stiffen; following one salvo of bombs a preternatural spectre had suddenly taken form amid the desolation. It bore the appearance of a phantom palace. The eldritch, ephemeral shape stood there for a second before it was shivered by the next burst and vanished.

From Monte Trocchio the cameras of the news-reel crews were turning, recording the spectacle for the delectation of audiences in the cinemas of bombed and beleaguered Britain. General Alexander, watching from Cervaro, successfully concealed his true feelings. He felt unhappy about the picnic atmosphere which had been created by the jubilant reactions of some of his staff.

In the American lines to the left of the New Zealanders the

troops entrenched behind the Rapido were cheering at the spectacle of the hated Monastery being blown to smithereens.

Mark Clark had declined to join the party watching the show from Cervaro. By remaining in his headquarters at Presenzano, fifteen miles away, he hoped to dissociate himself from the event. In this he was not entirely successful, for one group of aircraft mistook their target and bombed the army commander's headquarters. They caused no casualties but they earned Mark Clark's severe displeasure. His pet bitch had just presented him with a litter of puppies and was seriously distressed by these near misses. Another bomb-aimer unloaded his high explosive somewhat nearer the target on the unsuspecting heads of 4th Indian Division, who suffered forty casualties.

It so happened that at the time of the attack von Senger was paying a visit to the commander of 90th Panzer Grenadier Division. Baade's concrete pillbox was under the south-western slopes of Monastery Hill. As the bombs began to fall both Generals came out to stare in amazement at the rising pall of smoke. They were at a loss to comprehend this massive onslaught on a target where they knew there were no German troops.

The same morning in Rome a future Pope, Monsignor Giovanni Battista Montini, received a visitor in the offices of the Deputy Secretary of State at the Vatican. It was the German Ambassador who had come to inform him that the Germans were making no military use of Montecassino.

The first attack by Flying Fortresses had lasted for an hour and a half – from nine-thirty till eleven. During that period 135 aircraft had flown over the target. They had dropped 257 tons of high explosive in 500-pound bombs, topped up with 59 tons of incendiaries in 100-pound bombs.

One of the Flying Fortresses turned back early and six brought their bombs back. Perhaps not all the air crews relished the assignment and some found ways of not bombing this most defenceless of targets.

During the half-hour lull which followed the first attack, the Allied artillery poured shell-fire into the hulk of the stricken Monastery.

After the heavy bombers it was the turn of the mediums – Mitchells and Marauders. They carried heavier bombs and they flew much lower. Their attack began at about half-past ten.

During the next three hours, flying over the hill in echelons of six, they dropped 283 bombs, each of 1,000 pounds.

Once again a number of crews had excuses for not bombing the target. Of 70 Mitchells which set out, 23 returned early 'for unknown reasons'.

Nevertheless, the results were impressive. When the smoke finally drifted away towards the blue sky the profile of the Monastery was considerably lower. Wilfrid, watching from his OP, felt almost physically sick. There was something obscene about the grey-white pile of rubble, from which here and there rose up the remnant of a wall or a row of windows opening onto emptiness. There was the putrefaction of leprosy about it, a suggestion of decayed teeth in a decomposing skull.

'Cor blimey O'Reilly!' Lance-Bombardier Bliss handed the binoculars back to Wilfrid. 'Makes our 25-pounders look a bit stupid, don't it? I wouldn't give much for the chances of any Jerries in there.'

Wilfrid nodded his agreement and stooped to ruffle Dante behind the ears. It did not seem possible that anything could have lived through that holocaust.

*

After Prime and Terce the monks celebrated Mass. It happened to be the Mass appropriate for Santa Scholastica, because this was the week of her feast-day.

Even in this time of crisis and uncertainty the Opus Dei remained their first priority. Perhaps it would be truer to say, more than ever in this time of crisis. For the act of worship provided them with a structure of comfort and security in a world which had become terribly hostile and bewildering.

Baldovino had failed to buttonhole the Abbot or the *segretario* before the sequence of religious offices had begun. Richard, after failing to raise any response from Mignano on the morning transmission, found him waiting outside the Chapel of St Benedict, listening impatiently to the chanting voices within. Maria was beside him. She had left her patients in the care of Laura for a while and escaped to have some coffee and bread. She had been drawn towards the Chapel by the sound of the singing. When she realized that Mass was being celebrated she felt impelled to remain. She needed all the spiritual strength and comfort she could get.

When she saw Richard she laid a finger on her lips, then

stretched out her hand and drew him close to her. They stood together, listening.

Baldovino clicked his tongue in exasperation when the Abbot decided to go directly on with the offices of Sext and Nones. This whole performance was going to last an hour.

'*Porcamiseria!*' he muttered, and earned a disapproving frown from Maria. It had just gone nine-thirty when Richard began trying to identify a new sound in his ears. It was muted, yet powerful enough to make the floor beneath his feet vibrate. The source seemed to be somewhere up above and the volume of sound was increasing. In the chapel the monks were kneeling for the Marian antiphon which would end their devotions. They had just uttered the words '*pro nobis Christum exora*', when an explosion of mind-scattering force reverberated through the building. The sound was magnified and re-echoed by the long, empty corridors.

Maria screamed and clapped her hands to her ears. Then, blindly and instinctively, she flung herself into Richard's arms. He held her tight and knew in that moment that the mission of the Benedictine Commando had failed.

As a second detonation followed the first and the brutal, indescribably violent explosions succeeded one another, a figure in a black cassock burst from the door of the Chapel and rushed for the stairs leading to the upper level. It was Nessuno, going in search of Laura. Richard had seen fear on men's faces before but the monk's expression conveyed an emotion that went beyond physical terror.

Richard dragged Maria forcibly to the shelter of the crypt. Passing the Chapel door he saw that the monks inside were still on their knees. The Abbot, believing that death was imminent, was giving them absolution. From somewhere overhead came the sickening sound of masonry crumbling and the screams of terrified people.

*

The thunder of explosions overhead lasted for an hour and a half – at least, by the normal measurement of time. In the unearthly silence that followed the last bomb, the drone of aircraft engines gradually receded till it died away in the distance.

During a brief lull the Abbot had taken some of the monks to his own room, which he believed would be safer. As they gradually realized that the bombers had gone the braver spirits among them came up to survey the damage. Though it was hardly the total devastation desired by the advocates of aerial bombardment the injury was not slight. A high proportion of the bombs had fallen outside the walls. The upper floors had absorbed most of the damage inflicted by those that had dropped on the actual Monastery. Here and there fires started by the incendiaries were raging. The facade of the church still stood, but beyond it was empty sky. The Luca Giordano frescoes, the marble inlay, the Catarinozzi organ, the Florentine choir stalls no longer existed. The Bramante Cloister was a shambles. The statue of St Benedict stood headless, that of St Scholastica had vanished. The great staircase had suffered a direct hit and was like a badly organized quarry. The Loggia del Paradiso had gone sky-high. Men and women who had been caught in the open by the first bombs still lay there, skulls burst asunder by the suction effect of blast, their blood and brains spewed out on the stones.

From beneath the ruins of the church came muffled cries. When it had collapsed some hundreds of people had been buried beneath the mountain of rubble. Most were dead, some were still alive. None were destined to be dug out before 1947.

At this time a number of those who had survived the first hour and a half fled from the building. The Allied artillery observers assumed they were German soldiers and directed their fire at them. So, many who escaped the bombs perished under the shells.

Maria had insisted on Baldovino taking her to the chapel-ward. It was practically empty. Those who still had the capacity to move had fled, either to the illusory safety of some other shelter or to the slopes of Monastery Hill.

'I must go and see if there are wounded up above, Baldovino. Will you come with me?'

On the upper floor they saw a figure in a black cassock near the bakery working feverishly at a pile of fallen rubble, lifting huge stones and throwing them behind him, clawing at débris with his bare hands. His fingers were bleeding, his cassock covered with dust.

Baldovino stumbled over the stones towards him. *'Per l'amor di Dio, Padre, cosa sta cercando di fare?'*

Nessuno turned round. His eyes were wild, his lips creased back from his panting mouth.

'She is buried in there. She went to find Franco and the ceiling collapsed behind her.'

Maria was calling Baldovino. She was kneeling beside a man whose leg had been crushed by a block of masonry.

'If you could lift the stone off his leg, Baldovino, I can pull him clear.'

It was not safe to be out there in the open. The artillery were more accurate than the Flying Fortresses and most of their shells were falling within the Monastery. Richard and Nick, returning from the south-west corner, saw Maria in the Bramante Cloister with Baldovino, struggling to lift an enormous block of masonry. They went to lend a hand, and as they did so Richard again heard the rumble of approaching aircraft.

'They're coming again! You'll have to leave him, Maria. Everybody take cover quickly.'

He dragged Maria by force from the wounded and trapped man, who watched his saviours depart with an expression of hopeless resignation. As they hurried towards the stairs leading down to their crypt they met the Sacrist, Agostino, emerging from the doorway. He was bearing in his hands a platter covered with a white cloth. It was the Host. He had braved the shell-fire to go down to the Chapel of St Benedict to collect it from the altar. Now he was taking it to the Abbot's room. With their whole world collapsing in ruins about them, with hundreds of dead and wounded all around, with shell-fire descending upon them and fresh cohorts of bombers drawing closer and closer, the monks still clung to their priorities. The Apocalypse was at hand and they were going to celebrate the Divine Office.

Baldovino, following last behind the others, saw the priestly figure emerge and drew back with instinctive reverence to let him pass. As a consequence he was still outside the doorway when the first of the 1,000-pound bombs struck.

Inside the doorway Richard heard the heavy concussion and Baldovino's instant scream. He dashed back to the doorway. The Sacrist was hurrying unscathed across the cloister, still bearing the platter with its white cloth, but Baldovino lay writhing on the ground, clutching his thigh with his hands. Blood was spurting from a ragged wound.

'Nick! Baldo's been hit. Give me a hand.'

Feeling desperately exposed the two men ran out, lifted the Italian and carried him into the comparative shelter of the stairway. Bombs were now falling in salvos, but most were penetrating deep into the building before exploding. Richard had time for one quick glance upwards. He recognized the aircraft as Mitchells. They were flying much lower than the Fortresses. As he looked he saw three clusters of lethal black objects tumble from their bomb-bays.

'Let's get him down to Maria's hospital,' Richard shouted to Nick. 'This stuff they're dropping is much heavier than before.'

Force was lent to his words by the almost simultaneous impact of half a dozen thousand-pounders. The sensation was more like an earthquake than an explosion. The noise was too great for their ears to register. Richard felt his skull stretched and then a singing inside his head. But the ceiling over the stairway held.

Ruthlessly they carted Baldovino down to the chapel-ward. He was in a state of shock and was not yet feeling the full sharpness of pain. His wound left a trail of blood on the stairs and floor.

They laid him on one of the beds abandoned by the fleeing patients. Maria, cool and in complete control of herself, cut away his trousers from round the wound. Baldovino turned away from the sight of his own dirty, mangled flesh, tissue and blood. Maria looked closely at the thigh. Then she thrust a wad of torn-up sheet onto it, pushing hard to staunch the flow of blood.

'There is a big splinter embedded in his flesh.' She twisted her head towards Richard. He was standing behind her, watching. 'I am going to have to extract it. Will you hold this pad in place?'

He knelt down and pressed on the rolled-up sheet. Blood was being pumped from the wound and the pad was being rapidly stained red. Overhead the crash of bombs and the heavy rumble of collapsing masonry was unceasing. At any moment one of the four-foot long projectiles could come nose-diving into the chapel.

When Maria knelt beside Richard he saw that she had a short, pointed kitchen-knife in her hand.

She had gone absolutely white. Baldovino began to shout

212

'No! No!' He tried to heave himself up, thrusting the upper part of his body forward with his hands before falling back in despair.

'Have you any whisky, Richa?'

'No.'

'Any strong drink?'

Richard shook his head. 'I had a flask in the car but I left it.'

'You and Nico will have to hold him. You must be pitiless.'

'Oh, Jesus!'

'It is to save his life, Richa.'

Richard found it hard to look at Baldovino's tormented face. 'Sorry about this, Baldo, but we have to do it. Nick, you take his legs.'

While Nick knelt and put all his weight on Baldovino's legs, Richard sat on his chest. Maria bit her lip and then, after a second's hesitation, removed the wad. As she inserted the blade and probed for the splinter Baldovino's body squirmed with tormented strength. He began to scream. Resolutely Maria continued to probe. Then the body suddenly became limp.

'He's fainted.'

Maria nodded. She began to work faster, cutting and feeling. Then, at last, with a levering movement she gouged out a hard object about three inches long. Before Baldovino recovered consciousness she had used most of her remaining disinfectant to clean the wound, had placed a fresh wad over the gash to stop the blood and bound it in place with a tight bandage.

'That is the best we can do for the moment. I will have to think of some way of stitching it. If I can find a needle and strong thread I will need you again.'

'I'd like to get everyone down to our crypt.' Richard found himself shouting as a fresh blast brought a rain of plaster from the ceiling. 'It's the safest place in this building.'

Richard and Nick carried Baldovino down to the crypt and laid him on a palliasse. Maria brought what she could in the way of dressings and appliances from her improvised ward. It was a case of charity beginning nearest home. The pathetic human beings who had been unable to flee after the first attack were beyond help. Baldo's life could be saved, but only if Maria gave him her full attention.

Richard had learned a number of good soldiers' practices

from Mehan. One of them was always to carry a needle and thread stuck into the reverse side of his battledress blouse. He remembered it now and offered it rather apologetically to Maria.

She stared in astonishment and then burst out laughing at the incongruity of it.

'Oh, Richa! You English are even armed with needle and thread?'

The moment of light relief was brief. None of them relished subjecting Baldovino to yet more suffering. But he was more resolute now. The removal of the splinter had eased him, though he was still grey with pain.

'I can stand it. You need not sit on me this time.'

Nick had gone on a raiding expedition to the Chapel of St Benedict. He came back with a goblet of Communion wine and handed it to Baldovino.

'Knock it back. I don't know if it's been blessed or not but it will boost your spirits.'

Baldovino eagerly swallowed the wine, rubbed a hand across his colourless lips. He lay back and closed his eyes.

'All right, Maria. I'm ready.'

*

Richard did not feel in the least guilty about remaining down in the crypt during that second appalling bombardment. To judge by the sounds the building was being pounded to rubble. Even if they escaped a direct hit there seemed every chance that they would be buried alive.

Baldovino, after the ordeal of his stitching, had fallen into a state that was half sleep, half delirium. Maria knelt beside him, cooling his forehead with wet cloths from her meagre supply of water, monitoring the gradually lessening seepage of blood from the wound.

From time to time Richard and Nick exchanged a wordless look. There was no need to speak. Each knew what the other was thinking.

The second attack lasted twice as long as the first. When at last the shock waves and the echoing explosions ceased the silence was threatening, ominous. From up above there came no sound. Richard and Nick got up from their crouched position leaning against the wall. The question now was, had they been buried alive? They shook off their stupor and pushed their way out of the crypt through the gloom and dust.

By good fortune the Toretta under which they had been sheltering was the least damaged part of the building. The staircase leading up from it was intact and the entrance unobstructed. But once out in the open they saw that the Monastery of St Benedict was no more than a hulk. The only high wall standing was at the north-west corner and that was only a facade whose gaping windows were backed by sky. Here and there, as in the entrance cloister or at the former entrance to the church, the remains of an inner wall still stood. Whole areas of the site resembled a child's collapsed sand-castle. In places, horribly, the windows opened not onto sky but onto the rubble piled within. The internal cloisters were heaped with piles of stones, fragments of carved arches. Whereas the first bombs had accounted for the church, it had taken the thousand-pounders to bring down the principal blocks. Yet even they had failed to split the solid base on which the whole structure was founded.

Making their way back to the crypt they met Padre Nessuno. He had Laura and Franco with him. All three were covered from head to foot in white dust.

'It was a miracle, a miracle!' Nessuno, seemingly oblivious to the desolation around him, was triumphant. There was a strange light in his eyes as if some belief, held only tentatively until now, had been confirmed. 'One of the bombs opened the way for me and I was able to get through to them!'

There had been other miracles too, as Richard learned when he overheard the *Sagrista* and the *Segretario* telling each other what they had found. Not only had the most holy place in the Monastery, St Benedict's cell, escaped damage, but a heavy bomb, landing within two feet of the casket under the high altar containing the bones of Saints Benedict and Scholastica, had failed to explode. And though hundreds of refugees lay dead underneath the ruins, not one of the monks had even been scratched.

'Remember,' Agostino pointed out, 'that our Founder begged God to spare his monks, even if the Monastery was destroyed.'

An eight-inch shell landed on the south-east corner. The explosion sounded insignificant after the bombs, but Richard knew that these big American pieces were real killers.

'You will not be spared if you stay out in the open,' he advised the monks. 'It is going to be the turn of the guns now.'

They stared at him, surprised that a bedraggled refugee could speak with such authority. A second shell landing nearer confirmed the warning and prevented any questions. The monks retreated towards the shelter of the Abbot's quarters. Richard followed Nick as he made for the stairway that led to their crypt.

At the entrance he stopped and turned back towards the shambles that had once been the Abbey of Montecassino.

'Look at that, Nick!' He swept his arm towards the devastation. 'We've proved ourselves worse than the Nazis. You and I are fighting for the wrong bloody side.'

*

When they returned to the crypt they found that the lower levels of the Torretta were thronged with bomb-crazed refugees. The survivors had sought safety in the only part of the building which remained standing. At least three hundred of them were packed on the main staircase that led down to the ceremonial door. Tons of masonry on the outside prevented the door from being opened.

Not long afterwards the Abbot and the six remaining monks foresook the perilous sanctuary they had chosen in the Abbot's room. Bearing as much provender as they could carry they too made for the Torretta, settling themselves in the Chapel.

Maria had managed to protect the crypt from intrusion. Once Richard and Nick had rejoined her it was evident that there was no room to spare in the small space.

'What is going to happen?' Maria asked as the two men squatted down on their palliasses.

'What can we do except wait? The infantry will attack tonight. By tomorrow morning this place will be occupied either by the British or the Germans. Personally, I could not care less which it is.'

She studied him with concern for a long time after he had spoken. All the spirit had gone out of him. He was almost sick with fatigue and disillusionment, but she also felt that there was something else.

From the stairway came a hideous, sustained screaming. Two men were carrying down a woman whose feet and hands

216

had been severed. Maria made as if to go to help her. Richard put out a hand to stop her.

'Stay put, Maria. We must not attract attention to ourselves. If any of these people find out that we are Allied soldiers they'll tear us limb from limb.'

The waiting was not easy. From the crowded staircase came cries and lamentations. Overhead portions of the buildings were still collapsing, the thunder of falling masonry echoing through the Torretta and causing fresh panic. Baldovino had become feverish and was muttering deliriously. He was very restless and frighteningly pallid from loss of blood, but at least the heavy bleeding from the wound had stopped. Beyond the crypt the monks were moving about among the refugees, doing what they could to help them.

At eight o'clock Leutnant Deiber returned, this time not alone. The German propaganda machine was already at work. The Allies had presented Goebbels with a wonderful opportunity and he intended to make a meal of this 'desecration of one of the most sacred sites in Europe'. Deiber had brought a paper for the Abbot to sign, testifying that at the time of the bombing there had been no soldiers in the Monastery. He read out a high-sounding declaration which stated that Hitler, at the Pope's request, had asked the Americans for a truce to be observed so that the refugees and monks could be evacuated, the latter to the Vatican.

Abbot Diamare signed. Deiber departed with his paper. He was not seen again.

The survivors of the bombing settled down to endure a night of terror. Every now and again came the rumble of some other part of the building collapsing. Baldovino babbled nonsense. Maria never stopped cooling his forehead, checking the improvised dressing on his wound, easing him into a more comfortable position.

Nick was silent. He sat with his back to the wall of the crypt, covertly studying his young friend. He found himself suffering for the bitterness and disillusion which he could see written on Richard's face. He would have liked to find words to dispel the younger man's sense of failure, his rejection of his own cause. But he knew it was still too soon. So he watched and listened, trying to interpret every sound from within or outside the Monastery.

Whenever Richard dozed he fancied he heard knockings,

scrapings, scratching of nails, agonized pleas for release. He waited in vain for the sound of the great attack which must surely follow the 'softening up' of the Monastery. But from the town of Cassino came only the same sporadic noises as on previous nights.

And from Snakeshead Ridge the thud of grenades and the blare of machine guns told of a small-scale battle which came no closer.

None of it made any sense.

20

The grey dawn had ended a long night in the ruined Monastery. The steadfast demeanour of the monks under their aged Abbot contrasted with the hysteria of the refugees. Those who had remained most sane were haunted by the knowledge that hundreds of people lay buried under the débris. Many underground passages where survivors might still be alive would be inaccessible till the bulldozers came. A major disaster had occurred, comparable in scale to the blitzing of a town. But here in the middle of a battlefield there was no hope of help. The armies remained locked in their positions. Neither Germans nor Allies felt any responsibility for the plight of the wretched people in the stricken building. The expected attack had not materialized and for some reason the Germans had not moved in to occupy the ruins.

The coming of dawn saw the departure of some of the monks and most of the remaining refugees. Nearly all those who were capable of walking crept out into the grey light. Many perished in the shell-fire. Some were mistakenly shot by the German machine-gunners. The majority simply vanished into the landscape. A handful even found their way down into the town of Cassino. Anything to escape from the gaunt hulk of the Monastery. They knew now that no scruples would spare it and they dreaded to hear again the sound of the bombers.

Behind them they left their own helpless kinsfolk. Husbands had fled, leaving their wives. The old and feeble had been forsaken by the fit and strong. Parents had abandoned their injured children. The wounded were left without succour.

The bombers had destroyed more than masonry.

An icy wind was blowing over the ruins. Every now and again another wall collapsed, another vault caved in. Shell-fire was making it hazardous to venture into what remained of the open cloisters. The one safe place was the most ancient. Some said afterwards that it was because the Torretta was built on the huge cyclopean blocks of the primitive fort. Others affirmed that an almighty hand had diverted the bombs from the cell where St Benedict had worked and prayed a millennium and a half ago.

It was in this cell that the Abbot and the three monks who had remained with him took refuge. They had waited in vain for the return of Leutnant Deiber. The old man now saw that talk of the truce had been no more than a trick to persuade him to sign the paper. Abandoned by all men they prepared to face death in the spiritual presence of their Founder. *Non timebo mala quoniam in mecum est.* The accoutrements of their worship were destroyed or buried. All they had left was a breviary. Armed with this they intoned the morning offices, grouped round the altar and the precious de Matteis Madonna.

There were now five others with Richard in the little crypt. Nessuno had asked if Laura and Franco could join his group. They were not going to recover easily from the ordeal of their entombment. Franco would not consent to be separated from his mother. He spent the night clasped in her arms. Every time he fell into a fitful sleep he would wake up crying out in terror.

Baldovino became quieter and as the night wore on he seemed to sleep. Even Maria closed her eyes for half an hour at a time, but at first light she was already changing the dressings on the wound.

'Do you think he is going to live?' Richard whispered.

She put the old dressing to her nose and sniffed. She glanced at Baldovino's face before answering. His eyes were closed.

'I do not know. He has lost so much blood. He needs a transfusion. At least the bleeding has stopped but I am very afraid of gangrene and infection. If I could go outside, there is a moss that is said to prevent infection.'

'That sounds like an old wives' tale.'

'You do not believe in such things? Not even when you have seen miracles happen before your eyes?'

'Miracles?'

'Yes. Did you not hear what Padre Nessuno said? A bomb landed half a metre from the relics of St Benedict and St Scholastica and did not explode. And the cell of St Benedict is untouched. Not even one of the monks has been harmed. And still you do not believe in miracles!'

Her eyes flashed angrily as she spoke. He watched her roll up the dirty dressing with its greenish stains and put it aside.

Before he realized it he was saying: 'I really love you, Maria.'

Her head turned sharply. She searched his face and the two little lines appeared between her brows. Then she picked up the fresh dressing and applied it to the wound. Baldovino stirred and groaned.

'Maria.'

'Yes.'

'If we ever get out of here –'

She began to wrap the strip of torn sheet round Baldovino's thigh. 'Yes?'

'I must say this because I may never have the chance again. You are the most wonderful person I have ever met – or even dreamed about.'

She did not answer at once. Her head was bowed and he could not see her face. She finished the bandage, tied her knot and then sat back on her heels, staring at the huge blocks of stone that lined the crypt.

'I used to have a dream too. When I was a girl. I never really believed the dream could come true. But it did.' Her eyes moved to his face. 'But it did. I knew it that very first time in the farmhouse.'

★

Tuker's demand had been met for the Monastery to be levelled

220

before 4th Indian Division's attack. The bombers had done their work, though admittedly only ten per cent of the bombs released by the aircraft had fallen on the building.

The big attack, which would have been the logical sequence to such a massive air strike, turned out, in terms of numbers, to be a very small affair. It was mounted by only two hundred and fifty infantrymen, led by twelve officers. That was the total available strength of the 1st Battalion the Royal Sussex. The rest of the New Zealand Corps and their supporting arms stood by and waited for Glennie's men to clear Point 593. Fourteen infantry battalions and six hundred tanks remained impotent because a regiment of Paratroopers refused to be dislodged from the ridge dominating the northern approach to the Monastery. Even the eight hundred pieces of artillery available to support the attack were of little use to the men on Snakeshead. The Germans were too close to the start-line for the usual barrage to be fired. The gunners could only help by shelling enemy forming-up areas, supply routes, gun and mortar emplacements.

C Battery of the Greenshire Yeomanry had been given the task of neutralizing the machine-gun posts on a feature named Two Tits. It lay to the west of Snakeshead. Fire from that direction would enfilade the advancing troops.

Wilfrid had confirmed the gunnery programme with Glennie at 2110 hours, just before the CO left for his forward Tac HQ. It was the kind of situation which gunners relish least. The 25-pounders, sited on the floor of the Rapido Valley to the east of Snakeshead, would have to fire over the heads of the Royal Sussex with very little margin for error. Wilfrid had registered his targets in daylight, but the GPO's fears had been realized and the ammunition had not come up till after dark. There had been no opportunity to 'lot' it.

'How much crest clearance have you got?' Wilfrid asked his GPO. He had opened up with his own 18 set and was talking on the Greenshire frequency.

'Damn little. If the Royal Sussex were Guardsmen we'd be parting their hair. It's like trying to chip over the roof of a house with a niblick. Why's the attack not going in till 2300?'

'We're waiting for grenades. Everything has to come up by mule train and Jerry is shelling the supply routes.'

Glennie's plan sounded simple. B Company would attack and capture Point 593 from the left. A Company would make a diversionary attack on the right. When B Company had taken the hill, they would send up a Verey light signal, two greens over a red. D Company would then move up onto Point 593 to repel the counter-attack. C Company, so badly mauled the previous night, would remain in reserve.

2300 hours came up on the synchronized watches and still the mules bringing the essential grenades had not arrived. The attack was postponed for half an hour.

At 2330 hours there was still no sign of the mules. The attack was postponed another half hour.

None of this helped the nerves of the men waiting in their slit trenches with bayonets fixed. No chance now of brewing up a quiet 'cuppa chow'. The night was bitterly cold and the fingers that would have to pull triggers on rifles or the pins from grenades were becoming stiff and clumsy. They had got themselves keyed up to go over the top at eleven o'clock. It was hard to summon up the courage all over again to make that suicidal gesture. In low voices the officers and NCOs did what they could to keep up the morale of the men. Here and there a butt-end glowed in the darkness, a low chuckle of suppressed laughter greeted some sally by the platoon wit.

Dante was restless and unusually nervous. He kept standing on his hind legs with his forepaws on Wilfrid's knee, whimpering and looking into his eyes.

'He's a demon for punctuality, is Dan.' Lance-Bombardier Bliss nodded proudly at Dante. 'He knows it's not going right, doesn't he, sir?'

Wilfrid was disturbed by the dog's edginess. He was sure that Dante was trying to tell him something and he could not get the message.

'Down, boy. On your bed. That's a good boy.'

Dante tried one last meaning look, then let his paws slide to the ground. Glumly he lay down on the old sheep's pelt and turned his face to the wall of the slit trench.

At 2330 the mule train arrived. Half of the animals and their precious cargoes had been lost on the journey up from the valley.

'We will attack at 2400,' Glennie told his company commanders. Then he rang through to the Gunner OP. 'We're attacking at 2400 hours.'

As midnight came up there was quiet on and around Snakeshead Ridge. The guns which would support this attack

222

were holding their fire. The eight 25-pounders of Stockwell's battery knew their targets and sights had been carefully tested. The only unknown quantity was the newly delivered ammunition. The term 'gunfire' meant that each gun would fire, reload and fire again as soon as it was ready. By that method the battery could deliver 120 rounds per minute onto the target.

At a minute to midnight the C O came through on the blower to the OP where Wilfrid and the FOO of 31st regiment were waiting.

'Just confirming. We're kicking off in one minute.'

Sixty seconds later, as the sweep hand of his watch came round to the horizontal, Wilfrid heard from down in the valley the distant staccato crack of the 25-pounders opening up. Dante started barking. The German artillery seemed to be answering very swiftly. Shells were landing on Snakeshead Ridge already.

It took five minutes for the information to come back. The Adjutant rang through to the OP on the field telephone from Tac HQ.

'Could you please stop shooting?' he said with extraordinary calm. 'Your shells are landing on our soldiers.'

Wilfrid spoke one word into the set: 'Stop!' To gunners that stark monosyllable was the most imperative word of command.

A moment later the distant chorus of guns was silenced. Out on Snakeshead Ridge there was an ominous hush. Wilfrid got through on the blower to Tac HQ. The CO himself answered.

'Colonel. I understand some short shells landed on your chaps. We're very sorry. We had a new lot of ammo. We think it must be—'

'Can't be helped,' the CO answered tersely. 'It happens to the best. But I think we'll go ahead now without artillery support.'

Ten minutes later, after evacuation of the casualties and some hurried reorganization, the attack went ahead. This time there was no gunfire to make the machine gunners on Two Tits keep their heads down. In the FOP Wilfrid had turned away from his two assistants. He could not bear Lance-Bombardier's eyes on him. Dante jumped up onto his knee and started to lick his face. This time Wilfrid did not stop him. Dante went on licking for a long time. He felt he was helping and there was an intriguing salty flavour on his master's cheeks.

Even at Tac HQ it was hard to tell how the battle was progressing. The darkness was too intense and the ground too broken for there to be meaningful co-ordination. The night was hideous with the detonation of grenades and the roar of machine-gun fire. Streams of tracer slashed the black velvet backcloth. Sometimes came the heavy crump of an exploding mine. Wounded were coming back into the Regimental Aid Post in increasing numbers.

On the right A Company, mounting their diversionary attack, had run up against a forty-foot precipice which was not marked on the map. Edging to their left they encountered a crevasse fifteen foot deep and twenty foot across. The best they could do was go to ground and give supporting fire to help B Company.

B Company, thanks to many feats of individual valour, had destroyed the machine-gun posts on the slopes of Point 593 and got onto the top of the dome-shaped feature. Some of them, in the impetus of their thrust, pushed on past the summit and fell down a precipice. Others, penetrating further, met a party of reinforcements coming up and were liquidated. On the dome itself a fierce hand-to-hand battle with grenade and bayonet was being waged. The reserve company, D Company, was sent in to reinforce.

Then fate played one of its most ironic tricks. A German officer of 3rd Parachute Battalion sent up a light signal. Two greens over a red. It was the same signal as the Royal Sussex had pre-arranged to indicate a withdrawal.

The companies on and around Point 593 thankfully obeyed the signal and extracted themselves. The time was 0130. At 0215 confirmation came in that the enemy was still on Point 593. The attack had failed and in the CO's opinion it was too late to mount another.

Not with what was left of the Royal Sussex. The toll on officers had been very heavy. Only 2 out of the 12 who had started off at midnight now survived. Of the 250 other ranks no less than 130 had been killed, wounded or taken prisoner. In two nights four-fifths of the officers and more than half of the men had become casualties. A fine English battalion which had fought its way through from the beginning of the war had been cut to pieces on Snakeshead Ridge.

And still no major attack had been mounted on the Monastery.

★

It was dark inside the Monastery when the Abbot and his three remaining monks said Matins in the Chapel of St Benedict. Outside, the sky was beginning to turn a sullen grey. The usual early-morning hush lay over Monastery Hill and the battle-grounds around it. It was the second dawn since the bombing. There was still no sign from the Germans and still no advance by the Allies.

In the crypt Richard rubbed sleep from his eyes and shook Nick into wakefulness. Laura was giving Franco some bread and a little watered-down wine. Maria had already lit the lamp and was examining the dressing she had taken off Baldovino. The injured man was carrying on a conversation in his own language with some unseen person. He did not appear to know where he was.

'How is he, Maria?'

She shook her head. 'I feel so helpless! This wound is badly infected, and has started to go gangrenous. That is not surprising. The typhoid infection is everywhere.' She put a hand on his brow. 'His fever is very high. That is putting a great strain on his heart.'

Baldovino's head swivelled and he stared at Richard with his sunken eyes. Richard knew he was seeing someone else.

'*Nessun maggior dolore . . . che ricordarsi della felicità . . . nella miseria.*'

Nessuno had come straight from Matins to reassure himself that Laura and Franco were safe. Franco turned and stretched out his arms to his 'padre'. Nessuno picked him up and hugged him. Before he put him down he met Laura's eyes over the boy's shoulder. Richard marvelled that a woman could endure so much and still preserve that extraordinary serenity and calm beauty. If he had been a painter he would have tried to memorise her face at that moment. Even Leonardo had never captured such an expression of inner fulfilment shining through suffering and apprehension.

Then Nessuno put Franco down and turned to Richard.

'The Abbot has decide to leave the Monastery.'

'When?'

'As soon as it is light.'

225

'Where is he now?'

'In the Chapel of St Benedict.'

Nick asked: 'What does he say?'

Richard translated.

'You'd better go and find out exactly what's happening. If the monks are leaving that's our chance to get out of here.'

'We can't abandon Baldovino.'

'Then we'll take him with us,' Nick said decisively. 'You go and ask the Abbot if he'll agree to us coming with him.'

Richard nodded and made his way to the little chapel.

The Abbot was standing in front of the altar. He had a deep forehead and close-cut grey hair, a slightly pendulous lower lip and overhanging eyebrows. A pair of tortoiseshell glasses lay sideways on his nose and on the back of his head was a small black skull-cap. Richard knew that he was praying, even if he was not kneeling. Or at any rate seeking strength and guidance. In the corner lay the body of an old woman who had died a few moments before. The toothless mouth was open but the eyes had been closed. The lines etched by a lifetime of toil had deepened in the yellow-grey skin.

The Abbot heard Richard's step and turned round.

'Padre Abate,' Richard murmured respectfully.

The Abbot made a gesture with his hand.

'Speak, my son.'

'I have a confession to make to you. I am not a refugee, as I have been pretending to be. I am a British officer.'

The old man started visibly and his eyes hardened into hostility.

'British? Did you come here to guide your bombers to their target?'

'No. I came to try and save the Monastery.'

'To save it?'

Richard briefly explained the purpose of his mission, but did not elaborate on how they had gained access to the Monastery. He did not want to betray the confidence of Padre Nessuno.

'You risked your lives to try and save the Monastery?' The Abbot shook his head in bewilderment.

'Yes, but we failed, Father. I'm even beginning to wonder if we have been fighting on the wrong side in this war.'

'In war all sides are wrong,' the Abbot said angrily. 'There is no right side. It is all evil. Our Lord taught us that nineteen hundred years ago and man has not heeded. Now, look at the world!'

'You do not blame us for deceiving you, then?'

'No, my son.' The Abbot's hand stirred but he did not raise it. 'You have my blessing for what you have tried to do.'

Richard would have liked the blessing to have been administered in the ritual form but he could not bring himself to ask for it.

'Father, what do you intend to do?'

'I have decided to place our lives in the hands of God.'

'You are leaving the Monastery?'

Diamare inclined his head. 'What else can I do? The Germans have evidently forgotten us. And where are the British and Americans?'

'I can't understand what's happening, but I think you've made the right decision, Father. All last night more and more parts of the building were collapsing. Even this Torretta is not safe.'

The Abbot's hand moved to the crucifix hanging on the front of his habit. 'My heart bleeds for those we cannot take with us, but there is nothing more we can do for them. There is usually a lull at first light. We will leave then.'

'Padre Abate.' Richard hesitated and let his eyes go over the Abbot's shoulder to the de Matteis portrait of a young woman propped in its frame on the tiny altar. 'Will you allow me and my three friends to come with you? Our only hope is to pass ourselves off as refugees. If the German catch us they will shoot us as spies.'

'Shoot you?'

'We are soldiers in civilian clothing. We took off our uniforms to enter the Monastery.'

★

'Good,' Nick said, when Richard told him. 'Seven o'clock? That gives us damn little time to get ready. You and I can carry Baldo, Richard. We'll fix up some kind of stretcher.'

'You think the krauts will give him proper medical attention if we take him into one of their posts?'

'I'm not talking about handing him to the krauts.' Nick shook his head in exasperation. 'There's a nice Mercedes-Benz parked down the hill waiting for us. We're going to use the monks and their hangers-on as cover to get out of this place.

227

Then when we're clear we'll peel off and go down by the same trail as we came up. It'll be easier going back down Route 6 than coming up. If we can get Baldo back to the partisans they'll know some Italian hospital where he can be fixed up.'

But when Richard explained what was happening to Maria she shook her head firmly.

'He cannot be moved. The shock and the cold would kill him. He has lost a lot of strength in the night. You have only to look at him.'

Richard had to agree that Baldovino's appearance was ghastly. 'But we can't just leave him. That would be certain death.'

'I will stay with him.'

The quiet statement jolted Richard like a douche of cold water.

'There are other wounded too,' Maria went on. 'I cannot abandon them.'

'Then I will stay too.'

It was Maria's turn to look shocked. 'No, Richa. You are a soldier. If the Germans come they will make you a prisoner, maybe kill you.'

'But I can't go and leave you here! I just can't!'

'You have your duty to do.'

'Damn my duty!' Richard exploded. 'I've had this bloody war.'

Maria put a hand out and placed her fingers on his lips. He might have been seeing for the first time those extraordinarily expressive eyes, the high arched brows, the cropped and resilient Titian hair, the strong cheek-bones now brought into higher relief by fatigue.

'Please, Richa. I ask you this. Each of us has our part to do. Mine is to stay here. Yours is to go, to continue the fight. Please be true to my dream.'

Somewhere up above a gust of wind struck the flank of a tottering wall. The thud of falling stones lasted for nearly half a minute.

Baldovino stirred and opened his eyes.

'*Non mi lasciare! Non mi lasciare!*'

Maria turned her head towards him. '*No, caro. Io non ti lascio mai.*'

Richard took a deep breath. The pain was already in him, the pain of a deep wound which no surgery could heal. He reached for her hands, made her turn to face him.

'If I go now it is only because you ask me. But I will come back when our forces conquer this place. And if I don't find you here I will find you somewhere. You will wait for me?'

'Yes, Richa. For me there will never be anyone else. I promise it.'

*

It was a strange procession which formed up in the passage leading to the door of the Monastery. The rubble blocking it had been cleared away. Outside, the dawn light was growing stronger.

At the head of about three dozen assorted souls stood the old Abbot. For protection against the dangers beyond the door he was armed with the whole armour of God. To symbolise it he bore a large wooden cross. It was less than life-size, but nevertheless heavy enough to be a considerable burden for ageing arms. At his shoulder, ready to support the frail figure, were Martino and Agostino, who had remained by his side through the long ordeal and were ready to share whatever fate now awaited him.

The woman who had lost her legs and hands had been placed on a section of ladder. The two men who had offered to carry her were at either end. Near them a tall, middle-aged peasant had hoisted a small boy onto his shoulders. The boy's brothers had been left on the main staircase; one was on the point of death and the other beyond human help. Behind these were lined up the last of the refugees, torn between their terror of the Monastery and their fear of the bare mountain outside.

Nick and Richard were able to attach themselves to the tail of the column without attracting attention.

Nessuno had Laura on one side and Franco on the other. He was holding each of them tightly by the hand, drawing them forwards as near as possible to the protection of the Cross. He had been watching surreptitiously as Richard took his leave of Maria and had shared the agony in the Englishman's heart. But the sight of the soldier leaving the nurse had ended his own struggle. He knew now what he would have to do.

It was 7.30. The Abbot turned and gave absolution to his followers. Then, holding the cross aloft, he stepped out into the

229

cold light. One by one the others followed him, picking their way over the fallen masonry.

By some chance, or perhaps some miracle, the gunners were leaving the cratered hillside in peace that morning. As the file of people stumbled down towards the church of Sant' Agata the only sounds were the rushing of the icy wind and the strong voices of the monks intoning the fifty-seventh Psalm.

'I am frightened, Padre.' Franco was staring up fearfully at the bleak sky. 'What if the bombers come again?'

'They will not come,' Nessuno told him firmly. 'We are under the protection of the Cross. Remember the words I taught you: In God have I put my trust, I will not be afraid what man can do to me.'

'But where are the Germans?' Laura was peering in all directions. There was nothing to be seen but bomb craters, rocks, thorny bushes and uprooted trees. 'There is nobody in sight! Where are all the soldiers?'

Indeed the utter solitude of the mountain top was uncanny. Had it not been for the occasional crump of an early-morning shell in the Liri Valley it would have been possible to believe that the war had ended and the armies gone home.

'Perhaps this is the truce which the Germans promised us.'

Nessuno turned to look back at the place where he had vowed to live out his life and end his days. He felt his heart contract. The golden building was now a black and jagged husk. At his side Laura stumbled. He put an arm round her waist and drew her closer to him. She looked up into his face in surprise. It was the first time he had ever made a gesture of affection to her in public.

It took nearly an hour for the slow procession to reach the head of the mule-track that led down to the Via Casilina. Nessuno saw the Abbot halt abruptly. Four Paratroopers, in pot-shaped helmets and camouflaged smocks buttoned under their crotches, had scrambled out of their dugout. The machine-gun they were manning covered the approach to the Monastery from the west. They stood there, jaws dropping at the incredible spectacle of the approaching procession – the monks with their black cassocks whipped by the wind, the limbless woman on the improvised stretcher, the tall peasant with a boy astride his shoulders, the straggling band of halt and lame, and at the head of it all the plain wooden Cross. None of this was in any military manual.

230

The Abbot called out, asking them for permission to proceed. They continued to stare in total disbelief. Not one of them could find a word to say. After a moment the Abbot moved on. The rest of the procession followed. As the two men at the tail passed the weapon-pit one of the soldiers, in a gesture of shame or respect, was draping a ground-sheet over the evil-looking machine-gun. The others were still staring at the receding Cross.

Nessuno did not look back till the mule-track had turned a corner. He saw that the flank of the hill now hid the Monastery. Two men had detached themselves from the rear of the column and were striking laterally across the slope, following the curved line of the olive terraces. He thought he recognized the Englishman and the American. One of them stopped and raised his arm in a farewell salute.

Nessuno put up his right hand in reply, three fingers extended, and slowly waved it to and fro.

The two men carrying the woman on the ladder had fallen behind the rest of the party.

'*Corraggio!*' he called out to them. 'It is not far now.'

'*Ne siamo stufi,*' one of them shouted. '*Non possiamo più.*'

He would have gone back to help them, but Laura and Franco were already round the next bend in the path. He hurried on to catch them up.

It was ten o'clock when the head of the straggling procession reached the Via Casilina. Down here the shelling was more frequent and the final part of the journey was the most hazardous. By good fortune they had stumbled on a first aid post. The Germans had put up a tent beside a peasant's house and a huge red cross had been painted on the roof. Orderlies were moving to and fro, stretcher parties were bringing in wounded and from time to time an ambulance moved away towards the rear.

Surprisingly the peasant family had not abandoned their home. They preferred to risk death where they had lived rather than face an uncertain fate in some distant camp. And as this was von Senger's sector the Germans had not forced them to go. They had however been relegated to an outhouse.

When Nessuno asked them if they would shelter Laura and Franco they reacted with typical peasant hospitality. The old

231

grandmother showed him a cowshed where there was enough hay to make a bed.

'You must excuse us, *reverendo*,' she apologised, showing toothless gums. 'It is all we have to offer.' She shrugged and spread her hands in the timeless gesture of resignation. '*Ma, cosa vuole? Sono tempi brutti.*'

Nessuno gave her his blessing and helped Laura to improvise a bed from the straw. Neither she nor Franco had rested the previous night and they were so exhausted that they would have slept on a stone floor. Franco's eyes were closed almost before he curled up in the hay. Nessuno would not permit Laura to sleep yet. He made her listen. There were things he wanted to say to her and now was the only time.

'The German High Command has given orders that the Abbot and his followers are to be taken to a place of safety. Tonight you may be in Rome.'

'Will we be in the Vatican? Shall we see the Pope?'

'You will probably be in the Vatican to begin with, yes. And who knows but you might see the Pope. Laura, have you friends to go to in Rome – friends who will look after you and Franco?'

She was too tired to comprehend the implication in his question. 'I know no one in Rome. But I am not worried. I fear nothing when you are with us, Nessuno.'

The cattle-shed was dark. Somewhere in the gloom at the far end he could hear sounds of munching and the stir of hooved feet. He thought he saw the movement of a pair of pointed ears beyond a wooden partition.

'These past days in the Monastery,' he said, very slowly and carefully, 'terrible things happened but I shall always remember them as the most wonderful in my life.'

'Yes. I can believe in miracles now. During those hours when we were buried alive I never doubted that you would come and release us.'

'That was done by a mightier hand than mine.' Nessuno examined his fingers. The nails were torn and there was still clotted blood on some places where the skin was broken. 'Laura.'

'Yes?'

'You will always remember what I told you? That I loved you more than anything in heaven or on earth? I really meant it. You will always believe that?'

'Of course. But we are nearly out of danger now. When we are all safe you will not leave us, will you?'

Nessuno put his hand on the curly head of the sleeping boy.

'Franco will soon be a man. In less than ten years. He is a fine boy. I know he will be a good son to you.'

Laura's head had fallen back onto the pillow of straw. He was not even sure that she had listened to what he was saying. He put a hand out towards her and then withdrew it. The act of separation had already taken place.

'You are very tired. Rest now. They will call you when the vehicles come to take you to Rome.'

She nodded and smiled back at him trustingly. Her eyes closed on the image of his face gazing down at her. She was too sleepy to try and understand why he was so deeply troubled.

It was mid-afternoon when she awoke with a start. The image of his face was still before her but now she understood what his expression had meant. She sat up, shivering. Franco was still fast asleep at her side. The tall man who had carried the boy down the mountain on his shoulders was stretched out on the floor, dead to the world. There was no sign of Nessuno.

Filled with a desperate premonition she hurried over to the peasant's house. She found the three monks making ready to board an ambulance that would take them to Rome.

'Have you seen Nessuno?'

The Abbot stared at her wild face. 'No. We have not seen him. We have been looking everywhere for him but the ambulance cannot wait. You do not know where he is?'

She shook her head, but in her heart she knew. She moved away clear of the buildings so that she could see the steep flank of Montecassino. Her eyes found the path by which the procession had descended and began to follow its zigzag course up the hill. Just before it disappeared over the crest she could faintly make out a moving figure, more easily distinguishable because of the bulky black garment blown by the wind.

Nessuno was making his way back to the Monastery. He had won his inner conflict, but he knew that there was only one way he could consolidate the victory and make it permanent. He had once made a vow to die in Montecassino and he was going back to honour that promise. He did not stop once to look back.

The sun was already setting when he crossed the crest and saw again the gaunt ruins rising above him. To his eyes there

233

was no menace in that sight, only an ineffable poignancy. Columns of smoke were again rising from the ruins. Forty Kittihawks of the Desert Air Force had flown across the Appenines to bomb the rubble and the 8-inch howitzers of the American artillery were pounding the hillside round the walls. The smoking skeleton of the Monastery beckoned him. Panting with fatigue he pushed on towards his goal. But this time there was no Cross to protect him, and God had no more miracles to spare.

21

Not long after Laura saw Nessuno disappearing over the crest of Montecassino, word reached the commander of XIV Panzer Corps that the Abbot was at one of his medical aid posts. He immediately sent a car and had him brought to the pleasant villa at Roccasecca where he had set up his headquarters. Von Senger was anxious to do all he could to make up for the terrible experience which the venerable old man had undergone and treated him as a distinguished guest. He had reckoned without Doktor Goebbels' propaganda machine. That evening orders came through that he must persuade Abbot Diamare to make a statement which would be recorded on tape. The old man was only too ready to launch into a tirade against the destruction of so much that was of artistic value. His vehemence embarrassed even von Senger.

Next day, on his way to Rome, Diamare was intercepted by agents of the Propaganda Minister and taken to a radio station. He was kept without food until he agreed to make the kind of statement the German radio columnists wanted. That evening newspaper placards in Italian, German and neutral cities again proclaimed to the world that the valiant German soldiers were opposing an enemy who had no regard for civilized values.

That same Friday Baade ordered units of 90th Panzer Grenadier Division to move into the ruins of the Monastery. In its demolished state it provided an excellent site for mortar and machine-gun crews. However, this did not affect the outcome of the second battle of Cassino in any significant way. It was the line of machine-gun posts across the whole width of Monastery Hill, each sited so that it could support and be supported by the others, which massacred the Gurkhas and Rajputs of 7th Indian Brigade who had now taken over from the Royal Sussex. Down in Cassino Town the Maori battalion which had captured the Railway Station was forced to withdraw when Baade sent in his tanks.

There was one bright spot for the Allies on 18 February. That was the day von Mackensen made his supreme effort to break into the Anzio beach-head. But the US 179th Infantry Regiment and the British 1st Loyals stood their ground and the German attack was broken up by a prodigious artillery barrage.

Alexander had been pressurized into making an attack on the Cassino Position under conditions which were favourable only to the defenders. The bombing of the Monastery had provided no tactical advantage and had not influenced the outcome of the battle. Freyberg's Corps had suffered heavy casualties. The New Zealand Division had lost more than the stipulated thousand men, but Freyberg did not easily admit defeat. He was ready to attack within a week of the débacle of 15 to 18 February. And now the Allied High Command believed they had a weapon to hand which would swing the balance of the battle. The Strategic Air Forces had shown their power in the attack on the Monastery. Their full fury would next be unleashed on the defenders of Cassino Town. The Paratroopers who were relieving the Panzer Grenadiers would be subjected to a softening up which would make any artillery barrage seem insignificant.

There was just one snag – the heavy bombers needed clear weather. On 23 February it started to rain again. And it poured with rain every day for the next three weeks.

★

It was early on the morning of Friday the 18th when Richard turned the Mercedes into the minor road that led up towards Peroli.

They had found the farm building where the Mercedes lay hidden about an hour after slipping away from the tail end of the column of refugees. Before then they'd had two hair-raising encounters with files of Paratroopers moving up towards the front. Richard had replied to their questions with dialect Italian and exaggerated gestures, while Nick had displayed a rare acting talent in his impersonation of a village idiot. Fortunately there was plenty of heavy shelling to keep the Paratroopers' minds occupied and the two men looked as wild and dishevelled as any of the refugees still lurking in the battle zone.

They waited till dark before uncovering the car. There were groups of soldiers moving across the slopes above them, who might have been surprised at the sudden materialization of a supercharged Mercedes-Benz 540k cabriolet.

Route 6 was not so crowded as on the night of the first attempt to reach the Monastery and when they reached it most of the traffic was moving up towards Cassino. Both had managed to preserve their service head-gear but the tunics which carried their badges of rank had been abandoned on Monastery Hill. So long as the Mercedes was on the move it provided them with adequate cover in the darkness.

'Seems more like five months than five days since we came down this way.' Nick said as the road began to wind into the hills.

'Yes. There were six of us then.'

Nick glanced at the face of his companion. Richard had shown no signs of throwing off the depression which had descended on him after the bombing.

'Now there's only you and me, Nick, left in one piece. It's not just the destruction of the Monastery, though that was bad enough. Viktor killed, Baldo with very little chance of recovery, Marcel wounded, Pat incapacitated. And all for what? I should have kept my big mouth shut when Alex talked about bombing the Monastery.'

'This is the turning coming up now. Well, damn sakes alive! We never removed that sign with Bennies written on it.'

Richard was about to swing out to make the turn into the track when he braked to a stop.

'Some heavy vehicle has been up here since we came down. Look, you can see the track of wide tyres. At least a three-tonner, I'd say.'

'We'd better case the place out on foot. Why not park the car in behind those bushes where it won't be seen from the road?'

When Richard switched off the engine they climbed out. For some reason they both shut their doors gently and quietly. The sun was about to rise. The birds were already wide awake and in full song. The rain from a recent shower was plopping from the trees. There was a smell of burnt wood in the air.

Cautiously they moved up the track, one on each side, keeping within the cover of the trees. When Richard emerged onto the patch which had been cleared round the farmstead he stopped. He stared ahead, sick in his stomach.

The hulk of the farmhouse was still smoking. All that was left were the blackened supports and tie-beams. The pink walls had caved in, the roof had collapsed on top of them, the tiles scattering untidily. There was no sign of people. The geese and hens had vanished. The donkey, still tethered on the side of the hill, raised its head to stare at them, its long ears rotating. From the far side of the ruin came a faint whimper.

Wordlessly Richard walked round the ruins. The woolly dog was still chained to his kennel. Richard released him. He fawned, squirming and whimpering, craving kindness and fearing blows. Then he lolloped round the west side of the house, tail between his legs, and stared back. His eyes were summoning Richard to follow.

Richard was used to the sights of war but what he saw now was different. The two bodies were slumped against a pair of windswept trees growing near the house. They were held upright by the ropes that bound them to the trunk. Emmanuele had been stripped of his jacket and shirt. His chest was lacerated by the weals of a beating from a metre length of hosepipe which had been flung on the ground near him. His head had lolled forward, mercifully hiding the toothless grimace on his face.

Costanza's hair was loose, falling down as far as her waist. There was a new bald patch on her head. She had been dragged by the hair so roughly that a bunch had been torn out.

Both of them had been shot in the chest at close range. Death

237

had certainly been a merciful release. The bodies were cold and stiff now.

'This happened yesterday.' Nick's years in the Dallas police had hardened him to this sort of situation. He was able to withstand it better than Richard. 'Looks like his wife was raped, probably in front of him.'

There was a mute accusation in the frozen, tormented bodies. Richard's mind went back to the night of the festive supper – the fine linen cloth, lamplight glowing on the precious crockery and glass, the roasted kid and hoarded wine. Must he add these two lives to the score of those who had died because of his impetuous outburst at Caserta?

'We can't leave them like that. It's an outrage against humanity.'

'But who would do a thing like this, Nick? It can't have been the partisans.'

Nick picked up some of the shells ejected by the guns of the killers.

'These are from a machine pistol. Could be the German MP40. This was not the work of partisans.'

'There may be other bodies. Even if Bill had gone off with Ram and Fen the other two must have been here – Pat and Spragg.'

Nick stared at the smouldering ruins. Richard knew he was wondering if Pat's body lay under there somewhere.

'My guess is Bill wouldn't have hung around here. And if they caught Pat and your escaped POW they as like as not took them away for questioning. Come on, let's get this job done.'

They found a spade and a fork in an outhouse untouched by the fire. The surface of the ground was frozen so hard that Richard had to go back for a pick. The dog sat watching them. It got on Richard's nerves. He took it away and tethered it out of sight.

They had to dig wide graves. The bodies had stiffened into grotesque postures and could not be laid out neatly. Before filling in the shallow trenches they found sacking to cover the faces. It seemed wrong to shovel earth directly onto them. Richard tried not to look at Costanza's features, but he had seen the eyes, the gaping mouth, the expression death had stamped on her. The memory remained to haunt him as long as he lived.

When they had filled in the graves they piled stones over

238

them, made two crosses with sticks and propped them upright as markers.

Before starting back for the road Nick went to untether the donkey so that he could roam where he wanted in search of grazing. Richard released the dog and persuaded the animal to accompany him. As he passed the well he saw the bucket standing on the edge. He dropped it down the circular opening and winched it up again.

'What's the idea?'

'Water for shaving – and breakfast.'

The Benghazi Burner was still in the boot of the Mercedes, as well as some tea and Compo rations. Both men became suddenly aware how hungry they were.

After they had breakfasted and shaved Richard said: 'I'm going up to the village. We've got to find out what happened to Pat.'

'If you're going up there I'm coming with you.'

'No, Nick. I want you to stay with the car. Keep well under cover. If I am not back within an hour find some way to make contact with Bill MacDonald and the LRP. If Pat has been captured by the Germans they're liable to hand him over to the Gestapo. The partisans may know where they take people for questioning. Something will have to be done to get Pat out of their hands.'

'I don't think we should split up. There's something about the feel of this place.'

'Please let me do it my way, Nick. I want you to be ready to start up and get out of here fast if I have to come away in a hurry. Here, look after my hat for me. I feel a bit conspicuous in it.'

Nick agreed reluctantly. Richard moved out from the shelter of the trees and started towards the village. He kept to the side of the road, ready to jump for cover if a vehicle approached. Just before he entered the deserted village he had to pass the gateway to a well-favoured villa. From down there came a strange murmuring sound. He went to the wall and peered over.

The house was about a hundred yards away. He saw a cart in the driveway, loaded with untidy greyish objects. A figure in white vestments with a coloured stole and black biretta was standing near, holding an open prayer book in his hands. At that moment two youths came round the corner of the house from the back. They were stooped by the weight of their burden. They swung it to and fro several times, then tossed it onto the pile of corpses already on the cart.

From up in the village came the sound of a bell slowly tolling. He was turning to stare in that direction when he realized that someone had come quietly up beside him.

'You! What are you doing here?'

He spun round to answer the challenge and found himself looking down into the carelessly shaved face of a small, dark man in a grey, belted mackintosh. As he had spoken in Italian Richard assumed he was a civilian. Taken by surprise he instinctively fell back on the aggressive manner which had been so successful in brazening a way up the road to Cassino.

'Speak with more respect when you address a German officer.'

The unprepossessing face creased into a smile. When he switched effortlessly from Italian into German Richard knew that he had made a fatal mistake.

'Ah, so? You are a German officer, are you? In that case let me see your *Wehrpass*.'

22

Kurt Sauckel was young for a captain. He had won rapid promotion because of his keenness and efficiency. He never questioned orders, content to serve his Führer with a blind loyalty. Born in 1914, he was just old enough to remember the misery in Germany after the Great War. He had seen the miraculous change brought about by Hitler's rise to power. A new Germany had been created by a man who must be regarded as a demi-god. The pride of a whole nation had been uplifted. In six short years the world had been forced to face the fact of Germany's might. The German people, purged of impure elements, was moving forward to its destiny. The set-back in Russia was temporary. The Wehrmacht only had to keep the Allies in check until Hitler's new secret weapon was ready. When it was, the war would be over in a month and the German people would march to their inevitable destiny – world domination by the thousand year Reich.

He managed to get away from the office early that Thursday evening. He wanted time to spruce up before meeting Lidia. There were a score of prostitutes in the local prison, refugees from Rome who had been put inside by the Italian police. He could have had his pick of them and some were not bad at all. But Lidia was something different. He had won her admiration by his own personal charm. She was slim, vivacious, mischievous. Such a contrast to his Gretchen, whose broad hips and ponderous breasts had spawned six lusty children, each one a paragon of the Aryan race.

He was lucky that his *Leitstelle* had its headquarters in such a beautiful spot. This special assignment at Fermine Fonte made an agreeable break from the stuffy atmosphere of Rome. It was a peace-time watering-place where wealthy and over-indulged Romans came to take the cure. It boasted a magnificent hydro and a great many luxury villas. Sauckel's billet was in one of the most opulent. The Signora, wife of an arms manufacturer who had unfortunately got himself embroiled with Badoglio and was now in the prison of Regina Coeli, had put at his disposal a self-contained suite of rooms.

'Such a charming man!' she told her friends enthusiastically. 'So clean and tidy – and so correct! The children adore him.'

She had seen the car arrive and opened the door with a welcoming flourish. Sauckel gave her his devastating smile, took her hand and raised it to within a centimetre of his lips. He somehow managed to give the impression that only respect for her absent husband prevented him from crushing her in his arms. The Signora would have been only too happy to be crushed in those arms. Sauckel stood six foot four in his jackboots and was a handsome stallion. But his hostess was plump and fair. She was too much the same style as the homely Gretchen. He was a faithful husband in the sense that he only dallied with women who were a complete contrast to her.

He turned as the two children came charging down the stairs to greet him. He scooped one up on each arm and lifted them high. They screamed in mock fear and then laughed. Signora Cerotti watched with smiling eyes.

'Will you play lions and monkeys with us?' Lions and monkeys was Sauckel's own invention. On hands and knees he made a fantastic lion and his roar was stupendous.

'Not this evening, *bambini*.' He put the children down gently and patted Angelina on her neat little bottom. 'The lion has to go out hunting tonight or there will be no food for monkeys.'

He and the Signora exchanged a secret glance. Sauckel made sure that the little family did not go short on rations.

After his bath he put on a record of the pilgrim's song from *Tannhäuser* and sat down at the dressing-table. His vanity kit was in an inlaid wooden box. He carefully filed his nails and pushed down the cuticles with an orange-stick. Then he sprinkled on a little pink powder and used a chamois-leather buffing pad to bring up a shine. Next he took the tweezers and plucked a couple of hairs from each nostril. Finally he smoothed his pale eyebrows with a tiny brush.

Before dressing he stood naked in front of the mirror and applied talcum powder to his crotch and armpits.

He put on the clean uniform which had been laid out in the bedroom by his soldier servant, brushed his hair carefully and inspected himself in the mirror. The ash-grey tunic was made to measure and emphasized his broad shoulders. The white shirt was spotless, the black tie without a crease. The badges and piping were crisply new, almost like jewelry.

Last of all he buckled on the black leather belt with the neatly holstered Walther P38 without which he never ventured out of doors.

His orderly had turned back the sheet at one side of the double bed and laid out his sleeping shorts. He put the shorts under the pillow, went round to the other side of the bed and turned the sheet back there, too.

Then he put on the curvaceous cap with the death's head badge, checked his appearance once again in the mirror and went down to the car.

The evening was a success. He drove Lidia a little way up the hills to a village restaurant where black market food was always available. The main course was roast kid, the wine an excellent estate-bottled Chianti, followed by champagne. It was evident that Lidia had succumbed to his blond good looks and the charm which he deployed. She made no demur when he suggested that she should come back to his billet and sample his excellent brandy.

*

At three o'clock the telephone began to ring on the landing outside. Kurt roused himself from his doze, pulled his arm out from under Lidia's waist. Her eyes opened, the full lips smiled at him. He heard the Signora emerge from her room and answer the 'phone. She came and tapped tentatively on the door, her voice unhappy and fearful.

'Capitano. It is for you. They say it is urgent.'

He rolled out of bed, reached for his dressing-gown and went out to the landing. The Signora threw him a reproachful glance before retreating to her room.

'Sauckel,' he snapped into the 'phone, then listened for a minute. 'All right. I'll be there in about half an hour. Keep him well occupied till I arrive.'

Back in the room he looked down at the woman in the bed, her outline suggestively contoured by the sheet. She moved under it provocatively.

'Come back to bed, *caro. Dammi ancora l'amore.*'

'You'll have to leave, Lidia. They need me at the office. It is urgent.'

'Do you have to go?'

'It is duty.'

Pouting, she dragged the sheet round herself and got out of bed. Watching her, Sauckel felt his desire mount again but he restrained himself.

Someone would pay dearly for this.

He drove her home on the way to the office. He always referred to it as the office, though in fact it was a great deal more than that. His *Leitstelle* had taken over the local gaol, turning the Italians out of all the offices and leaving them only one block of a dozen cells.

The two sentries, armed with machine pistols, sprang to attention and saluted him as he drove in through the gates. The Scharführer, a man with a close-cropped head and a roll of fat at the back of his neck, was waiting for him in his office.

'Right.' Sauckel's tone showed that he was not pleased at

243

being called out in the middle of the night. 'What's this about an important prisoner?'

'I thought it necessary to inform you, Herr Haupsturm-führer,' the NCO reported with self-righteous formality. 'But you always say we must not speak openly on the public telephone—'

'All right, man. Come to the point.'

'This prisoner, Herr Haupsturmführer. He was arrested at Peroli in very suspicious circumstances. First he tried to make out he was a German. Then he claimed to be a British officer, but the only military uniform he had were his trousers. Sergeant Weber thinks he must be a member of a partisan group.' The Scharführer could not suppress a smile of triumph. 'This may be the lead we have been looking for, Herr Haupsturmführer! If our *Leitstelle* can capture the killers of the Feldpolizei at San Gregorio and solve the mystery of what happened to Standartenführer Pohl—'

'Has he talked?' Sauckel interrupted impatiently. He led the way out into the corridor. He hung his hat on one of the pegs and from the other took a black garment like a mackintosh. He put it on, buttoning it up round the neck. His uniform was completely protected, only the boots protruding beneath. He took a pair of leather gloves from one of the pockets. He pulled them over the beautifully manicured nails and sensitive figures which had caressed Lidia's body with such patient sensuous-ness.

'Open the door,' he told the Scharführer.

The NCO opened the door and stood back. Sauckel marched into the room. The two SS men who had flopped down onto a bench sprang to their feet.

Sauckel hardly spared them a glance before he narrowed his eyes on the object lying in the corner. It was still recognizable as a human being. The face was bruised and bloody, the lips were split. One eye was closed. There were purple weals on its shoulders and chest.

'I told you to keep him occupied!' roared Sauckel.

'He fainted, Herr Haupsturmführer.'

'Then fetch a bucket of water, you fools!'

The sting of ice-cold water brought the prisoner to his senses gasping. There was no moment of bewilderment. He remem-bered at once where he was and what had happened. He was still lying on the stone floor fouled by blood, shit and piss. Now his hands were cuffed behind his back.

Above him a voice said: 'Stand him up.'

He was hauled to his feet and stood under an electric light bulb. He found himself facing a man who topped him by a good four inches. A faint perfume drifted from him. He was smiling.

Sauckel just looked at the prisoner for a half minute. Then he started slapping the man's face with his open hand, first one side and then the other. Next he bunched his fist and hit him again and again on the nose, eyes, cheeks.

Three minutes can be a long time.

★

February 18th. Friday. 5 a.m.

'Now, Sheisskerl, are you ready to talk?'

'*Do you – do you speak English?*'

'Why do you ask that? Not long ago you were trying to pass yourself off as a German. So we will conduct this interrogation in German.'

'I am a British officer. You have no right to treat a prisoner of war like this. All I am required to tell you is my name, rank and number. I demand treatment according to the Geneva Convention.'

'You hear that, Hans? Now he is demanding. This Schwein-hund has not understood the situation yet.'

'He is very obstinate, Herr Haupsturmführer.'

'Your job is to make him cooperative.'

'Shall we give him the bath treatment again?'

'Yes. But I want him revived more quickly this time.'

★

Friday. 18th February. 5.25 a.m.

'Now, Schwein Engländer, do you still made demands?'

'*Zadok the priest –* '

'What was that, man? Speak up, don't whisper.'

'*– and Nathan the prophet –* '

'We both know that you speak perfectly good German. Good enough nearly to fool that dolt Weber.'

'I am a British officer. I request proper treatment according to the Geneva Convention. Please.'

'Please. That is better. He is learning, Hans. But since when do British officers wear Italian dress? Either you are a partisan or a spy. Neither has any right under the Geneva Convention. Spies enjoy the privilege of being shot. Partisans die on a meat hook.'

'I am a British off – *Fuck you!*'

'Why did you say thank you?'

'Because we Christians are taught that it is a blessed thing to be struck on the cheek.'

'What have you been doing to this imbecile, Hans? He is raving mad. Now, Scheisskerl, you claim to be a British officer. How many more Anglo-Saxons are with the partisans?'

'Three.'

'That's a lie. We know there are more. Where is the headquarters of the partisans?'

'I do not know.'

'I think you do. What is the name of the leader?'

'I have no idea.'

'What arms, ammunition and supplies have they?'

'I can't tell you.'

'How are they supplied by the Allies?'

'I don't know.'

'Hold his head up, Hans. I want to see the swine's eyes. Who was it who killed the military policeman at Opi?'

'Oh, my God!'

'What was that? You call upon your God? Many have done so in this room but God does not enter here, my friend. You had better forget about your God, or anybody else's. What has happened to Standartenführer Pohl? ... You heard my question. What has happened to Standartenführer Pohl?'

'I've never heard of any Standartenführer Pohl.'

'You know very well who he is. Answer my question. Is he alive or dead?'

'I have no idea.'

'I think he is alive. Where is he being held?'

'You're talking poppycock, mate.'

'If you swear at a German officer you will be severely punished. Answer the question in German.'

'If I don't know who Pohl is how the hell can I tell you where he is being held?'

'You are shit and you are a liar. You are an English spy working with the partisans. You were captured in civilian dress masquerading as a civilian. You have no rights under the

Geneva Convention. You have no rights of any kind, not even the right to die—'

'I am a British officer—'

'Silence! You have been foolish enough to give untruthful answers to my questions. I am not going to repeat them now. You have had your chance for the time being, and I have other matters to deal with. In the meantime Hans and Fritz will be attending to you. I think that when we meet again you will be willing to answer my questions. Perhaps even eager to do so.'

'*My God, my God . . .*'

*

February 18th. Friday. 9 a.m.

'Now, English swine, are you ready to answer my questions?'

'Uh – uh.'

'I asked if you were ready to answer my questions properly?'

'Uh – I am a Brit—'

'Where is the partisan headquarters?'

'My name is Stewart – uh – my rank—'

'What is the name of the leader?'

'My rank is major and my number—'

'Who killed the military policeman at Opi?'

'My number is 6039287 and I request—'

'What happened to Standartenführer Pohl?'

'I request treatment according to the Geneva Convention—'

'Hold up his head for me, Hans. Your name is Stewart, your rank is major, your number is 6039287 and you no longer exist. The partisan group you were with is the Gruppo Manzoni. The name of the leader is Toro. You see, we know everything. What a pity you could not have gained credit by answering those questions yourself. Now, what has become of Standartenführer Pohl?'

'If you know everything what is the point of asking me questions?'

'Schweinhund!'

'*Fuck you.*'

'Take him back to his cell, Fritz. Hans, wait here a moment ... Goodness, this place stinks! Hans, we're not getting anywhere with these methods. I'm going to try something

247

different. Leave him to himself for a few days. We'll try deprivation. No communication, no light, no heat, no sleep. The minimum amount of food and drink to keep him alive.'

23

As the Ides of March drew closer nothing much had changed around Cassino. The hills remained, their peaks still mantled with snow. The clouds hung low. The rain went on and on. Now it was a ruined Monastery which overlooked the battlefield, and there was no longer any doubt about it being occupied by the Germans. The 1st Battalion, 3rd Parachute Regiment, had relieved the Panzer Grenadiers on 23 February, moving in with mortar crews and artillery observation officers.

Kesselring had been a staff officer in the Luftwaffe during the secret years of its formation and he knew what he was doing when he put 1st Parachute Division in to hold the Cassino Position. The division had been associated with the first operations ever to be carried out by means of parachute landings – at Stavanger in Norway, Rotterdam in Holland and the Albert Canal in Belgium. It had nearly met its Waterloo in Crete. Casualties there were so heavy that Hitler decided to use them henceforth as ground troops. Ironically at the same time the British decided to increase their own parachute arm.

As the Allies advanced up the boot of Italy the Paratroopers had fought like any other infantry division but always with the same pride and toughness, the same lethal hitting power. The British had learned to respect them in North Africa and Sicily and feared their tigerish counter-attacks. On the rare occasions when they took parachute prisoners they were surprised at the youthfulness of the faces in the pot-shaped helmets.

Now, they had been sent to hold Cassino. Behind them lay two hundred and twenty days of continuous fighting. They were dog-tired. Most of them were suffering from the effects of malaria. Many had had no leave since they'd been sent to plug the gaps in the Russian front in 1942. The full divisional strength of 16,000 was reduced to 6,000.

The fighting around Cassino had exercised a curious fascination on Adolf Hitler. It resembled the battles he had known in 1914-18 more closely than any other fighting in the Second World War and he identified himself closely with the troops in the Gustav Line. Already obsessed by his decision that if his cause failed he would drag the whole of Germany into the maelstrom with him, he had ordered Heidrich's division to yield not one inch of ground.

They were prepared to obey those orders.

By 25 February all of 211 Grenadier Regiment had left Cassino. Baade's 90th Panzer-Grenadier Division had gone back for a well-earned rest, and its eccentric commander had handed over the sector to the rugged, ruthless Heidrich. To Colonel Heilman's 3rd Parachute Regiment went the task of holding the town of Cassino and the hill behind it. He put his 1st Battalion on Monastery Hill and on the Rocca Janula. The latter was a hill at the back of Cassino on which a prudent Abbot had centuries ago built a castle to defend the road up to the Monastery; to the Allies it was known as Castle Hill. The 3rd Battalion was given the formidable task of defending Point 593, which the Germans called the Calvary Mount.

The 2nd Battalion was ordered to take over the cellars and blockhouses of Cassino. The three hundred men under Captain Foltin's command who relieved 211 Grenadier Regiment regarded this as just another tough assignment that had been handed to the Paratroopers. Yet, even if they had known that in climbing down into the buried defences of Cassino most of them were entering their tombs they would hardly have acted differently.

Rudi had been detailed to Major Kratzert's battalion on Point 593 and during the dying phases of the battle on Snakeshead Ridge he had more than once found himself evacuating wounded from the 4th Indian Division – men of the

Royal Sussex, Punjabis, Gurkhas – mostly with the head and eye injuries so characteristic of the fighting on Montecassino.

At the beginning of March he was transferred to Captain Foltin's battalion in the town and posted to 7 Company, commanded by Leutnant Schuster. During a period which in the military histories would be described as a lull there was still plenty of work for the stretcher-bearers. Rudi very quickly won the respect of the youthful veterans of 7 Company. Wearing a Paratrooper's camouflage smock, with a red-cross band on his arm and a water-bottle, slung from his belt, he seemed totally oblivious of shell, mortar or machine-gun fire.

Life in Cassino town was an existence hardly fit for sewer rats, let alone humans. Any movement above ground by day brought down immediate retribution. The choking fumes of the smoke-screen made breathing a penance. Supplies had to be brought in at night, when the lorries ventured over the pot-holes and craters of the Via Casilina. But Heidrich had given orders that, in order to spare them the merciless jolting, the wounded were to be evacuated by day in armoured personnel carriers, marked with the red cross. In the hell on earth that was Cassino the defenders on both sides developed a strange fellow-feeling and the red cross was scrupulously respected. German and Allied stretcher-bearers working under its protection frequently exchanged words and more than once swapped medical supplies.

'Sometimes I wonder if you really want to get yourself killed,' a young Fallschirmjäger said to Rudi after he had gone out under a particularly heavy stonk to bring back the one surviving member of a bazooka team.

Rudi smiled at the lad, who could not have been more than eighteen or nineteen. He had to take care with his comrades not to talk in a way that would betray the fact that he was really an officer.

'No more than you do. I've seen you in action.'

The lad's eyes were shadowed by lack of sleep. It was impossible to rest under the continous pounding of shells and mortars. There was a stubble of downy bristles on his chin and his mouth had the slack, drooping shape of utter fatigue. But the eyes were bright, almost fanatical. He was refilling the ammunition bandolier slung round his shoulders. He re-sembled a walking arsenal with stick grenades stuck into his belt, and a dagger sewn into a sheath on his chest. The Gewehr 42 automatic rifle he would take out on patrol lay beside him.

Perhaps because his own loyalty to the Führer and the whole National Socialist ethic had evaporated, Rudi was curious to know what had motivated a boy – he could still be at school – to become such a fearless fighter.

He asked: 'How long do you think we can hold Cassino?'

The boy's eyes flashed and Rudi knew that the question had been a mistake.

'For as long as the Führer wants us to! We're the parachutists, aren't we? Do you think we're going to give up what the Grenadiers held? I don't care for talk like that, my friend. If I hadn't seen what you've done I might think you were a quitter.'

Oh, dear, Rudi thought. I'm going to be treated to a lecture. He's one of those starry-eyed youths from the Hitler Jugend whose mission is to put us all straight on the glories of National Socialism.

'Perhaps you're one of those who think that Germany is going to lose this war–'

'No, I didn't say–'

'Because you're wrong. We've only got to hold them up until the secret weapons the Führer promised are ready.'

'You really believe there are such weapons?'

'Of course I do! Has the Führer ever failed in his promises?'

'No. Not even in his promise to liquidate the Jews.'

The lad spat. 'It was time Germany was cleansed. Not just Germany, but Europe, the whole world! Don't tell me you're a Jew-lover.'

'I can see that you are not. You feel happy about fighting for a regime that is killing thousands of our fellow-countrymen daily? Sacrificing your life for it?'

'That's foreign propaganda! You've been listening to foreign propaganda! I ought to report you. If that's how you feel why do you risk your own neck?'

Rudi realized that he had gone too far. It was hard to believe that a boy whom he had come to regard as a comrade could suddenly become so cold and hostile.

'I risk my neck because, like you, there's nothing else for me to do. We're all in the same boat – Germans, British,

251

Americans, Poles. We soldiers have just got to go on killing each other till the politicians tell us we can stop.'

'On parade, Binler!' The barked order came from the NCO who was to lead the patrol. 'Leave the political theory till we get back.'

Schütze Binler scrambled to his feet and picked up his rifle.

An hour later Rudi carried him in on a stretcher, his lower jaw removed by a chunk of flying masonry.

*

March 10th. Friday. Noon.

'Come in, Major Stewart. Sit down. You'll be more comfortable if you slip your hands over the back of the chair. You must forgive me if my English is not quite perfect.'

'Your English is excellent, Herr Obersturmbannführer.'

'Ah. So you know our badges of rank?'

'As I am sure you know ours. Do these handcuffs need to be fastened so tightly? It's stopping the circulation to my arms.'

'They are too tight? How very inconsiderate! Is that better?'

'Yes. Much better. Thank you.'

'Would you like a cigarette?'

'I'm not sure if I could manage it with my lips in this state.'

'Try it and see. I am sorry I cannot release you but I'll put it in your mouth and light it for you . . . How's that? You know, it really upsets me to see a brother officer in this condition, but you see the fact that you were in civilian clothes meant that you became a prisoner of the Sicherheitsdienst and not a Kriegsgefangene. We only have your identity disc and your word to prove who you are. Now, if you could give me the name of your regiment?'

'I am only required to give you my name, rank and number, and I've done that twenty times.'

'You have been very brave. What a pity if no one ever hears how brave. You know, this obstinacy does not help me to help you. I want to spare you the experience of being questioned by the Gestapo – . What did you say?'

'Nothing.'

'If we can keep this matter within the jurisdiction of Sipo I may be able to have you transferred to a POW camp, but I

252

cannot do that unless you are more cooperative. Now, I can understand that you do not wish to give me information about your armed forces but you cannot feel the same about a nation who were your enemies. We know that you had assistance from the partisans. Was it the Gruppo Manzoni?'

'I don't have to answer that.'

'Was their leader a man who called himself Toro?'

'I don't have to tell you.'

'Did your information come from a man they called Il Professore? While you were with the partisans did you meet two men called Attilio and Saturnino?'

'I don't know anything about such people. Listen, this cigarette is burning my lip and it's stuck to the blood.'

'How many British liaison officers are with the partisans?'

'This cigarette is stuck to my lips–'

'What arms have you supplied them with?'

'Could you take it out, please? Jesus, it's burning me!'

'We want you to give us the fullest possible information about this partisan group – numbers, locations, arms and equipment, intentions, contacts with the Allies – . *Get up off the floor*! Bloody English swine! Hans! Put him back in his cell and tell Haupsturmführer Sauckel to come in.

'Ah, Sauckel. I am afraid that you were right. He is not prepared to cooperate. We will have to proceed to "especially rigorous interrogation".'

'But if he really is a British officer, Herr Obersturmbannführer? We have already exceeded–'

'A colonel of the SS has been kidnapped and probably murdered. Do you want me to have to admit to our Gestapo friends in Rome that Sipo are not capable of solving this problem?'

*

March 10th. Friday. 11.30 p.m. 'Major Stewart . . . '

'Herr Haupsturmführer.'

'You do not think I like this, do you?'

'There were times, I confess, when you seemed to me to be enjoying it.'

'It is my duty. Some are called to fight at the front. Others to work for the security of the Reich and the Wehrmacht.'

'We all must do our duty as we see it.'

'You have slept well?'

253

'Yes. Thank you.'

'And the hot meal was palatable?'

'It was very good.'

'You see, we are not such brutes as you thought.'

'You do not know what I think, Herr Haupsturmführer.'

'No. I agree I do not. I must admit that you make me wish we were fighting on the same side against the Bolsheviks.'

'We could never be on the same side, Herr Haupsturmführer. You and I are enemies. Let us not forget that.'

'I do not forget, Major Stewart. And if I were tempted to do so my superiors would remind me. You have been allowed to sleep and have been given food because I want you to be in full possession of your faculties. You have to make a grave decision.'

'I am still in a position to make decisions?'

'My superior, Obersturmbannführer Eilen, has instructed me to proceed to "especially rigorous interrogation" . . . You did not think that there was a degree beyond what you have already experienced? I want you to understand what this involves. The history books tell us that when Galileo was shown the instruments of torture he agreed that the earth was flat. We don't want you to agree that the earth is flat but we do want full answers to all our questions. Hans is going to show you the devices we have at our disposal.'

'Jesus give me strength.'

'Put them on the table, Hans. Fritz, hold his eyelids open . . . You see, Major Stewart. Would you like Hans to explain exactly how they are used?'

'There's – no need.'

'You appreciate that this can only be used on a male? While this – ha, ha – is more suited to the female of the species.'

'Must I tell you again that I am a British officer and entitled to the protection of the Geneva Convention?'

'Oh, but we are not going to use these on you personally, Major Stewart. The injury would be too permanent. A young female partisan has very fortuitously fallen into our hands. An attractive girl in a full-blown Roman way. You and she are going to be placed in inter-connecting rooms so that you will be able to hear how she reacts to Hans's applications of these instruments. If the experience does not please you, you can always put a stop to it by – . Quick, Hans! Catch him! He's going to faint.'

March 11th. Saturday. 2 a.m.

'And there is nothing more you can tell us?'

'No. Nothing.'

'We will send a party to look for Standartenführer Pohl's body at the place you described. I hope for the woman's sake that they'll find it.'

'Are you going to give her medical attention?'

'She will get attention. Tell me. Why did you keep shouting Maria, Maria? The woman's name was Rosa, not Maria.'

'I was confused. I'm sorry.'

'You need not be ashamed of yourself, Major Stewart. No one has resisted me for as long as you. I have to respect that.'

'I've betrayed my friends . . . '

'Now that you have nothing more to tell us you are expendable. The rules require me to have you sent to a concentration camp or shot.'

'I'd prefer to be shot, if it's all the same to you.'

'In fact, I am going to do neither. I told you that you had earned my respect, and I am going to take a chance on your behalf. I am going to have you put in one of our cylinders.'

24

In the middle of March the weather began at last to let up. Heidrich warned his commanders to be ready to repel an attack and the word filtered down to all ranks. The Paratroopers braced themselves. Let howitzers, grenades, tanks, flame-throwers do their worst. They were going to deny their enemy the road to Rome.

They did not know that on the night of 14th March the New Zealanders had silently withdrawn a thousand yards from Cassino, leaving only a few suicide squads to share the town with the Paratroopers. At daybreak they heard the familiar rumble of heavy bombers, but still believed that the high-flying formations were on their way to bomb the railway marshalling yards or supply dumps further north.

In fact, what was about to happen was an event unprecedented in war. Upon the little market town of Cassino – or what was left of it – was to be unloaded a cargo of bombs greater even than the tonnage which the 900 bombers of the RAF had dropped on Berlin in their raid of mid-February. Exactly one calendar month after their visit to the Monastery the Strategic Air Forces were returning. From as far away as England the bombers were homing on a target which they knew was a small town at the foot of an insignificant hill near the confluence of two rivers.

455 aircraft from Mediterranean Allied Strategic and Tactical Air Forces took part – 164 Liberators, 114 Fortresses, 105 Marauders, 72 Mitchells. Between 8.30 a.m. and 12 noon, barring pauses of up to forty minutes, they delivered 2,223

bombs of a thousand pounds each. In one sense it was a compliment to the defenders that for each Paratrooper in Cassino there were one and a half bombers and a ration of three tons of high explosive per man.

As a first exercise in the use of strategic air forces to support a Corps attack it went off pretty well. Most of the bombs landed within the square mile of target area. The intention literally to pulverise the town had been realized. Hardly a wall was left standing and everywhere there were craters up to seventy feet in diameter. It was not expected that any human being would survive that cataclysmic onslaught and remain capable of offering resistance.

At precisely 12 o'clock the last bomber flew off on its way to a refuelling base in North Africa. It was the turn of the Allied artillery to take up the refrain. 610 artillery pieces, in many places standing wheel to wheel, began to 'carpet-sweep' Cassino town in a creeping barrage. Behind them 6th New Zealand Brigade moved forward on two parallel lines, spearheaded by the 25th Battalion and the tanks of NZ Armoured Brigade. The Kiwis had watched the bombing with awe and an involuntary compassion for the poor devils under it. So confident were they that the defenders must have been annihilated that the tank commanders had opened the hatches of their turrets and were standing up in them. General Eaker's official photographer scrambled over the ruins with impunity, photographing the results of the strike. Indeed, from 12 o'clock till 1 p.m. the heaps of rubble were as quiet as the grave and only the huge craters prevented the tanks from moving forward.

*

As the first bombs began to fall Rudi leapt for cover in one of the reinforced dugouts occupied by 7 Company. Hastily the Paratroopers grabbed their personal weapons and huddled under the new steel 'crabs' of which von Vietinghoff had spoken so proudly. Rudi had been under heavy bombardment before but he had never experienced anything remotely like this.

He was at the heart of a volcano in eruption. The concussions slammed the body and stupefied the brian. He felt a sense of unbearable violation and somewhere deep inside him the anger of outraged humanity. Time no longer had any significance.

The three and a half hours of bombing followed by an hour of intensive shelling was like a spell in the Inferno.

Even after the 'carpet-sweeping' barrage had passed over, the survivors of 7 Company still did not move. They were stunned, unable to believe that they were alive after all. But among those who had not died were Lieutenant Schuster and Sergeant-Major Richter. When the clanking and roaring of tracked vehicles was heard these two roused the survivors from their stunned apathy. From under 'crabs' and revetments they crawled out, still clutching their personal weapons. Cursed and exhorted by Schuster they pushed away the rocks that blocked the entrance to their dugout, crept out into the ruins and took up firing positions.

Rudi was with them. He had torn off his red-cross arm-band and picked up the rifle of a dead Paratrooper. It was a KAR-98K 7.92 mm fitted with a telescopic sight – the sniper's rifle. He was filled with a desire to hit back and avenge his dead comrades, the age-old motive that fuels battles and wars.

Two-thirds of Captain Foltin's battalion were dead, but the four score who still lived had slowly surfaced during that vital hour of respite. Now, motivated by their innate fighting spirit, they wiped the dust from their eyes and their weapons and prepared to kill the figures they could only dimly see in the swirling dust.

The outcome of the battle that followed hinged on two factors. The Paratrooper's own heavier weapons had been irretrievably buried and were useless. They still had personal weapons because they had clasped them to their huddled bodies. And by a stroke of chance General Heidrich had come forward to visit the command post of Colonel Heilman before the bombing commenced. When the New Zealanders attacked he was able personally to direct the full force of his divisional artillery onto them – and that included the 71st Werfer Battalion with their '88 barrels'.

The second factor was that the Kiwi tanks were not able to advance because the bombers had turned the town into an effective tank barrier, of which the vast craters formed an important part. Even though the New Zealanders had brought up scissors tanks to bridge these gaps, that one hour of delay gave the defenders the time needed to pull themselves together and reorganize.

By one o'clock the 25th Battalion had pushed forward

without opposition almost as far as the Continental Hotel, an important strong-point standing at the spot where Route 6 turned left to curve round the base of Monastery Hill. It was then that the first tank commander, standing up in his turret, was shot dead by a sniper. Then, from amidst the ruins, came the echoing crash of small-arms fire. The New Zealanders realized that not all the defenders had been obliterated. Even more extraordinary, they still had the guts to fight.

All over Cassino the story was the same. The whole might of the New Zealand Division, the vast apparatus of bombers, guns and tanks behind it, were rendered powerless because eighty German Fallschirmjäger did not know when they were beaten.

★

March 16th. Thursday. Time not known.

If I'm going to keep my sanity in this bloody cylinder I've got to remain active.

How can you be active in a pitch-dark space that's six foot long and two and a half foot high? It's got to be mental activity. I must somehow create a kind of pattern to my life. If I just lie in the darkness in my own filth I'll soon be a raving lunatic. . . .

It'll be important to keep a count of the days and to do that I've got to be able to distinguish day from night. I could keep a tally of the days by collecting pellets of hardened shit . . .

It was Friday the 18th – no, early in the morning of Saturday the 19th when they brought me in here. It was three weeks later that smooth English-speaking bastard came. They tortured the partisan girl the next night so I must have talked on the morning of – Let's see. Only twenty-eight days in February so I must have talked on the morning of Saturday 12th March . . .

They must have constructed these places with those circular pipes they use for sewers. If they don't clean me out I wonder how long it would take me to fill it with my own shit so that there's no air left for me to breathe? It's funny, but I can't smell a bad smell. Scheisskerl was right when he said these tubes are quite warm . . .

I'm wandering. Must concentrate. Keep my mental activity disciplined, or at least have certain periods of mental effort and periods of rest . . .

They've brought me food three times since I was put in here

so today must be Thursday, March 17th. In three days it will be Sunday. It would be good to observe Sunday in some special way ...

Must have fallen asleep. There go the guards in their bloody great boots. At least I learned something about the routine of the prison before they put me in here. The SS guard is relieved every morning at eight. They usually bring the women prisoners in late at night, around midnight ...

That was the worst thing of all. Hearing the women screaming, knowing what they were doing to them. At least I can't hear that from down here. I wish they had not shown me the instruments of torture. I keep seeing them in my mind's eye ...

Wish I could have asked Scheisskerl some questions. What makes people like that? How could any mother's son do the things he did?

Ah, grub up! Now, how to squirm round and get my head up the other end?

*

Dudley Fremantle was practising chip shots when Wilfrid reported. The third battle for Cassino had petered out and he was making the most of the lull to work on a tip from the CO of the Derbyshire Yeomanry. You started the backward swing with stiff wrists and only cocked them when the left forearm was parallel to the ground. It was working well, and the balls were rattling merrily into the bucket as Wilfrid saluted.

This Regimental HQ was below Fremantle's usual standard; he'd had to make the best he could of a ruined farm outhouse. There was hardly a building standing in the valley to the east of Cassino.

The CO gave Wilfrid a sharp, quick look. His Adjutant was right. Here was a clear case of battle fatigue. Fremantle began to wonder if they'd been asking too much of this young man. He'd taken the episode of the short shells very much to heart and then had gone through a grim week with the Gurkhas marooned up on Hangman's Hill.

He leaned the mashie against the side of his table. It was too early in the day for a drink.

Wilfrid's scarlet volume of sonnets still protruded from his battledress jacket pocket like some kind of badge. His trousers had lost any trace of crease and his tie was a tight little knot.

To a sergeant-major's eye he presented a most unsoldierly appearance, but Fremantle was experienced enough to know that the most steadfast courage was often shown by these apparently vague, poetic types.

'Still no word of Richard?' Fremantle asked, after he had glanced at the returns which Wilfrid had brought from the acting second-in-command of C Battery.

'Not a word. He's probably swanning about somewhere on Eighth Army's front or living it up with the ATS at Caserta.'

'I understand things were a bit uncomfortable up on Hangman's Hill.'

Wilfrid nodded vaguely in agreement. 'The worst thing was I'd lost my dog and couldn't do anything about it. We got separated in the darkness and chaos of Cassino that first night. I'm afraid he's bought it.'

'I've got news for you.' Fremantle brushed the ends of his carefully clipped moustache upwards. 'We've got him here. It was the oddest thing you ever heard. When the Paratroopers were counter-attacking Castle Hill the Punjabis cut them to hell. The German commander asked the colonel for a truce so that he could pick up his dead and wounded. It was agreed, of course. In fact, the Indians plied the Krauts with cigarettes and chocolates. But will you believe this? They had not enough stretchers so the Punjabi MO lent them three. He never thought he'd see them back but next day a couple of stretcher-bearers turned up waving a white flag. They'd come to say thank you and return the stretchers. One of them had your dog on a lead. Lucky you had that disc on him with your name and rank. You realize that was a breach of security, Wilfrid; you should not have put the name of the Regiment on it. Bombardier Stacey! Bring that dog in here, will you?'

Wilfrid's reunion with Dante lasted for five minutes. Fremantle watched with a smile as the dog, after a moment of ear-cocking disbelief, leaped into his crouching master's arms, then careered wildly round the small room in an ecstasy of joy. Then there was licking of hands and ruffling of pelt and communications of love in the secret language that the two had built up together.

'Sorry, Colonel.' Wilfrid was flushed as he stood up, but the drained expression had gone. There were still deep shadows under his eyes and lines on his cheeks but the eyes were more alive.

'That's all right.' Fremantle cleared his throat. 'Sit ye down. I want to hear about Hangman's Hill. Those Gurkhas must be extraordinary chaps. How the hell did they get up there?'

Wilfrid sat down, letting a hand drop to fondle Dante's ears. The dog squatted beside him, pressing his body close to the gaitered leg.

'Colonel Nangle had ordered two companies to pass through the New Zealanders and assault Hangman's Hill. The company I was with got separated from the other. It was pitch-dark in Cassino and no one had the vaguest idea what was happening and of course the rain had started pissing down. We just pushed on towards our objective and somehow slipped past the enemy positions.'

Fremantle picked up his mashie again and dropped four balls on the earth floor. Dante's ears pricked.

'When daylight came we were on an exposed lump of rock about two hundred yards square. Superb view! The town was 1500 feet below us, the slope so steep you felt you could throw a stone onto the houses.'

'How close to the Monastery were you?'

'Not more than 250 yards. It seemed very much closer.' Wilfrid was more talkative than usual and Fremantle listened with tolerance. He knew that when men have been subjected to extremes of danger and exhaustion they often become garrulous. 'We'd had to travel light, no greatcoats or blankets. There was an icy wind and freezing rain, temperature well below zero at night. We had to scoop shallow trenches out of the rocks and build sangars with stones. Jerry was all round us, above and below. The extraordinary thing was the Gurkhas' relationship with the Paratroopers. The soldiers of both sides had an amazing respect, almost affection for each other. We had three truces when the MO brought stretcher parties up the mountain in daylight to evacuate wounded.'

The CO had hit three balls smack into the bucket. The fourth one rebounded off the edge and skeetered across the floor. Dante intercepted it neatly, took it to Fremantle and dropped it at his feet.

'Well-trained dog. I think I broke my wrists too soon that time.'

'They saw us off Hangman's once but the Gurkhas retook it. After that they were content to shell and mortar us continually. We had over fifty per cent casualties.'

'We could see the aircraft dropping supplies to you. Damn! Missed again.'

'Yes. Most of the stuff dropped outside our positions and trying to fetch it back in daylight was just not on. The Germans were very grateful for our rations – and the blood plasma. The worst problem was water. The Gurkhas found a well a little way down the mountain. The water tasted rather rich and rare but it wasn't till we'd drunk it dry we discovered there was a dead mule at the bottom.'

Fremantle laughed, as he stooped to collect his golf balls from the bucket. 'I saw something of the Gurkhas in North Africa. Knee-high to a grasshopper, but when they get their kukris out and prepare for an up-hill assault they make your blood run cold. Ah, thank you, Stacey.'

The provident Stacey had brought in two mugs of strong tea, doused with tinned milk and sweetened with half a dozen spoonfuls of sugar.

'The programme we laid on to get them out of there seemed reasonably effective.'

'It worked like a charm, Colonel. We came down between two curtains of fire. No trouble at all.'

'Your fire orders had a good deal to do with that, Wilfrid.' The Colonel stirred his tea and took a sip. Then he added casually: 'I suppose there's no harm in you knowing. I've put you in for an MC.'

Wilfrid stared at him with a shocked expression. 'But I didn't do anything to deserve a gong! Goodness, every one of those Gurkhas deserve it more than I do!'

'They'll get their fair share. Let me be the judge where my own officers are concerned. And I've another bit of news for you. You're going on a spot of leave. We've got an allocation at the rest camp in Sorrento. You and an officer from two of the other batteries will be going for a week. You can take that baksheesh Volkswagen we liberated in Tunis.'

*

March 19th. Sunday.

Sunday today. I make it the 20th March. I wish I had Wilfrid's capacity for memorizing verse. He can carry whole sonnets in his head without effort. Takes me about an hour to learn one verse. I've got quite a few verses of hymns and psalms in my head, though. God, we must have sung them hundreds of times! Might sing a hymn and some of the psalms around mid-morning. . . .

It was a good idea to divide the day up into canonical hours.

Matins at 5 a.m. when the internal guards make the rounds of the cells.
Prime and Terce at 8, when the SS guard is changed.
Sext at 12 when the sentries on the gate over my head are relieved.
Nones at 1.30 when my daily ration comes.
Exercise in the afternoon after that, stretching and flexing muscles, getting leverage on the sides of the cylinder.
Vespers at 4 when the sentries are relieved.
Then I let myself think about Maria.
Compline at 8 when the main gates clang as they close. I must not let myself sleep until then.

So long as I can keep that up I can kid myself that I have not been buried alive.

★

The rest camp turned out to be a very pleasant hotel on the slopes above Sorrento. It looked out over the Bay of Naples towards the island of Capri. Wilfrid had a room to himself and that night savoured the rare pleasure of taking a hot bath before slipping between clean sheets. Dante occupied a liberated bread-basket in the far corner of the room and appeared to enjoy the comfort and silence as much as Wilfrid. For a long time after he had put the light out Wilfrid could hear him making contented chopping noises with his mouth and noisily swallowing saliva.

He had trouble in getting to sleep. The silence was eerie. For months the sound of gunfire had been a constant background.

Next day his two companions took the VW into Naples in search of 'talent'. Wilfrid had discovered that a public bus ran along the coast to Pompeii. He spent the day examining the excavated houses of the city. The sun shone for him and, close to the sea, the air was spring-like.

He was back at the hotel by mid-afternoon. The other Greenshire officers had not returned from Naples and most of the occupants of the rest camp were either sleeping on their beds or still out on expeditions. Wilfrid procured a glass of wine from the bar and took it out onto the southward-facing terrace.

A girl sitting in a deckchair reading a magazine glanced up as he came out and then quickly dropped her eyes. She was wearing a coloured blouse and skirt, not uniform. Wilfrid assumed that there must still be a few Italian guests in some part of the hotel. He sat down on the balustrade of the terrace and began to drink his wine. Three miles away the Mediterranean was a shimmering, rippling sheet of silver. Already the bougainvillaea tumbling from the terrace was coming into bloom. The afternoon sun was warm enough to have brought out the frisky bees.

He sat, closed his eyes and let the sun warm his face. After the freezing cold of that comfortless cliff-face on Hangman's Hill this was an intimation of heaven. His mind was rich with the colours of Pompeii's interiors, and the delicious Madonna he had found in a church on the walk up from the bus stop.

A half-muted bark from Dante broke his reverie. He glanced round. The dog was beside the girl, looking up into her face, his tail going like a windscreen wiper, everything about him conveying his interest in the home-made pastry she had charmed the Italian waiter into providing with her tea.

Wilfrid stood up, feeling in his pocket for the lead, and went towards the deckchair.

'*Scusi, signorina. Non deve mendicare.*' He slipped the lead on Dante's collar, gave the girl a nervous smile. She was very attractive indeed. Dark, with a marvellous skin and a stunning figure and legs. She smiled back at him and he felt himself flushing. He dragged Dante away.

That evening before dinner in the bar he saw her again. His two fellow officers were round her, chatting her up in a big way and laughing a lot. She glanced towards him and he quickly swung his eyes away.

God! She was English! He'd made a fool of himself, talking to her in Italian.

In the dining-room he saw her at the far end sitting in the midst of a group of obvious civilians. The men had long hair and the three other girls were very good-looking.

'They're an ENSA party,' Charlie Ward informed the table knowledgeably. 'I can't see why they need leave. Entertaining the troops can't be all that exhausting.'

'Depends on how you understand entertaining, Charlie,'

Mike Higgins remarked with a suggestive grin. 'I should think anyone who'd entertained you for a night would need at least a week in a good clinic to recover.'

The Greenshire pair had come back from Naples titillated by the talent they had seen in the streets but with appetites unassuaged. They'd taken a brief look at what was available in one of the licensed establishments and had got out of there as fast as their dignity would allow.

'I wouldn't mind a week in a clinic with that female we saw on the road up to the hotel. God, you should have seen her, Wilfrid!'

'How *do* those Italian women manage to move their bottoms in that marvellous way, sort of turning their heel to make the muscle of their rump flex with every step?'

'That little ENSA bit we were talking to's not half bad.' Charlie was looking in the direction of the civilian group. 'Wouldn't be surprised if she had some foreign blood in her. I got the impression she might be amenable. I think I'll test the temperature again after dinner. Pass the wine, please, Wilfrid.'

Dinner and the drinks that had preceded and accompanied it had livened everybody up. The atmosphere in the bar afterwards was very convivial. The babble of conversation rose to a roar. The ENSA girls were penned into a corner by eager suitors. Charlie was not the only one who had decided to test the temperature. Wilfrid kept well away from it and after a time took his drink out onto the terrace. Looking up he saw the floor of heaven thick inlaid with patines of bright gold. The conical shape of Vesuvius broke the sky-line to the north. There was enough moonlight for him to see the plume of smoke drifting from the dormant crater.

Next morning he took a bus to Naples on his own, and lunched at an Italian *trattoria*. The art galleries were still closed but he found a few pictures in churches. Best of all, he discovered that the opera was functioning. They were doing *Aïda* the next day. He went to the box office and found himself buying two matinée tickets. Perhaps he'd find a friend to go with him.

He returned early because he did not like to leave Dante alone for too long. He'd just finished giving him his run when the ENSA girl came out of the hotel with her book. She had evidently opted out of all the expeditions that had been planned

266

for the day. Dante ran straight to her, as to an old friend, his tail wagging the whole rear end of his body. She stooped to save her stockings and ruffled his neck.

'I say, I d-do want to apologize for yesterday,' Wilfrid stammered awkwardly. 'Mistaking you for an Italian, I mean.'

She smiled up at him, still crouching to parry Dante's attentions.

'I was pleased to be mistaken for an Italian. That was a compliment. You speak Italian, obviously.'

'A bit. No, Dante, down. Down boy!' She straightened up with a lithe movement.

'What's the matter with his leg?'

'He was nicked by a piece of shrapnel,' Wilfrid said casually, then changed the subject. 'I see you're reading *Sparkenbroke*. You like Charles Morgan?'

'He's my favourite author. But I'm not quite sure about the poetry.'

'Last night I flew into the tree of death.'

Dante, leading the way down the steps in the terrace to a neglected garden below, looked back. Without thinking they began to follow him.

'You didn't go on the expedition to Amalfi?' Wilfrid said, knowing that he was stating the obvious.

'No. It's so marvellous to have a chance to be on one's own, and I find this place so peaceful.'

He wondered if that was a hint to push off, so he made no comment.

A moment later she said: 'What have you been doing? I noticed you didn't go with your friends yesterday or today.'

He glanced round at her shyly, surprised that she had noticed.

'I went to look at Pompeii yesterday. It's really miraculous how those colours have lasted all these years. Have you been?'

'No. Ruins don't attract me all that much.'

'But these houses are as fresh as the day they were built!' Wilfrid exclaimed. 'They've been preserved by the volcanic dust, you see. The wall-paintings look as if they were done yesterday. You really ought to go. There's not much to see in the way of pictures in Naples. I tried today but it was a waste of time. But the opera has started up again.'

She stopped. 'Has it? What are they doing?'

'It's *Aïda* tomorrow. Should be fantastic. Do you like Verdi?'

★

Sitting in the fifth row of the stalls waiting for the curtain to go up, Wilfrid experienced one of those rare moments when happiness wells up untrammelled within the spirit. After Cassino, to be in an opera house, listening to the wild gaiety of an orchestra tuning up, staring at a curtain which would soon rise on a world of magic, was delight such as he had never expected to experience again. He turned to smile at Rachel and found her already smiling at him.

After the opera was over, in a kind of daze, they wandered along the street, hardly caring where they were going. It was only half-past five. Neither of them spoke. They were still full of the music. To break the spell with small talk would have been sacrilege. Never before had Wilfrid known this brimming sensation of being on the threshold of some wonderful discovery. Then at a cross-roads she stopped and looked southwards. Her fingers tightened on his forearm.

'Look!'

He followed the direction of her gaze. The street ran towards the open country. Beyond where it disappeared the conical shape of Mount Vesuvius rose, seeming quite small at that distance. From its summit there poured a surging, muscular mass of smoke and dust, orange, grey and blue in colour. It pulsed upwards into the unbroken blue of a clear sky to a height of ten thousand feet, swirling, powerful and awesome. The volcano had at that very moment blown its top.

They stood watching the extraordinary spectacle for half an hour, gazing and wondering, and when at last they turned away they felt bound by a unique experience.

'That was the most inspiring and awesome thing I've ever seen,' Rachel said. 'I'm glad I was with you when it happened.'

After a minute Wilfrid asked: 'Why me? You could have had your pick of the officers at the rest camp.'

She laughed and her nose wrinkled. 'I did have my pick. It's because you're different. You stood aloof when all the others were crowding round me. You've no idea what a relief it is to escape from those same endless questions. The invariable verbal passes. We've been at it for six months now.

'Sometimes I'm afraid I'm going to scream.' She squeezed his arm. 'Don't worry, darling. I'm not going to scream. With you for the first time since we left home I can be myself.'

*

Next day the other Greenshires, exercising unusual tactfulness, took the bus into Naples and left Wilfrid with the VW. He drove Rachel along the Costa Amalfitana. They stopped many times to gaze down at the small beaches below, or back at the still smoking mountian.

Dante wore a permanent air of proprietorial satisfaction. He was well aware that the whole thing had been his doing.

By the end of the week Rachel and Wilfrid were totally in love.

'You'll write to me, won't you?' he said, as his kit was being brought down to the VW. 'You've got my BFPO, haven't you?'

'Yes, darling. Every day. And you'll do the same?'

'I promise. Whenever I can. Let's try to have our next leave at the same time, shall we?'

Rachel's brow puckered.

'I'm afraid we may have to go back to England before the Second Front. It could be a long time before we meet again. You won't forget me, will you?'

'No.' Holding her hands he looked down into her face with his serious, thoughtful expression. 'I shall not forget you for one single moment of the day or night. You won't lose my home address, will you? Even if we can't meet till the war is over I'll feel just the same.'

'So will I. Goodbye, darling.'

As the VW drove away he twisted round to wave. She was standing on the terrace where he had first seen her. Charlie and Mike studiously avoided looking at him, but Dante's eyes never left his face.

25

The April sun had melted the last of the snow. The migrating birds, heedless of battles, were beginning to wing their way northwards. Swallows from North Africa were heading joyfully towards the eaves of houses in Germany that had been blasted into dust since last year's nesting.

The valleys were turning green with wild corn and the streams were bursting. Compassionate spring spread her ephemeral mantle of beauty over Cassino town, but it lay like a threadbare embroidery on the corpse of a long dead man. Flowers sprouted miraculously from the rubble, tinting the wasteland with brush-strokes of vermilion, cobalt and indigo. The stagnant water in the bomb craters brightly reflected the azure sky and its bosomy drifting clouds. Here and there oily patches displayed all the colours of the rainbow. On the slopes of Montecassino the surviving Judas trees were sucking blood from the soil and squeezing it into their reddish sprouting buds.

But over it all hung a constant pall of smoke and the hammering of mortar-bombs was constant. It was hard to believe that there were men living beneath those ruins.

Behind the fitfully dormant front line Alexander was preparing for Diadem – the master-stroke which was to smash the German armies in Italy once and for all. He and Kesselring had one thing in common. Both knew that they would have to fight their Italian campaign with depleted forces. Alexander was to lose the whole of the French Expeditionary Corps and up to five US Divisions. The French colonial troops would be needed for Anvil – the cosmetic invasion of the Côte d'Azur which was intended to link up with the Resistance and restore the self-respect of the French nation. Eisenhower wanted the Americans for the cross-channel invasion of Fortress Europe, code-name Overlord.

In the eyes of the higher commands, Italy had become a side-show. For those taking part it was a bloody side-show.

On the German side too there was re-deployment. To von Senger's chagrin the Cassino front was split. The inter-corps boundary between his XIV Panzer Corps and General Feurstein's L1 Mountain Corps was moved south. As a result the Cassino Position, which .von Senger had so successfully defended, became the responsibility of staff officers in Feurstein's headquarters who had not the same experience of it. But Heidrich's 1st Parachute Division still held Montecassino and Cassino Town, faced in the latter by 1st Guards Brigade.

Alexander's deception plan was working like a charm. As the multi-national divisions of Fifth and Eighth Armies re-grouped, elaborate steps were taken to mislead the enemy. Whilst false formations exchanged what appeared to be normal wireless traffic, the real formations maintained wireless silence. Spies observed Canadians carrying out beach-landing exercises at Salerno, whilst the mustering 1st Canadian Corps preserved anonymity by removing all its markings. Reconnaissance of the front was severely rationed, lest the capture of a Pole near Snakeshead Ridge or a Frenchman in the Aurunci mountains should give the game away. Virtually no written orders were issued in Eighth Army. So successful were these measures that Kesselring informed his army commanders that no major offensive need be expected before 23 May. At the beginning of May von Vietinghof, von Senger and Baade, obeying a summons from Hitler, departed to attend an investiture at Obersalzburg, followed by a senior officers' indoctrination course. Before 11 May von Senger's deputy had allowed his Chief of Staff to go home on leave. By a coincidence, unfortunate for the Germans, Kesselring's own Chief of Staff was on sick leave at the same time.

On Snakeshead Ridge the Kreswan and Carpathian Divisions of the Polish Corps had crept up into the positions from which 34th US and 4th Indian Divisions had vainly assaulted Point 593. Under General Vladislaw Anders their appointed task was to cut through the Paratroopers, reach Route 6 and isolate the Monastery. This would be their first action since the exodus from Poland and they were prepared to die for the cause that would liberate their homeland. They did not know that at the Teheran Conference the Big Three had already agreed how they would parcel out Europe when final victory was achieved. They did not know that Roosevelt sought to appease the Russian bear by throwing Poland to him. They did not know that four thousand of their officers had been liquidated in the forest of Katyn. They did not know that few even of the survivors of this battle would ever see Poland again.

The French Expeditionary Corps had been switched to the Aurunci Mountains on the left flank. Now they occupied the narrow bridge-head over the Garigliano which had been won by British 10 Corps. Though no one realized it yet, except perhaps General Juin, they were the ace in the pack, with their rations on the hoof, their capacity to subsist for days on minimal supplies, and above all their ability to scale the steepest mountains. These North African troops were to exert pressure where the line was most vulnerable, at the boundary between L1 Mountain and X1V Panzer Corps.

Beyond them on the seabord was 11 US Corps, commanded by General Geoffrey Keyes and consisting of the fresh 85th and 88th US Divisions.

The flat valley of the Liri still offered the best road to Rome. The Italian capital lay seventy miles away, with all that the Eternal City meant in terms of propaganda for both Allies and Germans. Here was where the main thrust would come. 13 British Corps, commanded by Lieutenant General Sir Sidney Kirkman, was poised for an assault across the Rapido, that Bloody River which had destroyed the Texas Division. But whereas the Americans in January had attacked with two divisions Kirkman would attack with four – 4th British Infantry, 78th British Infantry, 8th Indian and 6th British Armoured.

The 1st Canadian Corps under General Burns were waiting at the rear of Eight Army and would not take part in the first phase of the battle. Their task was to sweep through when the first objectives had been secured and smash into the defensive line which the Germans had prepared further up the valley. The Allies still referred to it as the Hitler Line. These Canadians would be fighting as a national corps and taking part in a major offensive for the first time in the Second World War.

With so many divisions committed to the attack the only formation available as reserve was 6th South African Armoured Division, newly arrived in Italy.

The Polish, British and Canadian Corps, together with the South Africans, were under command of Lieutenant-General Sir Oliver Leese's Eighth Army. The French and Americans, along with the troops in the Anzio beach-head, belonged to General Clark's Fifth Army.

Concealed within the arsenal of 13 Corps there was a dagger. It was aimed ready for a thrust which would be made as soon as the German line was broken. Its role was a hazardous one – to drive swiftly between the boundaries of von Senger's and Feurstein's Corps, swing right and cut off the retreat of the formations in the Cassino Position. Built round the light tanks and armoured cars of the Derbyshire Yeomanry it comprised elements of other arms, including gunners. Artillery support was provided by a battery of 25-pounders from the Greenshires. The CO had allocated C Battery for the task, Major Stockwell having returned from convalescence. Captain Wilfrid Stewart would act as observation officer.

So they faced each other, these opposing hosts, comprising with their support and supply units some two million persons. To the Allies' 25 divisions the Germans were opposing 23, and they were numerically much smaller divisions. In everything except the suitability of the terrain Alexander had the advantage. 1660 guns, 2000 tanks and 3000 aircraft were available to boost the infantry assault. But in the end it would come down to man versus man, body and heart against body and heart.

In the May sunshine the ruins of the Monastery brooded over the killing-ground. It all looked quite peaceful now. The mist that hung over Cassino could have been the normal exhalations of the Rapido. After nightfall fireflies cruised luminously through the corn and nightingales sang in the trees of the Liri Valley. In a few days the moon would be full.

There was going to be another battle – more guts to be spilled, skulls to be split open, eyes to be blinded, hands to clutch the earth, life's blood to soak into green grass.

26

The passage of time, or rather the recording of it, had become an obsession. It was immensely important to recognize the Sabbath and to observe it. He always rested on Sunday. That is to say he let himself off the physical exercises, which he scrupulously carried out every afternoon between Nones and Vespers, and allowed his body its sparse, pathetic indulgences.

It had been a great triumph when, after two weeks and three days in the cylinder, he had prised a piece of concrete from a joint in the huge pipes. His taps on the side of his prison had evoked no response for two days. Then at last he had heard an answering tap from a few feet away. The confirmation that there was another living human being sharing this purgatory with him was a wonderful uplift for the spirit. Whoever the other prisoner was he knew no Morse. Their communication was limited to varied patterns of tapping, almost like simple tunes.

According to his 'records' today was Monday the 9th of May. It seemed a very long time since the mid-day relief of the guard at the main gate. It was becoming more and more difficult to concentrate, to keep track of these things and a score of times he had been tempted to let it all go hang. The fear haunted him that he had counted days twice. In the darkness and silence it would be easy to make a mistake like that.

When he heard the food trolley clanking along the corridor outside he began to salivate, like an animal. Foul as the food was its arrival provided the highlight of his day, the one concrete proof that the outside world still acknowledged his existence. He turned his body round so that his head was at the lower end, towards the small flap through which his daily ration was pushed.

He ate the bread, holding it in his filthy, long-nailed hands, chewing it till it had the consistency of soup, resisting the urge to wolf it down. It was important to squeeze the maximum amount of pleasure out of this great event.

He had just finished, had squirmed round and was reaching for the stone to signal his neighbour that he had finished eating when the building was shaken by a heavy explosion – then another, and another. He heard the distant rattle of machine-gun fire, the crashing of the food containers, the thud of running feet.

There followed a pause of perhaps two minutes. Then the concussions came again, as if some storm of retribution were swirling over the prison.

During the second pause he waited, bewildered, not daring to hope. Then he heard again the sound of running feet, the jangling of keys. An Italian voice shouted: *'Ecco, capitano! E qui dentro!'* The circular door to his cylinder was opened. Light flooded in. He cried out and covered his eyes.

'Richard!'

God in heaven, the voice was Fen's!

'Fen,' he croaked. Screwing his eyes up tight he scrabbled towards the light.

'Man, you're in a mess! Where are your clothes?'

'Took them.'

'We've no time to worry about that. Phew! What a stink!'

All along the corridor partisans were opening the doors of the cylinders, hauling out the naked, bearded and filthy prisoners. Richard wanted to see his friend from the next-door cylinder but he was cowering at the far end, too broken and terrified to come out. Fen had to drag the almost blind Richard along the corridor and up the stairs.

'Bill! I've got him.'

Richard heard Bill's voice, echoing the exultant shout.

'Ram, Fen's got him.'

The upper floors were a shambles. As the power to see returned, Richard saw that the bombs had made great breaches in the walls. Prisoners as well as SS men lay dead amongst the debris, but many gaunt, wild figures were limping to their freedom. From the roof a sentry was shooting as many as he could. Some died at the very moment of liberation. The whole scene was illuminated by the orange glow of the half dozen fires which had started.

Hans was tottering against a wall, tied in the Jap way Ram had learned in Burma – a fine cord binding elbows tight behind his shoulder-blades, head yanked back and the free end passed between his teeth. Hans was staring at the ceiling, grinning bloodily as the cord ripped his lips.

Sauckel was hanging from a beam by a pair of his own handcuffs.

There came a roar of sound as a squadron of Mustangs flew low over the building. Richard cowered.

'It's a dummy run,' Bill shouted. 'Next time they'll be dropping bombs. Let's go.'

Ram gave Hans a push. He could not keep his balance and fell gurgling, the cord splitting his lips.

Bill was aiming his Tommy-gun at the dangling body of Sauckel. The SS captain's teeth were bared in a grimace of fear or defiance.

'No, Bill!'

Bill swung on Richard in disbelief.

'What?'

'No. Don't shoot him.'

'You must be mad.'

'I don't want you to kill him.'

Bill's jaw dropped. From the door Fen shouted: 'Come on, Bill! What the hell are you waiting for?'

Bill grabbed an SS greatcoat from a hook, put it round Richard's naked body. He was still dazed by the violent noise and movement coming unexpectedly after weeks of isolation and immobility. Somewhere near he recognized the stentorian voice of Toro ordering his partisans to withdraw. The prisoners had been released from their cells. Now they would have to take their chance to escape.

Richard's legs were atrophied. Fen swept him up in his arms and carried him out of the place like a baby. As they crossed the forecourt Bill turned and shot the sentry on the roof.

At the prison gate Bill put two fingers into his mouth and gave vent to a piercing shepherd's whistle. From where he had been waiting a couple of hundred yards away Nick came tearing up in the Lancia Lambda. Around them the partisans also were piling into getaway cars, hauling on board as many of their own people as they had been able to find in the Sipo gaol.

As the car roared away through the empty streets the Mustangs swept low again. This time they were strafing with machine guns and dropping bombs.

'Why didn't you let me kill that bastard?' Bill demanded, as they left the streets behind and headed out into open country.

'Don't know.'

'Wasn't he the officer in charge, the one who tortured you?'

'Yes.'

'Then why did you stop me killing him?'

'Don't know. We – he . . . respect for me.'

'*Respect*! Jesus, you've gone round the bloody bend.'

'Douse it, Bill,' Nick said, without taking his eyes from the road.

'Nick,' Richard said with sudden cogency, 'what day is it? Is it Monday 9th May? Please say it is!'

'It's Monday all right.' It was Bill who supplied the answer. 'But it's the 8th, not the 9th.'

'How can it be? If I've got my days . . .'

'Richard, old sport, what the hell does it matter? Aren't you glad to be out of that shit-house?'

The three in the back seat lurched sideways as Nick took a sharp bend with the tyres screaming. Ram twisted round to look out through the rear window.

'Did the bloke in the next cylinder to me get out?'

'Everyone had a chance to escape. We opened all the cell doors. But it was you we were after and we had not much time.'

Richard was recovering the use of his eyes. He could see that it was a beautiful spring day. The land was green and colourful, the sky white and blue. It was as if he had been born fully equipped, like Athena in the Temple, but instead of the weapons of war he had the senses of perception. He tried to control the flood of emotion. He did not want to break down and weep.

Nick was driving with the window beside him wide open. In the front passenger seat Ram was cradling a Tommy-gun. In

277

the back seat beside him Bill was holding his nose and Fen had a handkerchief pressed over the lower part of his face.

'Bill. . . . don't know what. . . . ' Richard prodded one eye with his knuckle. 'Feel a bit funny. Can't believe I'm out of it.'

'Don't worry, old boy. I'm sorry we kept you waiting so long. We made at least six plans to spring you but had to abandon them. In the end we had to coordinate our attack with the RAF. That took a little time.'

'Hell of a – of a risk.'

'Not really.. We arranged with them that they'd make two bombing and strafing runs. That softened the Germans up a bit. Then they made two dummy runs, flew low but did not bomb or strafe. That made the Krauts keep their heads down so that we could go in. They made another dummy run while we were inside just to discourage any interference. The fifth run was for real. We knew we only had five minutes to get in and out again.'

'Of course!' Richard's lips had been moving as he listened. 'Leap year!'

Bill shook his head as if to clear it. 'What?'

'Leap year! Why I was a day out.'

Fen and Bill turned their heads inward to stare at him, then exchanged a glance of pity.

'Nick, must you have your window open?'

'Don't you realize, old man,' Bill explained. 'You smell ten times worse than any pole-cat?'

Fen asked: 'How long did they keep you in that shit-hole?'

'Seventy days, if you count – .'

'Ten weeks.' Fen for once was not smiling. 'Left to lie naked in your own filth.'

'Oh, wasn't so bad. Better than their interrogation rooms. I was left in peace and reasonably warm. Couldn't hear the screaming of the women they brought in. That was the worst thing – up above – those women screaming. Bring them in late at night and – '

'Okay, Richard,' Nick said loudly from the front seat. 'Take it easy. Don't try and tell us about it now. You're in bad shape, you need time to readjust.'

Fen said: 'I'd never have recognized you.'

'Yes, how . . . You knew where to find me. You came straight to my cylinder.'

278

Nick had turned off the road following the valley and the car was now climbing into hills. Beyond were high peaks but the snow had vanished from their crests.

'We had our informant – the Italian who cleaned out the interrogation rooms. Through the partisan network he let us know where you were. We'd never have found you otherwise. You were among the Italian criminal prisoners.'

'SS captain to thank for that. Should have been shot or sent to a concentration camp. Wonder how many of those poor sods got away.'

'All who were capable of running,' Bill assured him. 'There were some too far gone to move.'

'What I'd like more than anything in this world is a long, hot bath. No, two long hot baths. Suppose I'll have to make do with –'

Bill chuckled and Ram turned from the passenger's seat to flash his brilliant smile. 'My lad, you don't know what lies in store for you. You are the blue-eyed boy of the Gruppo Manzoni.'

'Bill, I –'

'Yes?'

'Have to tell you. I broke under questioning. Told them everything I knew.'

'We know what you told them,' Bill replied equably. He had shown no surprise at Richard's admission. 'We know quite a few other things too.'

'For instance,' Fen joined in, 'that you stood up to the most brutal interrogation for two weeks and refused to speak; that you only talked in the end to save a woman partisan from hideous torture –'

'I let them start on her, they had her in a connecting room and I could hear everything. God, it was –'

'Forget it, Richard.' Nick slowed the car and spoke over his shoulder. 'It did not make all that difference you talking. When Toro heard they'd got you, he said we must assume they'd break you in the end, so we made our dispositions accordingly.'

'Nick's quite right,' Bill agreed.

Richard was swung against the reassuring bulk of Fen's body as the car took a hairpin bend. 'You haven't said anything about Pat.'

Bill and Fen exchanged a grin.

'Pat's fine,' Fen assured him. 'He and Spragg got away from the farm before the SS came. Thanks to some persuasion from Toro he was admitted to the clinic of one of the best orthopaedic specialists in Italy – as an Italian, of course. When they heard how he got his injuries nothing was too good for him!'

'Is he still in hospital?' Richard could not understand why the others found this so hilarious.

'No, they chucked him out. He's up at the partisan camp.'

It was after half an hour's driving that the Lancia stopped at a luxurious Swiss-type chalet set on the slope overlooking a mountain valley. It belonged to a rich Roman lawyer who was not in a position to leave the city. The couple of retainers who looked after it for him were sympathetic to the partisans.

'This is where we leave you, pal,' Nick explained quietly. Bill had gone to the gate and was staring back down the road. 'These people will look after you. We'll be back in a couple of days to pick you up.'

Standing on the gravel driveway Richard looked down at his bare legs and feet sticking out below the greatcoat.

'But you can't leave me like this!'

The Lancia accelerated away towards the gate, spurting gravel from its wheels. Richard heard the door of the house open. He turned to find himself facing a middle-aged, buxom woman with an apron tied round her waist.

He was shown to a magnificent guest suite with a bathroom as big as a small studio. It was equipped with all that he needed. As in a dream, he cut his beard and shaved the bristles off. His wish for two hot baths had come true. In the first he washed the dirt off his body and let the filthy water drain out. In the second he lay and luxuriated for half an hour. He dressed in the Roman lawyer's holiday clothes which had been laid out on a couch, then sat down to a meal which must have taxed even the resources of the Italian black market.

When he had eaten he stood for a long time staring out of the window. His strength and balance of mind were coming back; but it was still embarrassingly easy to be moved to tears. The trees were coming into blossom. The weather was warm. Streams sparkled in the sun. Mountains were majestic against the blue sky.

He felt an irresistible desire to sleep. He went to bed, revelling in the delight of slipping between clean sheets.

He woke, believing he was still in the cylinder. He blinked at the light, stared round him striving to get his bearings. Daylight was fading beyond the drawn curtains. The sound of water running in the bathroom reminded him where he was.

'*Chi è?*'

The water was turned off. He saw a woman appear in the doorway. She was wearing a long, silk housecoat. Her hair had been loosed and fell down her back. Against the light he could not see her face.

It's a dream. I'm still asleep.

He said again: 'Who is it?'

She came forward into the room on bare feet, the silk swishing as she moved. She went to the curtains and opened them a chink. The light of a setting sun fell on her face.

'Who are you?' he asked again.

'My name is Corina. I am from the Gruppo Manzoni. We heard what happened. We know that you held out for fourteen days and only gave in because they were torturing a girl partisan. So I have come to help bring your poor body back to life.'

She came towards him, unfastening the belt of her silk coat. She withdrew her arms from the sleeves and let it fall to the floor. Then she pulled the sheet off him and knelt down on the floor at the end of the bed.

She began with his feet and he realized for the first time what responsive members they can be under sensitive fingers. Then she stood up and began to stroke the insides of his legs with slow circular movements, gradually moving up towards the top of the V.

'You like that, *tesoro*?'

'Yes, but –'

'Be patient. There is no hurry.'

She continued her upward progress till she came to his head. Her tongue explored his ears, her lips brushed his mouth gently. Her full breasts hung over his chest. He could feel her nipples against his own.

'Turn over. I want to massage your back.'

Her hands eased the tension of the muscles at the back of his neck, then worked their way down the length of his body again till they came to his feet.

He rolled over onto his back. 'Signorina, I –'

'Shh – .' She reached up and put a finger on his lips. 'I have not finished yet.'

She was deploying the full range of a well-schooled seductress. The *faena* of the fingers was over. It was time now for the mouth. Again her lips slid softly over his, no more than hinting at kisses to come. She took a nipple at a time between her sharp teeth and bit gently.

As the mouth treatment became even more intimate he was ashamed at his lack of response.

'It's no good,' he said at last. 'I don't know what's wrong with me.'

'You are tired. You need more rest.'

'No, it's not that. It's what happened in the prison, the things they did to the women. I keep hearing those terrible screams –'

She began to move away but he held her. 'Please stay with me. I want to go to sleep holding you.'

*

It was dark when he woke. This time he knew where he was. The warm, soft form was in his arms. She was lying with her back to him. When she felt him stir she tightened the muscles of her rump. The luxuriance of her breasts filled his hands. The nightmare memories had gone. His body was liberated.

He flung the sheet away and pulled her onto her back, wanting now to be the dominant one. She lay waiting. There was enough filtered moonlight for him to see her eyes staring up at him and her lips parted. He controlled his impatience and began to caress her, wanting to return the tenderness, the slow prelude which she had given him.

'Come, *tesoro*! I am ready for you. Don't wait! Come quickly!'

*

'Who is Maria?'

'What?'

'Maria. Who is she?'

'Why do you ask that?'

282

'You spoke her name while you were asleep.'

'Did I?'

It was daylight again. She had put on the silk housecoat and was lying beside him, her head tilted, gazing at him with a smile in which he thought he saw a wry sadness.

'Who is she? That is an Italian name and I do not think you were referring to the Virgin.'

'I'm sorry.'

'Were you thinking of her when we made love? Pretending that I was Maria?'

'No, Corina. I promise you I was not. But there is someone called Maria.'

'And you love her?'

He hesitated. 'Yes. But I was not thinking of her when we made love. Please believe that. And you will never know what you have done for me. You gave me something that I needed very fundamentally.'

She bent over and kissed him gently.

'*Addio, tesoro.* I do not think we will make love again. I do not want to take any more of you from this Maria, whoever she is.'

★

When they arrived at ten that morning Nick and Bill had Pat with them. They found Richard sitting up enjoying a late breakfast in bed.

'How's the patient?'

'You sure look as if you'd got your tail over the dashboard.'

He smiled up at the ring of grinning faces. They knew perfectly well what the cure had consisted of. The bed was topsy-turvy and Corina's perfume still hung in the air.

'Pat can vouch for the effectiveness of Italian nursing, can't you?'

Pat reddened and looked self-conscious.

'Tell Richard about that masseuse who worked you over.'

To save the Irishman embarrassment Richard cut in: 'You really are OK, Pat?'

'Never better.'

'What about the leg?'

'Och, I've still got a bit of a limp but I can use it fine.'

Bill was sniffing the air. 'I must say you smell a lot better

283

than when we last saw you. Was the – ah – treatment satisfactory?'

After the inevitable pleasantries and ribbing Nick became serious.

'We'd like to give you longer but something's come up. Do you feel whack enough to take on a job of translating?'

'A job! God, don't you realize I'm completely clapped out?'

'It sounds urgent, and looks like you're the only one can handle it.'

'I don't know if I can. You'd better tell me about it while I shave.'

He put a towel round his middle, went into the bathroom and stropped his Rolls Razor. While he shaved Bill explained.

'It's to do with some information that came through partisan channels. Toro heard that there was an ex-officer of Badoglio's army in Subiaco. He was one of a group that volunteered to do a job in Germany, somewhere in the Harz Mountains. Most of them were shot, no one knows why. But this chap managed to make his way back through Germany and into Italy. Christ knows how he did it. He must have practically dragged himself on hands and knees. He's in the advanced stages of terminal tuberculosis –'

'You've seen him?'

'Yes. I went over with Toro and Il Professore yesterday. He's hanging onto life by a whisker. His intention was to go through the lines to the Allies, but when he got as far as Subiaco he collapsed. Only one thing is keeping him alive. He says he's got information of such vital importance that he'll only give it to an Allied officer in person.'

'Didn't he tell you what it was?'

'He tried to, but I couldn't make out what he was talking about. I suggested he let Il Professore translate but he shook his head. He's very suspicious. I'm not surprised after what he's been through.'

'Is he sane?'

'Yes. I think so. He's very insistent that his information is so vital that it will determine the outcome of the war. If you feel up to it Toro wants you to talk to him, but it's got to be soon. I've never seen anyone who more obviously ought to be dead.'

'I think I'm up to it.' Richard swished his razor through the water and carefully dried it on the towel. 'How far away is Subiaco?'

'Ten miles as the crow flies. Thirty by road. Since we sprung the prison the Fascist police are everywhere and they've got road blocks on all the roads. The partisans will take you and me across country and get us into Subiaco. This Italian is too ill to be moved. He's holding on by a thread.'

★

The party of four ate at the partisans' new camp before setting off across the hills on a bee-line to Subiaco. Toro had detailed two of his men to act as guides and escort for the two British officers. One of them was Guido, the same lad as had met them when they first arrived at Peroli. The other was nicknamed Saturnino, which suited him well. He was a tall, dark man with aquiline features. Richard did not feel he could easily come to trust him. Bill and Richard had their service revolvers but the two partisans were as usual armed to the teeth.

Richard soon found that he had over-estimated the strength of his legs. The party stopped at a farm, borrowed a mule and put him astride it. They climbed half a dozen steep slopes and descended into as many valleys before they at last looked down on the red roofs of Subiaco.

'We must wait till dark,' Saturnino warned. 'There is a curfew at six, but we can avoid the patrols by using back streets.'

'You know the town?'

Saturnino's gaunt face twisted into his concept of smile. 'I was a lay brother in the monastery here. That was where I became familiar with Saint Thomas of Aquino's doctrine of the Just War.'

They waited in a wood on the outskirts of the town for night to fall. Richard and Saturnino filled in time arguing about Dante Alighieri's sympathetic treatment of Francesca da Rimini. As the town disappeared in shadow they tethered the mule and followed a footpath into the town. The streets were deserted. Only cats were prowling the alleys which Saturnino followed. Once they had to cross a main street. As they were about to dash over a patrol of Fascist police came round the corner and they ducked back. At sight of the uniforms Richard had an attack of the shivers. He felt an

285

irresistible urge to run for it. Bill had to hold him by main force.

When the patrol had passed they crossed the street in a tight bunch. After a quarter of a mile Saturnino stopped at a house in a narrow lane. He looked both ways before rapping the door – rat-ta-ta-tat. It was opened immediately. The four men tumbled in.

A frightened woman and two very nervous men received them in a small room. The woman insisted on offering *vin'santo* and biscuits.

'How is Antonio?' Saturnino asked her husband.

'He is sinking fast.'

'Is this the doctor?'

'Yes. This is Doctor Comastri.'

An old but alert man with a triangular patch of beard on his chin came forward out of the shadows.

'*Buona sera, dottore*,' Saturnino said. 'Can you revive him?'

'I cannot revive him.' Doctor Comastri's voice was little more than a husky whisper. 'All I can do is give him an injection that will strengthen him for a short while. But it will be only temporary and will impose a severe strain on his heart.'

'But he is going to die anyway?'

'Oh, yes.'

'Then, doctor, that is what you must do. He has come so far only for this.'

The doctor nodded and peered nervously from Richard to Bill. 'Which is the British officer who will speak to him?'

'I am, *dottore*.'

'You must let me go in to him first. He insists on seeing you alone. I will call you when he is ready.'

Richard followed the doctor upstairs, waited on the landing while he entered a room where a low light was burning. He could hear laboured breathing, the murmur of voices, a heavy cough.

Then the doctor came out and said in his whispering voice: 'He is ready for you now.'

'How long have I got?'

The doctor shrugged. 'Who knows? Five minutes. Perhaps ten. He has the courage of a lion.'

Richard went in. On the bed was a man so shrunken and

286

wasted that it was hard to see what was left to support life. But the eyes were bright.

'You speak Italian? You are a British officer?'

Richard answered in Italian. 'Yes.'

'How can I be sure of that?'

'I promise you he is British, Antonio,' the doctor said from the doorway.

'Leave us alone, *dottore*.'

'But you may need me –'

'Please. My last request.'

Doctor Comastri nodded, went out and closed the door.

'Sit down. Close, where I can see you.'

Richard pulled a chair up to the bedside and sat.

'Let me feel your hand.'

He gave his hand. The other grasped it in his own cold hand. He retained his grip all through the conversation that followed.

For a time he stared into Richard's eyes, breathing with an effort. He was summoning up the strength to talk.

'We have not long. The doctor warned me. You have a good memory?'

'I hope so.'

'When I have told you, you will write it down immediately?'

'Yes.'

'And you will take the information to Mr Churchill?'

'I will see that he gets it.'

'You will cross the lines?'

'Yes.'

'Good. Now, where to begin?'

The eyes remained open but turned inward. The hand tightened its grip on Richard's.

'After the Armistice, in October last year, I was one of a group of Italian soldiers who volunteered for work in Germany. We were allowed to keep our own uniforms and had our own officers. They were our Allies, remember. We were sent to the Harz Mountains, near Nordhausen. It was a camp, code-name DORA, part of a much bigger camp at a place called Buchenwald.'

He stopped to cough, leaving blood on the handkerchief made from a torn-up sheet.

'Buchenwald, did you say?'

'Yes, but this was a sub-camp called DORA. Except that it was not a camp. It was the interior of a mountain.'

Richard wondered if he was listening to a man in delirium.

'Yes. There were 125,000 square metres of chambers and tunnels hollowed out of the solid rock. A vast factory. When we saw the work that we were called upon to do most of us refused to do it. We had not agreed to help manufacture such terrible weapons of war. Those who would not cooperate were shot by the Germans. I decided to cooperate and try to escape later.'

Another pause for coughing. Richard wanted to ask questions, to try to come to the nub of the matter. Time was running out. But he felt he must let the man tell the story in his own way. He had to lean close and concentrate very hard to hear the words and comprehend them.

'The inside of that mountain was a hell on earth. There were 11,000 prisoners – Poles, French, Russians, even some German criminals. There were Gestapo spies and informers everywhere. We had twelve hours hard labour a day, six hours roll-call and queueing for food. We slept for the few hours we could on four-tier wooden bunks. It was cold, very damp, always dark. They took away our uniforms, made us wear striped suits. There were no latrines except for empty carbide barrels. It was a kilometer walk to the water taps. Many died or were executed. They carried the corpses away in trucks to the crematorium at Buchenwald. For bad work the punishment was flogging. For sabotage it was strangulation by hanging, in public.'

'Oh, Jesus.'

The coughing again. After the paroxysm Antonio closed his eyes. It seemed that he was too exhausted to continue. He fought for breath, then opened his eyes again.

'Listen carefully now. Can you find my boots?'

'They're under the chair here.'

'Take the right one. Got it? Now, rip the heel off. There's a knife on the tray there.'

Richard ripped the worn heel off. Inside was a piece of thin paper, wrapped in the kind of waterproof tissue used for poultices. He unwrapped it carefully and smoothed the paper on his knee. It appeared to be a drawing of some kind of bomb.

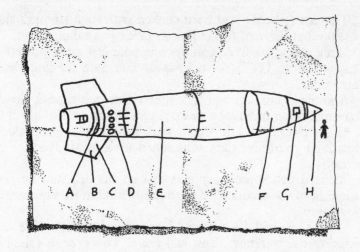

A B C D E F G H

'That is what we were constructing inside the mountain. I only made that drawing when I had reached Italy. The human figure gives you the scale.'

Until then Richard had not noticed the figure.

'But it is gigantic! It must be fifty feet long.'

'At least. My estimate is twenty metres.'

'Is it an aircraft? It looks more like a bomb.'

'It is a rocket. You see the letters? I will tell you what they mean. A is a rocket motor. B external vanes. C stabilisers. D pumps. E oxygen tanks. F alcohol tank. G the automatic pilot. H is the war-head. Yes, you are wise to write it down.'

'How much explosive does it carry?'

'You must not think of ordinary explosive. This is the important part. The German scientists are working on a new explosive. Not even the Germans themselves know of this. But one pound of this explosive is more powerful than a ton of TNT.'

'That's not poss –.' Richard bit off his objection. He was remembering how German prisoners had talked of Hitler's new secret weapon.

'This rocket has a range of several hundred miles. With it the Germans will be able to bombard London and other English cities. In October last Hitler ordered production to be increased to 900 a month. When they are ready England will be obliterated from the face of the earth – and Europe will be enslaved for a thousand years.'

289

The last sentence had been spoken with such strength and passion that Richard forgot he was talking to a dying man.

'This new explosive. You say one pound is more powerful than a ton of TNT. What basis do you have for that? It is incredible.'

Antonio began to cough. The sheets were stained with blood. Through the coughing he was trying to speak.

'You release –.' The words were gasped out. He paused, breathing painfully, then summoned up a great effort. 'You release – .'

Richard could only suppose that in his delirium he was thinking of the comrades he had left behind in the concentration camp.

'Yes, they will be released,' he reassured him. 'We are winning the war now. You just relax. This is very valuable information you have given me. I will see that it reaches Mr Churchill.'

'You release – .'

'Doctor, can you come in? He's having trouble breathing.'

The doctor came in, shook his head. 'There is nothing more I can do. To give him another injection would kill him.'

Antonio's eyes were closed. He appeared to be unconscious. Then unexpectedly they opened and focussed intently on Richard. He raised his head from the pillow. When he spoke the words were blurred.

'You release the energy in the atom.'

He fell back. His eyes were still open but lifeless. The breathing had ceased. The doctor reached across and pulled down his eyelids.

After a while Richard asked: 'Did you catch what he said, doctor?'

'Yes. He said: "*Liberi l'energia nella tomba*".'

'"You release your energy in the tomb." What did he mean?'

The doctor pursed his lips and adopted a serious, pious expression. 'I believe that the spirit often moves across to the other side before physical death takes place. I base this on statements of patients who have suffered clinical death and then been restored to life. What this poor soul had glimpsed was the glory of the life to come.'

Richard stared down at the dead face. The mouth had slackened into the mould of final repose, but the cheeks were more hollow and shrunken than before. The stress of that final communication had left lines of constriction on his temples and forehead. He raised his hand in a salute to one of the anonymous and unsung heroes of the war.

★

It was not till they were back in the partisan camp and alone in the tent with Ram, Bill and Nick that he was able to speak without risk of being overheard.

'Was it worth all the trouble?' Bill asked.

'Yes. In fact, I learned something incredible.'

Richard was having trouble in keeping his eyes open. The effort of getting to Subiaco and concentrating on Antonio's story had completely exhausted him.

'Spill it.'

Richard thought for a moment. 'I don't think I should, Nick. This is so hot that only those who have to know ought to be told. It's no exaggeration that if it's true it could affect the whole outcome of the war. I've simply got to find a way of getting back to Alex with this information. Bill, can you get me through the lines again?'

'You may not have to go through them,' Bill said tersely. 'All you'll need to do is hole up somewhere and let the advance absorb you.'

'Does that mean –'

'Yes,' Nick supplied. 'The big attack has started. It came through on the news this evening.'

291

It was because the moon would be at the full that Alexander had chosen 11th May for his big attack. On that Thursday night it was due to rise at midnight. The sky was clear and stars twinkled in the cool darkness. The scent of flowers strengthened in the night air. Over Cassino and the surrounding landscape all the air held a solemn stillness. By an odd coincidence the German guns were as silent as the Allies.

Three seconds before the BBC time signal for eleven a single Allied gun fired two shells, a pre-climax to the full-blooded bombardment which was to come. Then, as the first pip sounded, 1,659 other guns opened up. Forty-five minutes later the British infantry walked forward into the thickening fog hanging over the Rapido.

*

It was not till dawn that the four Corps' operational staffs were able to piece together the events of the first night. The reports they had received presented a depressing picture.

The British and Indian infantry trying to cross the Rapido in boats had suffered very much the same fate as the Texas division four months earlier. To the difficulties of the fast-flowing river was added the chaos caused by a dense fog compounded of natural mist and shell-smoke. It was so thick that the soldiers could not even see the direction-giving tracer shells. Only because of many personal feats of valour was a foothold obtained on the far bank. That night nineteen-year-old Kamal Ram of the 3/8 Punjabis won his Victoria Cross, braving the withering fire of Bode's machine-gun battalion.

On the sea coast the two new American divisions – the Oklahoma Wildcats and the Custer Division – had been stopped by the 94th German Division. Juin's Moroccans, after making initial gains, had been driven back by the machine-guns and flame-throwers of Raapke's 71st Division.

The Poles had not attacked till one a.m. so that their supporting artillery could thoroughly soften up the Paratroopers. When they did advance they found that Heidrich's men, sheltering in their caves and well-constructed sangars, were impregnable. To their cost they discovered how deadly was the carefully co-ordinated system of heavy machine-guns and multi-barrelled Nebelwerfers. They learned also what a Parachute counter-attack was like. Point 569 was lost to the seventh such attack. The company holding Point 593 was reduced to one officer and seven men.

At first light it seemed apparent that all along the front the familiar story was about to repeat itself. The Germans were too professional, too courageous, too well dug in to their excellent defensive positions for the superior weight of the Allies to dislodge them.

★

As the Mercedes-Benz bumped its way slowly down the uneven track Bill walked a little way after it. His emotions were a mixture of exasperation and concern. This was the second time he had watched Richard set off on a foolhardy journey which promised to be more than hazardous.

Only when it had disappeared found a bend did he turn and walk back to where Toro, Saturnino, Fen and Ram were waiting.

'I still think it's crazy.' He shook his head in exasperation. 'Now that we've got our wireless communications going we could have sent a message in code.'

'Codes can be broken,' Fen pointed out, defending Richard's decision to go back through the lines.

'It's as secret as that? Did he tell you what the Eyetie gave him?'

Fen hesitated. 'Yes. He did.'

'Then why all the secrecy? Am I supposed to be a bad security risk?'

The two partisans had walked on ahead to where the cars were waiting behind the barn.

'It's not that, Bill. With a thing like this the fewer who know the better. You can understand if Richard is particularly aware that people can be made to talk. He only told me so that there will be someone else who has the information. If we don't hear he's got through safely, I'll have to try and make it, even if I have to go it alone.'

'Well, you'd better start planning,' Bill told him. 'I wouldn't give much for Richard's chances.'

Toro had turned and was waiting for them to catch up. He addressed Bill in the usual pidgin Italian he thought the LRP man would find easier to understand, with every verb in the infinitive.

'Now, your friends to depart.' A gesture in the direction of the vanished Mercedes. 'You and I – to discuss how the partisans to assist the Allied armies. We – *partigiani* – to blow up bridges – to ambush retreating Germans – to kill *Fascisti*.'

*

In one way Richard found it a relief to get away from the partisans. Il Professore in particular was insistent in his attempts to find out what he had learned from Antonio. Toro was taking it as an insult to the partisans that he would not share his information. Even Bill had been stuffy about it.

Fen had been the only one he felt he could really trust to keep his mouth shut. He was also one of the original Benedictine Commandos. The New Zealander had wanted to accompany him. He was concerned that Richard had not recovered strength enough for such an undertaking. It was only when both Nick and Pat insisted that they were going back with Richard that he agreed to the plan.

'Though it's a slight case of the blind leading the blind,' he'd pointed out, watching Pat as he moved towards the tent with a pronounced limp.

As Bill would not consider parting with his Jeep and the partisans were guarding all their 'borrowed' vehicles jealously, Richard had little alternative but to use the Mercedes-Benz' again, at least till he was in the front-line area. After Nick had made contact with the partisans the German staff car had been skillfully concealed inside a haystack a few miles from Peroli. It was brought out and given a jump start from the Lancia. Richard carefully checked oil, battery, tyres and water. He poured a five-gallon Jerry-can of petrol into the tank and checked the gauge. It showed three-quarters full, which should be enough for the hundred and fifty mile drive to Gaeta. They had decided to recross the lines in the coastal southern sector.

This time they had no uniforms, except for one of the long-peaked Meyer caps which Toro had given Richard to make him look more Krautish. To preserve some anonymity the windows of the Mercedes were splattered with mud, leaving free only the segment swept by the wiper blades.

It was evening on 13 May when Richard, Nick and Pat set off. The attack at Cassino had been in progress for two days now. The news bulletins stated that the German defences were holding firm at all points. They encountered little difficulty for the first thirty miles and passed through Frosinone at nine o'clock. So far from being stopped the impressive cabriolet attracted several precautionary salutes. Even though it was carrying no flag the long bonnet and aggressive radiator suggested high rank. From Frosinone to Ceprano the traffic was heavy. A lot of stuff was moving up towards the Liri Valley.

The only map they had was one of those road maps which filling-stations used to give away free to motorists in peacetime. Its scale was 1:500,000. In the passenger's seat Nick had it on his knee and was trying to read it by the light of a small torch. The road that led across the Aurunci Mountains through Itri and Pico was in a very bad state. Every few hundred yards were wrecked vehicles, victims of MATAF's air strikes. Traffic was moving in both directions and there was an air of panic and confusion not customary in the Germans. No one thought of challenging the staff car. Everyone was too immersed in his own problems.

Those fifty miles took five hours.

At 2 a.m. they reached the sea coast at Formia and immediately encountered a jam of traffic moving west. There were heavy lorries, light trucks, motor-cycles and side-cars, infantry trudging in files up the gutters and an astonishing number of horse-drawn vehicles. To Richard, who had come to think of the Germans as more efficiently equipped than the British, this was the most surprising sight of all.

'This is a full-scale retreat!' The traffic was double-banking in its haste to withdraw towards Rome, the lorries impatient to get past the horse traffic.

In fact, it was 94th Division fleeing before the advance of the US Corps. Stemnitz was pulling out to avoid being cut off by an enemy who had pushed rapidly through the mountains to the north. But Richard did not know this. He had to bully and horn-blast his way against the tide and in the next hour only covered five miles.

Once he met a Mercedes 320 moving west. At sight of the 540K coming the other way its driver stopped and the occupant of the back seat opened the door. Richard squeezed past, splattering mud on a booted and breeched leg, and accelerated away with spinning wheels.

'Looked like a goddam general.' Nick began to turn round but realized he could not see anything through the muddy windows. 'I guess he thought we were Kesselring.'

By Santa Croce Richard had had enough of it. The road ahead was even more tightly jammed but there was a turning to the left which seemed clearer.

'Where does this road go, Nick?'

'To Cassino – through Ausonia.'

'Right.' Richard made a snap decision. 'We'll take it.'

It was now 3 a.m. There was very little traffic on this road. Mountains were soon rising on either side. Richard reckoned that if the front had held firm they were still five miles behind it. In fact, they were moving into the gap between 94th and 71st Divisions, which were being prized apart by the advance of the Moroccans.

There are few sensations more disturbing than to be in a battle zone without knowing what is happening nor where the lines are drawn. Richard began to feel really worried when a crump-crump behind told him that the road was being shelled. Parties of German troops were withdrawing across it, moving to positions in the hills on the other side. The war was evidently very near.

Richard decided to risk stopping for information. When he saw a group of battle-weary soldiers debouch from a lane on the right he put his brakes on and drew up beside them. He pulled his Meyer cap down over his brow and lowered the window.

'Why are you retreating?' he demanded aggressively.

'Those are our orders, Herr General,' the Feldwebel answered, trying to see through the window who was addressing him.

'What regiment are you?'

'74th Fusilier Battalion, 71 Division. The front has broken. We are under orders to fall back on the Senger Line.'

'How far away are the enemy?'

'Not far.' The sergeant glanced back at the hills behind him. Under the Stahlhelm his face was dark with bristles. His uniform was mud-stained and baggy. The pockets bulged with ammunition. A ribbed gas-mask canister, water-bottle and leather map-case dangled from his shoulders. 'In those hills behind us. We had not expected them to attack over such high ground.'

Some Allied gunner had decided that this road junction was a likely point to shell. He had not registered it accurately but stuff was landing not far away.

'Is good,' Richard said magnanimously. 'Carry on.'

Gratefully the Feldwebel signalled his men. Toting their Spandau they clanked across the road and took to the hills on the other side.

'I can't understand this,' Richard said, when his heart-beat was back to normal. 'Their troops are so thin on the ground here. This is the sort of fluid situation we used to get in North Africa.'

'A sight too bloody fluid!' Pat remarked from the back seat, as the car was spattered by earth from a shell that had landed close. He had been so silent during the trip that Richard had almost forgotten he was there. 'It was in a spot just like this I got my game leg.'

'OK, Pat. Point taken. I'm going up this lane.'

The section they had met appeared to be the last to pull out of the hills to the right of the road. The moon was giving enough light for Richard to drive without lights but he knew that it also made the Mercedes visible. The hills ahead seemed mysterious and threatening. The road behind was still being shelled, but up here there was silence.

Rounding a bend in the narrow road they came on a Kübelwagen, knocked out and abandoned. It completely blocked the road. Richard stopped and switched off his engine.

'Those aren't 25-pounders.' He was listening to the detonation of the guns firing from the east. The shells whined over their heads before landing in the valley behind. 'Could be howitzers, I suppose.'

It was an eerie feeling to be in this empty countryside. One army had slipped away under cover of darkness and the advancing army had not yet arrived.

'Sure, we can move that,' Pat said, opening his door. 'Those Volkswagens don't weigh much.'

'No, Pat. We're going to leave the car. I don't want to stop an anti-tank round. I'll reverse into that farm behind us.'

Craning out of the driver's window he reversed back down the lane a hundred yards, then drove into a farmyard and parked the Mercedes under an open-sided shed.

He did not enjoy leaving the car. It had served him well and so long as he had been in it he had felt a certain sense of security. In a way he had come to believe it was his own property now.

The sky was lightening to the east as they went past the Volkswagen. Just beyond it the lane topped a crest before descending into a dip beyond. They were walking in file. Richard was leading and Nick was bringing up the rear. Even after a few hundred yards Pat's limp was more pronounced.

Pat had just said: 'You'd better take off that cap, sir,' when three figures came out from behind a wall ahead of them. There were no shots, no challenge, just the silent menace of the three men. In the feeble light Richard could make out the striped woollen garments they wore over their uniforms, the French-style helmets and the dark, whiskered faces.

'They're Goumiers!' he muttered. 'Put your hands up quick!'

From behind them another dozen Moroccans had materialized from the shadows at the roadside.

Pat and Nick already had their hands up. The Moroccans advanced on them suspiciously, guns at waist level, fingers on the trigger.

'*Nous sommes des officiers alliés,*' Richard said clearly. Then he said it again.

Teeth gleamed and the whites of eyes shone in the dark faces. One man, scorning a helmet, was wearing the pointed hood of his *cachabia* over his head. They were talking in their own Atlas Mountain dialect. Richard realized that his French had made no impression on them.

298

'*Kamerad!*' the hooded one said and laughed.

'God, he thinks we're Germans.' More loudly he insisted: '*Pas allemands. Américains. Anglais. Brittaniques* – '

They were not listening. The main body had quickly moved on down the lane, or rather down the hedges and walls on either side of it, trying to re-establish contact with the retreating Germans. The hooded Goumier, who seemed to be some kind of junior NCO, had produced a coil of rope. By signs he indicated what he wanted them to do. In turns Richard, Nick and Pat lowered their arms and had their hands tied behind their backs.

Richard could not help thinking about the German head in the helmet some of these same Moroccans had procured for him. For a moment Pat seemed ready to resist but he changed his mind when he was prodded by a bayonet.

When they were all secured they were strung together by one length of cord.

'*Marchez!*' the NCO commanded. '*Schnell!*'

Following them with his rifle at the ready he herded them on down the lane. Daylight was growing. The sun was already tinting the under-sides of the clouds overhead. From the valley below, the guns which had been shelling the Ausonia road were still firing, the sharp crack of the detonations reverberating round the hills. Soon they met more files of Goumiers hurrying forward to exploit their advantage. Some of them were leading pigs and goats on ropes. There were a few American helmets to be seen but most were wearing the old French helmets. On a motoring tour in France Richard had seen them all along the road from Paris to Verdun – one on top of every kilometre stone. They met a mule-train, the beasts straining forward under the weight of the pack-howitzers which gave these troops their extraordinary mobility.

The spectacle of the Moroccans hastening forward so eagerly was astonishing. What had happened to the usually dour German defence? And where was British 10 Corps?

After half a mile they came to a small village which was bustling with activity. There was no shelling. The retreating Germans had not had time to get their guns turned round. Not surprisingly the Tabor had set up their headquarters in the *trattoria*. The three captives were halted outside while the hooded NCO went in to report. There was nothing they could do except stand there and wait, roped together and surrounded by a curious ring of staring North Africans.

A few minutes later the NCO came out with a French warrant officer. He was a little unsteady on his feet, either through fatigue or over-indulgence in the *trattoria*'s stock of wine. He had a day's growth of beard on his chin.

'*Vaut mieux les fusiller tout de suite,*' he was saying. '*Nous n'avons pas le temps de nous tracasser pour ces cons.*'

'Listen,' Richard spoke up in French. 'For God's sake don't talk about shooting us. We're Allied soldiers. Two British and one American. We've been a mission across the lines and we're trying to get back.'

'Let me see your identity disc.'

'It was taken from me by the Germans. I was a prisoner of the Gestapo.'

'Oh, yes?' The *Adjudant*'s tone was sceptical. He nodded at Nick, who had grown a beard while he was with the partisans. 'And this grand-dad here, I suppose he's General Eisenhower in disguise. You expect me to believe that crap? You know what we do with spies? We shoot them. I'll give you five minutes to say your prayers.'

The man's speech was so fast and his accent so atrocious that Richard had trouble in understanding him. But there was no mistaking the gist of his remarks.

'No, wait!' he appealed as the other turned away, presumably to drum up a firing squad. 'You're not the 8th Moroccan Infantry by any chance?'

The *Adjudant* swung back.

'How the hell do you know that?' he damanded more suspicious than ever. 'That proves you are spies.'

Richard said: 'Do you know a Captain Marcel Duval?'

'Le Capitaine Duval? How do you know that name?'

'Because I visited you when you were north of Cassino in January. He was a member of a patrol I took behind the German lines. He was wounded in the leg and decided to try and come through the lines to you from the Liri Valley. Did he make it?'

The *Adjudant* nodded.

'He made it.'

*

It took most of the day for Marcel to be located and brought

300

to the village. Richard and his companions were not sorry to have been locked in the cellar of the *trattoria* for eight hours. The German artillery had registered the village and were subjecting it to intermittent shelling.

During one of the lengthy lulls the door at the top of the stairs was unlocked. The voice that called them out was a strange one. The Tabor which had captured the place had moved on and it was now occupied by service units.

Richard was the first to come out of the darkness into the bar of the *trattoria*. Before his eyes had readjusted to the light he felt himself seized and hugged.

'But this is *formidable!*' Marcel exclaimed in delight. 'And they thought you were spies!'

'Your *Adjudant* was about to shoot us.'

'Oh, he would never have done that. But you do not look very soldierly, *mon vieux*.' Marcel shook his head sadly and held Richard's shoulders at arm's length. 'And you have grown so thin! What have you been doing to yourself?'

Before Richard had time even to avoid the question Marcel had noticed Nick and Pat. They received a Gallic welcome only slightly less demonstrative than Richard's.

'*Formidable!*' Marcel said again. His face was sun-tanned by a month's convalescence in a North African rest-camp. 'Tonight we will have a big feast at my headquarters. We have liberated a sucking pig and there is excellent wine in this region –'

'Marcel, you've got to get me back to AFHQ as fast as possible. I have some very urgent information for General Alex.'

'More urgent than a sucking pig?'

'A lot more urgent, I'm afraid.'

'That is a great pity. Especially as I have at my billet some nice Italian girls who are quite friendly.'

'Can you fix me up with some transport? Do you think your Corps HQ will know where I can find the C-in-C?'

Realizing that Richard meant what he said, Marcel became serious. 'If it is as urgent as that I will take you to General Juin myself. You see, I am a staff officer now – temporarily, I assure you.'

Marcel's means of transport to this inaccessible mountain village had been a 350 cc Matchless, scrounged from a friendly

Eighth Army A/Q. There was no way he could convey more than one passenger back to Corps.

'You and Pat will have to follow on foot or mules,' he told Nick. 'I will leave instructions for an orderly to accompany you. Till you are dressed in proper uniforms again you are likely to be arrested as spies once more.'

'I'll see you back at AFHQ,' Richard told his two friends as he sat himself astride the box-shaped pillion seat of the Matchless and put his heels on the foot-rests. 'Don't worry, Pat. If General Alex takes me on again you'll get your old job back. So long, Nick.'

'Watch your step,' Nick warned with forced casualness. 'Try not to get run over by any hearses.'

Marcel was exultant about the success of the French Corps. While Richard held on with hands clasped tight round his waist the Frenchman shouted the news over his shoulder.

'We are going through them like a dose of laxative! The Boches could not believe it when our Moroccans and Algerians appeared on the top of peaks of fifteen hundred metres in height.'

He took his hand off the grip for a perilous moment to point towards the 4,700 foot peak of Monte Petrella to the north. A squadron of aircraft were flying over the hills dropping supplies by parachute to the columns which had outrun their own lines of communication.

'Has the Monastery been captured yet?'

'No. Only the French have made progress. And the Americans on the coast to our left. Everywhere else the Boche is holding.'

'Mind out!'

Richard's shout was just in time to prevent Marcel running down a goat which had escaped from the Algerian *tirailleur* who was leading it up the mule-track.

'When we cut the Ausonia road,' Marcel went on, as he straightened out the wobbling bike, 'they will have to fall back or risk being cut off. Juin is forming a Mountain Corps to drive through to the Itri-Pico road.'

'That's miles back!' The Itri-Pico road was the route across the mountains which the Mercedes had followed to reach the coast. 'How can your troops advance so fast through this sort of country?'

'We don't encumber ourselves with too many prisoners. The

302

Moroccans and Algerians are mountain people. They drive their rations before them. We fight hard. For us the war is not the gentlemanly game of you British. And we let our troops taste the fruits of victory.'

This recipe for success was communicated in snippets over a distance of a quarter of a mile. The steeply-descending track was very bumpy. Richard had to hold on as if he was riding a bucking bronco. He had not the breath to argue.

As the Matchless passed through a village he saw that the Goumiers resting there had run a coil of Dannert wire round a paddock and herded all the women and young boys they'd found in the village inside it. He could hear them wailing as the motor-cycle raced past.

'*Povera Italia!*'

'What?'

'I can see you do take women prisoners.'

'Oh, that.' Marcel laughed. 'They do not harm them. Italian women like it, you know.'

Richard was not sorry when they arrived at General Juin's headquarters. He was feeling slightly sick and his crotch was very sore. Marcel took him straight in and presented him to the General, a small, puckish man with eyes that slitted when he smiled. He was wearing field boots and breeches and a voluminous Jeep-jacket over his service-dress jacket. The four stars of a Général de Corps d'Armée gleamed on the front of the peasant-style beret which was his trade mark. Juin had voluntarily sacrificed one star to fit into the Allied chain of command.

'Only for General Alexander personally?' he said when Marcel had passed on Richard's request. He subjected Richard to a shrewd appraisal. The British officer's smart salute had belied his bedraggled appearance. 'If you wish it I can pass a message for you. I have direct communication with AFHQ.'

Richard shook his head and stuck to his guns. 'With respect, sir, it is for the C-in-C's ears only.'

Juin nodded acceptance and made his mind up immediately.

'You will take him, Duval. Use a Jeep from the Corps pool. But this officer looks as if he would relish a good meal. He will have dinner with us first.'

28

It took a whole day to struggle back to Caserta. The Bailey Bridge over the Garigliano had been knocked out by shell-fire and when it was repaired priority was given to traffic moving towards the front.

Not till nearly eight o'clock did they reach AFHQ. To his frustration Richard learned that the C-in-C had gone forward that day to Eighth Army HQ and was not back yet. As they had pressed on without stopping for lunch the next priority, since Alexander was not available, was to eat.

Marcel, his manner a little evasive, declined Richard's invitation to dine in B3 Mess. His excuse was that he preferred Italian *cucina casalinga*, but Richard was sure he was after a bit of Italian tail.

Entering the dining-room at B3 Mess gave him an odd sense of unreality. A few eyebrows were raised as he stared round, searching for a familiar face. The place was full of officers he had never seen before. Then he caught sight of Diana Canning. She had her back to him. He sat down beside her.

She glanced round briefly, then went on with her dinner.

When he'd given his order to the Mess waiter he ventured a tentative: 'Good evening.'

This time she turned to give him a proper look.

'Oh, it's you,' she said in a cold voice. 'I didn't recognize you.'

'I want to apologize.'

'What for?'

'That business about the German helmet. It was very thoughtless of me.'

She was studying him with a puzzled curiosity. 'It was stupid of me to ask for it. You must have thought me awfully wet. What's been happening to you? We heard you had been returned to unit.'

'Actually – ,' Richard began, but she had touched his arm.

'Watch out,' she murmured. 'I think our new Mess Secretary is coming to have a word with you.'

The Mess Secretary was a very smart officer with a battledress that had obviously been adjusted by a tailor, knife-edge trousers and highly-polished boots. His sandy hair had been clipped indecently close to the back of his head and he had a nasty little fair moustache.

'Sorry to interrupt but – ah – are you authorized to use this Mess?'

'Yes, I think so,' Richard said over his shoulder. 'I was before I left, anyway. I've just come back from a mission. My name's Stewart.'

'I can vouch for him,' Diana cut in a little breathlessly.

A pause. Then: 'Well, Stewart, even if you are a member of B3 Mess we like officers to be reasonably correctly dressed – you might at least wear a tie and badges of rank.'

'I know. I'm very sorry about it. I got separated from my kit. Do you want me to leave the table?'

'No, you can finish your meal. But do spare us embarrassment by indenting for new battledress trousers and a pullover that does not reveal large areas of shirt.'

'I'll do that. Sorry to cause trouble.'

He was amused to see that Diana was blushing for him. They kept their eyes down till the Mess Secretary had left the hut.

'He's an awful fuss-pot. But you do look very outlandish, you know. And it was because you're so gaunt that I did not recognize you.'

He ran a hand self-consciously through his long hair. 'Do I smell?'

'Only a little. Nothing that a cigarette won't cure. Will you have one?'

She was offering him a silver case stocked with Turkish cigarettes.

'Balkan Sobranie! I haven't had one of these for a long time.'

305

He smoked for a minute or two, enjoying the sense of luxury that the Turkish cigarette induced. She was watching him covertly, trying to make up her mind to say something.

'You said you'd been on a mission?'

'Yes.'

'Very secret, I suppose.'

'Just a little trip behind the German lines. Nothing to write home about.'

'Gosh, how exciting! Old AFHQ must seem very dull after that.'

'On the contrary,' he said, looking her directly in the eye. There was something about her which produced in him an irresistible desire to shock.

'It seems like Paradise when you've spent nine weeks in a Sipo gaol.'

'Sipo? That's not the Gestapo, is it?'

'Twin brothers of the Gestapo. The same charming family characteristics.'

'But you escaped?'

'I was released – mostly thanks to the RAF.'

'Had they been – were you interrogated?'

'Yes.'

She finished her cigarette, then crushed it in the ash-tray. 'You – er. You're not free this evening, are you? One doesn't often have the chance to talk to someone who's been behind the lines.'

His surprise must have showed. She dropped her eyes, blushing again. He guessed it was his starved and beaten-up appearance. It had aroused the mothering instinct in her, or perhaps something more primitive and deep-seated. A pleasant thought, to cushion his head on those pneumatic breasts, now so severely constrained within the uniform jacket.

'I wish I could but I can't make any plans before I've reported to Daddy Jenkins –'

'But – . Haven't you heard?'

'What?'

'Vyvyan Jenkins. He killed himself.'

'*What?*'

'He poisoned himself. In his office. It was ghastly. They said it was cyanide.'

'My God!' Immediately Richard began to regret all the hard things he and Nick had said about Daddy Jenkins. The poor old sod must have used one of those tablets which they had refused. 'When did this happen?'

'Oh, three months ago. In fact, three months to the day. It was Tuesday, 15th February. I remember because that was the day the Montecassino Monastery was bombed.'

'It was suicide, of course?'

'The Court of Inquiry concluded that his death was due to the strain of his job. But that was for the sake of his widow. She gets a better pension if it's Died on Active Service. Everyone knows it was suicide, but in a way he was a casualty of war.'

'Yes.'

The Benedictine Commando. It had certainly taken its toll. Erle and Tucker almost as soon as they'd crossed the lines. Viktor and Baldo at the Monastery. And poor old Daddy Jenkins who'd been dead for three months and they never knew it.

'As a matter of fact,' Diana was saying, 'I was talking to him only a couple of hours before he did it.'

'How did he seem then?'

'He was drinking pretty heavily and not making much sense. At least, it did not make much sense at the time —'

'Like what? Please try to remember.'

'Well, when he got to his most advanced state he grabbed my arm, blew a blast of whisky breath on me and said: "You knew him, didn't you?" I said: "What are you talking about?" "My Benedictines," he said. "I dropped them in the shit." Sorry, but that was the word he used."'

*

Richard could not bring himself to seek out Jenkins's successor. He excused himself in his own mind by reasoning that he would be put under pressure to divulge all his information and he did not want to give it to anyone except Alex — now more than ever.

Instead, he went to find a GSO1 on Alexander's staff whom he'd known in North Africa. He found Maurice Cartwright on duty in the Ops Room. Cartwright listened with astonishment to Richard's abbreviated account of the Benedictine Commando's mission and how he had come back through the French lines.

'S10 kept that all very quiet,' he remarked. 'You were actually in the Monastery when it was bombed?'

'Yes.'

'That's incredible.'

'But it's something completely different I have to see Alex about. Do you think he'd see me tonight?'

'No. The C-in-C's not back yet. We don't expect him back before midnight. He was supposed to be going to Eighth Army but you know Alex. Wouldn't put it past him to go swanning about on the other side of the Rapido.'

'Has the Monastery been taken, then?' Richard had a sudden sinking feeling that he had missed the boat, had been stuck here at Caserta when everything was happening at Cassino.

'No such luck. Things are going well on Fifth Army front. The Americans have got 94 Division on the run up the coast and the French have deepened their bridge-head across the Garigliano to five miles. We heard this evening that the tricolour has been hoisted on Monte Majo. That's the one bright spot in a gloomy picture. We've got five Bailey bridges over the Rapido but our front line's only a mile and a half beyond that. And of course the whole of 13 Corps area is overlooked by the Monastery.'

'Whose pigeon is that?'

'The Polish Corps. They've been having a bad time these last four days. The Paratroopers are still up there and as B-minded as ever.'

'I suppose you've no idea where the Greenshire Yeomanry are?'

'That's your old regiment, isn't it?'

'Yes. I've got a brother with them.'

'Actually, I do know. They're with the Derbyshire Yeomanry Group, under command of 6th Armoured.'

Cartwright could see that Richard was on tenterhooks and wanted to get clear of AFHQ without delay.

He said: 'I could arrange for you to see the Chief of Staff, you know. It would save you waiting around for Alex.'

'Thanks, but it must be Alex personally. Maurice, could you fix it for me to see him as soon as possible? I have some information which could affect the whole course of the war.'

The GSO1 smiled.

'And I don't just mean this campaign,' Richard continued with great seriousness. 'I mean the whole war.'

'Come in, Stewart. Do you know General Harding?'

Alexander was as courteous and urbane as ever. No one would have guessed from his imperturbable manner that the outcome of the offensive he had been planning since March hung in the balance. The room was the same except that the chinagraph lines on the maps had moved fractionally. Pale morning sunlight slanted obliquely through the windows.

Richard, who had waited for an hour and a half to see the Commander-in-Chief, inclined his head respectfully towards the Chief of Staff. Harding was a small and compact man with remarkably keen eyes. He wore two rows of medal ribbons by contrast with Alexander's five. His brow was lofty and slightly wrinkled. On his left hand he wore a woollen mitten. It was evident from the atmosphere that between these two men there was a strong understanding.

Harding returned Richard's nod with polite wariness.

'Now then,' Alexander began briskly. 'What's this story Maurice Cartwright has been telling me about you being in the Monastery when it was bombed?'

'That's right, sir.'

'But how the devil did you come to be there?'

'The Benedictine Commando, sir.' It was perhaps not surprising, Richard thought, that with two armies to command Alex had forgotten about such a minor operation. 'We made it in the end, sir. A bit late, as it turned out.'

'Stewart, what on earth are you talking about? I understood you had some very important information –'

'But I thought you knew all about it, sir. Colonel Jenkins gave me to understand it was your idea.'

Alexander stroked his moustache thoughtfully. 'Jenkins sent you on a mission to the Monastery?'

'Yes, sir.'

The two Generals exchanged a glance. Alexander said: 'This may explain a lot of things, John. Sit down, Stewart. Tell me about this Benedictine Commando.'

Keeping his account as brief and terse as possible, Richard related how the Benedictine Commando had come into being, how they had crossed the lines and succeeded in entering the Monastery. Alexander listened to the account of the bombardment without apparent emotion.

'Of course, I had no idea there were a thousand refugees in the place. I must say the Vatican's role in all this was a little puzzling. You say the bombs did not do much damage to the lower structure?'

'No, sir. The main walls collapsed but the lower floors were not very badly damaged, apart from being buried under rubble.'

'That's interesting, John.'

Again Harding nodded, but without taking his eyes from Richard.

Richard was glad he'd asked one of the Mess waiters, who'd been a barber in civvie street, to give him a haircut.

'And I'd like to say, sir,' Richard found the words pouring out, though he had not planned to speak like this, 'that I know I was mistaken to query your decision. I realize now that we must let nothing delay our victory over these people. It's not the fighting troops, it's what's going on behind the lines. Sir, you have no idea what the Nazis are like, what they are doing to the civilian population –'

'Thank you.' Alexander managed to stem the flow without raising his voice. He smiled slightly. 'I too am confident that I made the right decision.'

His left hand touched the side of his battledress blouse and for a moment his expression became very intent, very serious. 'When a choice has to be made between buildings, however artistic and valuable, and men's lives – there can be only one decision.'

It was a moment before Harding said: 'Would I be right in assuming that something more than the ill-treatment of civilians has made you change your mind? If I may say so, you look, not exactly battle-weary, but ... '

'Bruised,' Alexander suggested. 'Mentally and physically bruised.'

'I spent eighty days in a security police prison.'

They waited, realizing that he might want to unburden himself but too well-mannered to remind him that they had a large-scale battle on their hands.

He said: 'It would be a waste of time for me to try and tell you about that. The reason I made such a fuss about seeing you, sir, was something else.'

They listened with close attention while he told them about

310

his encounter with Antonio and the extraordinary story of the dying Italian.

'I promised him I would get this to Mr Churchill.' Richard smiled as he laid the sketch on Alexander's desk and smoothed it out with his hands.

'I know Mr Churchill will be very interested indeed.' The C-in-C had given the sketch a rapid and searching scrutiny. 'You can leave this with me.'

'It was what he said about a new explosive that made me decide I must get back to you with this information. Do you think it could have anything to do with the Commando raid on the heavy water plant on the Lofoten Islands?'

'It well could, Richard. It well could. And I don't have to stress that this is Top Secret information.'

'I understand that, sir. In fact I've only shared it with one other person – in case I did not make it back through the lines.'

'Well, you did make it, Stewart,' Harding said. 'A damn good show. I know Tommy Rankin would like to have a word with you. You must have some very useful stuff for the Intelligence boys.'

'Yes, quite a bit,' Richard agreed.

'Then I should think you could use a spot of leave.'

'Not yet, sir.' He turned towards Alexander who was contemplating him with a thoughtful expression. 'I wonder if I could resume my old job – at any rate until the Monastery is captured.'

'Your old job is still open.' Alexander was not going to say that he felt he had been a little hard on his young liaison officer, and had decided to make it up to him. 'And if you don't wish to take leave that's your own affair. But if you want to be there when the Monastery falls you'd better move fast. The Canadian Corps are already driving for the Hitler Line and 78th Division are very near to Route 6. The Poles are attacking the Monastery again tomorrow and the Paratroopers are in danger of being cut off.'

*

When Richard had saluted and departed to report to the GS01 (Intelligence), Alexander picked up the sketch and handed it to his Chief of Staff.

'This must be the rocket that chap Jones told us about.'

311

'Jones?'

'That young chap who runs Scientific Intelligence. He was present at the last conference we had with Winston.'

'Oh, yes. I remember him. A civilian. Do you think the Germans are going to be able to put an atom bomb in one of those things?'

'God forbid! We know they are working to develop an atom bomb but so far we're ahead of them.'

Alexander tapped the sketch. 'I'd like to send this information back to Winston without delay. Ask Terence Airey to come in and you'd better send for Tommy Thompson. This had better be passed through Ultra channels.'

29

On 16 May, while Richard was being debriefed by Colonel Rankin and members of his Intelligence staff, the battles were moving towards their climax. The French Mountain Corps continuing its relentless advance was threatening to cut the Itri-Pico road and roll up the whole southern flank of the German line. In the Liri Valley, Burns's Canadian Corps was given orders to pass through 8th Indian and begin its assault on the Senger-Hitler Line. Under the shadow of Montecassino, 78th Division were carrying out a wheeling advance aimed at cutting Route 6. The code-names of their successive objectives reflected the tally-ho attitude of the divisional staff – Grafton, Pytchley, Fernie, Bedale.

Up on the heights around Point 593, that blood-drenched crest, the Poles were licking their wounds and preparing for a final thrust. In the first three days of the attack they had discovered, at fearful cost, how tough the Paratroopers were and how well organized these hills were for defence.

Opposite them the Paratroopers were in an even worse case. Before the battle began the division had been milked of one third of its strength to form new units in France. Regiments were reduced to two weak battalions with strengths of two or three hundred men. On the heights above Cassino there were seven hundred of them to resist the attacks of two divisions. After those battles the Poles claimed to have captured Point 593 and the Paratroopers claimed never to have lost it. Both were right. Attackers and counter-attackers suffered such heavy casualties that at times a handful of survivors from each side were huddled in caves a few yards from each other.

By the night of the 16th it was clear that the Cassino Position was becoming untenable. While Oliver Leese, commanding Eighth Army, was ordering 78th Division to attack towards Route 6 at dawn the next day, von Vietinghoff was telling Kesselring that Cassino would have to be abandoned.

Yet even when Heidrich received authority to withdraw from the positions 1st Parachute Division had been holding since February, he was reluctant to admit defeat. He decided to hang on for one more day.

*

Rankin's debriefing had been thorough and painstaking. Richard suffered it with mounting impatience. For reasons which he could not explain even to himself he felt a tremendous urgency to get to Cassino before the Monastery fell. There had been letters from his parents waiting for him. His father reported that Wilfrid had been writing 'strangely'; the boy sounded at the same time excited and apprehensive. And who was this Rachel who meant more to him than life itself?

By the time he was cleared by Rankin it was too late to arrange transport from the AFHQ pool. It was not till eight o'clock the next morning that he bumped out of Caserta in a brand-new Jeep with a fresh driver. He was wearing the battledress he had drawn from the stores. He'd sewn on badges of rank and medal ribbons during the small hours.

He had not seen Marcel again and there was no sign yet of Nick or Pat. To his relief Diana Canning had not been in the Mess for dinner. She had presumably found someone else to hold her hand, or her breast.

The driver he had been allotted from the transport pool was a nervous lad just out from England. The nearer they got to Cassino, the slower he drove. At Mignano, when they were within sound of the guns, Richard told him to move over and took the wheel himself.

It felt odd to be driving along Route 6 towards Cassino yet again, this time from south to north. When he caught a brief glimpse of the Monastery through a gap in the hills, it gave him a shock, almost a thrill. How long ago it was since he had stared out through that farmhouse window on Bare Bum Ridge and seen it for the first time! He wondered whether the Fusilier he'd seen being carried down on a stretcher had made it or gone for a Burton.

The road was comparatively clear this morning. The special Indian sapper company had turned it into an excellent highway. The sun was warm and the small towns, now four months into peace, were beginning their resurrection. All around, the Italian spring was burgeoning.

It was still only half-past ten when he saw the sign of the mailed fist and an arrow pointing to the headquarters of 6th British Armoured Division. Maurice Cartwright had advised him to check up on the tactical situation there before going any further forward. The armoured command vehicles were drawn up in a rough rectangle on the side of a hill leaning away from Cassino. Although most units of the division were committed to the battle 6th Armoured was not yet involved as a formation and so its headquarters had not gone forward. Richard was made welcome by an academic-looking G3(I) and an Intelligence Officer who wore a KOYLI forage cap and a permanent air of good-humoured amusement.

They were sitting in their ACV drinking a mid-morning cup of tea. 'Not much room in here,' the G3 apologized when Richard had made himself known. The interior of the ACV was indeed rather like the cockpit of an aircraft. 'You can sit on that box. My name's Calvert and this is Bertram Aykroyd.'

'The Monastery had not been captured yet,' Aykroyd said, referring back to the first question Richard had asked. He pointed a chinagraph pencil at the map on the wall, which showed the foremost line of the Allied troops and the enemy order of battle. 'But it won't be long now. The Poles got onto Phantom Ridge last night and saw the Germans off Colle Sant'

Angelo. It's not clear whether they or the Paratroopers hold Point 593.'

'What do you think my chances are of getting up there? I'd like to be with the first troops to go into the Monastery.'

Aykroyd looked at his visitor through half-closed eyelids. He was shrewd enough to realize that there was some personal reason for Richard's eagerness to be in the most uncomfortable place on the whole front. But he did not ask any questions.

'You'd be unwise to try and get up there in daylight.' A twinkle of amusement accompanied the understatement. 'The Germans are still on Monte Cairo and they overlook the supply routes. The mule and porter trains only go up at night.'

He saw from Richard's expression that this was not going to deter him. 'In any case, you might get up there and find that the Monastery had been taken from the west. 78 Division are very close to Route 6 and 4th Division may enter Cassino today.'

Richard peered at the complex pattern of red, blue and green lines on the situation map. 'You don't know where the Greenshire Yeomanry are, do you?'

'Yes. As a matter of fact they've come temporarily under our command. One of their batteries is supporting the DY Group, which is on the southern flank of 78 Division.'

'Is it C Battery?'

'Yes, I believe so.'

'I think if I can't get up to Monastery Hill I might push on and pay them a visit. I have a brother in C Battery.'

Aykroyd shook his head. 'I wouldn't go forward of the Rapido if you want to be on hand when the Monastery falls. The Liri Valley is one huge traffic jam. Our Field Security Officer went up to the DY Group yesterday and it took him eight hours to get back. And of course the whole area is under observation from Monastery Hill. You'd do much better to stay with us and watch how the battle goes. Then you can move forward as soon as we get word that the Monastery has been taken.'

The advice was sound, but only with the greatest difficulty did Richard curb his impatience. He had this illogical sense of urgency. Some instinct was telling him that time was short. It had become an obsession to be among the first to reach the captured Monastery.

'I guess you're right,' he said, unconsciously apeing Nick's trick of speech. 'If I'm not going to be in your way.'

The day seemed to pass swiftly. The headquarters of 6th Armoured were receiving constant reports and could maintain an up-to-date picture of the progress of the battle. It was a change for Richard to be able to take this Olympian view of a major offensive. Sometimes when Aykroyd entered a message on his log he would pass it over for Richard to read, and so he received a fragmented impression of events.

11.35 3rd Carpathian Division report one battalion on Point 593. Attempts to take ALBANETA FARM prevented by mines, machine-gun fire and counter-attacks.

11.52 Royal Inniskilling Fusiliers have captured 150 paratroopers in PIUMAROLA.

12.03 10th Brigade report two civilians stopped trying to cross bridge into Cassino.

12.17 Duke of Cornwall's Light Infantry have captured HQ of Parachute MG Battalion. 200 prisoners including 117 Paras. 3 Germans of 1 Para Bn carrying propaganda leaflets surrendered to sentry at Bn HQ, DCL1.

12.42 French Mountain Corps have reached PICO-ITRI road.

13.10 AMAZON Bailey Bridge knocked out by shell-fire.

13.42 Derbyshire Yeomanry report heavy counter-battery shelling in their area.

14.15 3rd Carpathian Division forced to abandon Point 593.

14.27 10th Rifle Bridge report surrendering Germans misusing white flag.

15.10 Canadians report stiff resistance from 90 PG rearguards.

16.07 78 Div report that prisoners state 361 and 376 Panzer Grenadier regiments at PONTECORVO.

16.40 12th Bridge supported by New Zealand and South African tanks near Route 6.

17.13 1st Canadian Brigade report Tiger tank turrets in concrete emplacements.

SUMMARY FOR SITREP

FIFTH ARMY SECTOR

11 US Corps. 85 and 88 Divs pushing on up coast past FORMIA.

94 German Div in full retreat.

FEC 1 and 4 Groups of Tabors have cut the ITRI-PICO road. But French Units have outrun their supply columns.

EIGHTH ARMY SECTOR

1st Canadian Corps. 1st Canadian Inf Div have passed through 8th Indian and are attacking Hitler-Senger Line.

13 British Corps. 78 Inf Div wheeling anti-clockwise have reached BEDALE line and anticipate cutting Route 6 by nightfall.

4 Inf Div pushing into CASSINO from the south, anticipate entering at dawn.

Polcorps. 3 (Kresowan) and 5 (Carpathian) Inf Divs have captured PHANTOM RIDGE, ALBANETA and claim Pt 593. Casualties total 4,000 approx. 900 dead, 350 missing, 3,000 wounded. Remnants will attack MONASTERY tomorrow.

ENEMY INTENTIONS

French advance threatens to roll up German line from the south but 26 Panzer Div reported moving to stop FEC. 1 Parachute Div threatened by encirclement may pull out of CASSINO Position.

*

That night Richard spread out his bed-roll beneath an olive tree and slept under the stars.

During his six hours of dreamless sleep the Paratroopers of Heidrich's Division, or as many of them as could still walk, slipped silently away from their positions in Cassino and on Monastery Hill. So tightly had the noose been drawn round them that the only escape route left was across the western slopes of Montecassino. The Allied artillery shelled all the known tracks throughout the night but when dawn came the seven hundred had vanished – to fight another day.

At dawn General Dudley Ward sent 10th Brigade of 78 Div into the ruins of Cassino town. From cellars and dug-outs remnants of 1st Parachute Division emerged to surrender and accept what they had been told was the fate of all prisoners taken by the British – execution by firing squad.

Richard was wakened not by daylight but by the hand of Bertram Aykroyd on his shoulder. He saw to his horror that the sun was already up.

'I thought you'd like to know, Stewart. Our troops are in Cassino. It looks as if the Germans have pulled out.'

With a stomach-knotting sense that he had missed the show, Richard snatched his clothes from under his pillow and dressed quickly. He took time only to swallow a quick cup of tea and,

317

without bothering to look for his gun-shy driver, climbed into the Jeep and set off on the three-mile drive to Cassino.

It was a glorious morning. The hills rejoiced in the sunshine. A faint benison of mist hung low over the ground. A lark began his ascent, soaring from tree shadow into the golden light.

Rounding the corner of Monte Trocchio he came in view of the Monastery and felt the old sense of flinching. It still had the power to inflict its most mortal blow.

Was she up there somewhere inside that shapeless hulk?

A military policeman on duty at the Bailey bridge at the start of the Mad Mile stopped him to warn that Cassino was not yet clear of the enemy. Pockets of Paratroopers who had not received the order to withdraw were still holding out. There were mines and bobby-traps everywhere.

Driving up the Mad Mile the Jeep was bouncing over the cratered surface. An eerie smoke-free silence hung over the town ahead. Though he did not know that Wilfrid had walked up this mile of road by night a month earlier, he felt the same sad loneliness. The fight for Cassino was over but the story was not ended yet. He knew that.

10th Brigade were mopping up the town. British soldiers were still dying in Cassino. Groups of suicidal Paratroopers were refusing to surrender. From trees on the hillsides snipers were deliberately trying to pick off the officers. Every now and then there came the crack of the sappers defusing booby-traps and occasionally the explosion of a mine going up.

Richard stopped near the temporary headquarters of a company commander of the DCLI to get the latest information.

'The Monastery?' the Major said. 'I don't know whether the Poles have gone in or not. But the Germans have still got Massa Albaneta and Point 569. And the road up to the Monastery is still exposed to machine-gun fire.'

'All the same, I've got to get up there,' Richard said. He had to crane his neck to see the ruins on the hill above him. 'Can I leave my Jeep with you?'

'We may be moving on. But there's an MP section putting up road-signs. I should ask them to look after it for you.'

Twenty minutes later he was bent forward as he began the ascent of the Via Serpentina. There were footpaths cutting off the elbows of the hairpin bends, steeper but quicker than the road. He had to watch where he put his feet because of the unexploded mortar bombs and shells and the risk of mines. Quite low down he passed Castle Hill, now silent and deserted. Then the landscape below gradually seemed to flatten as he climbed higher and higher. Corpses were sprawled around in abundance, perfuming the air with their unforgettable odour. From one he borrowed a steel helmet and put it on his head.

Once he had to go to ground when a burst of machine-gun fire from higher up spattered the rocks behind him. After that he worked his way more to the left, approaching the summit via Hangman's Hill.

For some time the actual buildings had been hidden by a false crest. He was sweating profusely and the muscles of his legs were aching. It was just after 10.15 when he came into view of the building, now quite close. As he stared up at it, the perspiration running into his eyes, he saw two flagpoles raised above the ruins. From one fluttered the Union Jack, from the other the Polish flag.

When he reached the Monastery ten minutes later it was to find that the 12th Podolski Lancers had beaten him to it by half an hour. They had walked into the Monastery without a shot being fired. The place was very different from when he had left it on 17 February. The interior had been turned into a fortress. Holes had been knocked in the surviving walls for mortars to fire through. There were dead bodies everywhere and the stench was indescribable. In one corridor lined with drawers for the storage of vestments the Poles had found a corpse in every drawer.

The Poles had taken thirty prisoners, half-crazed Para-troopers with bristles and gaunt beards, too badly wounded to walk. Their senior officer, Captain Bayer, had awaited the arrival of the Poles with stoic acceptance, expecting to be shot. He had remained for the simple reason that he had only one leg.

Richard found the officer commanding the Podolski Lancers standing on the heap of stones where the two flags had been planted. He was surprisingly young and had the same hawk-like features as Viktor Zygalski. He was wearing British battledress and a British steel helmet. His face showed no surprise when he learned that Richard had come up from Cassino alone and on foot. It was dulled by the fatigue of a week's continuous fighting. He kept looking back towards Point 593 and Snakeshead Ridge, his mind still on the carnage that these hills had witnessed. From Massa Albaneta and Point 569 came the sound of continued fighting

At last he turned and looked at Richard. He put a hand on the flagpole bearing the Polish emblem.

'Poland lives again,' he said. 'We have captured our first summit. There will be many more but each one a little nearer our homeland.'

A frisson ran down Richard's back. They were within fifty feet of the place where Viktor Zygalski had fallen.

They stood in silence for minutes before he dared to ask the question which was uppermost in his mind.

'Did you find any civilians here?'

The Lancer nodded. 'Yes. A woman.'

Richard's heart began to thud.

'An Italian woman. I think she must be a nun who stayed behind when the Monastery was evacuated. She has been attending to the wounded.'

'Do you – .' Richard cleared his throat. 'Do you know where she is now?'

The Lancer pointed towards the cloister inside the main entrance. That part of the structure had suffered slightly less than the rest. 'Our stretcher-bearers are bringing the wounded up from the basement. You will find her there.'

As Richard clambered over the rubble, holding a handkerchief to his nose, the Pole had turned to the north and was gazing towards some distant goal beyond view.

She was standing within the square formed by what had been the entry cloister. The Polish stretcher-bearers were bringing the German wounded out and laying them in the sunshine. She was still wearing the long nun's habit but the cowl was thrown back and he could see that her hair had grown a few inches. Her face was in profile as she watched her charges being laid out in a row. She was stooped with exhaustion.

He stopped twenty paces away to slow his breathing down. That dusty, threadbare figure was the woman whose image had sustained him during the interminable weeks in the Sipo prison.

Then, becoming aware that she was being watched, she turned. He took off the steel helmet. Her lips moved. She shook her head, not believing that this was true.

'Maria.'

The sound of her own name broke her incredulous immobility. She stooped to gather up the long folds of her habit and then came towards him.

The Polish stretcher-bearers looked on in amazement at the spectacle of an Italian nun running into the arms of a British officer.

When at last he released her he was able to see for the first time the extent to which the ordeal she had been through had left its mark. But though her cheeks were pale and pinched her eyes were bright and there was lustre in her russet hair.

'What about Baldo?'

'He died two weeks after you left. I had to nurse him in secret because he would not allow me to hand him over to the Germans. He put up a great fight but the gangrene won in the end. I buried him under stones in the crypt. After his death I helped the German medical orderlies. There were so many wounded – and such terrible wounds!'

'I am going to take you away from here. You need proper care yourself.'

She gestured towards the line of wounded Germans. 'I cannot leave my patients.'

'They will be evacuated to hospitals by the Poles. You needn't worry about them any more.'

By mid-day the last pockets of resistance on the heights around Montecassino had been subdued and the first Jeeps were making their way up the Via Serpentina. The news that the Monastery had fallen to the Poles spread like wild-fire to every soldier in Eighth Army, and was relayed to the world through the information services of all the Allied nations. Alexander issued a special communiqué and telegraphed the good tidings to Churchill. The Polish government in exile decided to strike a special medal with the inscription *Monte Cassino*.

Richard managed to persuade an American AMGOT officer to give him and Maria a lift down to Cassino. Frustrated at being deemed too old to fight, he had been one of the first into the town, on the excuse that there might be civilians needing help.

'If you can take the lady as far as Mignano you'll find there's a bus full of refugees going back to Naples,' he told them as he dropped them at the MP post in the town. 'I've got to get forward to see if Piedimonte has been captured.'

'It's all right. I'll take her. Thanks for the lift.'

Richard recovered his own Jeep from the MP post and drove southward out of Cassino. The sun was strong and there was a champagne quality in the air.

'I'm going to take you back to Naples. I can't just put you on a bus!'

She laid her hand on his arm. 'No, Richard. I need time on my own to recover my strength and my spirit. And you are a soldier. Your place is here, where the fighting is. Besides, it is important for you to see your brother.'

He needed no reminding about Wilfrid. Ever since he had assured himself that Maria was safe this compulsion to find Wilfrid had been growing stronger.

She saw his hesitation. 'I will be all right. The Sisters of Mercy will look after me.'

He drove on a quarter of a mile. It would take a whole day to go back to Naples and come forward again. In that time the DY Group could have been committed to the battle.

'I'll come back and see you as soon as I can get leave. Where will I find you?'

'The Sisters will know where I am. It is the Convent of the Sacred Heart.'

He turned his head to see the expression on her face. It told him nothing, but her fingers tightened on his arm. They did not talk for the rest of the drive into Mignano. An awkward silence fell between them as they waited with the score of bedraggled refugees for the bus that was going to Naples. The Italians cast respectful glances at the woman in the nun's habit who was escorted by a British officer.

Not till the matt khaki military bus drew up and the Cockney driver was urging the 'Eyeties' to climb aboard did she turn to him.

'Richa. I cannot explain to you what it meant to me when I looked up and saw you this morning. I had prayed that you would come and my prayer was answered.' She took his right hand in both of hers. Her brow was furrowed and her eyes very troubled. 'I never have and I never will love anyone like this. Will you believe that and always remember it?'

'But I'll be seeing you soon, Maria.'

'Promise me that you'll remember what I say.'

He nodded and after a moment managed to answer with a steady voice. 'Yes, I promise. Goodbye, Maria.'

322

She pressed her lips tightly together and her hands gripped hard before she let go her hold.

'Maria –'

'Yes, Richa?'

'You're not – you're not thinking of becoming a nun, are you?'

She stared at him in amazement, then put her head back and laughed till the Italians already aboard the bus were pressing their noses against the glass.

'No, Richa, I was not made to be a nun and I will prove it to you when you come on leave.'

'All aboard now!' The driver winked at Richard as he handed Maria up into the bus. Richard moved clear of the exhaust pipe as the Londoner climbed into the driver's seat and started his engine.

'Hold very tight!' he called back and let in his clutch.

Richard walked into the roadway as the bus gathered speed. He thought he could make out the back of her head through the rear window. A convoy of three-tonners was moving up Route 6 towards the front. Their wheels raised a cloud of dust from the dry, broken-up road, hiding the bus from his sight. When the trucks had passed and the dust settled the bus had turned a corner and passed out of view.

30

In the Liri Valley the whole atmosphere had changed. Now that the Monastery was no longer in German hands the teeth of the Cassino Position had been drawn. For four months it had been the dagger twisting in the flank of the Allied divisions. Now in the May sunshine it no longer had any importance. The onward rolling columns had left it to the dusty archives of history.

Richard travelled up the route known as Speedy Express and crossed the Rapido by London Bridge. The Derbyshire Yeomanry were five miles further on. The going was slow, the ground dry enough to make a lot of dust. In the scramble to get forward to attack the Hitler-Senger Line narrow farm tracks were serving as an axis for a whole division. There was a general mood of exhilaration in the air. Even the dullest private could smell the sweet scent of victory, mingling with that other sweetish smell which pervaded the valley.

He had picked up the signs for the DY group and could see the town of Piedimonte nestling on the hill to his right when he happened to spot the frog emblem of the Greenshires. It pointed up one of those typically Italian farm avenues lined with cypresses. As he turned into it he heard the familiar crack of 25-pounders opening up. It gave him a sense of homecoming. He was trying not to bank too much on finding Wilfrid at Battery HQ. He might very well be at a forward observation post. But the 2 I/C could tell him where he was.

Battery HQ had distributed themselves round the farm buildings. He parked his Jeep and walked towards the headquarters radio truck. The Battery Sergeant-Major took his head-set off and saluted as he came up. His was a new face which Richard did not know.

'I suppose Major Stockwell is at the Derbyshire Yeomanry headquarters?'

'Yes, sir. But Captain Webb is here. He's the 2 I/C. He and the padre are just –'

Somewhere not far away Richard could hear a dog barking and whimpering, obviously trying to break free. Nearby, a field of corn had reached thigh-height. From the far side of it came the sound of an orchestra. Some wireless operator with a taste for classical music had tuned in to a station broadcasting a Mozart concert.

'Could you tell him I'm here? I'd like a word with him.'

'Yes, sir. Er – I'm afraid I don't know your name, sir.'

'Stewart. You'd better say Richard Stewart.'

'Stewart, sir?'

'Yes,' Richard tried not to show his impatience with the warrant-officer's denseness.

The sergeant-major's eyes went over Richard's shoulder to

a small group that had just come round the corner of the farmhouse. It consisted of the RC padre, Captain Webb and a few other ranks. Among them was an NCO whom Richard recognized as Lance-Bombardier Bliss. He wondered why on earth the padre was wearing his robes. This wasn't Sunday.

As they approached, he saw their faces set.

'Major Stewart, sir,' the BSM said unnecessarily.

Webb nodded. He had been a subaltern in Richard's battery in North Africa.

'I just called in to say hello to my brother. I suppose he's somewhere further forward.'

Webb glanced at the padre. The padre took a pace forward.

'You'd better prepare yourself for a shock.' He paused. 'Your brother. I've just buried him.'

Richard did not take it in.

'Wilfrid?'

The padre nodded. 'Yes.'

They all waited. Watching him. Silent. Not far away a troop of 25-pounders loosed off ten rounds of gun fire. By the time the leaves and corn had steadied Richard had absorbed the Padre's statement. He lifted his eyes above and past the circle of faces, stared at the sky-line of the hills for a few seconds, then focussed on the Padre again.

'Did you say you've just buried him?'

Again the padre nodded. He had acted in this scene often enough to know that no words were any good. And this time it was not just a brother officer.

'What happened?'

None of them wanted to be the spokesman. In the end Webb decided it was up to him.

'He'd come back from the OP. Stockwell had relieved him himself. He was standing almost exactly where you are. I thought he was listening to something, but you know that odd habit he had of sort of drifting off into another world. Anyway, he suddenly turned and walked to the edge of that cornfield . . . You heard him say something, didn't you, Sergeant-Major?'

'Yes, sir. I heard him quite clearly. Haffner, he said. But we've got no one of that name. I was afraid he was going to walk into the corn. Jerry's left mines all over and the Sappers haven't cleared it yet –'

'But what *happened*?'

'It was one of those suicide snipers,' Webb said. 'You know, the Parachutists leave volunteers behind with a few days rations. They pop up when the front's moved on and try to pick off an officer or two.'

'He was in that tree over there.' The Sergeant-Major pointed to an ash in the middle of a field of corn. It was about two hundred yards away. There was a great black scar of scorched earth on the windward side of it. 'We set light to the corn to smoke him out. He tried to surrender but Lance-Bombardier Bliss wasn't having any of that.'

Bliss was standing a little distance away from the group, listening to the conversation but not wanting to take part in it. He kept moving his lower jaw and now and again wiped the back of his hand across his nose.

'He didn't say *the* Haffner, did he?'

'Well – . Yes, sir.' The BSM blinked with surprise at Richard's perspicacity. 'I do believe that's what he did say.'

Richard nodded. He could just see Wilfrid standing here with that faraway expression on his face, picking up the improbable sound of the Haffner Symphony floating across a field of corn in the Liri Valley. It would have acted like a magnet on him.

Behind him the dog's agonized barking continued.

'We had to tie his dog up,' the BSM apologized. 'It would try and dig up the body.'

'Do you want to see his grave?' the padre asked. 'Of course, it's only temporary. He'll be moved to a military cemetery as soon as possible.'

'Yes.'

'Would you like me to come with you?'

'No, thank you, padre.'

As he moved round the corner of the farmhouse the 22-set in the Jeep began to crackle.

When he came back a quarter of an hour later the padre had gone and Battery HQ was packing up. Webb was apologetic.

'I'm sorry about this, Richard, but we've had orders to move. Pretty pronto. I'm sorry.'

'That's all right.'

'Do you want to take his personal effects? We've got them all here. There's a bundle of letters.'

'No. Send them back through the usual channels.'

'There's just one thing. We don't quite know what to do with his dog. Sergeant-Major suggested you might take him.'

'His dog?'

'Yes. Do you think you could look after him?'

'Yes, I'll look after him.'

Webb nodded past him at the BSM. The BSM went into the farmhouse and came back dragging Dante on the end of a length of white marker tape. Dante's ears were back and his tail was between his legs.

Richard accepted the end of the tape. The dog sat down and looked up at him.

'I'm sorry,' Webb said again. 'We've got to be moving.'

Richard nodded. He stood while the personnel piled aboard their vehicles and watched them as they pulled out and moved down the dusty avenue between the cypress trees.

He waited till the dust had settled before starting back towards his Jeep. The tape tightened and jerked, dragging Dante for a couple of feet. He had his front paws dug in obstinately.

'Come on, boy,' Richard coaxed. 'Come on, Dan.'

Dante looked over his shoulder in the direction of the six-foot mound of earth with the plain cross and the tin helmet. In the end Richard had to pick him up and carry him. He could feel the dog shivering against the side of his chest.

Author's Postscript

This story is part fact, part fiction. The Benedictine Commando, the Greenshire Yeomanry, the Wessex Fusiliers S10, the LRP and all their personnel are fictitious. The battles for Montecassino are however based on historical records. Apart from the above exceptions, all the formations and units mentioned carried out the roles attributed to them in the story. The dialogue involving higher commanders is largely fictitious. The discussions about whether the Monastery should be bombed or not are built up from various sources, but the scenes between Richard and General Alexander are entirely imaginary.

Many incidents in the story are adaptations of personal experience, either of the author or of friends who have recounted them.

Padre Nessuno is a fictitious character but the description of events within the Monastery is based on both written and verbal accounts by monks who were there at the time. The Abbot of Montecassino kindly permitted me to visit the internal and private areas of the Monastery in 1979. It has been totally restored to its former glory in almost every detail except the irrecoverable frescoes. As no reparations were paid by the Allies the expense was met by the Italian government, supplemented only by a private donation from America. A great deal of the work was done by the Benedictines themselves, often with their own hands. The most notable example of this is the restoration of the high altar. I was fortunate in my guide, for he was Padre Agostino, who was Sacrist in 1944 at the time of the bombing.

Field Marshall Lord Harding of Petherton, who was Alexander's Chief of Staff, helped me to build up my picture of the Commander-in-Chief. While pointing out that the Commander-in-Chief would hardly have talked to a junior officer about his plans and decisions as described in my story he was kind enough to say that I had captured Alexander's character, appearance and personality. This already owed much to Nigel Nicolson's biography, entitled *Alex*. Nigel Nicolson was Intelligence Officer of 1st Guards Brigade in Italy and he lent me the very evocative letters which he wrote to his parents at that time.

At Downside Abbey I was able to meet Abbot Brookes. In 1944, as Father Rudisend Brookes, he was Alexander's Senior RC Chaplain in Italy. From him I learnt about Alexander's crucifix (now in his keeping). He also told me that, after the bombing of the Monastery, Alexander invited him to go forward with him on a visit to the front. They set off in the open staff car given to Alex by Eisenhower. Making a courtesy call at General Freyberg's headquarters on the way, they were dissuaded by the New Zealand Commander from continuing in such a conspicuous vehicle. He provided them with a Jeep and a packed lunch. They proceeded to the slopes of Monte Trocchio, where they sat down and had their lunch. Alex was wearing his scarlet-banded hat and they were within view of enemy observation posts, but this was standard practice for the C-in-C. As they gazed at the Monastery Alex confided to Father Rudisend that the decision to bomb it was the most difficult he had ever had to make in his whole military career.

The German side of the picture owes much to General von Senger und Etterlin's own book, *Neither Fear Nor Hope*, and to *Monte Cassino* by Rudolf Böhmler.

The Imperial War Museum was a rich source of material. The Library provided periodicals and books as well as personal diaries and records, including that of Squadron-Leader Thompson, who was Special Liaison Officer (Ultra) at AFHQ. The sound-records department let me hear the extraordinarily vivid radio reports of war correspondents. The film department made both German and British film of the bombing of Montecassino available. It was possible to see the whole horrific event in slow motion, even, godlike, to put the Monastery together again by reversing the film.

The Public Records Office at Kew gave access to War Diaries (subject to the information being used with due regard to confidentiality) and to the very intriguing Ultra files.

Antonio's experiences at Nordhausen were based on an account by Jozef Garlinski in *Hitler's Last Weapons*.

Brigadier David Block and Major-General Adam Block gave me valuable first-hand information on the operations of

Gunners, and General Sir Geoffrey Musson information about infantry operations at Cassino.

Mr Martin Windrow supplied expert advice on German uniforms and equipment and kindly vetted my script.

Mr Tony Oliver of Eton Wick allowed me to inspect his vast collection of military vehicles and Mr Mike Spicer advised on radio communications.

Penny Haslam gave valuable research assistance, especially in locating the books of the many distinguished authors and historians who have written about the battles for Montecassino.

To all who have helped me in the preparation of this book I offer sincere thanks.

James McConnell
Monxton, November 1980

Lissa Evans has written books for both adults and children, including the bestselling *Old Baggage*, *Their Finest Hour and a Half* (filmed as *Their Finest*), *Small Change for Stuart* and *Wed Wabbit*, both shortlisted for the Carnegie Medal, and *Crooked Heart*, longlisted for the Baileys Women's Prize for Fiction.